SELECTED FICTION

MANOJ DAS

PENGUIN BOOKS

An imprint of Penguin Random House

PENGUIN BOOKS

USA | Canada | UK | Ireland | Australia
New Zealand | India | South Africa | China | Singapore

Penguin Books is part of the Penguin Random House group of companies
whose addresses can be found at global.penguinrandomhouse.com

Published by Penguin Random House India Pvt. Ltd
4th Floor, Capital Tower 1, MG Road,
Gurugram 122 002, Haryana, India

First published by Penguin Books India 2001

10 9 8 7 6 5 4

ISBN 9780141007007

Typeset in AGaramond by Eleven Arts, New Delhi

Printed at Repro India Limited

www.penguin.co.in

This is a legitimate digitally printed version of the book and therefore might not
have certain extra finishing on the cover.

PENGUIN BOOKS
SELECTED FICTION

Manoj Das was born in 1934 in a remote village in Balasore district, Orissa. While still at school he published a book of Oriya poems and started bringing out a literary journal *Digantika*.

A Marxist youth leader who at one time spent time behind bars, he gradually turned away from politics and in 1963 joined the Sri Aurobindo Ashram at Pondicherry, where he is a professor of English literature at the Sri Aurobindo International Centre of Education.

His first collection of short stories in English was published in 1967, and several more have followed, including a novel, *The Tiger at Twilight*. He writes in both Oriya and English, and has published some eighty books. His work has been widely translated and he has been the recipient of many prestigious awards, including the Sahitya Akademi Award, the Orissa Sahitya Akademi Award, the Sarala Award, the Sahitya Bharati Award, the Bharatiya Bhasha Parishad Award, the Sri Aurobindo Puraskar, the honorary Emeritus Professorship of Berhampur University, the Padma Shri and India's most prestigious award for creative writing, the Saraswati Samman.

Contents

Acknowledgements

To the following for earlier publication of most of these stories, in anthologies and special numbers of their journal: Penguin Books; Macmillan, London; St. Martin's Press, New York; *New Orleans Review*, Loyola University, New Orleans; *The Malahat Review*, University of Victoria, British Columbia; *Hemisphere*, Woden, Australia; Batstone Books, Malmesbury, UK; the Sahitya Akademi, New Delhi; *The Illustrated Weekly of India*, Bombay; *Imprint*, Bombay; *The Statesman Annual*, Calcutta; *The Heritage*, Chennai.

To Anup Kishore Das and Somadutt for their valuable help in preparing the manuscript.

To David Davidar for undertaking publication of this compilation and to Ravi Singh for his editorial help.

The Misty Hour

In a provincial town of the third decade of the twentieth century, dogs still barked at motor cars, spectators kept sitting for hours gaping at silent movies, and signs of love were as simple as a rainbow: a young lady blushing violently at a fluttering look from a young man in the college corridors was evidence enough of her responding to his love. Thereafter the hero could safely take to versifying and the heroine to gazing at the sky when the sun was mellow and continuing to sigh, till her friends had hit upon the mystery of her mood and taken the routine initiative to bring the situation to its logical culmination. Nine times out of ten he and she belonged to the same caste. After a ritual fuss by their parents over horoscopes, dowry and date, they got married and lived happily ever after.

At seventy, Aunty Roopwati had enough bloom left in her cheeks to give the impression of blushing while reminiscing about those wonderful days when modernity meant a newly-wed lady, almost half her face revealed to the public, sharing a hand-pulled rickshaw with her husband, and when a monthly magazine highlighted the phenomenon of progress on its cover by showing a young lady cycling by (though the artist had forgotten to give a touch of motion to the spokes). Hence the storm that must have been caused by the beautiful Aunty Roopwati joining the freedom struggle can be easily visualized.

And she came of a well-known family and was a graduate. She claimed that she could even sing like a *shehnai*.

In fact she referred to a number of poems that had become immortal in our literature saying that their poets, her contemporaries, had composed them for the sole satisfaction of having them sung or recited by her.

No doubt, quite a few ladies from respectable families had come out to join the freedom struggle around that time. But none of them was as smart and dashing as Roopwati, none as fluent a speaker as she. Thus, endowed as she was with a rich assortment of virtues—any one of which could have brought renown to a lady in those days—Roopwati, her admirers thought, was destined to conquer great heights of glory. Roopwati herself had neither any doubt nor any false humility in that regard. She was sure no position was too high for her and she made no secret of it.

Those who had some knowledge about the intrinsic worth of most of the people in high places were not likely to dispute Roopwati's assertion. If there was anything wrong with her, it was her habit of extolling herself. Her colleagues in politics disliked this, though the clever ones among them were adept in using others' lungs-power to broadcast their own glory. As a result, although inferior to Roopwati in many respects, they bypassed her.

Roopwati asserted that all the budding leaders of the time had been dying to marry her. A little flattery and show of credulousness induced her to come out with a volume of anecdotes narrating how they had tried to woo her. Although Roopwati appreciated their idealism and patriotism, she had no faith in their personal integrity. There was only one young man who combined in his character both the virtues. He was Jagdishji. Roopwati at last condescended to marry him.

But the fact that she had highly underestimated Jagdishji's character became evident on the wedding night itself. This episode was not revealed by her but by her confidants among her compatriots, who were now becoming rare. Jagdishji, who was always clad in spotless white and spoke equally spotless prose, received his bride in their bedroom with a profound show of love and respect. After he had made her recline comfortably on the bed, what he opened with no less love and respect was a canvas bag containing three essays authored by himself, in a handwriting as distinct as his pronunciation.

A little past midnight, he finished reading his first essay, a profound treatise on the socio-economic benefits of the proposed prohibition on the trade in liquor.

By two a.m. he finished 'Reflections on the Gains of Adult Education'.

He had just read out the title of his third composition, 'The Role of Celibacy in Married Life', when the bride exclaimed, 'What a pity, the lamp is running out of oil!'

'Let me fetch some more oil,' said Jagdishji enthusiastically.

'Is that really necessary? Why not let your knowledge light us as long as possible?' observed Roopwati gravely. She snatched away the essays and burned them leaf by leaf.

In the spurting flames, her face must have looked as ominous as massed clouds lit up by lightning at night. In silence, the couple absorbed the realization that the fate of the essays was symbolic of the future of their relationship.

Also, the silence of the dawn seemed to have left an indelible impact on Jagdishji. Rarely did he talk for the rest of his life, which, in any case, was not very long. And when he did, he forgot his grammar. He died at thirty-five.

India won freedom. Roopwati's tongue, which till then was one of the main weapons wielded by the state unit of the party against the British Raj, was now active against her colleagues. Most of them had captured chunks of power, but they knew how ineffective their powers and positions were against Roopwati. She could strip layer after layer of their reputation with incredible ease, like peeling an onion, leaving nothing at the end. The younger generation of political aspirants, who tried to buffet their way to power partly through demagogy and partly through terrorizing or blackmailing their seniors, without the obligation to risk a thing, found it great fun to provoke Roopwati into her tirades. They flattered her by calling her Aunty. However, we pressmen felt that she had a soft corner for only one man, Chinmoy Babu—the lone gentleman in the

politics of the state. No doubt Chinmoy Babu was different from
the rest of his tribe. He had had a promising youth as an artist
and a classical singer, and had published a couple of books on
literary and cultural topics. His writings had originality. But
he was so reserved and humble that only those coming in close
contact with him knew that he was not only talented but also
intelligent.

He had made more sacrifices for the freedom struggle than
anybody else, but he hardly commanded any influence in the
party. He lived shy and aloof. But a time came when people
began to get disillusioned with their loudmouth leaders. The
party realized that its survival warranted the resurrection of
some ignored heroes of yesterday. It was at this juncture—our
town had lately been declared a city—when almost all the city
fathers made a beeline for the mayoral chair, each doing his
utmost to thwart the others and in the process all running, so to
say, naked, that some of the old freedom-fighters made it possible
for Chinmoy Babu to emerge from oblivion. He became the
mayor, uncontested.

Chinmoy Babu symbolized a new hope. Although such
hopes came to nothing much—and the people had already come
to realize this bitter truth—they needed the illusions from time
to time.

Chinmoy Babu was accorded a grand reception. The
mammoth public meeting was about to begin when Aunty
Roopwati was seen elbowing her way to the dais. Chinmoy
Babu felt happy to meet an old colleague and received her
with a show of courtesy.

'Would you like to say a few words, say for five minutes?'
the leader presiding over the meeting was obliged to ask Aunty,
but ignoring what he thought was a clever hint that she was
expected to be brief—she spoke for a full hour, heaping abuses
on nearly all the leaders, drawing frequent cheers from the
audience, but praising Chinmoy Babu to the skies. While doing
so, it appeared to us who were closer to the dais, that she blushed
more than Chinmoy Babu.

And she continued to blush till long after the meeting had
ended and Chinmoy Babu had left the venue, while we sat

surrounding her in a nearby restaurant and she gradually warmed up. She gave us a full dozen poignant anecdotes and, at last, over the third cup of tea, disclosed that even Chinmoy Babu had once been her lover.

A fortnight later, while Chinmoy Babu was presiding over a function held on the occasion of a foreign cultural troupe's visit to our city, Aunty pushed her way to the dais again and made for the chair by chance lying vacant by the president's side, her broad smile glittering in the floodlight.

Chinmoy Babu suffered her to sit near him, but was not as cordial as on the previous occasion. Someone had probably reported to him Aunty's latest claim.

It is difficult to say whether or not Aunty took note of Chinmoy Babu's indifference, but we observed that thereafter, on the slightest provocation, she asserted that Chinmoy Babu indeed loved her.

Six months later, when Chinmoy Babu abdicated his mayoralty in favour of his deputy and was elected to the Rajya Sabha, and chances of his induction into the ministry at the centre looked bright, Aunty began saying impatiently, 'Had I responded to his love and wedded him, he would have become a far greater man and that too much earlier!'

'Well, Aunty, what made you reject as brilliant a suitor as Chinmoy Babu?' we made bold to ask her with our tongues in our cheeks.

What Aunty said in reply in many words came to this: Not only had all the eligible youths of the time either fallen or come close to falling in love with her, but also a much revered leader of her father's age, at an opportune moment, had bared his bleary eyes of his thick spectacles and made a pass at her! Aunty, after all, could have bestowed her favours only on one. Forty years after the death of her choice, Jagdishji, Aunty was eloquent in his praise. Jagdishji emerged like a figure of mythical proportions—a Leonardo da Vinci in genius, a Caesar in courage and a Rama in character.

Aunty's presence at meetings, we felt, proved more and more embarrassing to Chinmoy Babu. There were whispers and exchange of knowing looks among us. Not that Aunty was insensitive to Chinmoy Babu's discomfiture or to our amusement, but she just did not care. She always reached for Chinmoy Babu with the display of a smile that she kept in reserve only for him.

A merry floor-crossing by a group of members of the legislature brought the state ministry crashing down. Chinmoy Babu had already been caught in the maelstorm of politics. His reputation as an incorruptible leader was the only hope for his party's return to power. He was induced to come down from parliament to steer his party to victory in his home state. Needless to say, he was to be the chief minister.

We learnt confidentially that Aunty met Chinmoy Babu and offered to manage his election campaign. Chinmoy Babu obviously did not think that to be a wise strategy. He spoke to her of other laudable missions that awaited her stewardship. But Aunty was too shrewd to be bamboozled. She returned fuming and cursing.

Within hours she had become the prize star in the opposite camp.

'Chinmoy for chief ministership? Pooh! This is what happened forty years ago. The party's working committee was in session. We went on till it was dusk. Suddenly, the lights went out. But we were in a spirit to defy every hurdle. Our president called upon us to continue the proceedings without bothering over the darkness. Chinmoy was by my side. He brought his hand close to mine. Slowly, his fidgeting fingers crawled onto my hand. We sat like that for a full hour during which he succeeded in spreading his hand over only half of my palm,' Aunty declared.

Nobody asked how a dusky hour of four decades ago was relevant to Chinmoy Babu's claim to chief ministership today. Had the country not seen chief ministers unfazed by formidable records of scandals?

It was strange that Aunty's statement became the talk of the town. Most probably it was because Chinmoy Babu was looked upon as a man above the propensities of an ordinary mortal.

However, nobody believed that the 'scandal' would affect the margin of votes by which he was expected to win, although it saddened Chinmoy Babu most certainly.

Just then there was a bolt from the blue. Old Dhani Chowdhury, out of the political scene for over two decades, came to us limping and groaned out a confession. He believed that his gesture, apart from serving the lofty cause of truth and of history, would help Chinmoy Babu regain whatever loss of face he had suffered.

Dhani Chowdhury took us back to the working committee meeting of the early thirties. It is true, he said, that Chinmoy Babu was seated beside Roopwati when the lights went out. But what Roopwati did not know was that Chinmoy Babu soon had to go out of the room to attend to some urgent work. The one to advance his amorous hand at Roopwati's was none other than Dhani Chowdhury, then the youthful treasurer of the party. The lights did not return before the meeting was over and hence Roopwati never found out who owned those audaciously crawling fingers.

Dhani Chowdhury became a victim of a kind of arthritis soon after and was deprived of all the fruits of freedom.

The remarkable gusto with which Dhani Chowdhury poured out his confession gave me the impression that he was not as remorseful as he declared he was, and that a secret sense of pride enlivened his narration. He was willing to donate a photograph of his own should Chinmoy Babu's election committee choose to print it on leaflets carrying his confession and distribute them liberally.

But before the election committee could take a decision on the conscientious offer and before we had any time to ascertain Aunty's reaction to the confession, she came down with high fever. The diagnosis that it was pneumonia came only hours before she died.

Frankly, we, the genuine well-wishers of Chinmoy Babu, had a feeling of relief for an unguarded moment. Indeed, how easily prospects of puny gains reduce mortals like us to utter meanness!

Aunty was cremated near the ruins of a temple by the lake on the city's outskirts.

Next day, we were on our way to Chinmoy Babu's constituency. While driving by the lake, I pointed out the deserted pyre to Chinmoy Babu. He nodded.

Five days of hectic campaigning, and a day more of silent
anxiety during which no canvassing was allowed, preceded the
polling. There was no room for any doubt regarding Chinmoy
Babu's landslide victory. But he was totally exhausted. As his
confidant, which I had become by that time, I arranged for his
other close companions to return to the city by vans and made
a comfortable car available to him. I sat beside the chauffeur.

It was evening, and cloudy and cool by the time we reached
the lake. The breeze was growing erratic. I was dozing.

'Will you please halt for a while? I wish to have a stroll in
solitude. The last few days have been so suffocating!' Chinmoy
Babu muttered from the back seat.

I appreciated his desire and let him go out alone and resumed
dozing. But, after fifteen minutes, when I noticed dark clouds
closing in on the patch of sky over the lake and anticipated a
shower, I stepped out to call him back.

There were only three or four men scattered around the
lake and I did not see Chinmoy Babu among them. I climbed
the embankment and looked towards the cremation ground
lying below it on the other side. I located him near the ruins of
the temple. He had gathered a bunch of flowers and was pruning
them. I was going to call out to him but stopped.

He advanced towards the pile of ashes—the remains of
Aunty's pyre. He knelt down and placed his bouquet on the
pile. He sat quiet and wiped his eyes again and again. Then it
began to drizzle. When he was about to get up, I took a swift
turn and reached the car in a few rapid strides.

It rained soon after Chinmoy Babu got into the car. We drove
on in silence. The swaying trees along the road looked like
phantoms whisking us away.

But the silence of that dusky hour had brewed a disturbing
question in my mind: was the confession of the former treasurer
Dhani Chowdhury true?

The Naked

Sapanpur-on-Sea, an abandoned port, showed no sign of modern times. It had few old buildings left to the mercy of raging winds, a row of shops and kiosks which always appeared to be in the red and a hamlet of fisherfolk.

Even the summer palace of the last raja was fast decaying. As the end of the British rule approached, Raja Sahib could foresee the end of native states too. He lost interest in everything and the mansion lay unused.

With the Raja dead, his son did not care to visit even their erstwhile capital twenty miles away, let alone the summer palace. It was Bhanu Singh, the scion of the hereditary *senapatis*—the commanders of the armies of the rajas of yore—who looked after the palace. The abolition of feudal rule had shocked him, and his receiving a quarterly allowance without interruption from the Raja's dwindling bank balance overwhelmed him. How ardently he wished he could do something to save the state for his master—as his forefathers had done, twirling their moustaches and swishing their swords—and repay this kindness bestowed on him by the Raj family!

No wonder that a personal message from the widow of the last ruler, now known as the Rajmata (though her son never had a chance to ascend the *rajgaddi*) should delight him. Some kind of a conference was to take place in the summer palace.

He was to receive a lorry-load of ladies and gentlemen who were to camp there for a full day. The conscientious Rajmata knew only too well how difficult it would be to provide the guests with the right kind of food at a place like Sapanpur. She was arranging to send the stuff from the city. All Bhanu Singh was required to do was to receive the visitors and to place himself at their disposal. The Rajmata had sent some money too, perhaps a little more than what he would require, to spruce up the mansion and buy some provisions.

Bhanu Singh had resolved to discharge his duty with great diligence. Half-a-dozen men and women were already at work inside the mansion, scrubbing the floors and dusting the walls.

The Rajmata's costly letterhead carrying the insignia of her dynasty, a conch flanked by a pair of lotuses, lay on the marble table in the spacious room, once the study of the princes when they came here for a holiday. 'There!' Bhanu Singh pointed at the letter after greeting Majumdar, the headmaster of the Middle English School, the highest educational institution in the locality. 'Read it and you will know why I summoned you so urgently.'

The headmaster read and re-read the letter and appreciated the quality of the paper as he held it against the skylight. Then he looked at Bhanu Singh. While unfolding a velvet preserved with naphthalene, Bhanu Singh said, 'They will number about fifty, right? I'm hopeful of getting ready with fifty simple garlands of jasmine. Can you supply fifty boys and girls to garland them as soon as they alight from the lorry? The kids should look smart and clean. I will give you a phial of pure English talcum left here by the Rajmata some five years ago. That will do wonders for their faces.'

Majumdar's attention had gone to the letter once again. 'Seems to be a new party of those "ists", or maybe a holy group,' he mused.

'Headmaster, why don't you consult the dictionary? I've not yet bothered about their creed.' Bhanu Singh opened the tall teakwood bookcase and identified the bulky dictionary. Majumdar dusted it, put it on the table and pored over it.

On locating the relevant word, he compared it with that in the message, pronouncing it aloud letter by letter. He nodded gravely. He was evidently no longer in any doubt about the import of the message.

His look baffled Bhanu Singh. The headmaster looked as if he had just been alerted by a team of doctors that his friend's disease had been diagnosed all right, but it was incurable.

'What is it?' Bhanu Singh grew anxious.

'It is an extremely knotty situation, Singh. "Nudist" means one who goes naked! Not a baby, mind you! In other words, you are required to receive and shake hands with a group of ladies and gentlemen, all emerging absolutely bare from the lorry.' Majumdar shut the dictionary with some force.

Bhanu Singh suddenly felt drained of all vitality. 'You mean fifty naked adults will assemble here for a conference?'

'Is it for nothing that they chose this solitude?' Majumdar sounded wise in accordance with his vocation. 'Imagine throwing garlands around the necks of fifty men and women— they must be quite important, with impressive moustaches and lipsticks—who do not have even a *langot* on them! Will it be ethical for a headmaster to expose his innocent students to such display of immodesty? Will they survive the shock? Well, brother, I must take leave of you.'

Majumdar turned to go.

But Bhanu Singh grabbed him by the shoulder. 'Take leave of me, eh? As if we had never been friends! Can you leave me in the lurch and just walk out on me? Is it not your sacred duty, at this juncture, to advise me as to what I should do?'

'What else is there for you to do except forget your clothes for a day and host the party?'

'What! Do you suggest that I too must go naked?' Bhanu Singh sounded like one receiving a knock on the nose.

'Isn't that as clear as the sunlight or the roar of the sea? How can a man of your maturity fail to see the incongruity in a host clad in *dhoti* and *kurta* shaking hands with naked guests? Won't that amount to insulting them? I'm sure the Rajmata is expecting the descendant of the brave generals of her ancestors to prove valiant enough for the occasion!'

Majumdar wriggled his shoulder out of Bhanu Singh's hold. Muttering some irrelevant observations on the weather and the migratory birds, he retreated towards the door and slipped out.

Bhanu Singh sprawled on an old sofa. The Rajmata had been educated in Europe and was known for her avant garde ideas. But Bhanu Singh had never foreseen a time when her modernity would suddenly engulf the forsaken summer palace at Sapanpur and hurl him into such a muddy whirlpool.

Mechanically shouting at the labourers to hurry up, he went out and walked towards Pratap Roy's house. In the golden age of the princely rule, when Raja Sahib would sit down for a few drinks with his chums and find fun in making some of his officials undress and dance before him to the rhythm of some gramophone music, Pratap Roy, the manager of the *taluk*, would come handy for the purpose. In fact, Pratap Roy and his colleagues were threatened with losing a few of their vital limbs if they refused to obey or failed to dance with abandon.

Pratap often came away with trophies. The retired manager now lived the life of a venerable citizen of Sapanpur. He gave a patient hearing to Bhanu Singh while enjoying a stroll in his garden.

'How can I help you?' he asked courteously.

'I'm in a bit of an awkward situation. My daughter's darling infant son has taken ill. I must leave for her village tomorrow. Will you receive the august nudists on any behalf? Well, Pratap, you're no stranger to the practice of occasionally shedding your clothes before others! In fact, you've performed far more complex feats in that condition than merely shaking hands with some guests.'

Pratap Roy laughed. 'I don't mind receiving the visitors in a manner fit for the occasion. But Bhanu, you surely haven't forgotten how the Rajmata used to address me!'

The Rajmata never cared to call an official of the Raj by his own name. She had allotted a special identity to each of them and used to call them by those exclusive names in a most natural manner. They were expected to respond in the same way.

'I remember. She called you Ravanasur.'

'Right. Pray, why?'

'Pratap, are we to expect logic in the whims of royalty?'

'Bhanu, you should not evade my question. I was, in the

eyes of the Rajmata, a debauch and a demon. Now, as I see it, there will be ladies among the visitors. Will the Rajmata approve of my hobnobbing with them? Why did she send the message to you? She trusts the decently dressed Bhanu Singh as much as the naked Bhanu Singh. The same is by no means her attitude towards me!'

Pratap Roy resumed strolling. Bhanu Singh did not tarry.

The seashore was without a soul but for a group of four or five young men and women waist-deep in the water. The waves splashed weakly on the wheels of their car parked beside a sand dune. They had come from the town. The youths of the locality were not accustomed to such scanty costumes, nor did the sexes mingle while bathing.

Those arriving tomorrow will be only a degree more modern than these bathers. These youths have a patch or two of foggy and revealing linen on them; those to come will be fully revealed. What radical difference would that make? And from a mystical point of view, even that much difference was nothing but an illusion, for all were equally naked beneath the garments. Mingling with these people might make it easier for him to mingle with the nudists.

With such thoughts, Bhanu Singh advanced towards their car. A man and a woman, emerging from the water, greeted him with smiles. Bhanu Singh smiled back. He felt encouraged, for he was quite at ease among them. But the depression returned soon. Would he be equally at ease when he had to shed his own clothes?

Suddenly his eyes fell on Kapil who stood on the other side of the car. Bhanu Singh knew that Kapil, a former servant in the Raj family, had been working for past some time as a kind of guide for the tourists, Indian and foreign, who were beginning to trickle into Sapanpur. He entertained them in various ways, not all of them decent, and earned fairly well. It was not easy to guess the lean, curly-haired Kapil's age and despite his new-found status and affluence his humility was exemplary.

Bhanu Singh's mind became charged with a new hope.

'Kapil, my dear Kapil!' Bhanu Singh suddenly felt great affection for him. He crooked his arm through Kapil's and led him away from his clients to brief him about the unusual situation.

'Pratap Roy is right,' he said in conclusion. 'The Rajmata would not approve of his taking my place, but she would have no objection to your doing so. Besides, I'm sure you can do it,' he concluded warmly.

'How much I wish that I could rise to the occasion, Singh Sahib! But I'm afraid, you've forgotten what the scoundrel of a bear did to me. Have you also forgotten the name by which the Rajmata used to call me?' asked Kapil remorsefully.

Bhanu Singh remembered. Kapil, in the Rajmata's nomenclature, was the Grand Neuter, an honorific earned by him after an unfortunate encounter with a haughty bear in the forest, during one of the hunting expeditions of the Raja. The beast had attacked his lower limbs and scooped out a chunk of them in such a horrid way that his survival was a miracle.

'You recollect, don't you? You realize then how ridiculous I'll look when I appear bare before those respectable nudes. I won't be surprised if they get the impression that I have been requisitioned to mock them!' Kapil sighed and, inspired by a profound goodwill, added affably, 'Of course, I don't mind baring myself before you privately.'

Bhanu Singh returned to the palace with brisk but unsteady steps. Never before had an evening by the sea appeared so desolate to him. The labourers had finished the day's work. Bhanu Singh paid them and went in, locking the gate and the main entrance behind him. He climbed to the terrace and sat there, gazing at the dark sea. He was hard put to absorb the reality that his friends had failed him in his crisis.

Would a prayer to any of the gods help? Which god? The great ones must be too busy with bigger and global problems to pay any attention to his predicament, however serious it might be for his own puny self. Whom to bother then?

The nearest shrine was that of Vishaleswar, built by a raja in the remote past. The deity, from all accounts, seemed to have been a powerful one in days gone by. But the bigger part of the shrine had collapsed for lack of maintenance. Since Sapanpur had lost its importance, the popularity of the deity had declined considerably too, though the essential rituals necessary to retain his presence had never been interrupted.

Bhanu Singh folded his hands and sent his obeisance to the deity. He hoped that Vishaleswar had enough leisure to pay attention to him.

His prayer should surely be able to travel two miles and infiltrate the stone walls and reach the deity's ears in toto, yet he felt it would be much safer to submit it to him personally.

Bhanu Singh set out along the seashore. Blasts of ice-cold wind planted blows on his back. He felt like weeping for they only reminded him of the blows given to him by his friends. His complaint to the deity grew more and more intense as the fierce wind pushed him forward faster.

He wiped his eyes as he reached the foot of the small hillock shouldering the shrine.

Some people were talking agitatedly. One of them switched on his torch straight on Bhanu Singh's face. 'Welcome, Singh Sahib, welcome! We did not know that the news would reach you so soon!'

The speaker turned his light on the other faces around him for Bhanu Singh to see them. They were respectable people of the adjacent village.

'News?' Bhanu Singh asked, intrigued.

'Oh, so you are still ignorant of the fact that the deity has been robbed of all his belongings—his copper utensils, his brass bell as well as the pair of old silver coins kept before him for ages! The pity is, the robber has even snatched away the yard of yellow silk the Lord wore, leaving him naked!'

'The Lord left naked?' demanded Bhanu Singh and raced up the hillock as fast as he could, followed by the others. Inside the pitch-dark sanctum, the priest moved his small earthen lamp several times from the foot to the crown of the deity to impress upon Bhanu Singh the pitiable condition in which the granite idol has been left.

Bhanu Singh said nothing. He descended at enviable speed, skipping several steps. The gentleman with the torch asked him something but he did not bother to answer him. He was beyond the weakening focus of his torchlight in no time.

He was now pushing against the wind. That was good, for the pressing wind helped him keep bottled up within his spasmodic sobs the outcome of his intense empathy with the deity.

Soon he laughed aloud. It was a strange sensation, hitherto unknown to him. He was in a sort of trance.

Naked was the infinite sky over his head and naked the sea beside him. The Lord too had gone naked. What did he care any more? Let the naked lot of ladies and gentlemen come! He would receive them, and without the slightest sign of shilly-shally throw his clothes to the wind.

'Come, come ladies and gentlemen! No longer am I afraid of facing you!' he thundered in a kind of ecstasy, joining the chorus of the waves.

A messenger with a telegram was waiting for him in front of the palace. 'Your family informed me that you were likely to be here.'

Bhanu Singh read the message under the light on the veranda. It was from the Rajmata's secretary. The proposed conference stood cancelled!

He re-read it, slowly beginning to shiver in an ecstatic reaction.

'They were frightened!' he shouted with extraordinary gusto, and laughed explosively.

'What's the matter, sir?' asked the messenger, bewildered by his historinics.

'Never mind, friend, but tell me which cloth shop is likely to be open at this hour? Lord Vishaleswar stands naked. We must have two yards of colourful silk for him—right now!' Bhanu Singh had once again become master of his voice.

But his eyes were filled with tears of gratitude. Who but the sky and the ocean would understand what the naked deity had meant to him!

The Crocodile's Lady

Miles and miles of marshland and sandy tracks, but nothing could disturb the curiosity of Dr Batstone, the distinguished sociologist from the West. After fifty miles the jeep had to be abandoned in favour of a bullock cart, and when the cart got stuck in a stretch of mud, we had to plod on to reach our village.

Dr Batstone who had lived in a city of skyscrapers practically all his life had expressed a keen desire to experience a real Indian village.

This was before our villages suffered the intrusion of huge red triangles glorifying birth control, politicians preaching patriotism, and billboards on the virtues of small savings and cigarettes, not to speak of loudspeakers blaring from community centres.

Dr Batstone relaxed in an armchair on our spacious veranda and muttered to himself, once every five minutes, 'Wonderful, fantastic!'

There was no need to ask him what was wonderful or fantastic. That one could drive for eighty miles without meeting a single automobile was wonderful. That a hundred cattle could march through fenceless paddy fields with absolute abstinence, obeying a tiny tot's hooting, was as fantastic as the Pied Piper's magic. Wonderful was the huge rainbow, fantastic the revelation that ninety-seven per cent of our villagers lived quite contented without having seen a locomotive or a cinema.

But his most wonderful experience had been an interview with the head pundit of the 'Model' Lower Primary School of our village, Shri Maku Mishra, who, Dr Batstone learnt, had taught for forty years without having heard of Hegel or Marx or Freud or Einstein, or even Bernard Shaw and Charlie Chaplin.

Nobody had ever dreamed that a day would dawn when a real Sahib would set foot on the soil of our insignificant village. The *Malika*, an ancient folk epic of prophecies and prognostications, which had foretold the great cyclone of half a century ago, the collapse of a local temple two decades thereafter and even the emergence of Mohandas Karamchand Gandhi, had failed to make a mention of such a possibility. No wonder that the two dozen daring, leaderly and scholarly males of our village sat in front of Dr Batstone throughout the afternoon doing nothing but gaping at him and smiling respectfully.

Dr Batstone realized how amused the people had been. He told me several times, 'Well, Baboo, I did not really know that I could mean so much! What a pity I can do so little to please them. I would have loved to perform acrobatics or even a dance, had I known any such art, for the sake of your wonderful people.'

Suddenly the professor asked, 'Tell me, Baboo, do all these people believe in ghosts?'

No sooner had I interpreted the Sahib's question to our people than they began shaking their heads. The professor leaned forward with a jerk. Now it was his turn to gape at the audience. 'Believe me, Baboo,' he confessed, 'your people are much more progressive than ours. At least fifty per cent of my countrymen believe in ghosts whether they admit it or not. Now, please find out for me, Baboo, do all these people believe in God?'

I translated the question. The villagers exchanged glances, but kept quiet, looking intrigued. But the professor had his own interpretation of their silence. 'Obviously, they are sceptical,' he observed. But soon, after some collective coughing, the villagers, one by one, began to explain their reactions to the question: 'Take it from us, Sahib, it is quite inadvisable to believe ghosts. How much conscience do they possess? I tell you, absolutely nil!' declared Maku Mishra.

'Will you believe, Sahib, that he was my cousin, my very own father's own maternal uncle's own son-in-law's own nephew? And hadn't I done everything for him, from sharing my pillow with him to doing half the shopping for his marriage? Yet who in this wide world does not know that this treacherous brother-in-law of mine, I mean his ghost, chose to harass me, out of all the thousands and millions of people of my village, within a week of his death? Who does not know that for a whole year, till his annual *shraddha* ceremony had fully satisfied him—and for your information I was obliged to share half of the expense—I never stepped out of my house at night even at the most pressing call of nature?' declared Shombhudas, the moneylender.

'No, Sahib, you, after all, are a stranger to them and a visitor from across the seven seas to boot. How much do you know about the native ghosts? You ought not to trust them. If they get a chance, they twist the necks of even the exorcists!' So revealed the second pundit of the school.

'Of course it would be libellous to say that there are no good-natured ghosts at all. As a boy I saw the illustrious Mahatma Languly Baba. Yes, I saw him with these very eyes. Baboo, would you kindly explain to the Sahib that the Baba wore not even a finger-long linen? I saw him when he was three centuries old. Isn't the history of his birth and his life most amazing? Once a terrible plague struck the land and the Mahatma's mother, taken for dead, was thrown in the cremation ground as people were fed up with burying or burning their dead with so many dying every day. And what do you think happened? The Mahatma was born right there in the cremation ground and howled for one full day and night beside his mother's corpse, until he was picked up by a couple of vagrants. Tell me, who protected the Mahatma for twenty-four hours? Jackals and dogs and vultures and ravens were all there, but all sat twelve yards away, watching the Mahatma in silent awe. Tell me, who threw an invisible cordon around the infant Mahatma?' One of our prominent villagers threw this question like a challenge to all and sundry, while inching nearer the professor, and promptly provided the answer himself, 'Evidently, a committee of enlightened ghosts! Did Languly Baba ever care to talk to human beings or did he care to wear clothes? Never! If at all he talked, it was with the invisibles around him.'

'And, Sahib, isn't the issue of believing in God or not quite absurd? Is God a moneylender or pawnbroker that the question of trust should arise? He created the earth, he brought us down here, he will take us away elsewhere, he will bring us here again, he will take us away again, he will . . .'

All heads swayed in rhythm, suggesting general approval of the head pundit's explanation.

I translated the observations faithfully. The professor leaned back. 'Fantastic!' he exclaimed.

'Beyond the river, Sahib, we can show you the spot where Languly Baba took birth. You can see the place yourself if you doubt the story!'

Dr Batstone brightened up at the reference to the river. 'No hot water for me tomorrow, please,' he told me, 'I must have a dip in your sweet river. The water looks so inviting! There are no crocodiles, I hope!'

My knowledge of my village was meagre, having lived in the town since childhood. I questioned my people about crocodiles. They seemed scandalized and put this counter-question to me almost in a spirit of protest: 'Crocodiles? Of course they are very much there in the river, Baboo! They cannot live atop trees or hills, as you should know better than us having read bulky books! But do they ever harm the people of our village? What have we to fear from a crocodile as long as the Crocodile's Lady is there?'

Several of them pointed their fingers in a certain direction. I had no desire to translate their statements in full. I simply informed the professor that there was no cause for fear from crocodiles.

But the professor must know everything the villagers said. Their pointing their fingers in a certain direction had not escaped his notice.

I had to tell him what I knew:

'Dr Batstone, that is a crazy story. You know how credulous our people are. Years ago there lived an old couple on the river bank. They had a daughter who had been married at the age of three and had become a widow at four. She lived with her parents and, people say, grew up to be a beautiful damsel.

'One day, while bathing in the river with the other women she was dragged away by a crocodile. She was given up for dead. But a decade later she suddenly reappeared in the village. Her father had died and her mother was dying. Their little hut on the river was broken-down.

'One morning, two days later, a crocodile was found crawling on the embankment behind her hut. The earth, loose at one place, gave way under its weight. The crocodile slipped down on the village side of the embankment and the people thrashed it to death.

'The young woman's mother died and perhaps she was too sad to talk to anybody. She wept and kept to her hut. Somehow a strange story began to circulate: the crocodile, which had carried away the girl, had in due course married her. Unable to bear the separation when the lady did not return to it, the crocodile had come to take her back!'

'Great!' exclaimed the beaming professor.

'And there is a sequel to the legend. Our people believe that out of respect for the woman who had once condescended to marry a member of their species, the crocodiles of the river do not harm the villagers! And this in spite of the fact that the chivalrous crocodile had been killed,' I added.

'And what happened to the woman?' asked the professor, agog with excitement.

'She is very much there—must be in her nineties—known as the Crocodile's Lady,' I replied. 'By turns the villagers feed her. They also repair her hut when necessary.'

'But what did the woman really do during that mystifying decade? What could have happened to her after the crocodile had carried her away?'

'I don't know. And I doubt if anybody ever took the trouble to investigate. She narrates some tales when asked, and that satisfies our womenfolk and kids.'

'Fantastic!' cried the professor, 'Please, Baboo, let us once interview the venerable lady. Let us dig out the facts. Let us solve the enigma to our satisfaction!'

✛

Moonrise was still an hour away. I led the way with a torch. The professor stumbled twice, first against a mildly protesting dog and then against a tortoise out for a nocturnal meander. But he did not mind the inconvenience.

The Crocodile's Lady sat crouching beside a kerosene lamp in a corner of her hut, softly singing to herself, with her chin on her knees. She smiled at us most affably. We sat down facing her and poured into her ancient stone vessel some crushed rice and sweetened milk with which her toothless gums should have no difficulty. She smiled again.

'Look, Granny, here is a Sahib, not a native baboo, mind you, but a pure Sahib, who has come to us flying through the blue. He desires to hear something from you.'

She showed neither surprise nor hesitation. 'I'll tell you about the wandering prince and the princess under a wizard's charm,' she offered.

'Oh no, Granny, we would like to hear something about yourself. People call you the Crocodile's Lady, don't they? But would you tell us what happened to you during the ten years you were away from the village—where exactly did you live and what did you do?'

She had no difficulty in hearing. And what amazed me was the ease with which she spoke, although her voice was no louder than a bee's drone. Dr Batstone asked me to translate every word she uttered. I did so as literally as possible:

'After the crocodile caught me, my son, he took me down, down, down—seven palm trees deep! I did not know what to do . . .'

'Oh no, Granny, we are not interested in tales. We wish to know what really happened. To begin with, how did you manage to escape from the crocodile?' I interrupted her.

There was no change in her tone. She continued, 'Under the seven palm trees deep water, my son, when I regained my consciousness, I saw the crocodile intently staring into my eyes. I don't know what happened to me. I could not take my eyes away from his . . .'

'Granny, if you don't remember how you escaped from

the crocodile, at least tell us all about your life thereafter,' I interrupted her again.

'But how could have I escaped, my son?' she asked. 'Could I take away my eyes? No! Under the seven palm trees deep water, there was no sun, no moon, no day, no night. How can I say how long I remained like that?'

I gave up, partly because I found her impossible, but mainly because of the irresistible curiosity and the rapt attention with which Dr Batstone was listening to her. I resigned myself to faithfully rendering into English whatever she said.

She talked for nearly an hour and a half. In the flickering flames of the lamp our phantom shadows danced on the mud wall and occasionally we could hear the oars stabbing the water in the river behind her hut. With great zest and earnestness, she went on narrating the story of her life with the crocodile in a deep pit at the confluence of two rivers, miles to the north of our village.

She would have tried to escape, but floating on the surface of the river she discovered a terrible thing—she saw her reflection in the water: it was that of a crocodile! Was it when the crocodile carried her, unconscious, to his home that the change had come over her? Or was it when they remained looking at each other? She did not know.

She felt miserable and wept. The crocodile tried his best to make her accept the condition in good humour. But he did not succeed. At last the melancholy crocodile told her: 'Well, then, take this mantra. Whenever you recite it thrice, you will resume your human form. But it will not work as long as I am near you, for, the moment you recite it, I cannot help reciting another mantra to counter its effect.'

The crocodile could not restrain his tears when he went out for his regular swim the next day. 'I know I will not find you when I return. But take care not to recite the mantra while you are in deep water so you don't drown. Recite it only after swimming up to your village *ghat*, close to the bank,' was his parting advice.

But the crocodile found her waiting for him when he returned. He was overjoyed. And he continued to find her there day after day after day . . .

They swam together happily from shore to shore and from

confluence to confluence. One day they entered a bigger river and swam for many miles until they arrived at the famous ghat of a holy city. The lady asked the crocodile, 'May I go into the city for a glimpse of the deity?' He gladly agreed and waited. She went near the ghat, recited the mantra, assumed her human form, visited the temple and returned by the evening. As soon as she jumped into the water the crocodile uttered his mantra and changed her into his mate. What a delight was theirs!

This was repeated several times, and she visited several holy spots on the river. But despite her great longing, she avoided visiting her own village lest she should fail to return to her crocodile.

It was only after ten years that she felt overwhelmed by the memory of her parents. The crocodile gave her permission to go and see them upon the condition that she would return within a day. She came and found that her father had died years ago. Her mother was on the point of death with no one to attend upon her. She remained in the hut for two days until her mother breathed her last. But in the meantime, the anxious crocodile had risked climbing the embankment, only to be killed.

The Crocodile's Lady had lived alone in her hut for nearly seventy years.

A pair of jackals howled right in front of the hut and the professor woke from his trance. The bright moonlight was softened by mist.

We walked silently. The professor stumbled against the same dog, which did not protest this time, and perhaps the same tortoise, now on its way back to the river. But his mind did not seem to register the encounters. He walked like a somnambulist.

He suddenly stopped on the river bank.

'Where is that confluence?' he asked.

'Which confluence?'

'Why, where they lived—the crocodile and his lady!'

I laughed and uttered the professor's pet word, 'Fantastic!' and added, 'Dr Batstone, I'm afraid, you took Granny's tale too seriously.'

The professor grew grave. We resumed our homeward walk. But now he walked like the intellectual he was.

Years later, the professor wrote to me from his city of skyscrapers: 'Often I pass into a reverie remembering the days and nights I spent in your village. Surely, I was under the spell of a mantra (who uttered it?) for a brief time. Fantastic!'

The Owl

A t Vishalpur, the sunset seemed to follow a certain rhythm, and the birds which flew back to their old trees on the marshland at the western end of the village did so beating their wings in time with it. As their vigorous review of the day's events would die down, the loud call of an elder would be heard, summoning a boy who had been late in returning from the fields with the cattle.

And when there was no doubt left about the sun having set, the jackals let out their ceremonial howl from several strategic points along the marshland. It was not possible to ascertain whether the sunset gladdened them or saddened them. Perhaps what their howl signified had nothing to do with the human notions of happiness and sorrow. Nevertheless, its impact was undeniable. At once it raised the spectre of the burial ground before the dimming eyes of the old folks, and once more realizing the futility of their worldly attachments their lips began to move as they hurriedly muttered several synonyms of God.

And children had a vague feeling that the dusk which overtook them at the height of their exciting game in the cosy lap of the dusty street was fraught with fearful possibilities. But the melancholy the howl wrought in the atmosphere was soon swept out by the sound of conch shells being blown rising in concert from different houses. Their drone restored faith and confidence.

At last, long after all the other noises had been silenced, from a hollow in the temple which stood in isolation between the village and the marshland was heard the hooting of an owl. Who all would hear the sound on a certain night depended on the course of the wind, the quality of one's sleep, and several other factors. But all the adult villagers were familiar with the hooting and that itself was considered important. Nobody ever asked why.

This was perhaps the owl with the most formidable personality among all the owls of the eastern region of the country. And so far as Vishalpur was concerned, the owl was believed to be the senior-most resident of the village. The temple had been built by a landlord of bygone days, who enjoyed a certain legendary reputation. After his successors ran out of luck and their estate changed hands, the upkeep of the temple naturally became the responsibility of the new landlords. But they showed no concern for it. When it appeared that its vault could collapse any moment, the priest carried away the deity, at the head of a small procession of devotees, to his own mud house. The deity took refuge in a small room, the floor of which was regularly washed with cowdung water in the morning. A generation had passed.

Every five or ten years, it was customary for the villagers to propose to renovate the temple through a fund-raising drive, but partly because the amount required for the purpose was considerable and partly because the deity confessed to the priest, in a dream, that he was quite content with the cowdung-washed floor, the proposal did not materialize.

In due course, the temple had come under the owl's possession. A parallel opinion asserted that the owl was very much there even as a co-resident of the deity. However, whether it was the same owl, meditating on whose hooting a certain old wise villager of half a century ago could prophesy drought, cyclone and noteworthy deaths, or a new one, probably a legitimate heir to the old one, could not be resolved as the villagers were not sure of the longevity of owls in general, not to speak of an owl with an occult standing

But the controversy did not really matter. The owl was looked upon as a supernatural presence and there was no sense in measuring the age of something supernatural.

It was a cloudy night though the clouds were not thick enough to hide the moon completely. The treetops formed a dark silhouette against the eerily lit sky looming over the roofs.

The hooting had duly commenced and two hoots had been heard. Just when there should have been another, a gunshot was heard. Before its echo had died down—say some villagers— they heard some indecipherable sound which could have been the owl's screech.

And an awful silence followed until inside the nearest hut, a furlong away, a newborn babe gave out its first shriek.

A group of villagers returning from the weekly market eight miles away, the wicks of their lanterns turned down, came to a dead halt. Once in a while, when the zamindar camped in his local cutcherry, gunshots were heard coming from the marshland, to be followed, an hour or two later, by the smell of cooked meat defiling the Vaishnavite atmosphere of the village kitchens. But never before had a shot been fired right inside the village.

The people knew about the visit of their paralysed landlord's young son. In fact, the exotic perfume he diffused as he walked by hung in the air for long, and that had been the talk of the village the previous evening. So the villagers, who had meanwhile raised the wicks of their lanterns, were not surprised to see him emerge form the clump of bushes behind the temple, gun in hand.

But they took time to speak. Even the prudent Balbhadra Das, who did ninety per cent of the total talking the villagers needed to do with the wide world, stood petrified.

A full year had passed since the news of the British Raj having been replaced by a native one had reached the village. People had ceased to be sceptical about the veracity of the report. They were growing conscious even of the changes taking place in their own outlook. They did not feel it necessary to prostrate themselves to the young zamindar as they were wont to do to his father.

Balbhadra Das offered a lifeless bow and asked abruptly, 'You killed the owl of the shrine, did you?'

His voice sounded uneven and unnatural.

'So what?' the young man's voice was no less awkward. He resumed walking after a moment's uncertainty.

The villagers followed him silently. Minutes passed.

'You killed the owl, did you? But how could you?' Balbhadra's tone had grown ominous.

'What happened if I did?' The young man made an effort to sound stern. He turned back and looked at them one by one, distributing his displeasure.

'What more is left to happen, Zamindar Sahib? You shot the owl of the shrine dead!'

'Whoever I shoot at falls dead. My bullet gives concession to none—bird or beast, giant or genie! Ha ha!' blustered the young man. But if his voice did not go well with his figure and gestures, his laboured laughter was at even greater discord with his voice.

The villagers did not seem to disbelieve him. Challenging his statement was out of the question.

'You can kill giants and get away with that, sir, but the question of the owl of the shrine is different!' several voices buzzed.

'But how is it different? I ask, how?' The young man's words were wispy and shaky.

'It is different, Zamindar Sahib, it is quite different.'

'Oh these fellows! They will drive me mad. Why are they pursuing me like hungry hyenas?' the young zamindar asked, looking at his clerk, the torch-bearing spineless companion of his nocturnal expedition.

Only then did Balbhadra and his party grow conscious that they were heading towards the cutcherry, leaving their diverse homeward lanes behind.

Not long ago one had to think twice before passing by the cutcherry if the zamindar happened to camp there. Their own conduct now assured the villagers that times had changed. However, they turned to go away.

'Gentlemen, listen!' the zamindar shouted at them, and when they looked back, showed them the veranda.

It was a custom to light a hurricane lantern when the zamindar passed his night at the cutcherry. It was burning now, growling like a wounded panther, its mantle growing alternately pale and bright at regular intervals. A servant pumped it vigorously from time to time.

The villagers put down their bags and bales and sat down on a hurriedly unrolled mat.

'What might happen if one killed the owl?' asked the young zamindar.

'We were raising the same question, sir. what might not happen?'

'Shut up!' yelled the zamindar. 'Tell me clearly what might happen.'

'Catastrophe,' quipped Balbhadra Das.

'You recite riddles again! Do not forget that I am the son—the only son—of your master, his only heir. Had my father not fallen sick I would have returned from the town only after I had graduated in law. How dare you bully me? Am I a rustic like you? Tell me, what might happen if one killed the owl?'

Balbhadra, while trying to divert a dragonfly which was making determined dives at the lantern, nudged an aged man, 'Pundit! Why don't you answer?'

The pundit, the highly esteemed teacher in the lower primary school, suddenly broke into a loud wailing. The shadow of his gaping face, enlarged on the wall, looked even more fearful than his real face.

The landlord took away his eyes from him and enquired anxiously, 'What is the matter?'

The pundit toned down his wailing to a whimpering and sat mute, his head resting on his unsteady knees.

'Huzoor! The pundit's too was an only son as you are your father's. One moonlit night, he happened to be around the temple when the owl began to hoot. The foolish lad had the cheek to mimic it. Well, the matter was clinched,' said Balbhadra.

'The matter was clinched! What do you mean?'

'The lad just vanished, believe it or not.' Balbhadra turned his palms upwards to illustrate the phenomenon and concluded, 'He went to the same weekly market from where we have just returned, but he never returned and five years have passed. Lost, sir, vanished!'

The pundit wailed again. From the direction of the temple came the howling of the jackals. At midnight it sounded lusty and purposeful. A quick gust put out the hurricane. Its growl was reduced to a hiss.

'And, huzoor, you did away with the owl, killed it, murdered it!' commented a third villager.

They now rose to leave. A couple of bats squeaked and flitted about under the roof. In the process, they touched the zamindar's head. He ducked.

'You mean to say, I shall die!' shouted the young man and sat down on the veranda. The villagers stopped and looked back. It appeared they wanted to say something. But they did not. Yet another gust which burst forth as though through a breach in the clouds, swept across the banyan trees in front of the cutcherry and engaged millions of leaves in an enchanted murmuring. Like a prompt response to their action came the rustling and whistling of the bamboo grove at the back of the house. The boom of distant thunder followed. The villagers realized the insignificance of their words before this mighty commotion in nature. They left quietly and seemed to dissolve into the night.

The servant who was trying to light the hurricane lantern failed in his effort and gave up. A swarm of dead leaves rushed onto the veranda. In the moonlight, their movement struck the young zamindar as somewhat macabre. Were they hunting for something, scurrying across the veranda? He hurried into his room as if escaping their invasion.

The wind continued to blow fiercely for the rest of the night. Once at midnight, the zamindar opened the door. A handful of the dead leaves at once came scampering towards him. They would have easily sneaked in had he not shut the door in time.

Through the window he observed each gust sending down showers of dry leaves from the aged banyan trees. The spiralling fashion in which they descended left no room for any doubt that although dead they, were possessed by some spirit.

The wind blew with the same force throughout the next day. The sandy stretch beyond the marshland recorded radical changes. Several sand dunes reformed their shapes. A multitude of rippled ridges disappeared, giving way to new forms and geometrical designs.

Despite the difficulty he faced in keeping hold of his flapping shawl, Balbhadra Das braved the wind and showed up at the window of the zamindar's room. From behind him peeped the pundit and a few other leading villagers.

'You have come to ascertain if I am already dead, haven't you?' the young zamindar screamed, furiously tossing on his bed. His voice sounded as though it came from a remote and alien world.

The villagers said nothing. Nor was there any sign of their desire to contradict him. Rather, there was about them an air of apology for their having to stand witness to the irresistible course of a terrible fate.

They found no cause to feel surprised at the confidential report that the zamindar had been frightened by an onrush of dead leaves at night and had contracted high fever, and that his temperature showed a continuous rise. Perhaps they would have felt intrigued had such a thing not happened.

And they did not fail to appear again in the evening. Still tossing on his bed, the zamindar was telling the village physician, 'I want to go to my mother!'

'Fie, huzoor! Should you utter words portending evil? How can a wise lad like you forget that your pious mother left for the other world a decade ago?' chided the physician apprehensively.

But the patient was in no condition to appreciate his concern.

The palanquin coming from the zamindar's house reached the cutchery late at night. A couple of extra hurricane lanterns had come. But they gave little light though they roared loudly and had to be vigilantly guarded against the wind. The grave and tired-looking doctor who came with the palanquin examined the patient and advised against carrying him home immediately.

The visiting party included an old maidservant of the zamindar's household, perhaps the patient's childhood nurse. Her moaning trickled out through the chinks in the door and windows of the patient's room.

She was heard crying at the same scale throughout the next day and till the following midnight. Then, suddenly, she burst into a loud wail.

The clouds had drifted away and the moon hung clear. The villagers had no difficulty in getting a good view of the dead young man when his body was carried into the palanquin. Some of them wiped their eyes and many more sighed.

It was a spacious palanquin and rather old; the colourful pictures of fairies dallying with flowers drawn on its planks were quite faded. During the time of the dead zamindar's grandfather, the founder of the dynasty, the palanquin was rumoured to have had strings of pearls hanging from its roof like bunches of grapes. Those who had seen the coloured glass beads decorating it until two years ago found no difficulty in accepting the legend as true.

The old maid ran behind the palanquin, sobbing. The doctor followed her, riding his bicycle whenever possible, otherwise pushing it through the sand, gasping and swearing.

With an umbrella tucked under his arm, the clerk ran behind him, flashing his torch from time to time. No attempt was made to light the hurricane lanterns which the servants carried back on their heads.

The villagers followed the palanquin up to the edge of the village and then sat down on a mound not far from the temple. They sat silent, mostly gazing at the palish moon.

'Tu-whit!' came the call from the temple.

'Oh God! The owl is not dead, after all!' muttered Balbhadra Das, his bewildered voice cracking.

The villagers sat agape, looking at the dark temple partly visible behind a row of palm trees. Nobody spoke.

The owl hooted for five minutes and fell silent.

The pundit gave out a few dry sobs. They forgot all about time until the east began to brighten. Birds on the marshland began calling to one another.

'Is the rumour I heard in the market the other day, that the zamindari system will be scrapped, true?' someone asked.

Nobody cared to reply.

The General

That April a highly exaggerated spring had burst upon our valley. In and around our small town, most of the trees had overdone their display and, consequently, now looked dumbfounded. A little moonlight was incentive enough for the cuckoos to begin cooing at midnight, infusing a new and disturbing element into thousands of dreams.

It was the assortment of fragrances in the breeze and the audacity of the cuckoos that had spurred us right up to the gate of the house on the hillock. Three large dogs began barking at us from the other side of the gate. But the season was in our favour. We tried to rouse their conscience through choice words and, in the process, attracted their master's attention.

'Good evening, General!' we greeted in a chorus.

General Valla appeared pleased. He kept his dogs under control with one hand and opened the gate with the other.

He was almost twice our height. His moustache looked like a pair of rusty hammers joined at their handles.

'Young men, don't believe in your textbook proverb that a barking dog does not bite. It is extremely doubtful if the dog itself has any idea of the proverb, warns a great man.' The general raised his voice and laughed like one of those automatic guns in action. The dogs fell silent and wagged their tails and looked at him in appreciation.

We stepped into the compound. As we sat down on the sofas on the veranda, the general brought out a ten-rupee note from his pocket and held it out to us.

'Sir?'

'Don't expect more. You are the third team of holy beggars this week!'

'But, General, we are . . .'

'Different from the others! I don't care. I don't even wish to know whether it is a night school or a library or a puja. I have fixed one rate for all the charity collectors.'

The dogs sensed our inability to see their master's point. They growled.

'Sir, we're, uh, artistes going to stage a play. We have been regularly doing so at this time of the year, and this activity of ours has come to be accepted as almost the other name for life in this town. Here is the writer, this very fellow,' Mardaraj said pointing at me.

'And I happen to be, uh, the director,' he added.

Mardaraj and I blushed together.

The general was not sure what he ought to do with the ten-rupee note and was squeezing it like a handkerchief.

'There is a role in the third scene of the third act, that of the royal commander, and our writer has executed the character well. He bagged an award in the state drama festival last year,' Mardaraj said again.

'And Mardaraj is a gifted director. The weekly *Lion's Roar* observed that a director like him could make even a dog act like a lion!' Bantoo informed the general and blushed, for it was he who had reviewed the production under a pseudonym.

We stole glances at the dogs to see if they took offence.

'And, sir, pardon us if we are talking foolish, but how wonderful it would be if General Valla himself appeared in that small but cardinal role! We have never known of a true commander enacting a commander's role,' said I.

'It will be a historic event, General sir,' said Bantoo.

It will be the most flattering experience for the audience, our townsfolk,' said Mardaraj.

The general slipped the note into his pocket and gave two

pats to his moustache and exploded into a laugh. So far only one bulb lighted the veranda. He switched on two more, illuminating the pictures along the wall which captured for posterity his various achievements. His face looked as chummy as a circus tiger's.

Not knowing what his laughter and the other gestures meant, we would have stood up, in preparation to our getting away. But the dogs had put their paws on our laps, determined to make us pet them.

Our ordeal, however, came to an end with the general ordering his dogs to behave like gentlemen. He then called out to his cook to bring us tea and biscuits.

Then, in many words, most of them swallowed up by his laughs, he indicated his acceptance of our proposal. We left his bungalow feeling overwhelmed.

Below the hillock, the town lay snug under a shawl woven of dim lights and fog. We felt that we had earned our adulthood. He, after all, was no ordinary general. Stories galore circulated about him, stories of valour and amazing exploits. In the frontiers, during the last war, once he deemed it necessary to survey the other side of a hill. The road to the hilltop was narrow and slippery, with a precipice on one side. Observing that his driver was hesitant, the general threw him out of the jeep, took over the steering wheel himself and drove up like a rocket, signalling twenty other jeeps to follow him.

He realized rather too late that he had been provided with a wrong map. There was no place atop the hill for a single jeep, leave alone the cavalcade following him.

His jeep rolled down the other side. The other twenty followed suit. It so happened that an advance party of the enemy lay in ambush along the slope, with a bigger battalion behind it. The sudden cascade of jeeps so terrified them that they did not know how to escape.

The general, who comprehended the situation remarkably fast, let out a laugh which was rumoured to be the loudest laugh in the military history of the century.

Thus did the general's move, appreciated by the enemy as a daring strategic manoeuvre, won us a victory on that front.

No one could have thought that the general, after his retirement, would choose to settle down in our sleepy little town. But since he had done so, we desired our town to have a taste of his epoch-making laughter. No wonder, we should we feel like conquerors.

Upon our meeting the general the next day, he suggested the rehearsal to be conducted in his bungalow. His family was away and there was no constraint on the volume of noise we could make. The suggestion was gratefully accepted.

The general's frequent laughter and the profusion of tea and biscuits soon helped us get over our shyness. There was some problem with the three dogs. Though chained up, they barked furiously when the king in our play had to thunder out his wrath, and they moaned when our whimpering princess had to expound her private anguish. But they rapidly learnt to put up with it all.

The princess had fallen in love with the enemy prince. While the battle was going on, she secretly met the commander of her father's army, a great warrior, and implored him to spare the prince's life.

The commander was required to say only a few words, but laugh aloud at this strange request.

Whenever the third scene of the third act came, a polite Mardaraj would tell the general, 'Please, sir, you don't have to stand up. You'll manage it all right.'

'Of course, I will,' the general would say, laughing. The rehearsal continued for six weeks and the general sat it out.

The news of a true commander enacting the role of the commander spread to every nook and cranny of the town. Walking through the bazaar, we could feel the silent admiration with which the townsfolk looked at us.

The general must have sent the news to quarters that mattered. We saw him receiving two telegrams, one from his wife and the other bearing the names of his daughter, his son-in-law and his month-old grandson, wishing him success.

At last, the big day dawned on our town and we assembled in the bungalow after hurriedly eaten breakfasts. To our consternation, we saw the general looking grave. By noon his

gravity had become so formidable—we learnt from his cook—
that after a quick consultation among ourselves, we decided to
question him about it. Mardaraj and I proceeded to his bungalow.

We ran into the general's close friend, Dr Ugrasen, on the
steps.

'I was looking for you chaps. Can't you postpone the drama?'
the doctor's words sounded ominous.

'Don't be silly, Doc!' cried out the general from behind,
emerging on the veranda. His smile was more of a grimace.

'Didn't I ask you to lie down?' Dr Ugrasen's voice betrayed
impatience.

'Listen to me, Doc, don't play foe to me. Haven't I been a
soldier to my fingertips? You surely haven't forgotten how I
blew off the aggressors and recaptured our camp on a stormy
night, or how I successfully led my men through a shower of
bullets to rescue a besieged outpost! Must I now retreat from a
mere dramatic performance? How dare you say that I am feeling
nervous? Who will believe you?'

The general pressed his hands to his chest and turned away.

'You are too obstinate for any doctor, Valla!' observed Dr
Ugrasen, and he drove away.

We stood befuddled. Mardaraj scratched his tousled head.
The spectre of a possible postponement of the performance, after
all the preparations and publicity, was driving us crazy. True,
we could do without the general. There were others who could
step into his small role, even though the change would prove
embarrassing. But how could we go about it unless the general
himself proposed it?

The cook beckoned us and showed us to the general's room.
The general lay on his bed. We, who were accustomed to seeing
him either grave or laughing, were drowned in remorse when
he smiled at us.

'Doc says I'm afraid of facing an audience. Who but a
numbskull can say so! I'm in fine fettle, I assure you.'

He gasped and dared us to answer, 'Do I look as though I
were in a funk?'

'Ho ho! In a funk and you! Aren't they antonyms?' we said.

We took leave of him after some forced attempts at making

light of the doctor's observations. Once outside, we looked like ghosts to one another.

By the evening, Dr Ugrasen had been able to fetch from the neighbouring town Dr Karmakar, the noted cardiologist. Dr Karmakar was accompanied by his assistant.

The doctors took up position in the wings well ahead of time. From our side, we let two budding doctors, our friends, to amble about in the prohibited area displaying their stethoscopes. Besides, Mardaraj's father, a celebrated homeopath, sat in a corner of the green room, his hand cupping his chin and his handy casket by his side.

Despite our great anxiety we acted out our roles rather well, no doubt because of the rehearsals held under the general's patronage. The general, costumed as a commander of old, looked magnificent. But he sat as still as a statue, flanked by the two veteran physicians.

Came the third scene of the third act. Mardaraj walked up to the general apologetically. But the general was alert. He stood up. So did his doctors. He stepped onto the stage at the right moment. At once, the buzzing audience was hushed into reverential silence.

After the brief dialogue between the princess and the commander, the princess moaned out her piteous prayer. That was the moment for the general to laugh.

But he stood silent. Slowly his right hand went up to his chest. Mardaraj looked like a pack of dry straw and I began to shake.

Dr Karmakar's assistant advanced towards the volunteer holding the curtain rope. Obviously he wanted the curtain to come down. Dr Ugrasen, unmindful of the audience, was about to rush to his friend's side.

But then the general started laughing. And what a laugh it was! The princess leaped back, startled. We stood amazed. The audience sat awestruck.

The general laughed and laughed, much longer and vigorous than we could have hoped. The curtain came down slowly to a thunderous applause and, at last, he stopped. The doctors closed in upon him immediately.

The play was a grand success. The general was carried home as soon as he had done his part and confined to bed. But he laughed again and again.

'He really enjoyed his laughter,' his cook told us in confidence. 'I could smell his joy as I can smell masala in the curry I cook.'

His family, informed of his condition, arrived the next day, resulting in our losing access to him. We rejoiced when he recovered. But he succumbed to another heart attack six months later. The newspapers, in their obituaries, recounted several of his heroic deeds. We, however, were not quite satisfied. Bantoo drafted a letter to the editors, claiming that the late lamented general's most heroic achievement had been his participation in our drama.

But then, on second thought, we did not mail the letter.

The Murderer

The moon rose rather late. We were still expecting the murderer. Mother had kept aside for him a quantity of rice which ordinarily would have taken two men to finish, and a matching quantity of *dal* and crushed potatoes, and even a cup of thickly boiled milk.

The night was somewhat chilly. From time to time, the wind howled in the bamboo grove at the back of our house. An already battered moon tried to cope with another threatening cloud. A lone moaning was heard from the bushes behind the temple of Lord Shiva, the place where we played hide-and-seek on Sundays.

'It is a vixen,' commented Uncle. The capacity to determine the sex of an animal from its cry revealed only the tip of Uncle's vast knowledge.

'It is going to rain,' observed Mother, looking at the sudden outbreak of cockroaches all along the veranda. 'I hope he'll arrive before it starts pouring.'

'What if it pours? For that matter, what if there is an earthquake, or even if a world war is fought between the market and our village? Binu shall be here all right. A murderer does not go back on his word,' announced Uncle.

Uncle was the only man in our clan to be in personal contact with the murderer. In fact, Binu had a lot of respect for him, he claimed. That explained how Binu had instantly agreed to his offhand proposal, made when they met in the weekly market, that he could spend the night in our house.

'There may be a storm, my child,' Mother told me, coaxing me to go to bed.

'But I am not scared of storms!' I exclaimed. 'Besides, I don't feel sleepy.'

'Not sleepy, eh? Two tons of sleep would descend on your eyelids as soon as it was sundown if there was the fear of the tutor making you do a little arithmetic!' cut in Uncle and, with a chuckle, added, 'I know what keeps you awake, son, but let me tell you that the one who is coming is to be tackled by adults only. You may not be afraid of a storm. There must be a full dozen lads in our village who are not. But how many can stand the sight of Binu? A murderer is no joke.'

I had never taken Binu to be a joke. He was the only living murderer in our region, lying between the canal in the north and the sea in the south and the two weekly markets in the east and the west. Over and above that, he had murdered not just someone but the famous Dabu Sahukar, moneylender and litigant.

Dabu Sahukar, no doubt, was an evil genius. Many could recite the long list of unlucky men who had lost their houses and lands to him. To be alert enough to escape Dabu Sahukar's trap was considered the height of prudence. People dreaded him as much as they dreaded an eclipse or the hour of Saturn.

It seems Dabu Sahukar enjoyed terrifying people. For no reason whatsoever he would snarl at a passer-by, bringing one's blood down to a freezing point. A notorious arsonist was on his payroll. To incur Dabu Sahukar's displeasure meant to be prepared to see one's house going up in flames, sooner or later.

For many, their most pleasant daydream had been to devise interesting ways to put an end to Dabu Sahukar. But even the most imaginative dramatist, if we had any such talent in our area, could not have thought of Binu, of all persons, doing it.

An orphan, Binu had grown up a lonesome young man. He owned a small patch of land and, at thirty, could boast of a saving of two hundred rupees. The father of a sixteen-year-old deaf-

and-dumb beauty named Sati had agreed to give the girl in marriage to him for half that amount.

Binu had been observed humming a tune or two during that phase of his life. 'Pity, his bride will never be able to appreciate his trilling!' the villagers observed sympathetically.

But Binu's humming stopped as abruptly as it had begun. Sati had been driven into Dabu Sahukar's household. Nobody could say exactly how much he had paid her father. But it was a safe bet to assert that it was more than Binu's entire savings.

Passers-by could see the emaciated and ever-silent girl devoting hours in the morning and again in the afternoon to cleaning utensils in the pond behind Dabu Sahukar's house. She looked sad and tired. She looked hardly any different when, one afternoon, she was found lying with half her body in the pond, as lifeless as the utensils scattered around her.

It had not been necessary for any physician to examine her and declare her dead. It was, however, a significant coincidence that around that time a mendicant, one of the holy tribe we often saw in our childhood, was passing along the road overlooking the pond, singing: 'The swan flies for the lotus lake that is far; the swan of my soul flies for the lotus feet of my master.'

The wise ones in the village believed that Sati would not be deaf once she was dead and that the mendicant's song must have given her the necessary guidance to the Master's lotus feet.

Nobody had ever heard Binu grumbling on account of Dabu Sahukar depriving him of a wife or for the fellow's inhuman treatment of the sweet Sati. Nobody had any chance to suspect that he had so much agony suppressed in his heart.

Famine struck the region not long after Sati's death. Binu himself was obliged to find shelter in Dabu Sahukar's establishment. His honesty was well known and Dabu Sahukar employed him for realizing his dues from his debtors. Also, Dabu used him as his bodyguard when he was required to travel with a fat purse.

Once Dabu, escorted by Binu, was returning from the sub-divisional town. He had won a victory in the court and had realized from his adversary five hundred rupees on the spot.

(Another opinion put it at five thousand.) They had covered the greater part of the distance by boat and only seven miles remained to be trekked.

There was a short cut through the woods. The sun was about to set. But eager to reach the village before dark, Dabu risked it.

Both entered the woods. But Binu alone came out!

Perhaps it was already night by the time Binu emerged in the locality. Next morning, he was seen sitting in the veranda of the zamindar's house, which was not far from the forest.

Two days later, when Dabu Sahukar's family grew anxious and looked for Dabu at every possible place but failed to trace him, the mystery began to clear. The zamindar, Bhupal Singh, had a long-standing enmity with Dabu Sahukar. However, whether Binu killed Dabu at Bhupal Singh's instigation or he resorted to Bhupal Singh's protection only after killing Dabu on his own, was a controversial issue.

Binu had been led to the police station. As it is, he spoke little. At the police station, he remained totally speechless.

It was rumoured that Bhupal Singh influenced the police to let Binu go. Nobody cared to explain why Binu should have been seen with varieties of marks on his back and with eyes and cheeks swollen if Bhupal Singh had exercised his influence. Be that as it may, if not before Dabu's murder, Bhupal Singh had developed a liking for Binu at least after that. Binu was appointed his *durwan*. All agreed that just as the murderer of Dabu Sahukar deserved to be the zamindar's durwan, the zamindar too ought to be proud at availing himself of the services of a murderer of Binu's stature.

There were many visitors to the zamindar's house. It was natural for all of them to pay special attention to the extraordinary durwan. Many offered him *beedis* and betel nuts. Humbler ones even greeted him with folded palms. Kids from nearby villages, when they had nothing more interesting to do, came to have a look at him.

Generally, the people made three significant comments about Binu. Maku Mishra, the head pundit, had opined that in view of his capacity to keep his thirst for vengeance suppressed for long, Binu could be described as a man of uncommon patience.

'While the world tolerated Dabu just as it bears with the fury of nature, Binu alone had the courage to conspire against him with as high a person as the zamindar. This showed that he was the only true male in the area,' said the proprietor of the well-known Shri Chandi opera troupe.

That Binu had succeeded in eliminating all the evidence of the murder after committing it showed that he could have been a great lawyer, said a retired *duffadar*.

Years passed. Binu was not required to be on duty as the zamindar's durwan all the time. He ambled about freely and partook of his lunch and dinner in respectable households, returning to the zamindar's veranda at night, sometimes not turning up at all.

When Bhupal Singh was no more, his pious widow and conscientious sons did not interfere with the arrangements the departed soul had made. Binu continued in his position.

I do not know when I had fallen asleep while waiting for Binu's visit to our house. Upon waking up in the morning, I realized that he had duly arrived and eaten and left our house in the dawn. Uncle taunted me with a sarcastic smile and an oblique look. No doubt I deserved it.

When I reported that Binu had passed the night at our house to my classmates in the primary school, several of them confessed they had wondered why there had been so many dogs barking throughout the night.

Even later, I narrowly missed a few chances to see Binu. Needless to say, the mental picture I had drawn of the murderer was marked by frightening traits.

At last, it was after fifteen years and in an unusual situation that I chanced upon him. Thirty years had passed since the murder of Dabu Sahukar.

One day, an old *sadhu baba* visited our area. Tall and bright, he sported a large beard and a dome of knotted locks on his head. His look was penetrating but warm. He was accompanied by a number of disciples who said that Baba, who had his hermitage in the Himalayas, was out on a tour of the country.

There was no reason for our area being included in a tourist map of India. Neither was it situated en route to any holy place.

Hence the prudent widow of Bhupal Singh grew curious as soon
as the Baba came to camp in her cutcherry. Her eyes were no
less penetrating than the Baba's.

'Sadhu Baba! I think I knew you in the earlier phase of your
life. Perhaps my husband and yourself looked daggers at each
other!' she observed.

'My mother, why should I come to pay my respects to you
otherwise?' was the Baba's cryptic comment.

'It is your kindness that has brought you here. A hermit, you
are under no bondage of any memory of the past,' observed the
enlightened widow as she prostrated herself to the holy guest.

Dabu Sahukar was not dead! He had turned into a hermit
and had emerged from the Himalayas after ages! The news spread
at lightning speed. Never before had our region experienced a
sensation of that magnitude. People continued to wonder at
the event for days together.

Several theories about the event were in hot circulation. The
most credible one among them said that while crossing the forest,
Dabu Sahukar had felt an irresistible urge to go inside a deserted
shrine. He asked Binu to wait outside and entered the enchanted
compound. Suddenly he came face to face with an ascetic. For
long he could not take his eyes off him. He was experiencing an
explosion in his consciousness. He shook like a blade of grass
and fell at the ascetic's feet. He got up after a full hour. The ascetic,
who had been his *gurubhai* in his previous life, was making him
wake up to the memory of his inner self.

At last, the ascetic planted a kick on Dabu. That snapped
Dabu's last knot of attachment to his lustful life. He followed
the hermit in silence. Both went out through a door opposite to
the one where Binu was waiting. It was getting darker. Binu
heard a lusty roar and concluded that his master was the cause
of the beast's delight. He took to his heels.

The nearest house to grant ungrudging asylum to anybody
in distress was the zamindar's. Binu had stopped there.

After the first shock had passed, our people realized the
illusion Binu had unwittingly created for them. They felt amused.
There were peals of laughter everywhere. People now wanted a
closer look at Binu who had enjoyed the status of a murderer
for three decades!

But Binu was not to be seen. By and by Sadhu Baba also heard all about Binu's reputation. It was reported that he too had a hearty laugh and expressed a wish to see his old servant.

The search for Binu became even more intensive, but to no avail.

Sadhu Baba's advent had made atmosphere festive. Hundreds came to have a look at him, among them his grandsons and relatives, who returned to his camp every now and then in the hope of getting some special recognition but went back disappointed. The disciples were chanting hymns and *bhajans* continuously, even in the dead of night. In this they had full-throated cooperation from an appreciable number of local devotees.

Then came the day for Baba's departure. More than a thousand men and women collected on the river bank to see him off. Holidays had brought me and two other collegians of my neighbourhood home. We were not willing to admit that our interest in mysticism was anything more than academic. Besides, we had never known Sadhu Baba in the role of Dabu Sahukar and so our amazement at his transformation was less than that of our elders. Nevertheless, his magnetic personality, warm smiles and tender words cast a spell on us. We too had walked miles to have a last *darshan* of the Baba.

A sickly old man crazily elbowed his way forward and fell flat before the hermit and clutched at his feet.

'Binu!' muttered a hundred voices.

That was the first time I saw Binu. Instantly the spectre, the legend of the murderer had conjured up in my imagination, was shattered to pieces. We understood later that by then Binu had starved for a week, hiding in the forest.

Sadhu Baba got to his feet and released himself from Binu's clutch with great care. Thereafter Binu kept his face covered with his palms.

Sadhu Baba waited with patience, his affectionate hands resting on Binu's head. In the crowd, the murmuring was growing louder, interspersed with giggles.

Sadhu Baba looked grave. Raising his head for an expansive view of the crowd, he said (he had never before sounded so loud and stern), 'Who says Binu did not kill me?'

There was a stunned silence. Said Sadhu Baba again, this time lowering his voice, 'You have no business to laugh!'

Binu slowly revealed his face. He looked visibly reassured. His face recorded the kind of satisfaction an infant shows when an elder kicks the floor on which it had slipped. Next, Binu hopped on to the Baba's boat and refused to budge.

'Let him come!' said Sadhu Baba, and the boat started to sail amidst shouts of '*Hari bol*'.

Binu continued to be an amusing memory in our region. But once I heard a granny informing her naïve grandchildren, 'Binu did, of course, behead Dabu Sahukar. It was the grace of the ascetic that joined his body and head together and gave him life—a new life.'

The Bridge in the Moonlit Night

A t times, the moon appeared so big and so close to Ashok's balcony that he wondered if he could say hello to it, and even reach it in a few bounds and shake hands with it. But since evidently it had no hands, he wondered if it would do to plant a kiss on it.

Relaxing in his easy chair, Ashok loved to chit-chat with the moon, particularly when it was full. He had just told it, 'I crossed eighty some years ago. What about you?'

There were moments on such moonlit nights when he could see elves and fairies—he was surprised that they never aged— playing hide-and-seek among the silver-rimmed clouds and atop the starlit trees on the faint horizon. He enjoyed their frolic to his heart's fill, but often dozed off in the process and, what was intriguing, still continued to see them. His only problem was, he could not say how much of those playful beings he saw while awake and how much while asleep.

He was aware that this queer forgetfulness had slowly begun to creep into his other activities too, even those gross in nature. For instance, this is what had happened that very evening: he had been delighted at the alluring colour of his cup of tea as it reflected the sunset sky. He had had a warm sniff of its steam. But his happiness drove him into one of those sudden snoozes. A little later, upon being reminded that his tea was going cold, he felt amazed that his satisfaction at having drunk the tea in his dream was not a whit less than the satisfaction he derived from actually drinking it.

But whatever be the condition of his memory, he was proud that age had not dimmed his vision to any lamentable degree. He attributed this to his feeding at his mother's breast till the age of five, being her last child.

But his pride had suddenly received a jolt and that was only a while ago. The bridge on the small river two furlongs away was no longer visible to him. Every time he woke up, he rubbed his bleary eyes and tried to locate the old familiar structure, but in vain. Was the moon playing tricks with him, withholding its beams? He glared at the moon. He then looked at the clump of trees on the horizon where he was accustomed to see the silhouette of the Taj Mahal.

But he could see that all right! This was an annoying problem. He solved it by quickly dozing off.

The footfalls dragging up the stairs, however, were enough to rouse him. They were Sudhir's—as familiar as the thwacks of his own walking stick. Although younger to him by a decade, Sudhir gasped for breath while climbing. But to Ashok the ascent was hardly more difficult than a leisurely walk. What was more, he had lately begun to have most unusual experiences while climbing the steps. For example, on the last occasion he had fallen asleep midway up the stairs, although for no more than a minute. But that was sufficient for his mind to lose the entire sequence of events. He had just returned from a delightful round in his son's car. But on reaching the balcony he had concluded that he had just got to the portico. He had looked for the car and had succeeded in rapidly recovering his sense of perspective and complimented himself on that score. To mistake ascent for descent and vice versa was no hallucination of any alarming proportion, he assured himself.

'Come, Sudhir, should we go out for a stroll?' Ashok extended his hands for Sudhir to help him stand up.

'Where on earth to go? The bridge was the only place,' Sudhir lamented, looking in the accustomed direction.

'Yes, yes, the bridge. Let us go there.'

'Look here, Ashok Bhai, you must shake off this forgetfulness of yours, what they call amnesia. Where is the blessed bridge? Why do you think we haven't enjoyed any stroll for a full month? They have pulled down the dear old bridge to its last brick. They plan to erect a new one—a stylish one with a number of jetties on both the sides for the taxpayers to enjoy their evenings around crotons and bougainvillaea, cracking nuts and sucking at ice-cream sticks. In no time it will turn into a fish market, I'll bet,' Sudhir spoke with some anguish.

'So that's it! The bridge is just not there! That explains why I couldn't see it. No doubt my memory is fooling me. Your case is different. You are young!'

'Not as young as you think, Ashok Bhai. I will be eighty in a year or two.'

'Well, at your age I could . . .' Ashok's muttering grew feebler and he began to doze halfway through his observation.

'You are under an exaggerated impression about your age, Ashok Bhai. It's so common to read about centenarians nowadays! What are you before them? A mere octogenarian! Ashok Bhai, are you falling asleep?'

'Oh no, Sudhir, I must confess though that I doze off from time to time. But that keeps me fresh. Now, should we make a move towards the bridge?'

'Ashok Bhai, did I not tell you for the umpteenth time that the bridge had disappeared? How fast you forget things!' Sudhir sounded disappointed.

From the restless movement of his limbs it was obvious that Ashok felt embarrassed. But soon he regained his composure.

'You are right, Sudhir,' he said, 'I keep forgetting much of what people tell me. There was a time when it was necessary to forget a whole lot of things. But then the memory proved too diligent to let a single item slip from its custody. And now when it is imperative for you to remember at least a few things— who else will care to remember for you when you are old and out of tune with the rest—memory betrays you!'

'But you lack no care, Ashok Bhai! Hasn't providence placed you amid a host of kind souls who will remember for you all you need to?'

'A host of kind but colourful souls. Despite all their goodwill for you they must dab your affairs with their own tastes and preferences, so much so that you'll fail to recognize what was yours. No, Sudhir, others can't remember for you, just as others can't forget for you!'

'Ashok Bhai, after a long time you are talking with as much sparkle as you used to when you were our professor. How dramatic it was!'

'Dramatic, was it? I don't remember. And look here, Sudhir, on second thought, there is so much peace in forgetting things! I am in peace, believe me, with my—what d'you call—amnesia. My instant snoozes of which you complain are nothing but symptoms of my peace. Would death prove gracious enough to close in on me while I was in one of those snoozes!'

Ashok's vibrant voice assured Sudhir that he would not feel sleepy for some time to come. He dragged his chair closer to him and, after a little hemming, said, 'Ashok Bhai, for a long time I have been trying to make a confession to you. No longer can I keep the anguish bottled up in my heart. Will you kindly bear with my babbling for a few minutes?'

'Go on, Sudhir.'

Sudhir hemmed again and rolled up his sleeves and changed his position. He passed a few more seconds ensuring that there was nobody in the vicinity to overhear him except for a cat on the sofa. He waggled his stick at it and it walked away more in disgust than in fear.

'Ashok Bhai, you remember Meena, don't you?'

There was no response from the listener.

'You remember her, don't you? Meena, my distant cousin, two or three years older than I, the beautiful Meena! Wasn't she a student when you were the star of our college—a young lecturer? Who could have outshined you in gait and glamour, in that spick-and-span look you had about you! But let me go back to Meena. We had put her up in our house. To cut the story short, I mean the very Meena you were in love with. Ashok Bhai, you are listening to me, I hope!'

'How can I do otherwise, Sudhir? Go on.'

'But will you first tell me whether you remember Meena or not?'

'What a silly question! Did you not say that I was in love with her?'

'Thank God. Yes, Ashok Bhai, you loved her and, I suspect, you grew thin yearning for her.'

'Never to grow fat again!'

'But you fattened me—and I have remained fat all my life—feeding me like a pig because you used me as the courier of your love letters to her. And how wonderful those letters were! I have rarely come across such moving sentiments either in fiction or in poetry!'

'Sudhir, don't tell me you were unkind enough to read my private letters to Meena!'

'Pardon this sinner, Ashok Bhai, but I did read them. I read not only your letters but also the one—the solitary one—she had written to you in response. Of course, that was how I learned that she too had come to set her heart upon you.'

'No, Sudhir, she had not. And she did never write to me.'

'She did, Ashok Bhai!'

Ashok sat silent without taking his eyes off the moon which had grown brighter after emerging from a fragile scrap of cloud. The lone eucalyptus that stood touching the balcony continued its whispering in the steady breeze. The grandfather-clock rang out a resonant half past seven.

'I am lucky,' Ashok's voice assumed an unsuspected vivacity, 'I don't care to call for any proof of what you say, Sudhir, but I wish you had told me of her love for me earlier. I could have considered myself lucky over a longer period, that's all.'

'There lies the knot, Ashok Bhai! What do you think I am feeling so awfully guilty about? You certainly remember how shy, how delicate Meena was. But she had at last yielded to your entreaties. She had written a small but sweet reply to your epic love letters. In fact, she had agreed to meet you at the bridge.'

Sudhir paused for a moment and then resumed, 'And indeed she did come, but had to go back feeling humiliated, for you did not turn up.'

'How do you say so, Sudhir? I never received any letter from her!' Ashok asserted in a trembling voice.

'How could you have received it, Ashok Bhai?' Sudhir faltered and tried to clear his choking throat. 'Did it not fly away, while I was crossing the bridge, in a sudden gust of wind?'

'Fly away? Let us go and look for it!' Ashok made an effort to get up.

'After sixty years?' Sudhir laughed nervously.

Ashok fell back into his chair. 'Ashok Bhai, I must confess that the letter flew away only after I had read it and torn it to shreds. In fact, I offered the shreds to the rolling flood under the bridge. I can still see them flying away like butterflies.'

Ashok sat silent.

Sudhir hung his head and muttered on: 'I do not know why I did so. You will certainly agree that I was not villainous as such. I admit that I was deeply attached to Meena. I could not have wished for anything but her good. My affection for you was no less, but that was tinged with a sort of fear. I was perhaps afraid that Meena would be entirely lost to me, and to herself too, if she married you. My apprehension, needless to say, was sheer stupidity. In any case, I was to lose all contact with her the moment she left our house—which she did before long— on the receipt of a message about her father's fatal illness.'

Sudhir played with his stick nervously.

'Ashok Bhai,' he resumed, 'all this hardly mattered to me as long as I was engrossed in my vocation. But since retirement, whenever I visited the bridge, the memory of my treachery became a terror and haunted me like a ghost. It has plagued me for ten long years. I still feel puzzled over my conduct that evening, sixty years ago. Ashok Bhai, I wonder if you will pardon me. But believe me, if I was a rascal, over the years, by pretending to be good, I have become good.'

Sudhir stopped. Someone was climbing the steps. It was Mahindra, tired but excited.

'Ashok Babu, if I am still capable of walking quite fast and can even climb steps without much difficulty, it is entirely due to the inspiration I draw from your example. Now, tell me, Ashok Babu, how on earth could you reach home so soon? I saw you from the other side of the dismantled bridge. I called out to you. It appeared you were too engrossed in looking for something on the dry river bed to respond to my call. I just took a turn to avoid trudging through the debris and came over to your side.

Alas! You were gone. You will overtake a hurricane, Ashok Babu. Who would believe that you were older than I?' observed Mahindra, still panting.

'But Ashok Bhai hasn't been out at all this evening! You must have seen someone else,' said Sudhir.

'Ha! Can I ever mistake someone else for Ashok Babu? And in this bright moonlight? Well, Ashok Babu, you must have been back here only a few seconds before me! Am I right?'

Mahindra waited for half a minute for Ashok to reply. 'Surely, he has fallen asleep!' he then observed.

'But he never sleeps so deep at this hour. Ashok Bhai, do you hear?' Sudhir called out, rather loud.

'Ashok Babu!' Mahindra joined in, louder.

'Ashok Bhai!' Sudhir gave a shake to his old professor and friend. Next moment he screamed out, 'Who is there? Phone up the doctor, quick! Where is the switch for the light, Mahindra? Oh God, I forget everything!'

The Tree

Right from the time the season began changing into the monsoon the village elders had begun to look grave. The sinister cloud formation on the mountains several miles away, and the eerie circular aura around the moon had indicated to them there were terrible days ahead.

The flood came at a little past midnight. The jackals, with their long moaning howls, managed to wake up several people who called out to one another and, reassured of a collective awareness, gathered on the river bank with lanterns or torches of dry twigs. The flames danced in the gusts of wind, making their faces alternately appear and disappear.

The moon was draped in clouds and the stars were as pallid as the eyes of dead fish. Nothing much of the river could be seen, but one could sense it swell and hear it hiss like a thousand-hooded cobra. The wind carried the smell of crushed raw earth.

The flood never entered this village, although hardly a season passed without the river playing havoc with the hamlets a couple of miles downstream. Down there the people knew when to go to their roofs or perch on the trees. They would quietly descend after three or four days and take root again.

But even though the flood did not enter the village, it nibbled at the high ridge and, once in a while, gobbled up a chunk of the grassland stretching along the bank.

The villagers felt scandalized every time the familiar tame river expanded and grew alien. It shocked them; as if a docile domestic animal suddenly had gone crazy, behaving wildly and not responding to any amount of endearment. One just looked on helplessly.

And that is what the villagers were doing when they suddenly realized that the situation was much more grave than they had imagined. From midstream they heard a chugging and cries already tired and cracking—as if from the world of dead. They raised their lanterns. At that the voices grew more plaintive.

The villagers strained their eyes to see through the darkness and the mist. A few of them could make out the dark shape passing by on the foaming ashen waters and shouted the only sensible advice that could be given to a boat caught up in the first rush of a flood: 'Have patience. As soon as it is dawn, people will throw ropes and save you. Keep on shouting. God be with you.'

Such boats generally came from the forest at the foot of the mountains, loaded with timber.

Sometimes they were given another stock advice: 'Throw away the load and make the vessel lighter, but don't get too light.' A very light vessel became a plaything for the rollicking waves.

The sounds from the darkness became faint and remote, random syllables blown away by the erratic wind.

The wind grew stronger and colder, and was soon accompanied by a thin shower. Everybody ran to take shelter under the banyan tree. The wicks of the lanterns had to be turned low so that the glass did not grow hot enough to crack at the touch of raindrops.

The leaves of the banyan tree chattered incessantly their familiar language of hope and courage. Its innumerable boughs spread out overhead had been the very symbol of protection for generations, affording shelter not only to those who bore love and regard for it, but even to those who had proved impudent towards it, of course, so far as the latter were concerned, only after humbling them to their knees. The elders would point at a mound covered with grass and shrubs, not far from the tree, while citing the ancient-most proof of this fact. The mound had decayed through centuries, but it was still 'as tall as two men'. They did not expect anyone to ignore a fact so emphatically displayed.

The mound contained the ruins of a certain king's palace. It was neither possible nor necessary to recall the name of the king who had built it, or whether he belonged to the solar or the lunar dynasty. What mattered was he had dared to cut down a few branches of the tree to make room for an extension of his palace. Perhaps he had planned to cut more, or even to totally destroy the tree, but before he could do so, a terrific storm levelled the palace to the ground. The royal family survived the catastrophe only by taking shelter under the tree. The king clasped the tree and wept. The storm subsided.

Further back in time, the tree had taken off and flown to the Himalayas and other such meaningful places at the behest of a certain great soul who lived under it. But that was in the Era of Truth and, in the absence of any concrete evidence like the mound to support this legend, elders of the present generation spoke relatively less about it than had their predecessors.

The trunk that had once been clasped by the king had decayed and disappeared long since, but after having sent down numerous shoots which had become new trunks. The tree, whose branches spread over an acre resting on these trunks, was the oldest institution in the village.

Beside one of the trunks rested the tiny Banyan Goddess. She had no regular priest attached to her. Whoever so desired could approach her and sprinkle vermilion on her, of which she was extremely fond. In the course of generations, the vermilion crust had come to account for the greater part of the goddess's person. Devotees ordinarily did not feel it necessary to prostrate themselves to her, but while passing before her bowed low enough for her to take cognizance of their respect. In matters complex and formidable, the villagers prayed for the intervention of famous deities of distant temples. But small issues were referred to her from time to time. Children of the primary school in particular found her helpful in crises arising from homework not done or the ill humour of the teachers.

The area before another trunk was the usual site for the village meetings.

Relaxing beside a neighbouring trunk, eyes shut and jaws moving in a leisurely rhythm, could be found the much-revered sacred bull. In the afternoon on market days, an old woman coming from a village on the horizon sat leaning against another trunk with a sack half-filled with greens and drumsticks. The market, still two miles distant, was her goal, but her knees, she would declare with a quiet, toothless laugh, refused to serve her any more, obliging her to sell her wares cheap while there. At sunset, she would rise and offer a handful of whatever still remained in her sack to the sacred bull.

In a hollow at the foot of another trunk resided a family of snakes which had earned the reputation of being kind and courteous, and in the branches above, a legion of birds.

The tree was taken to be immortal by all without anybody having to be told about it. Immortality being an attribute of the gods, it was godly. Nobody would easily flout a decision that had been taken in a meeting under the tree, for even when the decision was unpalatable to a party, over it there was the seal of a higher power, invisible and inaudible.

The rain stopped, though not the wind. The first touch of awe and excitement passed. They could all go back to their homes now and return in the morning. It was more out of respect for the river, to show that they had taken due note of its changing mood, than from any fear of the flood, that some people gathered at its edge.

A crashing sound stunned them. Suddenly the earth seemed to rock. The few who were nearest the river were splashed. Had they been standing a little closer, they would have gone for ever. In the dark, no one had noticed the crack in the ground before a huge chunk of the bank slipped into the water.

Nirakar Das, the retired head pundit of the primary school, shouted, 'Come away, come away, you all!' The authoritative voice was instantly obeyed.

Some snakes crept out of the hollow under the tree and wriggled away towards the mound. Some saw only one snake, some saw two and some three; but to all it appeared the exodus of a thousand snakes, a stream of life abandoning its ancient body.

It was now near dawn. Nirakar Das advanced towards the tree and looked up for a long time. 'My eyes are gone,' he declared again as he had on countless occasions during the past decade. Scanning the people who were now beginning to extinguish their lanterns and torches, he called one of his ex-pupils, Ravindra, the founder-proprietor of the village grocery, and asked him to look up and see if there were birds in the tree. Ravindra and others gazed up into the branches and reported their finding: 'No, not a single feather!'

Nirakar Das looked glum. 'Can any of you recollect another instance like this?' he asked the people of his age group. They too looked grave and shook their heads: 'No!'

'Far from a good sign,' Nirakar Das observed, 'snakes and birds fleeing this great shelter!'

Not long after this, Ravindra and others with better eyesight detected an extensive crack, in the shape of a sickle, with both its ends pointed towards the river. The semicircle embraced the tree.

'If the tree falls, it will carry this whole huge chunk along with it into the river, for its innumerable roots have made all this earth into a single cake,' a young man explained to his two friends. They were the only boys from the village studying in a college in the town. This was their first visit home after they had grown long hair and sideburns.

'What! The tree fall? How dare you say so? How much do you know about this tree?' an old Brahmin, notorious for his bad temper, shouted at them.

'They have developed bones in their tongues,' commented Ravindra. 'You are in college, aren't you? Come on, save the tree with your English, algebra and what not,' he challenged them.

'Why should we?' the spokesman of the trio said sniffily.

'Why should you? As if you could only if you pleased! Is this what you imply? Well, why not do it out of pity for us, out of pity for the fourteen generations of our forefathers? Will you?'

This time Ravindra was supported by a number of people.

The young man blinked and muttered, 'What I meant was, how can we save the tree?'

'Now it's how can we! If this much is your capacity, how did you dare to grow such obscene hair?' demanded the ill-tempered Brahmin.

'Look here, my young fathers! Take a solemn vow, not loudly, but silently within your hearts—let none but the spirit of the tree know—that if the tree is saved you will shorten your hair. Please, my fathers, make a solemn promise,' implored Shrikanta Das, the meek and mild Vaishnav, his palms joined in the shape of a lotus bud in humility.

As the sky in the east grew brighter, it was observed that the ground between the tree and the river had tilted towards the river.

The three young men tried to appear engrossed in discussing something highly sophisticated among themselves.

Shrikanta Das raised his voice: 'Hearken, you all! Not only these boys, but we all have our shares of sin. And if the tree has decided to collapse, it is because it cannot bear the burden of our sins any longer. Let everyone of us confess his sins, addressing the spirit of the tree, silently in our hearts! Let us pray to be pardoned. *Hari bol*! Glory to God!'

All shouted *Hari bol*. But it sounded like a cry of lamentation.

When they stopped, the silence grew biting. As the sky brightened, the seriousness of the situation became more and more apparent.

A few kites circling above the swirling waters occasionally pretended to swoop down on the crowd, as though to show their contempt—they being the creatures of the sky who could see from horizon to horizon—for the wretched men below.

The crowd swelled rapidly. Almost all the villagers, women and children included, were there. In different words everyone asked the same question: 'What is to be done?' A part of the tree was clearly leaning towards the river.

Once the college boys had been humbled, there was no hesitation in openly discussing the impending fall of the tree. Something, no doubt, had to be done. If one only knew what that was!

The crowd instinctively looked towards those who had claims to some sort of distinction, one by one.

Shridhar Mishra was a well-known homeopath, reputed to have pulled back a number of people from the jaws of death. When the people looked expectantly at him, his lips quivered as they always did in the process of diagnosing a disease. Patients and their relatives were accustomed to read in that quivering the promise of a remedy. But since the quivering did not stop even when the people had looked at him for a long time, they focused their attention on Raghu Dalbehera, the only villager who possessed a gun. He was rarely seen without his weapon, even though the list of his kills over two decades had been limited to a handful of birds and a greedy fox—the latter merely dazed by the sound and smoke from his weapon, and killed in an operation in which many had the privilege to participate.

When Raghu realized that the crowd had already been staring at him for five minutes, he raised his gun at an audaciously swooping kite, took aim and continued to take aim.

'Don't, Raghu, don't!' warned Nirakar Das and Raghu brought down his gun with relief.

People sighed and stopped concentrating on him.

Just then someone brought the news that the honourable member of the legislative assembly had been seen on a nearby road, perhaps heading for the next village.

'Bring him here at once; run, boys, run!' said the elderly villagers. Three or four young men started a race.

Freed from the obligation to think or do anything now that the MLA had been located and summoned, all stood peacefully looking towards the bend of the road where he was expected to appear.

The MLA arrived, walking at a running pace, his brows wrinkled.

'Do you see the situation, MLA babu? We are doomed!' more than one voice cried.

'Who says you are? Why this cynicism? People further down are really in trouble. The flood has entered their village and is threatening their houses. You are in paradise compared to them, and I wish you good luck,' said the MLA displaying the smile which he used to arouse the conscience of his listeners.

'We voted for you!' exclaimed a voice. The three college boys now elbowed their way forward, throwing glances back at the crowd as if defying it to stop them from confronting the leader. They were, of course, below voting age, but they were determined to regain face after their earlier humiliation.

The MLA paled, but ignored the boys. 'What would you like me to do?' he asked the elders.

There was no reply. Recovering his courage and flashing the conscience-rousing smile again, he repeated the challenge, but tenderly, 'Order me and I am ready to do it!'

'Do, eh! What can you do? Only remember that we voted for you and that it is during your reign that this divine tree, which has stood here since *Satyayug*, is going to leave us,' said an old man.

'Reign? Who reigns over our land today? Neither the British monarch nor the native rajas. You are the rulers now and I am only your humble servant!' retorted the MLA.

'Servant, are you? Let's then see you serve us! Stop this tree from falling!' It was again one of the college trio.

The MLA suddenly grew spirited. 'Why don't we all try together? Come on, gird up your loins. What were you fellows doing all the time? Fetch as much rope as you can—thick and strong. Run, run, I say!' He girded up his own loins.

'Run, run!' shouted several others. Though everybody knew how unrealistic the proposition was and how difficult it was to obtain even a few yards of rope such as the MLA had specified, several people were about to set off under the impact of the leader's clarion call.

But suddenly a part of the tree and the trunks it rested on slid into the river. Water shot up in fountains touching the wings of the startled kites.

'Oh God, oh God!'

The crowd stood thunderstruck. The silence was broken by an anxious voice: 'What will happen to the Banyan Goddess?'

No sooner had this question been raised than the ill-tempered old Brahmin was seen rushing towards the tree. He sat down on the muddy ground—a spot lately considered dangerous even by the snakes—and mustering all his strength pulled out the stone stuck to the spot for God knew how many years.

Holding the uprooted goddess close to his bosom as though to protect her from invisible enemies, he returned to the crowd that watched him breathlessly.

'Give place to the goddess!' the people shouted with excitement, thronging closer around the Brahmin. Someone spread a towel on the grass. The Brahmin put down the deity and patted her. All looked at her with the sympathy an orphaned infant would receive. They walked around her, stretching forward their hands in their eagerness to do something for her.

There was another terrific splashing sound. The entire tree was gone. The old branches wrestled with the mad waters, unwilling to be carried away.

'Gone! The tree-god gone! *Hari bol! Hari bol!*'

For a long time, under a continuous drizzle, they devotedly kept up the poignant chant, all of them looking stupefied and some weeping.

Old Bishu Jena had seated himself before the Banyan Goddess. Someone, who noticed that he had begun to shiver, cried, 'I think Bishu is falling into his trance!'

Several people rushed to their homes and brought out cymbals, drums and conch shells. In days gone by, when there was no vote, no college for village boys, Bishu used to be 'possessed' by the Banyan Goddess from time to time. Drums, cymbals and conch shells had to be played close to his ears as loudly as possible. He would start with shivering. Then he would fall down in a swoon and rise up with a face beaming supernaturally, eyes wild as he underwent indescribable experiences. Often, though not every time, he would utter words that were understood by only a few, who would listen to him and nod. Bishu was in a trance again, after at least two decades. Those who used to play the instruments close to his ears had now grown old; yet, their sagging skin flapping like empty purses, they were doing their best.

Bishu opened his mouth. The instruments stopped playing.

'I will be born again—again!' he said. He closed his mouth and eyes and resumed shivering. The instruments were played again. Again his lips parted and the instruments stopped.

'I will be born as a thousand trees—here, there, everywhere!'

'Hari bol! Hari bol! Hearken to the tree-god's message. He will be reborn as a thousand trees!'

The instruments played more loudly as younger hands took over from the tired old hands. Nirakar Das, Shrikanta Das the Vaishnav, and several others joined Bishu in a whirling dance, their hands raised in ecstasy. 'Hari bol! Hari bol!'

'My God! But the sun is rising!' a little boy drew the attention of those around him to a luminous crack in the clouds and clapped his hands.

Miss Moberly's Targets

It was ten minutes to five p.m. and time for Miss Dolly
Moberly to feel excited. She paced along the balcony throwing
restless glances at the narrow street below.

Robinson was already there, gazing up with the devotion
of a dog. Robinson, of course, was a dog, as were Mac and Badal
who were yet to arrive. They resided in the slum not far from
'The Rest'. Their owners, if they had any, must be calling them
by other names. One day Miss Moberly had thrown a crust of
bread to a dog and the crust had smartly landed in its mouth.
Delighted, she had forthwith named it Robinson. Thereafter
the dog would bound up to her with wagging tail and twinkling
eyes whenever she called it by that name.

One evening, while she relaxed in her easy chair on the
balcony and enjoyed the dog's vigorous tail-wagging below, she
gave some leisurely thought to this question: Why, of so many
names, had Robinson come so readily to her tongue? It did not
take long for her to remember the whiskered Mr Robinson,
her father's chum who sported impressive sideburns and was
the secretary of the local Anglo-Indian society. On the outskirts
of the town lived another Robinson whose poultry produce
was famous as the Sahib's Eggs. Both had departed long since.

From the parapet a middle-aged cat—one which reminded
Miss Moberly of a retired magistrate—watched the dog, disgust

writ large on its chubby face. Miss Moberly always felt uneasy at the sight of this cat. 'The Rest' was a home for the affluent aged and it was true that most of the inmates had no near enough relatives to care for them. But the organization which ran it was a sound one, and from the attendants right up to the health officers and the prefect, everybody worked with commendable dedication. For all their goodwill, however, and for the fat chunks they knocked off your bank-deposit month after month (or you could surrender your regular pension to them), they could not provide you with dear ones if you had none—none to visit you and warm you up with a few endearing words.

Did that mean that anyone could play uncle to you? But that was exactly what this cat was doing! It would appear on the threshold of her cabin near about midnight and give out a lusty mew, which evidently amounted to 'How are you?' but which also seemed to contain an arrogant hint that you were bound to be happy under the arrangements here, and that if you were not, none but yourself was to blame.

Miss Moberly used to answer the cat, 'I'm okay. Thanks.' But despite her perfunctory tone, the cat would hop on to her bedside table and cast a piercing look at her before jumping out through the window.

In the beginning, Miss Moberly had quietly put up with this offensive behaviour of her nocturnal visitor, although it had not taken her long to find out that the cat had nothing to do with the management of the institution. But the night she, quite by chance, found out that it was a male cat (and realized to her own amazement that all her life she had thought of all the cats as belonging to the female sex alone), she had told it straightaway, 'Your supervising is rather uncalled for. Please leave me alone.' She repeated her protest to the cat at its subsequent visits, but in vain.

This struck her as strange, for she was certain that cats had once been much more sensitive and humble. Of course, that was seventy years ago. She remembered at least one of her mother's several cats. They had at that time a young tenant on the upper floor of their house.

'There you are!' Miss Moberly told herself and grinned. 'He

was yet another Robinson!' In fact, the only Robinson that had once mattered to her!

Robinson used to return to his apartment in the evening and cook for himself, invariably inviting his landlady's cat to share his supper with him. The pussy would shoot up the stairs at his call and return an hour later, its tail raised in triumph.

After a few months devoted to an exchange of shy smiles with the tenant, Miss Moberly, then a teenager and beautiful, had tied a love letter to the cat's neck just before it was summoned upstairs. The letter was not long, but behind it lay a week's toil over numerous drafts.

When the cat returned, what it carried, tied to its tail instead of neck, was not a reply but the same letter, soiled with butter, jam and curry.

Seventy years later Miss Moberly called out from her balcony, 'Robinson!'

Robinson wagged its mangy tail and gave out a tender bark.

Once Miss Moberly had realized the significance of the name she had bestowed on it, she had consciously named the second and the third dogs as Mac and Badal. Mac deceived her, after carrying on an affair with her long enough to make it the talk of the town. It would have been hard to find a dignified match after the scandal and Miss Moberly did not bother to try.

It was a decade later that the millionaire Badal had come forward to propose to her. He was a widower with a clean reputation and, at fifty, had suddenly fallen in love, for the first time in his life, he declared on oath. 'What a headlong fall is here, my countrymen!' a professor friend used to tease them with a parody of Shakespeare. 'Then, religion, caste and kin sank down slain whilst bloody love flourished over them!'

Badal closed down his business in Saigon, but on his way back died in a shipwreck.

Badal, of course, could not be grouped with Robinson and Mac. But no longer did Miss Moberly bear any resentment even against those two. Not that she had ever formally pardoned them, but God must have. That alone explains her slowly transcending her anguish.

The gallant Badal died while he was at the peak of his

happiness. For a long time Miss Moberly loved to imagine that the ship had sunk while Badal was fast asleep, dreaming of her, and the next moment he had found himself in the heavens where he still awaited her, sporting the same milky smile under his bushy moustache.

But what about Mac? After he had squeezed out of her all he wanted, he joined an international gang of thugs. Injured in an encounter with the police, he died of gangrene. (Till she tired of the fantasy, Miss Moberly had nursed a faint hope that Mac's last message, to be delivered to her any day, was: 'Dolly dear, I'm sorry. I'm sorry. I'm sorry . . .')

And Robinson! Perhaps the chap had never been able to love anything better than a cat all his life. Miss Moberly was convinced, though she could not say why, that unheard and unsung, he had died of leukaemia in some mofussil town, and that his skeleton was dangling in the anatomy department of the new medical college attached to the impoverished local hospital.

Miss Moberly stopped pacing to and fro and, leaning on the railing, looked down. At once three tails began wagging and three tongues lolled. Robinson, Mac and Badal. Miss Moberly disappeared into her room and emerged, chuckling, with a small plastic tray filled with crumbs of cake, bread and biscuit.

'Would you now set the chairs on the balcony and prepare tea?' she called faintly to her attendant. It was time for her friends to arrive. Mr Doss was already in the park below, whacking his stick in the air and killing time. That was his virtue. If he arrived even half a minute early, he would kill that half-minute prayerfully looking at his watch, outside the door. 'You are almost an Englishman, Mr Doss!' his boss used to observe when he was in service. Mr Doss took the tribute as the crowning glory of his life and was never tired of repeating it.

Mrs Sawoo should be arriving any moment, accompanied or followed by Mr Jacob. All three, now in their late eighties, were slightly older than Miss Moberly. Her father had been an influential man in the town, with varieties of achievements and a couple of titles earned from the British Raj. Her acquaintances, naturally, were numerous. But these three were the last surviving members of an inner circle which had sighed at every phase of the tragedy that dominated her life. They claimed to be younger than she in spirit and had begun to insist that she had lately been prone to mild hallucinations and should be careful about it. Mrs Sawoo, for instance, asserted that it was wrong to imagine that a male cat could ever talk! Miss Moberly should have quipped that the cat talked in its own language and not in English! But the fitting rejoinder always evaded her when most needed and occurred hours after she had been snubbed.

All that the three had done for a good many years now was to sympathize with her. At last the day had come for them to realize that it was not just sympathy that was her due; she deserved congratulations too. Henceforth no one would be able to say that her life had been nothing if not a calendar of failures. She was now ready to demonstrate to all concerned her spectacular success in striking her target.

'Dolly darling!'

Doss, Mrs Sawoo and Jacob entered together, and Mrs Sawoo gave her a noisy kiss. Miss Moberly did not neglect showing her usual warmth but she remained thoughtful. She must demonstrate her feat in an artful manner; the guests should suspect not that she was making a deliberate show of it.

A crumb fell from Mrs Sawoo's hand. Miss Moberly stooped to pick it up.

'Sorry, but leave it there, dear,' murmured Mrs Sawoo.

Miss Moberly smiled and, holding the crumb in her hand long enough to draw everybody's attention to it, suddenly threw it over the railing. Robinson jumped up and caught it in its mouth. Mac and Badal, knowing that their turns were coming, licked their lips and gave out subdued barks.

'Excellent!' said Jacob and Doss.

'Thank you, but wait and see!' Miss Moberly turned her chair to face the road and, placing the plastic tray on her lap, began throwing the crumbs with style and verve. The dogs romped and hopped, catching the missiles with dexterity.

'Excellent. Wonderful!'

The guests were liberal with their exclamations. Miss Moberly did not recall at what point she had stood up. The rhythm of the romping dogs found an echo in her own motions. She almost danced as she threw the crumbs.

'Come on, Dolly, enough of it. Drink your tea!' said Mrs Sawoo in a matronly tone.

The plastic tray had been emptied. Miss Moberly sat down, satisfaction reigning on her face like a sunrise.

'Hah! you are surprised, aren't you? Believe it or not, rarely do I miss my target. Who could have thought that I would be able to achieve success ninety times out of a hundred,' she managed to say between mild gasps, and laughed.

'Why not, Dolly!' Mrs Sawoo remarked while stirring her tea.

Miss Moberly looked down and waved at the dogs. 'Still there, eh! Disperse, quick! See you tomorrow!' she said.

'It is a regular sport with you, is it, Dolly?' Jacob queried with a chuckle.

'Who could have dreamed that I would be such a success at it!' Miss Moberly trilled bashfully.

'Well, Dolly, is there a cleverer hunter among the beasts than a dog?' observed Doss.

'Exactly,' Mrs Sawoo took upon herself to elucidate the remark. 'A dog will snap up a crumb even if you throw it with your eyes shut!'

'Do you remember my Alsatian, Don Juan? Once he nabbed a robin from a branch two and half yards above the ground. Yes! he did so while I looked on,' reminisced Doss, drawing in the air with his stick the location of the bird's perch and the swiftness with which Don Juan had pounced upon its prey.

'And I believe you all remember,' he continued, 'Sweet Heart, my spaniel during my Simla stint, whose picture had appeared in vol. 3, no. 7, page 12, March 1921 number of *Dogs International*, with a feature by Mr Richard Whites. How diligently Sweet Heart would fetch the tennis ball with a bite as tender as a kiss!' Doss kept a slice of cake under his own tender bite for a while and then resumed, 'I just can't help recalling again and again the observation Mr Whites had made—that looking at Mr Doss, the ideal doggy, and Sweet Heart, his regal spaniel, one could suspect that Sweet Heart was the master and

Mr Doss was her dog! But I used to protest, "Such compliments, sir, are not my due!" Mr Whites would say, "Mr Doss! You were almost an Englishman, except for this humility of yours." Ha ha!'

For the next half hour they remained engrossed in discussing the great dogs they had known in their life.

Nobody marked how dead Miss Moberly's face looked and how awkward the movement of her limbs had become.

The guests stood up.

'Till next week, Dolly darling!' said the gentlemen, and Mrs Sawoo kissed her goodbye.

Miss Moberly, as brisk and breezy as an orchestra conductor only minutes ago, walked into her room holding on to the wall and sprawled on the bed.

'Despite all your glittering false teeth with which you try to smile clever, you are a fool, Mrs Sawoo. And despite your dyed moustache which you still strive to keep forked out in your damned desire to look dashing, you are a snob, Mr Doss. And, Mr Jacob, you are a nincompoop!' mumbled out Miss Moberly and that gave her the strength to sit up for a while. She did not know when sleep overtook her.

As soon as she woke up early in the morning and saw her supper lying untouched on the table and recollected the events of the evening, she began taking determined steps to tide over her anguish. At first she reminded herself for the thousandth time that it was vain to expect true understanding from human beings, including those who had been near and dear ones for decades. Then she tried to forget the matter and, failing, set about analysing the minds of her three friends. She concluded that since they had fallen into the habit of sympathizing with her for her missing the target all her life, they had grown chronically incapable of accepting her success even when it was so glaringly evident.

She was charmed by her own power to delve into the very crux of the matter and that gave her some peace.

But she soon hit upon the real mischief the deplorable episode had done. It had bred some misgivings in her mind about her own capacity and the doubts bred a deepening sense of frustration. But could she afford to lose her self-confidence just because of casual comments by a few silly fellows? 'No!' she told herself, 'No, no, no!'

She must prove, at least to herself, that her achievement was as real as her confidence in herself.

In the evening, Miss Moberly stole several peeps into David Dawson's room. The retired brigadier passed his mornings in humming or whistling ancient war tunes and his afternoons in snoozing against a huge bolster.

After strolling for a while along the balcony in front of Dawson's room during which she assessed the brigadier's condition, Miss Moberly stealthily entered the room and came out in a minute. Dawson did not open his eyes.

Back on the balcony she breathed deeply, inhaling a lot of oxygen and courage. She knew under which side of the pillow Dawson kept his pistol. She wavered for a moment and then entered the room again, picked up the weapon and tiptoed out.

Now she could prove it! The dogs might get the credit in the case of the crumbs. But surely, it could not be the same when it came to receiving a bullet! If she could hit one, it would be entirely due to her accuracy of aim, not the dog's.

Who should it be? Robinson, Mac or Badal? Any would do. Poor Badal! But what business had he to fall in love if die he must in a shipwreck? None of them deserved mercy. She could shoot down any of them. Couldn't she? Of course she could!— she assured herself, breathing in deeply several times.

'Damn it! Who the hell took away my pistol? Good God! Dolly, you!' Brigadier Dawson screamed and hobbled towards the door. Miss Moberly stood still, pressing the pistol to her breast, like a child stubbornly refusing to part with a toy.

'You meant to commit suicide, Dolly? Yo ho!' the old warrior screamed again, trembling all over.

'Suicide?' cried out Jayshri Mishra, former actress and one-time mistress of a prodigal prince, as she came rushing, her eyes ignited by the brigadier's exclamation.

'Suicide? Oh no!' cried out in a cracking voice the retired principal Jonathan Jana, who generally kept quiet during the day but at night taught Milton in his sleep.

'Suicide?' shrieked Miss Moberly herself and she broke into wild sobs.

The actress and the principal tried to take hold of Miss Moberly's tiny head. She obliged both, first leaning on the actress's breast and then on the principal's. She also allowed the brigadier, who showed remarkable consideration and patience in relieving her of the weapon, to fondle her.

It was the principal who first echoed her sobs. He was instantly joined by the actress and the brigadier.

Fifteen feet below, Robinson, Mac and Badal yapped politely. The well-wishers led Miss Moberly to her bed. Jayshri prepared coffee for all. The duty of hurling crumbs at the dogs was discharged by the brigadier. They all sat around Miss Moberly till late in the night, had their supper together, and talked of human goodness and God's kindness and exchanged anecdotes of profound significance.

'Now, go to sleep, sweet child, my very sweet child,' said the principal, stroking Miss Moberly's head and bidding her an affectionate goodnight.

When the male cat appeared at midnight and put its usual question to Miss Moberly, she did not feel offended at all. She had begun to see a guardian in everyone.

'I'm quite all right. Thank you,' she told the cat politely and fell asleep.

Prithviraj's Horse

It had been a fond habit with Mukund, the teacher of history and sometimes of geography, to offer his smiles to the tall, the burly and the brawny, by way of greeting them. He did not do it just as a safety measure, thin and weak though he was. 'These stalwarts roaming up and down the earth could cause even more trouble to the already harassed humanity if they so wished. But how harmlessly they move about! Don't they deserve a show of gratitude?' This was his thought. In fact, he thought on behalf of conscientious humanity.

One in every three such stalwarts acknowledging his greeting, by smiling back or giving a nod, was enough to tide him over his anguish due to the other two taking no notice of his gesture. Often he conquered those disinterested heroes with a second or third round of his undaunted smile.

Mukund was new at Parvatipuri. His lodge was four kilometres away from his school, the Goswami Academy. Far from grumbling on that account, he felt happy. Time had reduced Parvatipuri to a hick town, but it had a glorious past. And Mukund loved walking, exploring places.

What a thrill was there in finding a new route to his destination—discovering a blind lane on the way or taking a short detour for a closer look at a building that looked hoary! Who knew if the lane he had just covered did not contain the remains of a great king reduced to dust, or the nook he surveyed had not been the seat of a *yajna* performed by a great sage? Who knew if those old monuments did not still contain a stone or two of the legendary castles which adorned the city in remote golden age?

There was no dearth of time. He lived alone and had his meals at a small restaurant close to his lodge. His relatives had made several attempts at providing him with a consort. But in each case, the prospective bride appeared to be stronger than he. After running down the sixth proposal, he had conveyed to his tired well-wishers that he had resolved to remain a bachelor for ever. The cause of his grim decision, of course, remained buried in his heart.

He had retained and reinforced his reputation as a perfect gentleman as he changed schools. In every farewell meeting, the budding speakers, his favourite students, declared in voices choking with emotion that their only aim in life was to be as noble as their departing mentor. Mukund was the star—the Pole Star—to which they must hitch their wagons.

He was sure that few could equal him as a teacher—of history in particular. He tickled the dead past back to life. Students forgot even football and cricket, and sat gaping at him when he spoke of the great moments of history and went on speaking till well past the bell.

The character who fascinated him most was Prince Prithviraj. He was unhappy with the lacklustre manner in which the textbooks presented the remarkable story of the hero's elopement with Princess Samyukta. He retold the story with a vengeance, so much so that the students in the first row could see his hair stand on end and he thought he could see theirs do the same.

A normal Monday suddenly became a memorable day for him when, at the end of a period, he overheard a girl whispering to another, 'It looks as though Mukund Sir was a witness to the Prithviraj-Samyukta episode!' 'Indeed!' commented the other.

How many got to hear splendid appreciation of this kind? Mukund felt rewarded, delighted and grateful.

It was a quiet sunset and he took one of his newly discovered lanes, leading by an indirect way to his lodge. More important than the way itself was the new object of adoration he had found beside it. At the very first glimpse of the man, six times his girth if not more, he had remembered the mighty Bhim of Mahabharata. But as the man was young, he preferred to name him Ghatotcoch, Bhim's gigantic son by his demoness consort, Hidimba.

Mukund's first smile had evidently gone unnoticed. When he smiled at him at the second opportunity, the young giant looked intrigued. His reaction was not any different even to Mukund's third attempt. But Mukund did not give up. If anything, he felt even more fascinated by that mountain of a man and looked at him like a climber measuring a defiant peak he aspired to scale.

Upon Mukund throwing his smile for the fourth time at him—that was this morning—Ghatotcoch's lips had parted and his eyes had grown rounder. Maybe that was the fellow's manner of responding to his show of affection, thought Mukund, and derived some consolation from it.

Who could the giant be? His red round eyes and long sinewy arms gave one the impression that crushing men with a huge mace had been his pleasant vocation until the previous week.

Mukund slowed down his pace. He spotted Ghatotcoch on the veranda of an old house, a picture of Vir Hanuman pasted on the dilapidated door behind him. A few yards away sat four or five elderly men of the same clan, playing cards. He had not seen them there before. Obviously, they were all outsiders, living scattered in the town, meeting for a relaxed evening.

As soon as Ghatotcoch's eyes fell on him, Mukund gave him the broadest ever smile.

Suddenly Ghatotcoch jumped down and held him by the arm. Mukund had a feeling that his arm was fast turning to pulp.

'Why do you laugh at me?' demanded the man in a mixed language.

This was most unexpected. Mukund, always an inspiring talker, learnt for the first time what it was like to be struck dumb. Ghatotcoch's kinsmen paused in their game and gazed at Mukund and his captor. Mukund saw in them a troop of tigers making a silent allocation of his limbs among themselves.

'You find me funny, do you?' Ghatotcoch demanded again.

'Does he possess a pair of horns?' a card-player asked Mukund, baring his vampire-like red teeth.

'Is he a creature in the zoo and are you a mere toddler to feel amused at him?' asked another.

Mukund was shaking and seeing a thousand fireflies around him in a bizarre darkness engulfing him.

Suddenly he gave out a yell. Startled, Ghatotcoch released him. Mukund ran at great speed, feeling like a shuttlecock struck by a gorilla's racket.

'What's the matter, babu?' asked several voices, some curious and some anxious. Mukund did not stop.

On reaching home he lay down. He felt as if he had been scalded.

He who had successfully survived seven conspiracies to pin him down to a marital bed, he who looked ten years younger than his age, he whose farewell meetings drew a hundred streams of tears, he who could tell you from memory the exact dates of the Kalinga war, the coronation of Kanishka, and the confrontation between Dupleix and Clive, he who planned to go down in history as the founder-president of a cultural-cum-gymnastic club upon retirement—was about to get beaten up and unceremoniously thrown in a murky lane by a dunderhead!

Was his life a bubble for somebody to prick and see it vanish?

He was still shivering, no longer from the shock but from a brew of bewilderment and agitation churning within him.

'Who could have taken my life away so easily? Am I not invincible?' he asked himself and felt brave, and his lips curled in disdain of Ghatotcoch. Only if the chap had heard what the girls in the classroom had to say—that his soul dated back to the era of Prithviraj, if not to that of Vikramaditya!

And couldn't that be true? Why not? He felt the urgency for growing sure of it once and for all.

He sprang out of his bed.

It was dark by the river side and he jogged on comfortably.

'Tantrik-Astrologer, Gold-Medallist-Worshipper of Goddess Kali, Advisor to Kings and Emperors, Predictor of the Future, Expert in Reading the *Bhrigu Samhita* and Revealing your Past

Lives—Pundit Purandar Sharma' said the signboard with a flickering bulb dangling over it. The door was half open. Many times before had Mukund wished to meet the occultist. The right moment had come.

'Yes?' Sharma focused an owlish look on Mukund.

'I wish to know who I was in my earlier incarnations.'

'I have closed the sacred *Bhrigu Samhita* for the day. Once closed it cannot be opened before sunrise ordinarily, not even if King George the Fifth pleaded for it or promised a bit of his kingdom. However . . .'

'All I want to know for the moment is my status in the court of Prince Prithviraj, the last of the Chauhans . . .'

'Ten rupees.'

Mukund handed out the money. Sharma once again folded his legs into the lotus pose. He scribbled on a slate the numbers relating to Mukund's date and time of birth. He took the slate close to the table lamp and mumbled something for a couple of minutes.

Mukund stood breathless. The occultist shook his head and shut his eyes. A minute passed. He opened his eyes wide and at once fixed them on Mukund's.

'I saw you, sonny!'

'Really? How did I look? Was I by any chance Pr . . . Prithvi . . .'

'You were his faithful horse, my boy. Come again. The answer to the first query costs ten rupees. The subsequent ones cost only five rupees each.'

Sharma patted Mukund on the back. 'Yes, you used to bear Prince Prithviraj here!'

'And Samyukta too!' added Mukund. The occultist nodded. It was not clear if he understood Samyukta's relevance to Prithviraj. But he exclaimed, 'A monarch among stallions! Yes, that is what you were!'

Mukund was on the road again, his body charged with a hitherto unknown vim and vigour. He was no longer surprised over the speed at which he had run while giving the slip to Ghatotcoch. It was an ability that had come down to him from his glorious equine past. The yell that made the would-be assailant release his arm was an atavistic outburst of his stately neighing that had struck terror in the heart of Muhammad Ghauri in the year 1192.

What a stalwart among stallions, how handsome and stately he must have looked!

The darkness was only partially dislodged by the miserly street lights and a reluctant moon. Mukund began to run again. Despite the evolutionary metamorphosis of his two forelegs into arms, he was sure he could run like his earlier incarnation.

He was at his destination within minutes.

He peeped through the window. Ghatotcoch sat cross-legged before a lantern and munched chapattis meditatively.

Mukund stormed in. Ghatotcoch was taken aback.

Mukund grinned. 'So, baby, you take yourself to be really Ghatotcoch, eh? Scaring a mere teacher of Goswami Academy was as easy as shooing away a kitten, right? What a hero! Get up, boy, let's have a fight!' said Mukund, his hands resting on his waist. 'Yes, a real fight. I mean it.'

Ghatotcoch had instinctively thrown a whole chapatti into his mouth lest an opportunity for that should never come again, and was nervously trying to swallow the lump. It got stuck in his throat. He made a gurgling noise. Mukund saw his reflection in a cracked mirror on the wall. He looked menacing and weird. He laughed lustily.

'You nincompoop, you fat lump of ignorance, do you know who I am? Squeezing my arm, eh? Munching chapattis, eh? I can munch and munch and reduce you to a mouthful of syrup, and gulp the whole of you down. Do you understand that?' Mukund flexed his muscles, took a step forward and gave a shake to Ghatotcoch, who slumped.

Mukund laughed aloud again and jumped down to the road. His return journey was leisurely. He even whistled and hummed a tune. He ate twice his usual meal and sank into a sound sleep.

Next day, while he was zealously explaining to his students the phenomenon of heavy rain over Cherapunji—for, strangely, the geography teacher developed a sore throat and sneezed uninterrupted whenever the Cherapunji chapter came and took leave for a day—the headmaster summoned him to report to the teachers' common room.

The septuagenarian chairman of the school managing committee said, addressing the assembly of teachers, 'You might feel amazed to learn that a certain *goonda*, announcing himself to be a teacher of our school, manhandled a young man, a job-seeker from a faraway place. Is it not rather baffling that someone should try to tarnish the fair image of our institution? When the victim, his guardian and the secretary of their association brought the matter to my knowledge this morning, I straightaway offered to hold an identification parade of our teachers! Let them feel sure that we have no rowdy, no ruffian, or no brigand on our payroll! Please bear with the inconvenience.'

The chairman smiled and, through the window, signalled Ghatotcoch and his guardian to come in.

Ghatotcoch looked nervous. Directed by the chairman, he began surveying the teachers, one after another.

'Here . . . here . . .' he squeaked, pointing a feverishly trembling finger at Mukund.

'Who? Our Mukund babu?' asked the amused chairman.

All the eighteen teachers giggled while the chairman and the headmaster somehow managed to look serious.

'My boy, had you accused me of the crime, that would have made some sense,' commented the venerable chairman with a sigh. He then took Ghatotcoch's guardian aside and said as politely as possible, 'I suggest you take the young man to the hospital—I mean to the psychiatry department.'

Ghatotcoch, on the verge of weeping, was led away by his guardian. The chairman apologized to the teachers and left the common room along with the headmaster.

The eighteen teachers surrounded the blushing Mukund and burst into a laugh that surprised even the half-deaf watchman on duty at the gate a hundred yards away.

The Strategy

It was on a serene dawn, while the last star in the eastern sky was taking leave of Gouri through her window, that the brilliant idea flashed in her mind—the strategy to wake up everybody in the village, by giving them a jolt, to the fact that she was still there amidst them, as alive as ever.

The suspicion that she was being taken for granted, even cold-shouldered, had persisted in her mind for quite some time. It was time for her to act, she felt sure, to shake the villagers out of their complacency about her. Luckily, her bones were strong under her time-worn skin and her hands, at ninety-three, were only slightly less mobile than they had been till the other day when they did their magic with women in labour.

She had tried to impart her skill and dexterity to Ahalya, a young widow who addressed her as Granny. No doubt Ahalya was developing the ability—which needed more of ardour in the heart than skill in the hands—quickly. But a big dispensary had come up in the vicinity of the village and, by and by, the job had been entirely taken over by the nurses in immaculate white.

Ahalya, however, continued to attend upon Gouri. What was it that motivated her? The few silver ornaments Gouri had? Or only love? Maybe a combination of both and there was nothing wrong in it.

Gouri could have given her even the gold ring she had once

received as a reward for seeing the zamindar's daughter-in-law through a critical phase in the process of her delivery. Unfortunately, she had to sell it to save her adopted son, an orphan, from litigation. She could rescue the unworthy boy, fallen into evil company, from the clutches of law, but not from death.

That was half a century ago. For a while she thought that with the death of the adopted son her sole interest in the world had snapped, having lost her father even before her birth, her mother at the age of three, her husband (she had been married off by her late uncle when five) at the age of seven, and her grandmother, who taught her midwifery, at sixteen.

But, to her amazement, she saw her link with the world growing stronger by the day. For all the children of the region she became the golden bridge between their mothers' wombs and Mother Earth as they descended on her palms. It was she who responded to their first cry, in which she deciphered the infant's assertion of its blind faith that there was someone to hearken to it. And in her own spontaneous loving response she heard the reassuring voice of providence.

She emerged, every time, ennobled from the exercise. No one else was expected to know about it, but her memory teemed with numerous such moments, exhilarating and invigorating. Her days passed amidst those loving faces growing up around her and the recognition given her by their parents.

Times seemed to have changed. Where were those toddling golden cherubs? The one whose advent had brought her the gold ring had duly inherited his father's estates, but after the abolition of the feudal system, had grown addicted to opium. The local leader, now an MLA, whose voice resounded like that of a whole bazaar, had lain voiceless and benumbed for a long time after his birth, causing great consternation in all the women gathered around his mother, except, of course, in Gouri, whose feelings were moulded from deep within and did not depend on mere external signs of a situation.

The attitude of people was no longer the same—Gouri had been aware of it for a long time—and in their eyes she was perhaps in no way different from any other uselss, aged woman.

Only once during the last decade had she been treated differently when, at an appeal from the leading villagers, she willed her patch of land to be annexed by the adjacent school compound, after her death. In a public meeting held to discuss some important issues, this gesture of hers too was announced by the village chief and the audience burst into thunderous applause and a thousand eyes rolled in different directions to locate her. Some people even wanted to lift her and carry her over to the dais.

Gouri had been thrilled. At night she was unable to sleep even a wink.

Sleep, of course, had been evading her lately, but that was because of her age, she had been told. And it was towards the end of one such night with very little sleep that the right strategy to shatter the callous attitude of the villagers towards her had dawned upon her.

She sat up, inspired. Before long she was on the road, pacing along with her faithful walking stick. The first man of any importance she saw was Vanbihari Sahu, the moneylender. She saw him all right, but did he see her? He would have passed her by but for her deliberately stopping right in front of him and coughing.

'Hello Granny! How are you?'

Gouri looked up and smiled. Does the man know that it was she who had not only presided over his birth but also christened him with that excellent name—Vanbihari? The weeping infant of the other day had grown totally bald and half as toothless as herself! People say that he exploited his debtors mercilessly. Gouri hated such rumours regarding any of the souls born under her auspices.

So, Vanbihari was ordained to be the very first man to receive the shock she must administer! She was sorry, but she was not prepared to modify her grim decision in any manner.

'Sonny! you ask me how am I, do you? Well, let me tell you very categorically that I won't be amidst you for long. I am departing to the other world. Yes, I mean it!'

Gouri heaved a sigh and waited, sure of the moneylender's strong reaction—his anxious protests, his horror at her most unexpected, most unkind announcement, something like: 'Oh no, no, no. Granny! How can our life be the same without you? Oh, no!'

But Sahu only nodded and looked up and made a vague gesture raising both his arms towards the sky, which could either mean that the Lord's will be done or that it was going to rain! He then walked away.

It took almost five minutes for Gouri to bring a reasonable steadiness to her trembling walking stick.

'I tell you, to call the minister or even the chief minister is no problem. The question is, why should we? I don't believe in the formality of according receptions to anybody, however important . . . Who is this? Gouri Nani? Granny dear! How are you, sweet little girl? . . . So far as the minister's visit is concerned, well . . . are you all right Granny? . . . Yes . . . we must create an occasion for the minister or the chief minister . . .'

Gouri had stopped at the advent of that familiar gurgling preceding the party at the bend of the road. Baidhar Mirdha, the MLA, emerged in the company of a dozen men, some tall and some short, some fat and some lean, some dark and some fair. He loved to carry with him an assortment of human specimens.

'I can talk to the minister . . . but . . . yes . . . the occasion . . . Hello Granny, do you wish to speak to me? . . . You are looking as bright as a damsel about to wed . . . So far as the minister . . .'

'My boy! I am about to wed—to Death. No, I am not jesting. It's time for me to bid farewell to you all, my children. Am I not already ninety-three?'

Mirdha laughed like the first sound of a kick-started moped.

'Gentlemen!' he asked his followers, 'Do you suppose our Granny's death could be a strong enough argument to warrant the Hon'ble Minister's presence?' He laughed again and this time the specimens of humanity followed suit.

The MLA had begun to walk. 'Ours is a democracy. Any minister is bound to . . .' His voice faded like a distant thunder.

Gouri felt paralysed, a sensation she had never had before. But the zamindar's house was close at hand. She managed to climb to the dusky veranda of his fading mansion.

The zamindar relaxed on a worn out armchair. The last servant in his household was preparing the *hookah* for him.

'Who is it?' he queried without looking at Gouri.

'Nobody!' replied the servant.

'It is Gouri, Gouri the midwife, Gouri nani, Gouri granny!' Gouri announced aloud, correcting the servant, and added, 'My son, I must inform you that my days are numbered. Yes, truly so. I have resolved to desert all my dear ones like you . . . None can stop me!'

'Who? What's the matter?' the zamindar asked again, after his first puff at the hookah.

'Gouri the midwife. She says that she is going to die,' the servant said carrying his lips close to his master's ear, not without some irritation.

'Die? Was she alive?' The zamindar shut his eyes in order to relish the smoke better.

Gouri had forgotten that the zamindar remained under the effect of opium most of time. But it would have hardly made any difference even if she had remembered it.

Nobody noticed when she left. 'Granny!' Ahalya, back after a day's absence, called out early in the morning the next day. And five minutes later she was heard crying and announcing to the passers-by, 'Granny has left us, it appears peacefully in her sleep!'

The Submerged Valley

We became conscious of our village the day our headmaster asked us, the students of Class Three, to write an essay on the topic.

So far we had taken the village for granted—like our breathing or our mothers' love. But thereafter the elements that made the village—the trees, the pools, the Shiva temple and the hillock adjacent to it—had begun to look significant.

Our village had several other aspects to it. A lame crow perched on a crumbling stone arch of the temple and cawed on in an ominous way. Nobody ever dared to scare it away. A certain member of the Harijan community looked completely white because of congenital vitiligo. His fond grandparents had christened him Sahib. From some mysterious source he had secured a cork *topee* of the type the white men used to wear in colonial India. He visited the weekly market sporting the topee and invoked in the throng something of the awe that was due to the real Sahibs who ruled the country.

The trees that stood in front of our school used to appear as human to us as the wandering bull of Lord Shiva. One of the trees looked as if it was kneeling in meditation. Two more were never tired of chattering to each other. If the teacher had scolded or thrashed us, they seemed to be sympathizing with us. At

the approach of a vacation they seemed to be talking of the
many sweet moments in store for us.

Last but not the least, there was an insane woman who lived
on the hillock behind the temple. She had for her pets a mad
dog and a mad cat. Whatever be the standard applied to measure
the states of mind of the woman and her dog, it was intriguing
how our people had been sure of the lunacy of the cat. But before
I was of an age, all three had died.

The woman had left behind a son, crazy and no less arrogant.
He chose a house a day and planted himself in its courtyard,
refusing to budge until fed to his content. Somehow he had learnt
to claim that jackals and ravens talked to him. His incoherent
speech and enigmatic hints added a touch of weirdness to his
personality, and that was to his profit.

Serious-minded villagers had tried to harness him to some
constructive activity. One had introduced him to the spinning
wheel. He found running the wheel for its own sake good fun,
but not for spinning. An affluent farmer commissioned him to
guard a pile of paddy. An hour later people saw Lord Shiva's
bull lying in place of the paddy, ruminating with eyes closed,
and the young man entertaining it to a post-banquet song.

Hence he was called Abolkara, meaning the disobedient, the
funny hero of a series of folktales popular in our region.

I was five when my father, an engineer, moved our
establishment to the town. Soon the village became only a
memory for me. Even so, the day I heard that a proposed large
dam would submerge it, I became gloomy. Mother wiped her
eyes.

By and by, several respectable men of our area visited us and
not one of them went back without shedding tears. Although
Father was not connected with the project, my mother and the
villagers prevailed upon him to exert his influence to forestall
its execution.

Father had a solemn bearing and he talked or smiled little.
But if the situation warranted, he could be fluent, his solemnity
still intact.

Heaping their rain-soaked umbrellas and bales on our
veranda, once a delegation of elderly villagers recounted to

Father the glory of our ancestral area—tales of our pious forefathers who had toiled there and whose ashes had become one with the soil, of the several good gods who dwelt in the shrines even though rather ineffectual in the current *Kaliyug*, the era of falsehood, and of the fertility of the lands.

'Must everything end up in deluge, babu? Despite having begotten a worthy son like you, are we so unlucky that the cruel hand of the government will so unceremoniously tear us away from our God-given lands?' they repeated as they wiped their eyes more and more frequently.

Father heard in silence and that gave us the impression that he had been moved. But once he opened his mouth, I felt a certain heartlessness not only in his speech but also in the silence that had preceded it.

'Look here, for me the whole of history is made of only two factors, construction and destruction—be the latter planned or accidental,' he said. 'Where is Harappa today and where is Babylon? Time has licked them off—just for the sake of change. On the other hand, if we are losing our lands, it is for a change for the better, for the welfare of a larger population. And we ought not to ignore the fact that the government is ready to compensate for our loss and to provide us with every facility for rehabilitation. Who did not have pious forefathers? Where is to be found an area that had no shrines? Can a single project succeed if such sentiments were to be respected?'

Members of the delegation were too stupefied to say anything more. Mother sent tiffin and cool drinks for them through me and my younger sister Putu. If they showed reluctance to accept them, it was surely due to Father's attitude, and if they finally accepted them, it was due to their affection for Mother.

The next two years were marked by radical developments. After holding a few unreported meetings in the village, a few hundred villagers arrived in the town bringing their own food along, and went round in a procession. It was a pitiable show. The cars and motorcycles scared them, and they were too shy to raise slogans. The placards they held were written in a raw hand, with glaring spelling errors.

Their representatives met the leaders of the ruling party

but their arguments lacked the earlier vigour. Before long, they lost faith in their cause and were reconciled to the situation. Half of the people went over to an alternative site offered to them by the authorities, a valley eighteen miles away. They carried the deities with them and also led away the bull of Lord Shiva.

The rest chose cash compensation and scattered in bazaars and towns, seeking out sundry jobs or opening petty shops.

We heard that on the eve of their departure the villagers rolled on the ground, crying and beating their heads against it and smearing themselves with dust. We never saw our village again.

Five years had elapsed since the making of the dam. Three districts had now less to fear from floods. Regulated irrigation gave some boost to agriculture, though the increase in population did not let it mean anything more than a statistical satisfaction.

Then came exciting news. The monsoon had been delayed in the distant hills. The river had grown feeble and the level of the reservoir had fallen unusually low. Consequently the top of the Shiva temple and the hillock behind it could be seen. The small news item had been dispatched by a newspaper's correspondent in the dam area. Father read it out to Mother and said, 'I have to attend a committee meeting at the dam. Should you like to accompany me, I could arrange for a trip to the hillock.'

There were tears of joy in Mother's eyes.

We reached the dam the next day. The sky was overcast with more and more clouds taking up suitable positions. The locality had changed so much that Mother was expressing her shock and surprise every other minute. Two neat bungalows stood on two ends of the majestic embankment. There was a cluster of small buildings for the dam officials.

A bazaar too had cropped up. By then Father had reached the top rung of his career, and there were several eager smiles and hands to accord us a warm welcome.

We were accommodated in one of the bungalows. To the west stretched the vast lake. It was late in the afternoon and over the water hung a light fog. At a distance, the summit of the temple and the hillocks looked melancholy though charming, like two memories emerging from the mists of time.

Some more officers were expected by sundown. Father asked his assistant to schedule the meeting in the evening and commissioned a launch for us. He was in a hurry, for he had news of heavy showers at the source of the river. The water level could rise, submerging our destination.

Our launch soon left behind the three small boats which too were heading towards the islet. And we could see two or three boats already moored at the hillock.

'Sir, many of the former residents of this area have come rushing at the news of the old temple raising its head. They are thankful to you for allowing them to visit the sight,' said an assistant engineer who accompanied us.

'The permission was granted by your boss. You are being unnecessarily kind to me,' Father cut him short. The young officer's bright smile froze into an embarrassed grin.

The temple and the hillock had always remained green in my memory. Their reappearance in this novel setting aroused in me a strange sensation—an excitement tempered by sadness. But Putu, who was only a year old when we left the village, was even more excited. And Mother—she sat absorbed in her thoughts, her cheek resting on her hand. The clouds, the sombre lake, and her deep eyes combined to make it a serene experience for me.

Visitors who had reached the hillock before us gazed at our launch with curiosity. Among them were their boatmen who told our driver how to negotiate his way close to the islet.

We were there at last! Many in the crowd greeted Father, and Father returned the greetings warmly. I was patted and Putu fondled. I could spot several familiar faces.

Some old folks clustered around Mother and let flow the final instalment of the tears first shed five years ago. They also informed her that many of those venerable people who had met Father in the town had since then departed to the world beyond.

The boats we had passed began arriving one after another. There were more smiles and tears. Voices buzzed telling of erstwhile neighbours—who's who now and their fortunes and struggles.

'Babu, do you remember Abolkara? There he is!' Our

attention was drawn to a bearded, jolly looking fellow seated on a rock.

'How is he here?' asked Father.

'Babu, perhaps you won't believe ...' The observation halted midway.

Father looked at the speaker quizzically.

'He was here all along!'

Father laughed. Some others laughed too. But they did so as a courtesy towards Father. From the whispers and exchange of glances among the crowd I had gathered that quite a few of them were in favour of accepting this fantastic story as true. Some were asking Abolkara insistently, 'Do tell us—will you?—how did you manage to breathe under the water for five long years? What was your diet?'

'Like that, like that!' said Abolkara proudly, in his usual weird and indistinct tone and style, throwing his arms in the air.

Visitors who had brought light refreshments with them gave generous shares to him. The relish with which he ate only strengthened the theory that he had more or less fasted for five years, clinging to the submerged rock all the while.

Father did not pay much attention to Abolkara and discussed serious topics with the elite in the throng. Then, after concentrating for a moment on the water beating at the temple peak, he raised his voice and announced, 'Look here, everybody, the water has begun to rise. You should leave without delay.'

Father had hardly finished when a sudden gust blew away a middle-aged gentleman's shawl. He ran after it to the brink of the islet, but it gave him the slip in a highly tricky manner. I slapped Putu mildly in time to stop her from bursting into a savage laugh.

Rain came down, at first fine like dust, but soon to grow into the size of pellets. The visitors unfurled their umbrellas and boarded their boats hastily.

'Who brought Abolkara? Don't forget him, please!' Father shouted.

The boatmen of the six boats looked at one another. It was obvious that none of them was responsible for Abolkara. He must have been left there by an earlier party. However, every boat was willing to ferry him back.

'But I've been here all the time!' Abolkara repeated the statement with a chuckle, stressing each syllable. He was highly pleased with the story some innovative mind had floated.

'Is that so? Very well,' Father said sarcastically, and then looked towards the boats and said, 'You may go. Let him suffer the rain now and then whatever more is in store for him once the hillock has gone under the water.'

Father was sure, as the boats started to leave, Abolkara would come down, frightened.

The first boat left; the second, third and fourth ones followed suit. Abolkara sat quiet, dangling his legs and throwing nuts into his mouth.

'Come away, I say, or you'll die!' shouted Father, quite annoyed.

'But I'm here for five . . .!'

'Shut up!' Father looked at the last boat. The passengers were most anxious to leave. Their oars flapped at a slight wave of Father's hand. The leading ones among the departing passengers told Father, 'No use wasting time on that chap, babu, better you too leave. He will go on his own—maybe by swimming.'

Father did not give up coaxing Abolkara to come down. 'You are dreaming of more visitors tomorrow and more offerings for you, are you? But know that no one will be allowed to come here again. The hillock will have totally disappeared by morning.'

There was no result. Father took a few steps towards him. Abolkara slipped over to the other side of the rock, ready to plunge into the lake.

Father's command and the rain had driven the assistant engineer, Mother, Putu and myself into the launch. Father gave out a last roar, swore, and then joined us. The launch started.

It was raining heavily and the launch pitched violently. The lake looked fearful. Putu clung to Mother.

I tried to locate the boats we must be leaving behind. I could see the blurred shapes of only two.

Leaving us at the portico of our bungalow, Father hurried to his meeting. He had no time even for a cup of tea.

The rain grew torrential. Through the window—we occupied the upper floor—Mother stared into the lake time and again while Putu and I sat for dinner. She could have hardly seen anything except the turbulent hearts of the clouds laid bare by stabs of lightning.

'Mummy, what will happen to Abolkara?' It was Putu, on the verge of weeping after a smashing thunderclap. Mother walked to the telephone and tried to contact the other bungalow, the venue of Father's meeting. But the instrument was dead.

She sent us to bed and drew her chair close to the window. Putu, I assumed, had fallen asleep. But I could not help thinking about Abolkara and Father's brusque manner, and finding some way of consoling Mother. In the howling wind, I heard the cries of the ghost of the drowned village.

Father returned at midnight. Thoroughly drenched, he looked exhausted.

'Anything to eat?' he asked.

'Did you expect there'd be nothing?' asked Mother in turn, ready to lay out food for him.

'Not for me. I ate with the other engineers. How to inform you? The telephone wouldn't work!'

'Then?' Mother looked up, surprised.

'Why don't you go and see?' Father pointed to the outer room.

I followed Mother. There stood Abolkara, shivering like a wet squirrel, but smiling.

'Give him clothes to change, and a pair of blankets from the bungalow's stock in that almirah.' Father began to wipe himself. 'When it was certain that the hillock would get submerged at night, I had to take out the launch again. The temple had disappeared. All that remained was the rock with this gentleman on top of it. What a welcoming smile he gave when I focused my torch on him! On our way back, the engine stopped working and we escaped an accident narrowly. Well, I must lie down now. Have your dinner alone.'

Father went in to change his clothes. While feeding Abolkara, Mother looked glorious as a goddess.

The wind had grown erratic. 'Go into Father's room and see. If the west-side window is open, shut it,' Mother told me.

While shutting the window gently, I looked at Father's face with deep admiration.

I heard a giggle. Putu stood at the door.

'Father is wonderful, isn't he?' she whispered to me.

'Fool, how long you take to realize things that are obvious!' I quipped and, imitating Father's stern style, said, 'Naughty one, will you now return to bed?'

Bhola Grandpa and the Tiger

Bhola Grandpa and his wife lived at the western end of our village. Their hut was overshadowed by a large bokal tree which, with the advent of spring, grew luxuriant and continuously showered its tiny red fruit in their courtyard. The tree had become the permanent abode of a small troop of monkeys. Bhola Grandpa and his wife did not mind it.

I vividly remember the moonlit night when we were returning from the festival in honour of Lord Shiva. Still looked upon as a child, I had chances galore to travel perched on the shoulders of able-bodied villagers. The road was long and, far above the fog, the moon looked like suffering from a bad cold. I nodded off on the village chowkidar's shoulders.

Father was looked upon with awe and reverence, and the villagers considered it a privilege to walk in his company. Bhola Grandpa, senior to him by a few years, was always more prompt than the others in expressing his agreement with whatever Father uttered.

But suddenly Bhola Grandpa gave out a loud wail.

Taken aback, our party came to a halt. Enquiry revealed that Bhola Grandpa had led his daughter's son, who was of my age, to the festival. He piloted the grandson through the jostling throngs with two of the boy's fingers held tightly in his grip. He did not realize when those fingers slipped out. His grip, however, continued as before.

It was when someone queried about the content of his grip that he remembered the grandson and gave out the wail.

Father chose two keen-eyed escorts from our party and directed them to go back with Bhola Grandpa to the festival. The grandson, who had found a congenial shelter under a cow's belly and kept blinking at the unfamiliar people passing by, was rescued before long.

I remained alert for the rest of the journey and heard Father recount the following anecdote:

Bhola Grandpa, whose father and grandfather too had been in our employment, spent most of his time in our house. One afternoon, decades ago, he was found sprawling in a corner of our veranda with his tongue stretched out. A shiver ran through those who found him in that condition. They took him for dead.

What, however, had happened was this: an hour earlier someone had broached to him a proposal for his wedding. Modesty had made him stretch out his tongue. He had just forgotten to withdraw it while falling asleep.

I remember Bhola Grandpa blushing and looking down while Father narrated to an amused audience on our terrace the next day yet another episode of their younger days:

That had been a wet afternoon. Bhola Grandpa, looking wild with excitement, confided to Father and his friends that he had spied upon a gang of pirates burying a large box under one of the sand dunes on the lonely seashore by our village. He had also watched the gang disappear into the sea, their sleek dinghy shooting like an arrow into the mist.

Father and party at once began exploring the possible spots for the hidden treasure. Evening gave way to night. There was no light save for the moonbeams filtering through the clouds, and no sound except for the wind's moaning and the hooting of an owl from the hollow of a palm tree struck dead by lightning. A pack of jackals howled, indicating that it was past midnight.

Suddenly Bhola Grandpa was seen collapsing on the sand. His friends rushed to his side. Bhola Grandpa never spoke a lie. He soon composed himself and confessed that it was all a dream which he had had during his midday nap. He had somehow mistaken the dream to be a fact.

The locale of the most significant incident in Bhola Grandpa's life had been the Sundarbans. The region was marked by clusters of thick jungle. Royal Bengal tigers stalked the picturesque islands between the narrow serpentine branches of the Ganga. My forefathers, though belonging to Orissa, were among the few landlords who owned chunks of estates in that dangerous region of Bengal.

Bhola Grandpa was periodically sent there to manage the property.

In the Sundarbans of those days nobody would walk alone even in daytime. Tigers apart, alligators frequently sneaked in from the swamp. People took care to move about only in groups, particularly after sundown. Often they were led by a necromancer who, from time to time, gave out a piercing yell that could not be imitated by the uninitiated. The eerie sound was believed to drive away or immobilize all beings, natural or supernatural, hostile to man.

Bhola Grandpa was returning from the weekly market in the company of a group of people belonging to the neighbourhood of our camp. He did not remember when he had fallen behind the party.

He woke up to the fact that he was alone when, at a distance of about five yards before him, a full-grown Royal Bengal tiger gave a jolly growl, fixing his bright gaze straight on his face.

Bhola Grandpa instantly clambered up a banyan tree at hand. The tiger roared and circled the tree about a hundred times. Then it settled down under a bush and continued in that position without taking its eyes off Bhola Grandpa even for a moment.

With nightfall the forest grew dark and silent. Bhola Grandpa could hear the bored tiger beating its tail on the dry leaves and scratching the ground from time to time. He could see its bluish-yellow eyes rolling all over the tree. Hours passed.

Dawn broke with the cooing of a couple of doves. Bhola Grandpa came down. There was a hamlet of Santhals on a mound less than a furlong away. Bhola Grandpa climbed the mound and requested the first man he saw for a little fire to light his beedi.

The man had been a witness to all that passed between the tiger and Bhola Grandpa. In fact, he had spent the whole night sitting at the threshold of his hut, waiting to see what would happen next.

He eyed Bhola Grandpa with perfect bewilderment. 'What is your secret, sir, that you walked past that hungry beast and it just gaped at you and did nothing more?' he mumbled out his question at last.

Bhola Grandpa remembered the tiger and looked towards the bush. The tiger was seen stretching its limbs and yawning and preparing to leave the place as though its bewilderment was giving way to disgust.

Bhola Grandpa is said to have passed out for a moment.

Half a century later, one morning Bhola Grandpa was found to have died peacefully in his sleep. He was ninety-five. Even then we shed tears and lamented his death volubly.

But the most original of the laments came from the eighty-year-old granny, Bhola Grandpa's wife. 'The old man must have forgotten to breathe!' she said with a sigh.

Farewell to a Ghost

It was on moonlit nights that the deserted villa looked particularly fascinating. From the river bank we looked at it in long silence. When the fitful breeze made waves of the tall yellow grass around it, the house looked like a phantom castle floating on an unreal sea. Though pale, desolate and eerie, I must repeat, it was as fascinating as a fairy tale world.

Generally we didn't talk during the night. But the next morning, one of us would confide to another and we would all know by evening that he had caught a glimpse of the girl, standing on the broken terrace gazing at the moon or looking down at the river shedding tears which fell like drops of gold.

It was nothing new, yet we were thrilled every time and would gather on the river bank again the next evening.

Any of us village boys would have done anything to help her in some way. But we knew we could do nothing. She was so near, yet she belonged to a faraway world. Besides, we knew only too well that we ought not to be too enamoured of her. We had been repeatedly told about the gallant lad of a bygone generation who had fallen in love with her. There was a big banyan tree which stood in its mighty aloneness on the point of the river bank closest to the villa. The lad had often slipped away from his home and climbed the tree. Settling down on a branch, he would gaze for long hours into a crumbling room on the upper floor of the villa through its weather-beaten window.

Obviously, he could see her sitting inside the room lost in her melancholy. But did she ever look at him? Yes, occasionally. Why otherwise should the lad have fallen down from the tree, unconscious, not once but thrice? It is all right as long as you steal glimpses of a ghost without the ghost looking at you. It is only when the ghost looks into your eyes that you faint.

Finally, one summer noon, throwing to the winds all the stern warnings of his well-wishers, the lad had crept into the villa, climbed the decrepit stairs and peeped into the room. Perhaps the girl was asleep, for it was said that she wept the whole night and slept most of the day, sobbing in her sleep.

He should have behaved more prudently. Even a generation later, we boys censured his rashness and pitied him. To be in love was risky enough. And to be in love with a ghost was surely dangerous. How could he ignore this fact?

He had rushed up and kissed her before she could stop him. She had given out a shriek. Many had heard her sobbing and her mad babbling but that was the only time anyone had heard her shriek.

The shriek probably could not have been heard by you or me, but just then a popular mendicant known for his weird ways happened to pass by. He roamed about in the cemeteries of our area, coming into the village only once in two or three days, when he was hungry. He could understand the languages of crows and cows. Evidently, he could also hear what others could not. When the villagers discussed the missing lad, he revealed that he had heard the unusual shriek from the haunted villa.

A dozen brave men of our village entered the villa the next morning. They had sprinkled on their heads the sacred Ganga water and hidden pieces of iron under their girdles to check the ghost from coming too close to them. But, I can swear, no one even thought of carrying sticks or weapons. They would not do anything to offend the girl.

They found the lad prostrate on the cotton mattress that had lain unchanged for a hundred years on the cot in the room upstairs—dead. That he had kissed the girl was conclusively proved not only by the girl's sudden shriek but also by the faint streak of blood on the lad's lips which had flowed down to his chin. That, of course, was the price one must pay for kissing a ghost.

It was indeed a grim warning. But our villagers' affection for the ghost did not decline. What could she do if people fell in love with her? She had never asked them to! She had not killed the unfortunate lover! She could not undo the fatal curse that separated her world from ours. During the hundred years she had dwelt in the villa, not even once had she tried to lure anybody towards her or to possess anyone.

It could have been even more than a hundred years. Those were the days when the *feringhees* cultivated indigo over large tracts. They were concentrated in Bengal, but some had spread to the neighbouring lands of our state, Orissa. Their experiment did not succeed on our soil and they soon packed off, leaving behind the elegant house they had built.

As the legend goes, three young feringhees had brought a girl with them. Kidnapped or bought in the Sundarbans, she was the illegitimate daughter of a Sahib by a tribal woman, and she combined in her the ravishing freshness and wildness of her mother's race with the light complexion of her father.

Because of her strange origin she could not mix with our womenfolk. It was out of the question for our women to approach a girl with feringhee blood.

From the very beginning, the girl revolted against her masters. She was severely punished. After several attempts to escape had been foiled, she pretended to have been tamed and let several months pass without a murmur.

One day her three masters had to proceed to their headquarters on business. There was an epidemic of smallpox in the villages, and the feringhees, avoiding native contact, rowed themselves along the river. If the current was favourable it took only a day to reach the town.

They reached the town all right, though a little late, the next morning. A number of excited crows circled over the boat. The three young men and a crow lay stiff and cold around a carrier of half-eaten food.

The girl had prepared and packed their lunch. There was little doubt that she had prepared it with the choicest poison.

The girl had an accomplice in her desperate bid for vengeance and liberty—the keeper of the villa, a sly little fellow who had been with the company for many years. The girl knew where her masters had hidden their gold and money. According to the pact, the girl and the keeper were to escape with the wealth and share it. But once the girl had uncovered the cache, the rascal had stabbed her and fled.

Three days later, some outraged feringhees, accompanied by a group of native sepoys, appeared on the scene. They forced the villagers at bayonet point to bury the girl's body and searched every house for the killer. Potfuls of Ganga water had to be secured on loan from the neighbouring villages to purify the houses thus defiled.

But all these incidents had faded into a painless memory. It was only casually that people now referred to them. Neither the fate of the feringhees nor that of the girl's murderer interested us. It was only the girl that mattered—I mean her ghost. We always thought of her as one of us, although we knew quite well how different she was. Apart from being a ghost, she was of alien blood, blood from shores beyond the seven seas. We could not help being a little more respectful towards her on that account, though we knew that blood had lost much of its relevance once she had become a ghost.

No feast in the village, be it due to a birth or marriage or death, passed without the girl's share being duly offered to her. The ceremony took place in the dead of night. Some young men would carry the food in earthen pots. The party would always be led by a respectable elderly man, generally the head pundit of the primary school. We juniors were allowed to survey their actions only from a distance. After the pots and an earthen lamp had been placed between the villa and the banyan tree, the head pundit would intone: Unhappy girl, here is your share of the feast which has been held by the benevolent so-and-so on such-and-such occasion. Be satisfied with this. And, we ask you to guard the village from evil to the extent of your capacity. We have never tried to dislodge you or disturb you, have we?

No. Why not? Because we look upon you as one of our unlucky daughters. God grant you peace!

The party would leave the place without looking back.

Nobody was supposed to look into the compound thereafter. Nevertheless, hiding from our elders, from our favourite spot on the river-bank, we did look. In the flickering flame of the earthen lamp and the dance of the fluctuating shadows, we felt we saw something mysterious. Our hair stood on end.

The lamp would suddenly go out. 'She does not relish our watching her,' one of us would say, and we would leave her alone.

'But she obeys the head pundit all right, doesn't she? The pundit knows how to speak to her,' the head pundit's pet pupil would observe as we joined the feasting crowd. 'Who on earth does not obey him!' his rival would quip.

I had, however, a feeling that when the head pundit implored her to guard the village against evil what he really meant was that she herself should not cause any harm to our village. His words, I felt, even implied a threat. What else did he mean by reminding her that we had never tried to dislodge or disturb her?

I felt embarrassed. She was so innocent and so good. What business had the head pundit to be hypocritical in his speech?

A strong hot breeze blew during the summer noons for days on end. For an hour or two, everything was quiet except for the noise made by the wind. Doors and windows of the villa had disappeared since long. As the wind violently explored every nook and corner of the building, it produced varieties of squeals and whistles.

The sounds fascinated me. My father wanted me to take a nap, but I would sit up in bed listening to them intently. Once in a while, I must confess, I felt the urge to steal into the villa, for no other reason than to give the girl a moment's silent company. But, I was afraid, she might not understand my purpose. That checked me.

One day, feeling bold and a little proud, I admitted to myself that was almost falling in love and I blushed. Maybe, other boys of the village also felt like me. It never occurred to us that the girl was at least a hundred years older than us. Some wise man had told us that once one had become a ghost one never grew in age.

It was when we were preparing for the middle school examination that the shocking news came. The government had decided to demolish the crumbling villa and use the land for some other purpose. No wonder that we forgot our studies and hid behind the school wall to listen to the elders discussing the issue in the evening.

'Can't we request the government to spare the villa?'

'No. Once the zamindar was declared bankrupt, the land has become the government's property. The government does not provide for ghosts,' the village headman said, and his statement was followed by a prolonged silence and intermittent coughs and yawns.

Then a lizard tick-ticked and two or three people muttered, 'True, true!'

'But what will happen to the girl? She has lived there all these years and has never harmed us. Rather, there are reasons to believe that she is a benevolent ghost.'

The lizard tick-ticked again and this time more people said, and more loudly, 'True, true!'

The discussion continued for a long time. All agreed that something had to be done for the girl. But nobody had a surplus house to offer her. However good, a ghost, was still a ghost and keeping her with one's family was not a practical proposition. But if nothing was done for her, she would naturally settle in someone's house!

It was perhaps midnight by the time they came to a decision. By then, our mothers or uncles had found us out behind the wall and had driven us back to our beds.

At the request of the villagers, the demolition work was delayed for a few days. A renowned priest, well-versed in necromancy, arrived on the appointed day. He was tall and hefty, with a round red mark on his forehead. He wore a garland of beads which, we were told, were carved out of the spine of a wilful witch. He never smiled.

It was a sad day for us all. Outwardly too the day was

gloomy: it was cloudy and it drizzled from time to time. Almost every family had brought a little food—rice, bananas, coconuts, sweetmeats or cakes—to offer to the girl. Nobody was barred from witnessing the ceremony and so the villagers pressed near the villa. For many, particularly women and children, it was their very first entry into the haunted compound.

The presents were arranged in a semicircle on the veranda. The priest placed a parcel at its centre and slowly removed the red linen covering it. It was a complete human skull. He also held a stick of bone. He recited hymns while drawing figures in the air with the bone and then, his face flushing, shouted menacingly, 'But where is she? I have already pronounced my command thrice. She should have appeared before me immediately. How dare she be so impudent?'

The headman said apologetically, 'Look, baba, she must be asleep upstairs. She rarely sleeps at night, you know!'

'Very well, I will go up and drag her down by the ear. She must realize that I am not accustomed to going unheeded,' hollered the priest, and he climbed the stairs.

We looked at one another helplessly. I felt like crying. Should not somebody have told the priest that the girl was not to be treated rudely?

We could hear the priest's thudding footsteps upstairs. Then he roared something incomprehensible, and the sound and its echo made beads of sweat break out on our faces even on that cool morning. He returned triumphantly and said in a commanding tone, 'There. Eat to your heart's content and then leave the house!'

We had almost ceased to breathe. The priest looked at us with contempt and suddenly yelled at the top of his voice, 'What! You will not eat? Mind you, that will not soften me. Eat or not, you must leave the villa and the village now, instantly.'

The headman managed to say, 'Baba, you should perhaps wait a little. She had never disobeyed us. She will eat. Please tell her that it is our earnest request. Our womenfolk have brought these presents with so much love!'

But the priest did not seem to care. 'She is leaving. Make way!' he shouted at us. Immediately the crowd parted.

She did not eat. But when asked to leave, she did so without delay. We did not see her, true. But we knew how deeply wounded she must have felt. We felt extremely small.

'Halt! That's right. I will lead you,' the priest said, and slowly walked through the crowd, showing the invisible spirit the way with the pointing bone in his right hand. With the left hand he gave some directions to his assistant, who stayed back and collected the magic skull and, I believe, the foodstuff.

All followed the priest. The village was left behind and we walked through the meadow for nearly a kilometre, braving the drizzle and the fear of a heavy rain.

'There! Get into it!' commanded the priest, standing under a tall palm tree. Then he uttered some strange incantations and beat the tree with the bone and circled it a number of times.

'So, from now on this will be your dwelling. Understand?' the priest shouted, looking up to the top of the tree. He then grinned at us proudly and said in a pompous tone, 'She can never leave the tree. I have tied her to it!'

He turned back and we did the same. We boys walked with the women while the menfolk, surrounding the priest, walked faster and ahead of us.

We walked in silence. But at one point someone sobbed. Then everyone was weeping, though as quietly as possible.

When we reached the village, the workmen had already started pulling down the villa. The rain would make their work easy, the contractor informed the headman.

After three or four days of rain, the sky became clear. The moon shone bright and as on other moonlit nights we, boys, gathered in the meadow to play *hu-tu-tu*. But there was no life in our play. Eventually, someone said, 'The ground here is swampy. Can't we go farther up where it is dry?'

No sooner had he said this than we began to run. Soon we were near the palm tree and our hearts were back in the game. We played on till late in the night, happy to be near our lonely ghost.

And we returned there every evening till the last day of the summer vacation.

After the vacation, I was led to the town for admission to a high school. I had never known a town before. Soon I became engrossed in several interesting activities. I forgot the ghost.

Three months later came the puja vacation and I headed for home. From the bus stop I had to walk five miles to reach my village. I was in high spirits. Suddenly, while crossing the meadow, my eyes fell on the palm tree and for a moment I felt numbed. The tree was dead, struck by lightning. Its charred branches were crumbling.

With a heavy heart I resumed walking. During the fortnight's holiday none of the boys spoke of the girl. It being the rainy season, there was no question of our going to play in the meadow.

Gradually, I passed the age of playing *hu-tu-tu* and my visits to the village became rarer. And the new generation of village boys were so different, so ignorant. They were just afraid of ghosts.

Friends and Strangers

The people of our small town in the northern valley used to be classified, as anywhere else, according to their economic, social or educational status. But two of them, Tirthankar and Shivabrata, constituted an exclusive class. No third person belonged to it.

The two looked upon each other as unreal. Consequently, the townsfolk had gradually learnt to look upon both as unreal.

It was on an autumn evening that had set into motion the chain of events culminating in this bizarre situation. The moonlight on the lush outskirts of the town was so thick, one felt one could net a kerchief-full of it and pocket it for future use.

Tirthankar had arrived in the morning; Shivabrata in the afternoon. Year after year, around that time, they came home to spend their holidays. Every other time their visit coincided with that of a third friend, Pramath.

Pramath worked in a frontier town famous for its woollen products.

Tirthankar and Shivabrata sat on a rock, chit-chatting. The moon seemed to have risked coming so dangerously close to the tallest palm tree between the rock and the lake that the two friends feared the top branches of the tree, swaying madly, might scratch its delicate surface.

It was a forlorn area where even a mongoose running between the bushes looked quite a personage.

Fifteen feet below their rock and fifty yards away was a narrow road, used more by cattle and goats than by human pedestrians.

'Isn't that Pramath?' asked Tirthankar.

Someone in impeccable white, the kind of clothes Pramath usually donned on holidays, was walking slowly, carefully locating the road half lost in the grass. The wavering shadows cast by the trees often eclipsed him.

'Hello, Pramath!' called out Shivabrata.

Pramath stopped and looked at the two friends on the rock.

'Come up,' said Tirthankar. From the treetops a gust of wind swooped down upon Pramath's head and rummaged in his well-groomed hair. And there were lesser flurries around to smuggle away into the bushes half of the words from his response to the call.

But the two friends could still decipher his maimed reply. Pramath, they understood, promised to join them after handing over to Mrs Wilson the gift of a shawl he had brought for her.

'Listen, Pramath, can't the shawl wait till morning? Come up, it's important!' shouted out both the friends, putting a lot of vigour into their words to push them through the stubborn breeze.

But Pramath said—at least that is what Tirthankar and Shivabrata understood—that the old lady had seen him on his way home from the Railway station at sundown. She must be expecting him.

The old lady was in the habit of sitting out her afternoons and the early part of the night gazing at the road. She had nothing else to do and no one to talk to. Once in a while she would ask a familiar passer-by the time or the date, or would demand of him or her some small service.

She had cajoled Pramath to agree to bring her a shawl of quality wool. That was three years ago. Pramath would forget and regret. At last he had brought it. He wouldn't be at peace until he had delivered it to the good little lady.

Pramath resumed walking. The two friends looked at each other meaningfully.

'Just a minute, Pramath, do you mean to say you saw Mrs Wilson? Did you really see her seated as usual?' demanded Tirthankar.

'I did!' replied Pramath.

As soon as the reply, hauled up by the erratic breeze, reached the top of the rock, the two listeners felt a shiver, though as brief as Pramath's reply.

They strained their voices and advised Pramath to pay heed to their suggestion. He should postpone his visit to Mrs Wilson to the next morning and must come over to them now.

But Pramath was adamant. He did not even care to answer them again.

Tirthankar and Shivabrata kept sitting, nonplussed. Pramath did not give them an opportunity to tell him that Mrs Wilson was no more. Two months had passed since the evening she was found dead seated in her usual posture, apparently gazing at passers-by.

Had Pramath gone crazy? How could he assert having seen her?

Hallucination—caused by his habit of seeing her seated in that position year after year—they concluded.

They waited for Pramath to return. But their thoughts were in total disarray. They hardly talked.

Two hyenas fought and howled somewhere behind the tall bushes on the lake. Dogs in the suburbs moaned at that unfortunate strife.

And the moon slipped into a cloud.

'A cloud in autumn!' one of the friends murmured and both at once saw something weird in the phenomenon.

They came down from the rock and headed towards Pramath's house, sure that he had meanwhile received the shock of his life and gone home, perhaps avoiding the lonely short-cut through the rocky dale.

Pramath's home, consisting of his aged parents, a widowed sister, a cat and a parrot, was found plunged in gloom. His mother had been going into a swoon every half an hour since the receipt of the wire telling them that Pramath had died in an accident at noon.

The two friends left the place hurriedly and walked in silence.

They took care not to look into the compound of Mrs Wilson.

It was when they passed by the rock that the moon emerged from the cloud and flashed in their faces. And it was then that, looking at each other, each felt the other to be unreal—as unreal as Pramath.

And both parted even without saying good night to each other. In fact, they had been seen almost running to reach their homes.

Next day, Tirthankar was heard trying to ascertain from the others, at first tactfully and later directly, when exactly Shivabrata had died!

Before long Shivabrata was heard making the same query about Tirthankar.

Despite overwhelming proofs of their being alive and active, each continued viewing the other's existence as unreal. Both were nice chaps otherwise, agreed the townsmen.

Our town, though small, had at least one wise man to explain the episode rationally. According to him the passer-by whom the two friends had supposed to be Pramath was somebody else. He must have spoken something quite different from what the two friends heard. Once they had made the mistake, the moonlight played a trick: it showed the stranger as Pramath. The rest of the mischief was done by the wayward breeze that made them hear words which they imagined they heard.

But the wise man, while presenting his thesis, made gestures that did not go well with his explanation.

On nights when the moon looked somewhat wild and the wind went crazy, the two friends, if they were in town, kept to their rooms and peeped out through their windows looking perfectly bewildered.

The Martial Expedition

The prince had begun to show signs of depression within a fortnight of his marriage. His wife was no princess, but she came of aristocratic lineage, her ancestry linked to a dynasty more hallowed than his, its founder being a sage who had temporarily consorted with a nymph. She had charmed the prince through a classical dance performance at a certain golden jubilee celebration, and he had instantly resolved to marry her in total disregard of several proposals from the other princely families.

He had not been a loser by not marrying a princess. His father-in-law, an industrialist, was capable of buying two princely states the size of Haritpur, the domain of the prince's father. Besides, no princess was known to have practised Bharatanatyam or Odissi.

'What happened to that magic of yours—I mean that which inspired me to marry you?' the prince bluntly demanded of his wife on the tenth day after their wedding.

'I cannot really guess what I could have lost in such a short time!' the young lady wondered at the unexpected and embarrassing question.

However, she was intelligent enough not to remain bewildered for long. Although the prince did not quite succeed in explaining what he thought he missed, she found it out.

The prince expected her to smile, move her eyes and limbs, and dress too, in the manner she did during that hour's dance performance when she conquered his heart.

'That's just not practicable,' said the lady and tried her best, through loving smiles and other means, to lessen the shock her frankness might have caused her husband.

But the prince fell into a gloom. When months passed and he refused to smile, his wife left for Europe.

Raja Sahib died. The prince duly ascended the throne and was pronounced the new raja, although the throne had been reduced to an ordinary sofa. Midway to India, his wife became Rani Sahiba. On arrival at Haritpur, she found Raja Sahib as colourful in his dress as April and as jubilant as the spring birds abounding in their gardens. Even a simple answer like, 'I'm okay', to his simple question 'How are you?' inspired a roar of laughter from him.

Before the young Rani could decide whether to be happy or concerned at this total reversal in her husband's mood, India won freedom and the princely order was abolished. Like hundreds of other native states, Haritpur ceased to be ruled by its raja, though the ex-ruler was allowed to retain his title.

Raja Sahib refused to come out of his apartment for one full month. Those who could steal glimpses of him found it difficult to believe that he had ever laughed or even smiled in his life.

The couple moved to the city permanently.

Specialists diagnosed Raja Sahib's condition as manic depressive psychosis. His mood alternated between melancholy and elation.

Chowdhury, an old friend of the royal family, had gathered all this information about Raja Sahib from the latter's servant-cum-guardian, Mohan. The Rajmata had gone insane when her son was barely three. It was Mohan who had virtually taken on her role in nursing the infant prince. In fact, the prince called the bearded man Mummy till he was of alphabet-learning age.

Once the depressive phase was over, Raja Sahib indulged in a thousand lofty dreams. He planned daring business enterprises and launched a few too, shot a number of inedible birds and beasts in the forest, drove at great speed, caused accidents and reached the police station at even greater speed and reported his offences bursting with laughter and patting the officer on the back.

This, of course, was inevitably followed by a spell of depression when he either kept in bed or just blinked at everybody without speaking a word. He touched hardly anything but liquor. Mohan had to literally weep in order to persuade him to eat at least one meal a day.

Chowdhury, along with some of his friends, was then starting a new business. He wanted Raja Sahib to buy a share in the company, partly out of sympathy for the raja and partly for the company's benefit.

Chowdhury's was a personality like a huge, affable pussy cat's. His voice too carried the coquetry of a mew, craving and receiving your instant indulgence.

Raja Sahib appeared happy at the revival of the acquaintance. But his spells of melancholy were growing longer. Chowdhury soon forgot the pragmatic aspect of his interest in him and grew anxious to make him reasonably jolly.

He called a meeting of the partners of his company at Raja Sahib's bungalow. Rani Sahiba was then away at her father's.

The prudent and enterprising Chowdhury had arranged for a brand of liquor which Raja Sahib madly loved but could not afford. Raja Sahib came out of his gloom in one bound and was found basking in the glow from the bottles.

'Look here, Chowdhury, I'm going to treat your bloody partners to such laughter that they shall weep. I know a great joke,' Raja Sahib announced moments before the arrival of the guests. He had just gulped down a few pegs of his favourite drink.

'That'll be fine, Raja Sahib! This is the spirit we expect you to exhibit. You are so young. Why not just shrug off this corrosive melancholy?'

'Melancholy? I'll make the bellies of your bloody friends burst today. A fantastic joke; that's the bomb I'm going to explode on the numbskulls!' And Raja Sahib himself laughed wildly, holding on to his stomach.

Mohan looked at Raja Sahib with appreciation and at Chowdhury with gratefulness.

The partners arrived on time. There were eleven of them, but Raja Sahib received each with a fresh bout of laughter. He was unsteady and needed support. Chowdhury and Mohan flanked him all the time.

After the dinner had been ceremoniously laid out by the hotelier on contract, Raja Sahib stood up, supported by Mohan.

'I'll crack a joke the like of which none in your fourteen past generations could have heard,' Raja Sahib laughed.

'Take it!' he said in a muffled tone. 'Once a certain minister was invited to address a nudist association meet. The nudists came well dressed in honour of the guest, but the minister, to honour the nudists . . . wait, wait a minute!'

Raja Sahib shook off Mohan's support and rushed into his room.

'Don't follow me. I'll shoot you down if you do!' he told the hapless attendant.

Chowdhury knew the climax of the anecdote. He looked apprehensive and followed Raja Sahib into his room.

This was the dialogue heard:

'Raja Sahib, what's this?'

'A joke!'

'Look here, Raja Sahib, just say that the minister went naked to greet the well-dressed nudists. That will be enough to make all these gentlemen roll with laughter. You need not emerge naked yourself.'

'This is joke, you fool! A joke is a joke!' Raja Sahib shouted.

Chowdhury called out for Mohan and, leaving Raja Sahib under his care, came out of the room and bolted it from outside. Raja Sahib soon fell asleep, his head resting on Mohan's lap.

When Chowdhury met him the next day he looked as crushed as a mountaineer who has fought an avalanche. It was impossible to drag him out of his mood. Chowdhury gave up.

Business took Chowdhury out of the city again and again. He lost contact with Raja Sahib. A year later, during the India-China conflict, Chowdhury received a message from Mohan: Raja Sahib had resolved to join the war. Mohan and Rani Sahiba were unable to dissuade him from taking the step. Would Chowdhury try?

Raja Sahib had already left for the railway station by the time Chowdhury reached his bungalow. Raja Sahib, of course, was not heading for the frontier, but for Rohitpur, to take leave of his dear former subjects.

Chowdhury drove to the station. He discovered the inebriated prince held by Mohan on one side and Rani Sahiba on the other. They were struggling to locate his name on the passenger lists pasted on the coaches. Raja Sahib had folded up his legs and hung in the air, reposing his entire weight on his two miserable escorts.

Chowdhury ran along the platform and found out the berth allotted to Raja Sahib. As he bent down to take hold of Raja Sahib's legs to help lift him into his compartment, the Raja smartly straightened them and stood relatively steady. His look betrayed a queer combination of pride at his ability to stand on his own feet and glee at having made fools of his wife, Mohan and Chowdhury.

Chowdhury had earlier nurtured a faint misgiving: Did Raja Sahib's disappointment at having to leave the joke incomplete or his embarrassment at his own conduct inspire him to abandon the world and proceed to the war? The latest demonstration of Raja Sahib's ingenuity, however, set him free him from any such misgiving. He realized that external circumstance had little to do with the alterations in Raja Sahib's mood. The joy Raja Sahib evidently experienced by suddenly unfolding his legs seemed no less than that of the first man to set foot on the Everest.

'Bravo, Raja Sahib!' said Chowdhury.

Raja Sahib laughed and laughed till tears trickled from his eyes.

A week later there was an item in a minor newspaper of Raja Sahib's home state to this effect: As the Raja Sahib of Rohitpur, fired by patriotism, was heading for the front, he had summoned a meeting on the palace ground to bid him farewell. Raja Sahib presided over the meeing and spoke about the war.

At the end, Raja Sahib distributed *laddoos* to his audience and moved a vote of thanks.

Unfortunately, after waiting for days, at last when Raja Sahib was able to secure a First Class A/C berth for proceeding to the capital to notify the Defence Ministry of his momentous decision, the war was over.

Raja Sahib fell into gloom again. This time he did not survive it.

The Irrational

Subrato Das gave a start. That was nothing unusual. He suffered a momentary panic whenever Kakoli was mentioned.

'Kakoli? Can I make it? The winter is rather unkind this year and I must travel back to the capital after the function to attend the cabinet meeting the following morning. Otherwise our Hon'ble Chief Minister will misunderstand me,' he said and gave out a meaningful smile.

Kakoli was an insignificant town in a faraway corner of the state, probably without any suitable bungalow for a restful night. Subrato had got habituated to his comforts. In his late sixties, after unbroken service to the country for four and a half decades, that certainly was not something to feel guilty about. Unlike several other ministers, he had not become addicted to corruption and nepotism. To desire a warm, clean bed and a bathroom with arrangements for hot water, or to pass a full hour sitting on the bed and leisurely sipping three or four cups of tea in the morning, as if the murmurs of a motley crowd waiting in the outer room were no different from the chattering of the birds in the garden beside it, could not be called unpatriotic.

But it was not necessary to confess all that. The chief minister might misunderstand was a hint expected to be appreciated by everybody, for Subrato was the only one running neck and neck with the chief minister in the race for power. In fact, the regional newspapers, whenever there was no better incident to make a handsome headline out of, led their readers to see a Damocles' sword hanging over the chief minister's head, who could be toppled any day, and another one hanging over Subrato's head, who could be thrown out of the cabinet any moment.

Subrato, after his apparently casual statement hinting at the chief minister's animosity towards him, would pass a quick glance over his listeners and, from their reaction, determine how devoted they were to him, or at least how eager they were to show their allegiance towards him.

Generally, he found the reaction he expected. Members of the delegation from Kakoli looked and smiled at one another. Their spokesman cleared his throat in style and smiled in a manner suggesting that although what he was going to say was only a truism, he must say it, for Subrato, whose mind was preoccupied with thoughts sublime, would otherwise remain ignorant of such mundane facts.

'Does it really matter if the chief minister's misunderstands you? Men, women, even children over the entire state understand you and love you. Yes, even children in their mothers' wombs! True, today your rival lolls on that throne, but who can—ha ha!—prophesy about tomorrow? We the people know. Ha ha! We know, we know. But that's a different matter. What is relevant is, we will not let you drive back all that long way at night. This does not mean you must pass your night in that haunted house called the PWD bungalow, maintained by, thanks be to it, the chief minister's very own department!'

Subrato looked at the speaker with curiosity.

'You will be put up in the guest room of the Chowdhuries. Nothing luxurious, but as neat and clean as yourself, sir! The lady, I mean the Chowdhurani, has not lagged behind her late husband in maintaining the dignity of the house,' asserted the spokesman.

'She is noble, sir, and she knows the difference between gold and brass. When the question whether to invite you or the chief minister for inaugurating the dispensary came up and it was referred to her, she did not take even a second to announce her preference for you. She, after all, is the founder. We will be grateful to you if you respect her wish,' said a member of the delegation, stammering.

'The entire population of Kakoli will be grateful, sir,' said the spokesman, raising his voice. He did not relish the stammerer proving himelf very original.

'The people of Kakoli have never had the privilege of listening to you,' said their other two companions, sharing the statement between them, airing the deep sense of deprivation they had put up with for long.

The dialogue continued for still half an hour more, ending in Subrato condescending to oblige Kakoli.

A strong determination was forming within him during that half-hour—a will to conquer a bizarre weakness he had harboured for forty-five years. Must Kakoli continue to panic him like a ghost in the dark all his life? Yet how trivial was the episode behind it! And, no doubt, the only other character involved in the episode, if still alive, must have forgotten it long ago.

His eventful life had been marked by one after another acts of bravery; he had crossed numerous hurdles and had emerged victorious from a number of crises. But how come he had failed to shake a most irrational fear from his mind?

He was an untiring traveller. But he had never stopped at Kakoli during his long political life. If he was obliged to drive past Kakoli once in a while, that indomitable feeling would creep into him miles before entering the town. And once he entered it, he would invariably feel stripped of his clothes—a feeling that would continue to shame him till he had left the place miles behind.

He must put an end to this reflex. He must visit Kakoli and pass a full night in the town. Besides, the prospect of being put up as a guest of the Chowdhuries had a strange thrill about it.

Evening was about to begin when, at last, his car entered Kakoli, preceded and followed by a dozen more vehicles. The place did not seem to have changed much, except that new buildings had come up like anywhere else. The impressive, old-world mansion of the Chowdhuries, however, had not lost its lustre.

The PWD bungalow was the place where he was taken for his relaxation—that is the term used in his itinerary—to sit amidst the small-town dignitaries, sipping tea and drinking coconut water to strike a balance in his courtesy towards the two feuding groups in the local committee of his party, and answer a dozen questions in an optimistic vein but without making a single commitment.

Then he proceeded to the newly built charitable dispensary and inaugurated it, paying his tributes to the late Chowdhury whose memory it bore, and to his worthy widow, the Chowdhurani. The function concluded with a chorus glorifying Subrato, the lyric for which had been specially written by a local poet.

Since it was not easy for the important members of the audience to express their appreciation of his speech without each one of them making a brief speech before him, he was led once again to the same bungalow for another round of tea.

He was tired. The conscientious organizers arranged for an early dinner and retirement in the guest room of the Chowdhuries.

But once all was quiet, which was only at midnight, he came out to the broad balcony and surveyed the area.

The row of rooms, one accommodating the clerk of the household and another the tax-collector of the zamindari, and the third one in which he had been put up for a fortnight some forty-five years ago, had disappeared.

And where were the bushes on an acre of swamp behind which he sat shivering for hours? The swamp had become a colony of modest buildings. There were crotons and bougainvillaea, but no bush.

Last but not the least, where was that beautiful girl, the Chowdhury's daughter? She must have married into another feudal family. He had always checked his temptation to make such queries, for he was keen to erase that fortnight entirely from his life.

Subrato, who came of a poor family, had joined the high

school funded by the Chowdhuries as an assistant teacher. The school had not developed beyond the ninth class and the few teachers who came from outside Kakoli were provided with free board and lodging, on practical and compassionate grounds, by different affluent villagers. Subrato had the privilege to find shelter in the Chowdhury household.

The fourteen-year-old daughter of the Chowdhury, was a rosy restless fairy bereft of wings.

'Sir, would you please explain this to me?' she asked one afternoon, sailing into Subrato's room. What she presented was a simple arithmetical puzzle and though Subrato should not have taken more than five minutes to solve it, he took, in fact, some fifty minutes.

'Sir, do you relish these?' she dashed into his room another evening and heaped on his gratefully extended, slightly trembling palms, two or three varieties of berries. She ran away before he could thank her.

While munching those delicious stuff, Subrato wondered if the nectar-loving gods really deserved to be envied.

Alas, the fateful evening was only two days away.

For some reason most of the inmates and servants of the mansion were somewhere outside and all was quiet. A window of a room in the inner quarters showed the girl concentrating on a book with a lantern on her table.

Subrato stood gazing at the face from the outer veranda for five minutes. There was no movement around. The girl's face looked to him like the distant moon of his childhood which his mother's lullaby promised to fetch for him.

Perhaps it was time for him to try and catch the moon himself.

That was the only time when his legs behaved independently of his conscious will. Suddenly he found himself right inside the girl's room, although no employee or guest was expected to enter that zone unless summoned.

He felt the surging of some alien sensation in his veins. At first it seemed to flow from his heart, but before long it engulfed the heart, reducing it to an island about to be submerged.

Unknown to the girl, he stood behind her chair. But then?

He had no plan as such. He could surely employ his palms, which the other day had been lucky to receive those berries from her, to seal her eyes in a playful way!

He acted accordingly. He expected that the girl would giggle and feel his hands and probably her tender fingers would slowly crawl to his face, in order to guess his identity.

Alas, the girl did nothing of that kind. Instead, she gave out a shriek. Never again in his life was Subrato to know such a perplexing moment. Suddenly he discovered himself in the role of a thief or a criminal of sorts. Should he take his hands away and expose himself to her? Was there no magic way to clean disappear from the scene, even leaving his two arms behind if that was the price he must pay?

There was no time to lose, for he imagined the sound of rushing footsteps growing louder beyond the door opening to the backyard of the house.

Subrato made a bid to escape in the blink of an eye, but at the exit his *dhoti* snagged in a protruding wooden bar fixed to the door to serve as a latch. In the tug of war between himself and the obstinate bar, he lost his entire dhoti and sprinted into the dark.

He crouched behind a bush and shivered. For a moment he felt the impulse to continue to run through the miles and miles of paddy fields and get lost somewhere in the moonless horizon. But the coolness of the swamp was creeping into his body, almost paralysing it, the lower half of which was bare.

He got back to his room only at midnight. Now it was panic that kept him paralysed, as if he was to lose his head as soon as the sun rose.

Nobody came for his head, but he found it difficult to keep it straight and steady.

He left Kakoli. He got a better job in the city. The circumstances pushing him into politics, his election to the legislature and holding ministerial positions during the next twenty years, suddenly appeared to have carried only one secret behind them—his effort to recover the soiled, cheap dhoti he had lost decades ago, and all his daring moves and self-assertion were a long struggle to compensate for his bizarre humiliation of that remote evening.

The guest room was cosy and comfortable indeed. He slept the later part of the night well, dreaming of having a thorough bath in a murmuring brook, trying to cleanse himself of something he could not see.

What was that? He analysed his dream early in the morning and found the answer: an undercurrent of anxiety.

There was a gentle knock on the door. His personal assistant was followed by a servant carrying tea on a tray.

'The Chowdhurani would like to meet you for a moment. Can she do so now? I'm afraid there will be hardly any time afterwards!' said the personal assistant.

'She is welcome,' Subrato put on a shirt and moved to the sofa.

The Chowdhurani entered slowly, smiling. Subrato stood up and greeted her with palms folded. He was ready to listen to some request, perhaps for the transfer of a nephew or a cousin to a better place or post, or a complaint that she had not been fully compensated for a land or a building of hers acquired by the government. He must appear sympathetic and promise help.

'Did you sleep well?'

'Very well, madam, thank you so much.'

'It was good that the memory of that ticklish evening forty-five years ago did not haunt you.'

Subrato straightened up. He looked at the Chowdhurani with all the concentration at his command.

'Well . . . am I to believe that you . . .'

'How could I expect you to discover that fickle little girl you knew—and knew so briefly—in this old lady?' She laughed delicately and resumed, 'I had no brother. My husband who hailed of a house of our distant relatives took over our estates and I was spared the ordeal of having to be transplanted on another family. The dispensary you inaugurated was my husband's dream in his ailing last days.'

The Chowdhurani handed over a small parcel to Subrato.

'Your dhoti. I had hidden it before anybody had any chance

to wonder about its mysterious entanglement on my door.'
The lady laughed. 'For many years I did not know that the
leader known by that shy and timid teacher's name was none
other than the teacher himself. I knew it only after I saw your
photographs in the papers.'

'But why should you preserve this . . .'

'You are looking for logic! What was the logic behind your
impulse to seal my eyes with your palms?'

She stood up. She looked as fresh and serene as the morning
sky visible through the window. Subrato saw in a flash,
emerging from the white hair and wrinkled face, the moon he
had rushed at, once upon a time.

The Chowdhurani paused near the door.

'It was irrational of me to shriek, it was irrational of you to
run away; perhaps the most irrational part of the episode was
your running away from Kakoli.' She smiled and bade him
goodbye.

Subrato stood speechless. The personal assistant had to
cough and cough again to wake him up from his reverie.

It was noon when Subrato reached the capital, a noon
charged with tension. The central leadership of his party, in a
surprise move, had despatched an emissary to measure the
gravity of the conflict between the chief minister and Subrato.
The visitor had already had a long meeting with the chief
minister. He was eagerly waiting to meet Subrato.

Surprisingly, Subrato betrayed no anxiety, especially when,
at the end of the day, he was closeted with the emissary. The
meeting was very brief.

Reporters, their tape recorders switched on, surrounded a
smiling Subrato the moment he emerged from the meeting.

'Who, according to you, commands the central leadership's
confidence—you or the chief minister?'

'Have you accepted the chief minister's challenge to you to
prove your charges of corruption against him?'

'How many MLAs of the party are solidly behind you?'

'What is the size of the block of undecided members?'

'Should the chief minister advise the governor to dissolve
the assembly, are you prepared to face a by-election?'

Subrato was smiling, paying equal attention to all the questions.

'How come you look so happy?'

'Because no longer do I stand stripped,' Subrato spoke at last.

The reporters laughed while groping for the meaning of Subrato's statement which, they were sure, was figurative.

'Will you please explain?' asked an owl-faced senior, after casting a contemptuous look at his laughing compatriots.

'I will. I am resigning my cabinet post, resigning my membership of the legislature and retiring from politics. This is a decision which has nothing to do with all our quarrels and conflicts, and, I assert, the decision is irrevocable.'

The reporters stood stunned for a moment.

'Is this true?' several voices buzzed.

'True.'

'What is the rationale behind it?'

'Well, since I know no rationale for my birth, no rationale for my inevitable death, why should I look for a rationale for this and why should I be under any obligation to formulate and produce a rationale for your consumption?'

'It appears from your answer that the decision could not have been made off the cuff. Since when were you preparing for such a momentous step?'

The reporters were fast recovering from their surprise.

'From the day I took up politics. But I was not aware of it.'

Subrato Das had nothing but smiles for all the other questions, as he pushed on towards his car, exuding an aura of liberation.

The Different Man

The fearful apprehension that more and more people were growing crazy, if not quite mad, began to darken, like chunks of aggressive clouds, the otherwise sunny mind of Pratap Singh.

All that he had asked his colleague, Hemant Babu, was, 'You don't seem to suffer from any kind of cold. Why then have you started coughing at the beginning, middle and the end of every sentence you mumble out?'

That made Hemant Babu, known for his sobriety, blurt out menacingly, 'What then should I do if not cough? Yes, what else is there to do?'

Pratap Singh's was nothing more than a casual query. He was, naturally, surprised and embarrassed at that old familiar voice raising the issue to the lofty plane of the very basic whys and hows to which there were no answers.

Walking along the river bank in the evening, he had observed no less than five pedestrians engrossed in soliloquies. One of them was engaged in a loud argument with himself, gesticulating in a defiant manner. Pratap Singh hoped that the man looking a decent kind of clerk accustomed to sitting behind some glass counter, or an affable broker, would come to his senses if he knew that someone was observing him. Pratap Singh walked closer to him and deliberately looked goggle-eyed at him. But the man did not even notice him and went his way, as charmed by his own voice as a musk deer is by its fragrance.

It was getting dark. Pratap Singh stopped near a kiosk and asked a young trio buying cigarettes, 'When did you take to smoking?'

'Well, we didn't record the date. Say, a year or two ago,' they replied, a bit intrigued.

'My young friends, long before that the cartons had begun announcing that smoking is injurious to your health. It may be all right with those who had already grown addicted to smoking before the warning became statutory, but what about you? Why did you pledge your health to the vampire of tobacco?' he demanded.

'Whose health, yours or ours?' the one who looked like the male monkey in the troop retorted with a sneer.

'You consider yourself very clever, do you?' shouted an irate Pratap Singh. 'Tell me, are you the maker of your health, your body? Did you know whether you would be male or female, short or tall, fat or slim, dark or fair? Is it you who gave your body the immunity against the effects of adulteration and pollution? Must you vaunt it as your health?'

Pratap Singh seemed to have impressed his small audience, including the shopkeeper, with his harangue. But the one who looked absolutely a nincompoop among the three, asked in a deceptively calm tone, 'Pardon me, sir, but are you married?'

'What do you gain by putting such a question to a man of your father's age?' Pratap Singh sounded exasperated.

'I gain nothing. But you could have gained from the statutory warning against sex pronounced by the seers and sages for thousands of years. I wonder what made you ignore that!'

The audience, led by the shopkeeper, burst into a guffaw. There was nothing surprising in the shopkeeper's elation, for Pratap Singh's stand went against the chap's interest, but why should the others prove so irreverent?

'Listen, young man,' Pratap Singh assumed the most sagacious tone possible. 'What you advance is hardly an argument. Nature had endowed all creatures with certain instincts. They were there even before man appeared. Can you say the same thing about the cigarette? Can you classify smoking as an instinct? Don't make faces. Argument must be met with argument and not with giggles and guffaws!'

'Will you please tell us what inspired you to come out with such sermons against smoking?'

'What inspired the authorities to print the warning on the cigarette packet? Duty. Am I clear?'

'Please go on with your duty. Cheers!' The young men hopped on to their bicycles and pedalled away.

Pratap Singh was extremely vexed. A sage had said that five kinds of people are not expected to be governed by reason: the child, the stupid, the wicked, the lunatic and the mystic. These fellows were neither children nor stupid nor mystic. They had to be either wicked or lunatic.

He would prefer them to be lunatic rather than wicked. That way there was some hope for mankind.

He remembered his destination—a bookshop. It was closed. But the airport was nearby. He could perhaps buy the book he needed at the stall inside the airport. He bought an entrance ticket. Book or no book, he could relax for a while in the air-conditioned hall.

A major flight had been delayed. People waiting to receive the incoming passengers and those waiting to take the flight crowded the lounges. Pratap Singh saw no vacant chair. And the bookshop hardly had any room for standing.

But he did not mind walking up and down for a while through the rows of comfortably seated ladies and gentlemen.

Suddenly his eyes fell on a young man in an exquisite suit and gleaming shoes whose foot-long necktie looked like a tiger's tail, but whose glistening hair was in total disarray.

Pratap Singh felt uneasy. To be that Bohemian with one's hair one should be in soiled pyjamas and a tattered shirt. What sense was there in being so tip-top right from the boots to the necktie, and then leaving the lush crop of hair in a mess?

In an effort to forget the nagging question he stepped into the bookshop once again, but the realization that it had not been a wise course dawned on him in no time, for he had the misfortune to see an elegantly dressed gentleman, at least twenty years older than himself, turning the pages of a recently published pictorial edition of Vatsayana's *Kamasutra*. The walking stick dangling from his left elbow exaggerated the shaking of the hand holding the heavy book.

'Well, venerable sir, of what use is the book to you at your age?' Pratap Singh managed to hold back his surging question and hurriedly came out of the bookshop, in the process forgetting the very purpose of his visit to the airport.

But once again Pratap Singh's attention went over to the young man with the puzzling state of his hair. The young man could not have left his hair like that for the sake of style. What then could it be?

He found a possible answer. The young man, a bit late for his flight, had left home in a hurry. His wife being away at her maternal uncle's house—for the fellow did not look either a bachelor or a divorcee—there was nobody to remind him that his hair was uncombed. By the time he realized this, which was only after coming to learn that his flight was delayed, he found to his dismay that he had forgotten his pocket-comb on the dressing table. What could he do?

That's right. What could he do? The argument calmed Pratap Singh. He went over to the small stationery shop and bought a plastic pocket-comb, paying four times more than what he would have paid for it outside.

He waited for an opportune moment for his next act. It came when the young man strained his neck to survey one who could be among the ten best-dressed women of the century yelling out her distress at the delayed flight.

Pratap Singh dropped the comb right at his feet and sat down in a chair just fallen vacant opposite him. Singh was happy when the young man noticed the comb and picked it up, and held it prominently enough for those near him to see it. Honesty, no doubt, impelled him to trace its owner. Pratap Singh had to struggle once again to check himself from blurting out, 'Young man, why don't you use it on your hair first, before thinking of giving it away?'

He was shocked to see the young man calmly put the comb in his pocket.

Did the chap forget that he had a head and that the head was blessed with a profusion of hair and that it looked uncannily uncared for in relation to the rest of his well-groomed person?

Singh tried his best to stop exercising his own head on the issue but failed. For a moment he had an impulse to ignore it all. He even walked up to the exit, but did an about-turn and was soon back on the scene. He had realized that to abandon the puzzle was simply impossible.

The chap had a glistening bush of hair on his head and a brand new blue comb in his pocket. What stood in the way of his applying the latter to the former?

He could feel the quiz swell within him. Soon it seemed to take complete possession of his being. He went and stood before the young man, staring at him.

'Would you like to sit down here?' The young man was courtesy personified.

'Oh no, thank you. Please keep sitting. But if you don't mind, would you please comb your hair?' Pratap managed to say, though he sounded nervous to himself.

'I beg your pardon?'

'I mean, it looks so unkempt. Won't you care for your head?'

The young man shifted his disconcerted look from Singh's face. 'If you are speaking of my head, well, I'll beg you to leave it in peace, for it is my head!' he said, his facial muscles stiffening.

It was frustrating for Singh. Why does everybody fail to read sense in a suggestion born of plain goodwill? Why is everybody so eager to be sarcastic, so ready with retorts?

But he controlled himself. 'Look here, my friend,' he began, trying to sound as affable as possible. 'How many are blessed with such a treasure of silken hair? You have not neglected an inch of your person; even the face is so well-rouged except for that blotch of undiluted powder—never mind that—on your nose. Why should you be so unkind towards your head?'

The young man's eyes, which looked so tender with concern only a moment ago when he was appreciating the screaming lady behind him, began to give out spooky sparks.

'What had I done to you that you must deride me?' He stood up.

'Believe me, I had no intention of deriding you. I mean what I say, sincerely. You have—don't you?—a comb in your pocket, a brand new one!'

'Who said I have?' asked the young man through clenched teeth.

This was too much for Singh.

'How dare you challenge the truth, you liar?'

'How dare you call me a liar?'

'Must you know how? Who do you think paid for the comb you have pocketed?' Singh's voice was growing shrill.

A crowd was collecting around them. It included the damsel in distress, now rapidly puffing at her cigarette and leaning against a colourful companion sporting a crimson beard, two elderly European ladies equipped with movie cameras, their arms around each other's waist, a tall Grecian figure leading a very short and fat woman in a half-veil holding a tennis racket for him, and eight or ten men and women without any special traits.

'So much ado just about a comb, eh!' commented someone.

'Not about a comb!' shouted Singh.

'Then?'

Pratap Singh began to stutter in his effort to explain.

The aged gentleman from the bookshop stepped forward, his manner suggesting that if he leaned on his stick, it was on account of the sheer weight of his wisdom.

'Who is the loser?' he asked, coughing benevolently. 'Let him come with me. I will buy a comb for him.'

'Venerable one, will you please return to the bookshop and spend your remaining eyesight on those erotica on Italian art paper?' shouted Singh.

'Oh, a mental case!' commented the tall man, and he left the scene, nudging the woman in veil to follow him.

'Mental case? How dare you? Do you take me for mad?' Singh was about to rush upon the man when he was stopped by an airport official. 'Excuse me, which flight are you boarding?' he asked, so polite as to be almost pleading with him.

'No flight.'

'Which flight do you propose to attend? Two are arriving almost simultaneously.'

'How do I care!'

'Why then are you here?' The official now sounded quite matter-of-fact.

'I willed to be here; that's all! But I'm no intruder. Here is my entry ticket!'

'Strange!' sighed the venerable old man, looking askance.

'There are people who buy tickets in search of quarrels.' He was sure of support and protection from his audience should Singh turn violent. His listeners exchanged smiles in mutual recognition of sanity, courtesy and such other qualities warranted in as civilized a place as an airport lounge. And, of course, they indicated their agreement with the observation that the world had queer people galore ready to buy quarrels.

It was announced that the flight announced as delayed had been cancelled. The crowd dispersed and regrouped in front of the enquiry counter.

Pratap Singh came out into the open. He felt the atmosphere outside cooler than inside, though it could not be factually possible.

He inhaled some peace and walked along the pavement skirting the dimly lighted car park.

Suddenly his eyes fell on the young man with the tousled hair about to start his car. He had rolled down the glass and was looking for passage.

Here was the fellow for whom he had been branded a mental case and buyer of quarrels. An upsurge of vengeance maddened Singh. He thrust his hand in and caught the young man's hair in his grip.

Panic wrought a ghostly mutation on the young man's face. His eyes betrayed the fright of a goat about to be butchered. He started the car and shot away.

Pratap Singh stood aghast. He had never visualized such a metamorphosis. The man who slipped away from his grip seemed to have changed into a totally different man in the twinkle of an eye. Then his eyes fell on his own hand, which for a moment looked alien to himself, like that of an assassin, for it held something unexpected, something like a part of a head—a complete wig of glistening, dark hair!

He kept standing there, absorbing the shock, and moved only when obliged to give way to a honking vehicle.

All his senses seemed to have grown mellow with a sweet melancholy and a feeling of empathy. Silently, he apologized to the young man and all the others concerned.

He also remembered Hemant Babu and spoke to him in his mind: 'Cough on, my esteemed colleague, cough on! What else is there to be done, after all? Yours is a million-dollar question, indeed!'

Had he been familiar with the man who walked along the river bank talking to himself, he would have given him a pat on the back and said, 'Go on, my friend, go on with your soliloquy. To who else but yourself can you explain yourself? Who understands anyone else?'

The Concubine

The small brick house with a thatched roof at the western end of Sumanpur, which one could reach by trudging past acres of marshland, had a past, but the members of the Progressive Club were not at all in favour of discussing it. Citizens of the small town, however, knew it till 1951 as the Slaughterhouse. In order to rid them of the deplorable habit of referring to it by that uncomfortable name, my friends had crowned the house with a signboard bigger than any in the bazaar, bearing their club's name, the sombre letters looking like a parade of undertakers.

As the post-independence Sumanpur had shown an encouraging growth in the number of goats along with the population of goat-eaters, the affluent and patriotic butcher had shifted his workshop to a spacious accommodation and had allowed the ambitious youths of the town to use the old place for their proposed cultural revolution.

It was my second day at Sumanpur. In the evening, one of the leading progressives, Sujan Das, cordially led me to their club. He briefed me on our way about the project to be discussed: they were going to launch a fortnightly devoted on the one hand to the wonder that was Sumanpur of yore, and on the other to the burning issues of the day. The paper was also to wage a crusade against social evils like dowry, child-marriage and every kind of orthodoxy.

He also informed me that the elite of the town had been entrusted with the task of suggesting an attractive name for the journal. Among the proposals already received were 'God is Good' coming from the venerable Sanskrit scholar Pundit Pundarik Panda, which, Sujan Das confided to me, the executive committee of the club had rejected with regrets, and 'The Thunderclap' and 'The Earthquake' suggested by two promising entrants to their club.

Under a roof that badly needed repairs, the assembled members displayed a palpable excitement on their faces. The president of the club, Makhan Roy, introduced us to the cause of that excitement—one Pradeep Bishoi—who was on the staff of a daily published from the state's capital and who, while on a visit to his old friend Makhan Roy, had kindly consented to educate the members of the club on the making of a newspaper.

Bishoi brought out a beedi from a cigarette case and Makhan Roy lighted the match for him.

'What you need for a fortnightly is not just paper or ink or a printing press, not even money, but . . .' Bishoi paused to blow out an impressive puff of smoke.

All were nodding their heads to denote their agreement with Bishoi, but when he stopped abruptly and left it to his listeners to complete the sentence, assuming the look of the chairman of a public service commission. Some gave knowing nods and some others coughed, while the rest sat smiling though embarrassed.

Bishoi resumed, 'What is needed is an extra pair of eyes. One pair won't do, Mr Roy!'

Makhan Roy, the would-be editor, blushed. Bishoi planted a rather unkind whack on his head and said again, giggling indulgently, 'You need to cultivate a pair of eyes here, right at the back of your head. Only then you'll learn how to see, what to report!'

'But ours is a small place, nothing more than a bazaar, though we flatter ourselves by calling it a town. Events to merit report rarely take place here!' grumbled Roy.

Bishoi almost thrust his smouldering beedi into Roy's face and bellowed, while the would-be editor hurriedly shut his eyes:

'Closing whatever eyes you have, eh? Didn't I tell you about the need to cultivate even more eyes to do justice to a newspaper?' Bishoi laughed but soon his voice rang with compassion. 'Never mind, one pair of eyes should do. After all, even I do not possess more, do I?'

Makhan Roy looked hopeful.

Bishoi threw away the beedi, already reduced to a stub, and explained: 'What I mean is, you must develop a subtle vision. You suspect dearth of news. But I tell you, I could have filled half a page of a daily with whatever I saw even while coming from your house to your club here!'

We stared at Bishoi, our looks betraying reactions ranging from total disbelief to amazement.

'Should I give an example? Should I?' he provoked his audience.

'Please do,' Roy pleaded on our behalf.

'What happened near the sub-registrar's office?' Bishoi demanded, squinting meaningfully.

'What?' Roy stared blank.

'Nothing?'

'I . . . well . . . I must confess I can't exactly remember!'

'Ha ha! Don't you remember that hand-pulled rickshaw with two passengers, and a third one, fat as a gorilla—you informed me that he was a local capitalist—squeezing in? Didn't you mark the miserable condition of the rickshaw-puller struggling with the giant weight and the people around laughing, thereby obliging the capitalist to get down?'

There was a pensive silence.

'I know, you're unable to catch the import of my observation. Listen. This should be the headline of the item, 'People's laughter triumphs on Broadway: Capitalist relents!' Ha ha! Do you now realize what you were missing?'

Makhan Roy and his collaborators looked amused as well as enlightened.

'And, needless to say, the forthcoming elections should mean a great opportunity for you.' Bishoi rolled up his sleeves. 'You should forthwith launch an attack on the candidature of

the young prince of the erstwhile Sumanpur state. Tell the people
that although the Raj has gone, as the scion of the dynasty, he is
the symbol of a reactionary feudal past, a reminder of tyranny
and exploitation!'

Bishoi gave attention to a fresh beedi as his audience sat
whispering to one another.

It may be almost impossible today to discover a young man
who is not aligned with one political party or the other. But
then the situation was different. The progressives of Sumanpur
had not yet been fired by any radical idealism. I suspect Makhan
Roy alone had some ambition in that direction. However, all
of them sat convinced that if Sumanpur were to find for itself
a dot on the map of the modern world, it must take a big leap
out of its foggy feudal past and the sooner it did so the better.

Unfortunately, the young prince appeared popular. People
had forgotten, in a deplorably short period, all about the misrule
of his late father.

Not that the rival candidate was a paragon of virtue. But
he represented the forces of anti-feudalism, having once raised
his voice against the Raj. It was not necessary that one who
represented a valuable ideal should be ideal himself!

The prince had one day paid a surprise visit to the Progressive
Club and had greeted the members affably and requested their
help. The overwhelmed progressives were about to promise him
their support. But Roy hastened to mend matters. 'Please don't
mind, but you were a raja; we wouldn't like to vote for an ex-
raja. We have no grievance whatever against you personally. It
is only a question of principle.'

The prince had meanwhile pushed cigarettes into several
hands. While helping them with his gold-studded lighter, he
rejoined in a remarkably calm tone, 'Mr Roy, if I say that you
were once a baby and it is not proper to offer a cigarette to an
ex-baby, would you appreciate my logic? I should expect you to
reconsider your stand.'

The prince left Roy discomfited. The report of the encounter
spread like wildfire and the people of Sumanpur were all praise
for the prince's wit. The humiliation made Makhan Roy a

progressive with a vengeance. He inspired his friends to resolve to work for the prince's defeat, 'If not in the forthcoming election, in the next election or in the one thereafter.'

'But the prince is hardly making any propaganda. Either he does not care or he is too shy to address the public. Others speak for him. Our womenfolk have been requested to gather tomorrow at noon in the grove on the eastern outskirts of the town,' one of the members informed.

'Who is going to address them?' Bishoi queried.

'Sati Dei.'

'Who is that?'

'A woman from the palace, a concubine of the late Raja.'

'A golden opportunity!' Bishoi screamed out and clapped his hands.

He then briefed the youths on how to exploit the situation. Sati Dei must be exposed. She must be told to her face that she was a concubine, in the full hearing of her audience. Humiliated, she would hang her head or beat a hasty retreat. And Bishoi explained at some length how to make an exciting story of the episode for the lower half of the first page of the first issue of the fortnightly.

'Issue-oriented but imaginative, yes, that's what your paper must be—and you have to be vigilant,' was the parting advice of the valued guest.

The progressives stood up gratefully and bade Bishoi a farewell just short of tearful.

While returning from the club, my companions descended on a young homeopath of the town, Dr Subudhi, and realized from him five rupees in advance for a quarter-page advertisement in the inaugural number of the publication.

This is how Roy impressed Dr Subudhi: The print order for the first issue shall be twelve thousand copies. If one copy is read by ten people on an average, the paper will command a readership of one lakh and twenty thousand. Half of that number must be suffering from one ailment or another. At least one-third of that half, that is, twenty thousand people, must be having faith in homeopathy. If one-fourth of them came to Dr Subudhi for treatment, and if the doctor realized one rupee on the average per head, he should earn five thousand rupees. The cost of the insertion deducted, he should be left with a clean profit of four thousand nine hundred and ninety-five rupees!

The charmed physician had mildly protested, 'I'm afraid it'll be less. In case of such a rush of patients, I must appoint an assistant. Besides, we have to keep in mind the cost of the medicines.'

On the road again, I asked Roy, 'Don't you think it might prove rather tough for the lone hand-press of your town to turn out twelve thousand copies?'

'The print order of a paper is a secret,' observed Roy gravely.

I had to desire of go to confront Sati Dei. But Sujan Das and Makhan Roy would not spare me.

Among the progressives, Roy no doubt possessed a heart of steel. The others were hardly excited at the prospect of humiliating Sati Dei. It was only a sense of sacred duty towards the cause of progress as well as the demands made by the lower half of the first page of the first issue of the fortnightly that led them, profusely sweating under a stern sun, towards the grove.

Some five hundred women and a number of children had collected in the grove when we made our unexpected appearance there. They were surprised. I am afraid several members of our delegation too were growing nervous.

We faltered to a halt under the gaze of the women.

'Who are you?' Sati Dei, seated in a chair under a big mango tree, threw the question at us. There was no rancour in her voice, only curiosity.

Roy took a determined step forward. 'We are the representatives of a progressive newspaper. But may I ask who are you?' Roy looked askance at us. He was in dire need of some moral support.

'Me? Well, I'm Sati Dei, of course! You kids won't know me . . .'

'We are no kids!' Roy tried to thunder, but his voice cracked.

'You kids won't know me,' Sati Dei continued, totally unmindful of Roy's protest. 'You were born only yesterday. Your mothers should know me.'

'But we know!' bellowed Roy, mobilizing all his stamina,

though gasping in the process, 'You were a concubine of the late Raja!'

'I was what, my son?'

'Concubine, that's to say, a—well—what's called a kept—a woman of the old Raja.'

We lowered our heads. There was complete silence for a moment, except for a koel calling persistently from a nearby tree.

Would this be the end of the confrontation? Would Sati Dei, exposed and insulted, sit stupefied or retreat as quickly as Bishoi had prophesied?

But we stood bewildered. The old and serene Sati Dei, in a milk-white saree, slightly stooping, was seen quietly advancing towards us, all smiles.

Makhan Roy looked back. I could feel how eager he was to locate the way out.

But there was no chance. Sati Dei caught him by his shoulder, touched his chin tenderly and patted him on the back. 'Live long, sonny, how did you know so much about me? You're right. I am the same Sati Dei.'

Her tone was marked by a deep emotion. She wiped her eyes and resumed, 'I was under the impression that you wouldn't recognize me at all! But, my sons, you know so much! No wonder, for you are an educated lot! While in her deathbed, the Rani had entreated me, "Sati, take care of my son!" That's why I'm doing my bit. I go from village to village asking the women to vote for the boy. Were the Raja alive, he would have skinned me alive. But let us not speak of that demon. The boy, however, is as gentle as a calf!'

Sati Dei caressed Roy again and called out, 'Nrutya!'

Nrutya, her servant, came rushing forward.

'Give my children a pair of laddoos each. Don't you see how they have come here braving the summer sun?' She apologized for having called the meeting at noon: 'You know, this is the only time your mothers have a little respite!'

After we had consumed a couple of laddoos each and taken leave of Sati Dei, duly bowing to her, we felt that the day had suddenly become extremely tender and pleasant.

The long silence was broken by Sujan Das, 'I think the right thing for us will be to publish a cultural monthly and not a fortnightly newspaper.'

All the progressives jumped at the idea. Unlike on other occasions, they did not wait for Makhan Roy's ruling on the issue. And that very evening they unanimously accepted the name I proposed for the magazine 'The Monthly Jasmine'.

Mystery of the Missing Cap

I t is certainly not my motive, in recounting this episode of
two decades ago, to raise a laugh at the expense of Shri
Moharana or Babu Virkishore, then the Hon'ble Minister
of Fisheries and Fine Arts of my state. On the contrary, I wish
my friends and readers to share the sympathy I have secretly
nurtured in my heart for these two gentlemen over the past years.

Shri Moharana was a well-to-do man. His was the only pukka
house in an area of twenty villages. Whitewashed on the eve
of India achieving independence, the house shone as a sort of
tourist attraction for the folks of the nearby villages. They
stopped to look at it, for none could overlook the symbolism
in this operation that had been carried out after half a century.

Shri Moharana had a considerable reputation as a
conscientious and generous man. He was an exemplary host
with two ponds full of choice fish and a number of pampered
cows. He was a happy villager.

Came Independence. As is well known, the ancient land of
India has had four major castes from time immemorial. But
during the days immediately preceding Independence a new
caste was emerging all over the country—that of the patriots.
Independence day—15 August 1947—gave a big boost to their
growth. In almost every village, besides the Brahmins, Kshatriyas,
Vaisyas and Sudras, a couple of patriots came into being.

It was observed that the small fisheries of Shri Moharana were often exploited in honour of these new people. And observers began to notice that Shri Moharana himself was fast growing into a patriot. As I found out later, he had even nurtured an ambition to be elected to the state legislature. The incident I relate occurred at the outset of his endeavour in that direction. A small boy, I was then on a visit to my maternal uncle's house which was in the immediate neighbourhood of Shri Moharana's.

In those early days of indigenous ministries, there were no deputy or sub-deputy ministers. All were full-fledged Hon'ble Ministers and, since Babu Virkishore hailed from our district, the sponsors of Shri Moharana thought it proper that the latter's debut into politics should have his blessings.

That was a time when a minister's daily life was largely made up of speech-making at public meetings. There was no need for any specific occasion to accord a reception to a minister. A reception was arranged for Babu Virkishore with Shri Moharana as the chairman of the Preparatory Committee.

Shri Moharana's huge ancestral cane-chair was laid with a linen cover, on which the most gifted village seamstress had laced a pair of herons holding two ornamented fish in their beaks. The children of the village lower primary school were made to practise a welcome song every afternoon for a fortnight.

Among the many strange phenomena wrought by the great spirit of the time was the composition of this song, for the composer—the head pundit of the school—had lived for fifty-five years without any poetic activity. The refrain of the song still raises echoes in my memory. Its literal translation would be:

O mighty minister, tell us, O tell us,
How do you nurture this long and broad universe!

The rest of the song catalogued the great changes nature and humanity experienced on the occasion of the minister's visit: how the morning sun frequently blushed in romantic happiness, how each and every bird chanted a particular salutation-oriented *raga*, and with what eagerness and throbbing of heart the womenfolk waited to blow their conch shells in unison when the minister would set his foot on village soil.

I know that nowadays ministers do not enjoy such glory. But it was very different then. We, the rustic children, wrangled over several issues: What does a minister eat? What does he think? Does he sleep? Does he ever suffer from colic or colds as ordinary mortals do?

Shri Moharana himself was excitement personified. He used to be very fond of his hour-long afternoon nap. But he gave up the luxury at least ten days prior to the day of destiny. He devoted all his time to examining and re-examining details of the arrangements; even then he seemed nervous and uncertain.

At last dawned the big day. The minister got down from the jeep as soon as it reached the very first welcome arch on the outskirts of the village. He was profusely garlanded by Shri Moharana but was requested to re-enter the jeep as the destination was still a furlong away. But the minister smiled and made some statement which meant that great though destiny had made him, he loved to keep his feet on the ground! Moharana and his friends looked ecstatic.

While hundreds applauded and shouted 'Babu Virkishore ki jai' and 'Bharatmata ki jai', the minister, double the size of an average man of our village, plodded through the street, it seemed to us, to the embarrassment of the poor, naked earth. And I still remember the look of Shri Moharana when the minister's long round arm rested on his shrunken neck, a look which I have seen only once or twice later in life on the faces of dying people who had lived a contented and complete life. Shri Moharana's look suggested: 'What more, what more, O my mortal life, could you expect from the world? My, my!'

All the people—even invalids, for many of whom it was the experience of a lifetime—were alternately shouting slogans and gaping at the august visitor. We, the half-naked, pot-bellied, uncivilized kids walked parallel to the minister at a safe distance and could not help feeling extremely small and guilty.

At Shri Moharana's house, the minister and his entourage

were treated to tender coconut water, followed by the most luxurious lunch I had ever seen, with about twenty dishes around the sweetened, *ghee*-baked rice mixed with nuts and cloves. Soon the minister retired to the cabin set apart for him. Though it was summer, the cabin's window being open to a big pond and a grove, there was enough air to lull even an elephant to a sound sleep. Volunteers had been posted to see that no noise whatever was made anywhere in the village to disturb the ministerial repose.

I had by then separated myself from my companions. Being rather ambitious, I was eager to be as physically close to the great man as possible. And the minister sleeping was surely the most ideal condition for achieving my goal.

I mustered courage and slowly approached the window facing the pond. This was the rear side of the house. The minister's personal assistant and entourage were on the opposite side.

While I stood near the window, suffering the first shock of disillusionment in my life regarding great men, for the minister was snoring in the style of any ordinary man, something most extraordinary happened. Speechless I was already; the incident rendered me witless.

Through the window I had observed that the minister's egg-bald head rested on a gigantic pillow while his white cap lay on a table near his bed. Now I saw the mischievous Jhandoo bounce towards the window like a bolt from the blue and pick up the cap. Throwing a meaningful glance at me, he disappeared into the grove.

Even when my stupefaction passed, I was unable to shout, partly because of my deep affection for Jhandoo (knowing that the consequences of his crime could be fatal to him), and partly for fear that the minister's dream—must be on a patriotic theme—might cease. At that crucial moment, I was in a dilemma as to which I should value more—the great man's cap or his snoring.

I retreated, pensive. But before long I heard an excited if subdued noise. Crossing into Shri Moharana's compound again, I saw the minister's personal assistant flitting about like a butterfly and heard his repeated mumbling, 'Mysterious, mysterious!' The minister was obviously inside the cabin. But nobody dared to go in.

Shri Moharana stood thunderstruck, as were his compatriots. The public relationships officer was heard saying, 'The Hon'ble Minister does not mind the loss of the cap so much as the way it was stolen. Evidently, there was a deep-rooted conspiracy. The gravity of the situation can hardly be exaggerated. In fact, I fear, it may have devastating effects on the political situation of our country.'

I could see Shri Moharana literally shaking. He was sweating like an ice-cream stick, so much so that I was afraid, at that rate he might completely melt away in a few hours.

The conflict within me, as to whether I should keep the knowledge of the mystery to myself or disclose it, was resolved. I signalled Shri Mohavana to follow me, which he eagerly did. A drowning man will indeed clutch at a straw.

I told him what had happened. He stood dumb for a moment, eyes closed. Then wiping the sweat from his forehead, he smiled like a patient whose disease had been accurately diagnosed but was known to be incurable. He then patted me and said, 'My son, good you told me. But keep it a secret. I will reward you later.'

The incident had thrown a wet blanket on the occasion. The sepulchral silence in the minister's room was broken only by his intermittent coughing. Every time he coughed, a fresh wave of anxiety hit the people in the courtyard and on the veranda.

I went away to join my friends. They were wild with speculations. One said that the thief, when caught, was to be hanged on the big banyan tree beside the river. 'Perhaps all the villagers will be thrown into jail,' said another. Among us there were naïves who even believed that the minister's cap was a sort of Aladdin's lamp, that anyone who put it on would find himself endowed with ministerial power the very next moment.

But the situation changed all of a sudden. I saw the minister and Shri Moharana emerging on the veranda, the former all smiles.

It was the most remarkable smile he had hitherto displayed. By then, at least half a dozen caps had been secured for him. But he appeared with his head bare. Even to a child like me it was obvious that his bald pate wore an aura of martyrdom.

Not less than five thousand people had gathered in front of a specially constructed stage when the minister ascended it, that remarkable smile still clinging to his face. Shri Moharana's niece, the lone high-school-going girl of the region, garlanded the minister. A thunderous applause greeted the event, for that was the first time our people saw what they had only heard in the tales of the ancient *Swayamvaras*—a young female garlanding a male in public. Then the chorus 'O mighty minister' was sung in *kirtan*-style to the accompaniment of two harmoniums, a violin and a pakhauj drum.

Now it was Shri Moharana's turn to say a few words of welcome. I saw him (I stood just in front of the stage) moving his legs and hands in a very awkward fashion. That was certainly nervousness. But with a successful exercise of will power, he grabbed the glittering mike and managed to speak for nearly an hour, giving a chronological account of Babu Virkishore's achievements and conveying gratitude, on behalf of the nation, to the departed souls of the great man's parents but for whom the world would have been without the minister.

I was happy that Shri Moharana did well in his maiden speech. But the greatest surprise was yet to come—in the concluding observations of Shri Moharana. Well, many would take Shri Moharana as a pukka politician. But I can swear that it was out of his goodness—a goodness confused by excitement—that he uttered the lie. He said, his voice raised in a crescendo, 'My brothers and sisters, you must have heard about the mysterious disappearance of the Hon'ble Minister's cap. You think that the property was stolen, don't you? Naturally. But not so, ladies and gentlemen, not so!' Shri Moharana smiled mysteriously. The minister nodded his big clean head which glowed like a satellite.

Shri Moharana resumed, 'You all are dying to know what happened to the cap. Isn't that so? Yes, yes, naturally. You are dying. Well, it is like this: a certain nobleman of our locality took it away. Why? That's what you ask, don't you? Well, to preserve it as a sacred memento, of course! He was obliged to take it away secretly because otherwise the Hon'ble Minister of Fisheries and Fine Arts, the brightly burning example of humility that he is, would never have permitted our friend the nobleman to view the cap as anything sacred!'

Shri Moharana stopped and brought out of his pocket a handkerchief full of coins and, holding it before the audience, said, 'Well, ladies and gentlemen, the nobleman has requested me to place this humble amount of one hundred and one rupees at the disposal of the Hon'ble Minister for some little use in his blessed life's mission—the service of the people—through fish and fine arts.' Shri Moharana bowed and handed over the money to the minister who, with a most graceful gesture, accepted it.

Applause and cries of wonder and appreciation broke out like a hurricane. Even the minister and Shri Moharana, both looking overwhelmed, clapped their hands. The minister spoke for two and a half hours thereafter, drinking a glass of milk in between, at the end of which he declared that as a mark of respect to the unknown lover of his, he had decided to remain bareheaded for that whole night although the good earth did not lack caps and, in fact, a surge of caps had already tried to occupy his undaunted head.

Soon my shock gave way to a double-edged feeling for Shri Moharana: praise for his presence of mind and a regret for his having to spend one hundred and one rupees to cover Jhandoo the monkey's mischief. At night, the respectable people of the area partook of the dinner that the Preparatory Committee threw in honour of the minister. Glances of awe and esteem were frequently cast at the minister's head and homages paid to the honourable thief. But when I saw Shri Moharana in the morning, I could immediately read in his eyes the guilt that haunted him at least whenever his eyes fell on me. Shri Moharana perhaps had never spoken a lie; and now when he did speak one, he did so before a gathering of thousands! God apart, at least there was one creature, myself, who knew that he was no longer a man of truth.

The minister, however, exuded sheer delight. He did not seem to notice with what constraint Shri Moharana was conducting himself before him.

At last came the moment of the minister's departure. He was served with a glass of sweetened curd. While sipping it leisurely, he said, in a voice choked with curd and emotion, 'Well, Moharana, ha ha! the way things are moving, ha ha! I'm afraid, ha ha! people would start snatching away my clothes, ha ha! and ha ha! I may have to go about, ha ha! naked! ha ha! But I don't mind! ha ha! That is the price one must pay for winning love! ha ha ha!' The minister came out to the rear veranda facing the pond and the grove to wash his mouth. Shri Moharana followed him with water in a mug.

Except for me, there was nobody on the veranda. My presence was not accidental. A few minutes before I had observed that the rascal Jhandoo, playing with the minister's cap, was slowly emerging from the grove. Seldom had I wished for anything so ardently as I wished then for Jhandoo to go unnoticed by the guest. He was a monkey not in any figurative sense, but a real one. When he was an infant, his mother had taken shelter inside Shri Moharana's house in order to save her male child from the usual wrath of his father. Shri Moharana had not been at home and his servants killed the mother monkey. Shri Moharana felt extremely upset, did not eat for one and half days, and, to compensate for the wrong done, nurtured the baby monkey, christened Jhandoo, with great affection.

Jhandoo, when he grew up a little, would often escape into the grove. He was half domesticated and half wild. He played with everybody, and everybody tolerated him. We children were extremely fond of him.

To my horror, I saw Jhandoo rushing towards us from the other side of the pond. I made an effort to warn Shri Moharana of the impending crisis, but in vain. Jhandoo got there in the twinkling of an eye. He sat down between the minister and Shri Moharana. He put the cap once on his own head, then, taking it off, offered it to the minister in a most genial gesture.

My heartbeats had trebled. Looking at Shri Moharana's face, I saw an extremely pitiable image—pale as death.

The bewildered minister mumbled out, 'Er ... er ... isn't this one the very cap taken away by the nobleman?'

And something most fantastic came out of the dry lips of Shi Moharana who seemed to be on the verge of collapsing: 'Yes, yes, this is the nobleman ...'

His eyes bulging out, the minister managed to ask, 'What ... what did you say? ... Well?'

But Shri Moharana was in no condition to say anything more. He broke into tears. Next moment, I saw the Hon'ble Minister of Fisheries and Fine Arts weeping too. The personal assistant's voice was heard from the opposite veranda, 'Sir, the jeep is ready, Sir.' The minister gulped the mugful of water and walked towards the jeep. Shri Moharana followed suit. Their reddened eyes and drawn faces were interpreted as marks of the sorrow of separation.

Shri Moharana's political endeavour is not known to have gone any further. And it is strange that the Hon'ble Minister, Babu Virkishore, who was willing to be robbed of his clothes, was soon forgotten in politics. I have a strong feeling that it was this episode of the cap that changed the courses of their lives.

The Birds

Kumar Tukan Roy knelt down, as he had done evening after evening, at the end of a stroll along the marshland on the river, while the red sun, as though shot at, sank down behind the hills. Amidst the new offshoots of the topmost bough of the old banyan tree sat a pair of green pigeons. A son of the late Raja Sahib of Mandarpur, born to a lady other than the Rani, the now-sixtyish Tukan Roy, who had forgotten whether it was in love-making or in hunting that his genius had bloomed first—and how easily—knew well that a pair of birds seated meditatively on a bough at that hour of the day would not choose to disperse unless provoked.

He took position as discreetly as possible. His knees had long since become immune to pricks and pebbles. He closed one eye and strained the other and took aim. Behind the birds was a patch of dark cloud, its borders gilded by the hidden sun. Roy's finger hooked the trigger.

Just then a third pigeon flew in and settled with a flutter on the branch next to the one occupied by the pair.

This was luck! A little patience and adjustment and the fall of all the three is ensured! There was no need for him to be in a hurry. The cool twilight itself taught patience. Roy changed his position as slowly as a caterpillar and took a fresh aim covering all the three birds.

The golden line around the cloud was fading fast and the cloud was swelling up. Against that quiet grandeur, the three tiny heads of the birds looked like three tender bubbles offered to Roy for him to burst them at his sweet will.

He began feeling the thrill he always had when the birds came down—their wings, which had flapped over hundreds of miles, from horizon to horizon, flapping desperately for the last few times against the gravitational pull.

The colour of such deaths, smoky and red, mixed well with that of the twilight. Over the hundreds of past sunsets, hundreds of such sweet deaths had steeped Roy's eyes in the same kind of smokiness and redness.

At times, dusk swooped down rather swiftly upon the valley. That is what it was doing today. Since the past year Roy had been slowly losing faith in the sharpness of his own vision. He was anxious to press the trigger. But a sudden lightning across the clouds dazzled his eyes for a moment. Just when his targets should have been visible to him once again, thunderclaps burst across the valley and they flew off.

For a while Roy stayed put with the unashamed nothing-to-do-ness of a lizard when a prey escapes its leaping tongue. The experience was not unusual; even then it annoyed Roy every time. It was different today, however. He felt no irritation at all. Passing over the deserted bough his eyes reached the swelling cloud that seemed like a mighty heart in turmoil. Birds and more birds flew across it and melted away in the infinite.

Roy kept on gazing at the clouds and the birds.There was lightning once again; a spray of misty rain tickled his eyes and cheeks. Yet he kept on gazing at the birds—hundreds of them.

He stood up abruptly and, leaving his gun on a rock, set off running, pacing himself with the flight of doves overhead. He was pacing inwardly too, for he felt that the joy he was experiencing was not entirely new—it inspired a remote memory of something similar. He felt a strong curiosity for tracing its origin.

He succeeded before long. The joy he had just felt was the echo of a sensation he had had fifty years ago, when the Raja who exercised over him all the authority of a father but was not willing to allow him the status of a prince, had suddenly collapsed of a heart attack.

It was the thrill of freedom.

The birds were in too much of a hurry. It was not possible to keep pace with them. Roy stopped and rolled his eyes across the sky from horizon to horizon. He had never known that his eyes were so big that they could grasp so much of the vast sky. The birds which had just flown across the sky and across his eyes had brushed away from the latter the accumulated dust of many years, and had left them pure and young.

In spite of the deepening dusk, he spent a long time in the valley before returning to the palace. And, on the dinner table, he did not feel the disgust he usually felt at a vegetarian meal. His whole being was elsewhere, though he did not know where. But he was happy to be there.

He had captured an elegantly green parrot only a week ago. In the morning, he served it with its breakfast, a banana, and opened its cage. It hopped experimentally and took to wings in no time. It circled twice or thrice over Roy's head and then disappeared in a headlong flight towards the woods. Roy smiled and wished that he had many birds to free, or rather, he had the power to make every creature on earth run or fly to its heart's content towards the God-knows-where of freedom. He stood entranced in his own thoughts for quite some time.

The afternoon was cloudy again. Roy went out to the valley as usual and fired several shots. But not a single bird fell. In fact, every time he fired either below or above the covey of birds, just to startle them. And after every shot he followed the flying birds on foot as far as he could.

Old Giloo—also an illegitimate son of the late Raja, though lesser in rank since his mother was not one of the recognized concubines but only a maid servant—was surprised to see Roy returning empty-handed for two consecutive evenings.

Roy was a bachelor. So was Giloo. During the good old days of the Raj, these little potentates had no need to marry. But time had changed and the hoary system had collapsed. Their step-brother, the present Raja, continuously sick and sad, lived in a city. The old palace of Mandarpur, apart from a few of its corners occupied by invalid and good-for-nothing dependants, lay largely deserted and was believed to be freely used by ghosts, particularly at night.

Besides the invisible ghosts and, for all practical purposes, its equally invisible human inmates, the palace had another resident—a tiger. It was during the last days of Mandarpur State that the Raja, spurred by what was perhaps his last whim, had built a small private zoo inside the palace compound. With his state gone, the government took charge of the animals and transferred them to a public zoo in the city. But on the insistence of Giloo, they had spared a tiger cub that was unwell at the time. The cub had grown up fully and perhaps grown a bit old prematurely. However, Giloo had fostered the animal as carefully as he could with the blessing of Tukan Raj the shikari.

Giloo used to cook for Roy. For two days now, both had to do with vegetarian dishes since the meat Giloo could secure was barely sufficient for the tiger. Giloo was saddened at the thought that Roy was getting old, perhaps he was failing as a hunter.

Roy left his bed at midnight. He walked quietly up to Giloo's bedstead and picked up the key for the tiger's cage from a hook on the wall above Giloo's head and stepped out, tiptoe.

The tiger lay asleep inside its cage. The moonlight focused on its big face. In spite of its familiarity, it would have been a fearful sight but for the moonlight. The magic of the moon reduced it to a tiger in a dream or to one drawn in watercolour.

Roy never imagined that there could be so much joy in turning the key of a lock. In a choked voice, he addressed the tiger that just raised its head inquiringly. 'Come on, my boy, you are free. Now, run into the forest. Well, don't waste your time yawning, hope that's what you're doing and not gaping to measure my damned head! You should behave as a grateful boy, shouldn't you? Now, come out.'

Roy held the door wide open. The tiger stood up and, with hesitant steps, came out into the open and stopped, its eyes fixed on Roy's.

Roy crossed the palace gate and stood on the road. The tiger did the same and stood behind him. Roy pointed his finger at the hills and the forest and said, 'Run, my boy, run. There—that's your natural habitat.'

But the tiger only moved closer to him, fondly smelling him and swinging its tail with some reservation.

'What are you surveying? I'm useless. There are deer galore in the forest. Run! Forgotten to run, eh? Well, it's like this!' Roy began to run and soon gathered speed, for, after all, he was setting an example to none other than a tiger! The animal began to overcome its hesitation or lack of practice and gathered gusto.

'Good. This's how you are to run, right? Go on! Only a mile and you'll reach your true home,' said Roy as he struggled with his breath. But the tiger had stopped, motionless except for its tail.

'Who's there, please? Two thieves, are you?' The exclamation, obviously made by somebody still sleepy, woke up Roy to the fact that he stood before the police station and the block development office. A number of dogs had begun barking from several directions.

Before he could think out his next course of action, a torchlight flashed on him and the tiger, and the stern voice from the police station changed into an abrupt howl.

Roy started running again. The tiger followed suit. They ran along the rocky meadow and through the prickly bushes. Roy had realized that the tiger would not run without him. And he could not stop before convincing the tiger that it had been granted the supreme thing—its freedom. Nor could he stop before feeling sure that the dear beast had truly appreciated the gift.

Once reconciled to the inevitability of his having to run into the forest, Roy ran with a wild enthusiasm—with the forest ahead, the night around, and the tiger sometimes behind him and sometimes beside him.

They had run for about a quarter of an hour when he realized that a jeep was rushing up at them. The officials of the police station and the block were pursuing them with the intention of rescuing him from the tiger!

He stopped and told the tiger, 'Go ahead, you fool! Here is the forest, spread over miles—over districts. Now you must make it alone!'

But the tiger did nothing of the sort. Roy had to resume running. He certainly did not wish to be discovered by the rescue party!

The jeep had moved off in a slightly different direction. Roy entered the forest. He stumbled and stopped, and ran again till he came to a thicker area. He was unable to run any more. A patch of moonlight showed a relatively clean block of rock. He stretched himself over it. The tiger stood close to him, surveying its novel environment and its liberator's face, alternately.

With every cool breath of the forest air he inhaled, Roy felt like he was taking a wave of freedom into his veins. The feeling was great as well as tranquil.

He slapped the tiger. 'Still don't understand, eh? How stupidly naïve you are, my boy!' he said.

But the tiger was probably waking up to the spirit that ruled the forest of the night. It suddenly gave out an impressive roar.

Birds tittered and flew away from the nearby trees. Also there was the sound of panicky footsteps of some small animals. The roar produced distinct echoes in the hills.

Roy felt happy, but he slapped the tiger once again. 'You fool!' he said, 'Won't they hear you?' He pulled the animal down by the neck as though in an attempt to hide it within himself. The tiger was obliged to sit down, its forelegs on Roy's chest. Roy saw in the tiger nothing more than intimate cat. He closed his eyes with satisfaction.

And in his vision were flying hundreds of birds—green, white, and many hues. The hundreds became thousands. They were scattering into ever-expanding heights and horizons like silver arrows and golden bullets. Roy, his eyes still closed, recognized them as the vibrations of the freedom that electrified him—freedom vast and vaster.

At last the two were caught under the jeep's headlights. Next was heard a booming shot. The tiger was staring at the light. It lowered its head slowly to rest on Roy's chest.

'The scoundrel had finished Mr Roy. After chasing him all way, at last it must have pounced upon him here.'

'He might still be alive.'

'No. Both are dead.'

'But isn't it strange that Mr Roy seems to be without a scratch? How did he die?'

'Er—well—a ferocious beast pouncing on him would've been enough to fell him.'

'Pity! Giloo will weep. Both were so dear to him!'

The Shadow

Professor Anjan Sharma was on the ascent as a scientist, thinker and an articulate orator when, within an incredibly brief span of time, he practically disappeared from the public view and, before long, from the public memory. The three independent incidents that brought this about, when viewed retrospectively, seem to have had a fearful conspiracy behind them, as if aimed at totally demolishing him. To begin with, the middle-aged professor, whose only love hitherto had been his laboratory, fell madly in love with a truly charming and kind-hearted young lady and married her. Secondly, his laboratory went up in flames. Thirdly, the lady died as suddenly as she had come into his life. Like most of his younger admirers, I too had forgotten him and could not have dreamed of waking up to his existence after thirty years, and that too in a remote Himalayan valley. It was a discovery to reckon with.

A chance meeting with a classmate of mine at Simla brought me to the isolated guest house not far from Manali. The experience was exciting. My friend had been an artist. Having come to the Himalayas in search of inspiration, he got captivated by solitude and stayed put, and had probably forgotten his art. For a living, he looked after this solitary summer mansion of a raja built on a lovely lake. He generally passed his time, clad in a shawl, gazing at the snowy hilltops, the lush green forests frequently changing into different splendid hues, and a sky which somehow looked very personal. He had nothing much to do. The raja had sold the mansion to a wealthy merchant soon after the abolition of the princely states. Lately, it had been acquired by the tourism department of the government. My friend had been allowed to stay on as its manager. But rarely did any tourist avail of its comforts, though the authorities advertised it, with expertly coined phrases, as an ideal health resort with swimming facilities in a natural lake, and breeze and sunlight that acted like a tonic.

'Only once in a while I receive a visitor who loves silence and solitude for their own sake. I thought of proposing to the government to close it down, but then where would Professor Anjan Sharma go?' mused my friend, drawing my attention to the lonely figure on the other side of the lake. 'Does he never come out of his seclusion?' I asked my friend, looking at the lovable man in tattered pyjamas, stooping rather prematurely, ambling towards the hills. A mild gust of wild wind would be enough to sweep him into the lake, I feared.

Only once earlier—when I was in the college—had I seen Anjan Sharma. 'If any Indian scientist deserves a Nobel for his original research today, it should be Professor Anjan Sharma,' our principal had observed to our great amazement by way of introducing the speaker.

The professor had just made public some hints regarding his revolutionary concept of harnessing the laws of gravitation for running factories, trains and all kinds of machines. His highly sophisticated technical thesis covered a couple of thousand pages. What was encouraging, an inspired millionaire, a friend of his, had already come to his aid, financing him to make a few basic instruments necessary to prove his point! But soon it had been realized that the fabulous amount of money required for the fruition of his dream could be provided only by an affluent western country or some international organization.

The professor's well-wishers began exploring such possibilities. But catastrophe struck all of a sudden. A fire destroyed his laboratory, along with all the documents and instruments he had prepared over the years.

The professor's shock was beyond description. The irony was, he had seen the arsonist moving about in the moonlight and knew that he was no ghoul or zombie, but human. He had even seen the fellow sprinkling petrol in the laboratory. But being too strong a believer in man's good nature, the professor had failed to imagine that the stranger's action could be anything but constructive.

Many of his friends felt that they could see the reflections of those flames in his bewildered eyes for days thereafter. He hardly spoke and, after a short while, resigned his job.

For sometime, the arson was the talk of the town. From petty jealousy of a colleague to transcontinental conspiracy, many were the causes imagined. And then, the incident was forgotten.

The millionaire friend dispatched the professor and his wife to the mansion in the Himalayan valley. Despite the changes in ownership, the professor was not asked to leave the small suite he occupied in the upper storey of an outhouse. The millionaire paid his bill, which in any case did not amount to much.

He had just settled down to a different plane of living—serene and peaceful—and the tranquillity was beginning to inspire in him some other kind of creativity, when his wife died. It was impossible for my friend to gauge the professor's reaction to the tragedy, for there was no visible reaction!

The professor's last companion was a faithful and intelligent dog nurtured by his wife. Depressed, the creature gave up eating and died after a month. The professor's stoicism was shattered at last. He cried like a child.

And this is the summary of the subsequent events, as narrated to me by my friend:

At times, Anjan Sharma took walks amidst the woods, totally oblivious of the world around him. Anybody could feel the impenetrability of the wall of silence surrounding him.

Days passed. One afternoon, during one of his habitual strolls, he suspected that someone was following him. Needless to say, there was no one or nothing, only his own shadow. He suddenly burst out, casting a stern look at his shadow, 'Why must you keep me company when everybody else—even my dog—has deserted me? Get lost, I say.'

Such was the poignancy and intensity of his admonition that his shadow leaped up, in the process suddenly getting detached from him, and scampered away and hid in a bush. The Professor could hear its faint sobs, like that of a timid child, for a while.

My friend was the only man to whom the shadowless savant had narrated this unusual incident.

The professor stopped coming out in sunlight or moonlight. He ventured into the valley only after dusk fell or if the sky was clouded. If he observed the clouds receding, he literally ran back into his suite. If anyone knocked on his door in the evening or at night, he switched off the lights before opening the door, if at all he opened it.

'Why this caution?' I asked.

'He did not wish anyone to know that he was bereft of his shadow.'

'But you know the absurdity of the proposition, don't you? Why didn't you flash a torchlight and convince him that his shadow was very much there with him?'

My friend, to my surprise, gave such a start as if I had proposed a treachery. I explained, 'I mean, someone should have put an end to his weird delusion!'

'Delusion?'

'What else? Surely you don't believe that one's shadow could desert one! You must have seen him with his shadow intact!'

'How could I?'

I grew impatient. 'What do you mean? You might not have seen his shadow because he did not come out in light. But did that prove his having cast his shadow away?'

My friend kept silent. I repeated my observation, hiding my uneasiness as best as I could.

'I don't know,' he hissed reluctantly.

'What do you mean?'

'I mean, I never put his proposition into any test.'

'Good heaven! Where was the need for any test? What does your common sense say?'

He fell silent again. Normally, it should have irritated me. But somehow it did not.

There was no exchange between us for a while. Evening

was giving way to night. A little moonlight on the nearest peaks created the illusion of their being the frontiers of some floating isles carved out of diamond. I tried to divert my attention to the strange chirpings and whistlings of birds unknown to me. Then, looking at my self-absorbed friend, I told myself like a wise man that one needed some quaint notions, some fantasy, to pass one's days in this uncanny solitude.

The next day I took leave of my friend. I had a great desire to see the professor once more, but there was no chance.

Five years later, I ran into my friend once again. He had returned from his Himalayan sojourn and had devoted himself to agriculture in his native village. He told me in a very natural tone, 'Life became intolerable once Professor Anjan Sharma was gone.'

'Where did he go?'

'In search of his shadow. That is the message he left for me.'

'Then?'

'How far could he go? We found him lying unconscious at the farthest end of the valley, at the foot of the hills. He died before long.'

'Then?'

'We cremated him.'

'I hope he found his shadow!'

'Oh no!'

'How did you know? Did you observe his body casting no shadow even after you found him?'

'The sky was clouded all the time. We were shivering even under our heavy overcoats.'

'But how did you conclude that his shadow had not returned to him?'

My friend did not answer me, but I could feel that he had something to say, though he was undecided whether to say it or not. Then he muttered as if in an aside, 'I felt that I heard some faint sobs from the bushes—for days together.'

'Do you mean to say the professor's shadow was looking for its master, weeping all the while?'

Again he avoided answering me and continued in the same

vein, 'How could I live in peace? But I am not sure if I did the right thing. Sometimes I am overwhelmed by an urge to return there.'

I was going to shout him down. But suddenly my eyes fell on my own shadow. I felt it forbade me to do anything rash.

Son and Father

The rain continued unabated. Through the window Samir could see the sombre contours of the distant horizon, but only occasionally, for the showers pounded by the fierce breeze wiped them off as soon as they had begun to take shape.

Alone in the forest guest house, Samir kept gazing at that drama of appearance and disappearance. Nature seemed determined to demonstrate to him how thin and flimsy was the difference between illusion and reality. If the idea of reality was highlighted when there were bright flashes of lightning, the darkness that followed asserted the power of illusion.

Never before had Samir imagined that the sky had so much energy in store—to go on and on with the display of such awfully long fireworks of lightning, booming all the while at variant scales.

And Samir sometimes wondered which was the reality and which the illusion!

The meadow extended up to the hills. Lush green palm trees stood in a scattered fashion, like a lyric broken into haphazard lines. There were dwarf rocks and bushes and shrubs galore for erratic punctuation marks.

What kind of theme and plot can make the best use of such a scene? The writer in Samir tried to figure out. Can this be the backdrop to a romance—for a chance-meeting between the hero and the heroine, both taking shelter under a banyan tree, the heroine shivering partly because of cold and partly for fright? The story narrated from a third person point of view, the narrator seeing them inching closer, then losing sight of them because of a heavier shower and then finding them even more close to each other . . .?

Or should it begin with an emphasis on the terror the intermittent thunder aroused in such solitude?

But that strange boy approaching the bungalow at the speed of a shooting star did not leave him in peace with his musings. Samir saw him for the fifth time. He had earlier seen him flying with the wind, like its coach, as if inspiring it to gather momentum! Once again he had seen him under the focus of a dazzling outburst of clouds, as if eager to catch hold of a string of lightning and swing it up to the clouds!

Yet again he had seen the boy climbing to his veranda and spinning around a pillar, with the dry leaves spiralling up in the whistling and howling breeze.

And during a lull in the thunderclaps, the boy had laughed. But the laughter was not meant for Samir who watched him so intently. It was an item in the lofty catalogue, to which the breeze and the rain and the lightning and the thunder belonged.

Wrapped in the costly Kashmiri shawl bestowed on him at a literary conference, Samir came out to the veranda. The boy saw him but did not seem to consider him relevant to his world. Samir was disappointed, for he had never suspected his own importance. Only a few people outside the circle of top officials of the forest department were eligible to check into that bungalow. That itself could be a matter of awe for the boy, if not anything else.

But the boy's attention obviously riveted amidst far more important events in the meadow and the forest and the hills.

'Hello, boy!' he called rather loudly. A hurried glance was all he received as the boy's response. He realized, unhappily, how futile his Kashmiri shawl, his well-built physique and his carefully groomed moustache—not to speak of his literary eminence— were. Even his baritone voice failed to elicit the respect it deserved.

'What's your name?' he asked, unwilling to give up.

'Don't know.' A gust of wind engaged the mango, the tamarind and the jackfruit trees, standing close to the bungalow, in a rapid conversation, and the boy whizzed off into the meadow. Samir kept gazing at him till he disappeared beyond a mound of earth.

Samir's friend, the chief conservator of forests, had arranged for his regular supply of food from the camp of a wealthy timber merchant. The caretaker-cum-watchman of the bungalow arrived with his afternoon tiffin and tea, the tiffin-carrier and the flask carefully protected from the rain under a tattered raincoat. From the start Samir felt in this silent tribal the natural poise and confidence of one who never failed in his duty, but was greater than his duty.

'Who was that?' Samir asked, pointing at the way the boy had gone.

'Son.'

'Is that your son? What is his name?'

'He does not respond to any name, sir.'

'Don't you—or his mother—try to keep him under check?'

'He is motherless, sir.'

Samir groped for words.

'Must he romp and horse around in such riotous weather?' he demanded at last.

The watchman made no reply. But his look dampened Samir's spirit. He seemed to challenge Samir to explain what was wrong with the boy's doings.

He went away. Samir shut the door and resumed reading the novel he should have finished three days ago, for he had brought seven books for his proposed seven days of solitary sojourn.

He could not proceed with the text. The nameless boy haunted him. He looked through the glass panes again and again, and as they were hazy, he opened the window. Two dogs, miserably drenched, had taken shelter on the veranda. Suspicious of his motive, they jumped down, but just then the boy came dashing on to the veranda, and the dogs, emboldened by the boy's company, climbed it once again.

Except for the loose shorts, perhaps gifted to him by a well-wisher, the boy was bare-bodied. He was talking, but it was not possible to say whether to the dogs or to the trees.

Samir could resist no more. He hurried out to the veranda even without his shawl. The wind slapped and thrashed him, but he advanced towards the boy.

'What are you doing?'

'Talking.'

'To whom?'

The boy did not care to reply.

'Won't you tell me with whom you were talking?'

'With me.'

'You're strange. Come in. You will talk to me.'

'In the evening.'

'Well, if you are in no mood to talk, I will talk to you. Come.'

'In the evening.'

A fresh blaze of criss-cross lightning tore the sky apart—like a demoniac wizard spreading all his ten fingers and hypnotizing the prostrate earth. The boy raised his arms and scampered off, as if to catch hold of the lightning or to wrap him up with it!

He ran through the rain. The two dogs kept pace with him. The wind seemed to change its course suddenly so that it could blow in his favour. Or was the boy pulling the wind with him?

For a moment Samir forgot himself. In fact, he was about to jump down, but the splash of rain on his face and a stronger whip of wind reminded him of his convalescence and his Kashmiri shawl. He stepped back and strained his eyes looking into the valley. The boy and the dogs had disappeared. The boy had promised to come in the evening. Weather, of course, had transformed the entire day into an elaborate evening. But the real evening was not far either—Samir's wristwatch informed him. Back in his room, he tried to concentrate on the novel, but could not. He was feeling a vague urge to write, but could not decide on a theme. He spoke aloud. That gave him some satisfaction. He realized that to express himself in some way—like the clouds or the wind or the nameless boy—had become very urgent for him.

What is it that the boy was mumbling? There was a lure in

his intonation. Samir resolved to pay all his attention to him even if he talked nonsense.

It began growing dark. The rain subsided, but not the wind. Samir, waiting for the boy, had dozed off in his easy chair. More than an hour must have passed before he heard someone's footsteps; he lighted the table-lamp in a hurry.

'I'm late, sir,' said the watchman, placing the tiffin-carrier on the table. 'I reported at the merchant sir's house late.'

'Doesn't matter. Where is your son?'

'Gone.'

'Where?'

'Gone, sir, with the lightning.'

'What?' a stunned Samir managed to ask.

'I found him on the river bank, holding on to a palm tree. But he was gone—whisked away by the lightning,' he reported.

Samir stood speechless at least for five minutes. If the news was a bolt from the blue, the father's manner of narrating it baffled and bewildered him as nothing else had done in his life.

'Where is he?'

The man raised both his arms first towards the sky and then pointed at his hut.

He walked away slowly, stooping a little.

Samir collapsed into his easy chair. He passed the night in a daze. The moment he tried to think, he received a jolt equal to a fall. But the thoughts could not be warded off for long. Why was the boy there at all? What was the purpose in his appearing like a string of lightning, playing like a string of lightning and disappearing like a string of lightning?

The memory of the boy's eyes assumed some new significance. As if they asked: how could you measure me with the yardstick of your mind and thoughts? Samir wondered what those eyes could have reflected. Certainly something that was much more than a mere mind. Something deeper and luminous—something with which one could probably gather in a brief moment experiences of aeons. Samir made a bid to find out if he too had something nearer to that splendour in himself—somewhere deep within—and in the process fell asleep under his Kashmiri shawl. By morning, the sky had become thoroughly clear of clouds. Samir went out for a stroll after three days of confinement. The otherwise weak rivulet looked rejuvenated.

'Sir!'

The watchman stood leaning on his shovel between the rivulet and a rock. Samir walked up to him. He had dug a small pit and had already lowered into it his son's body, turned a bit bluish. Samir remembered that no relative of the watchman lived nearby. His native hamlet was on the other side of the forest, miles away.

Samir suddenly felt like his kin. As the man began filling the pit with his shovel, Samir joined him, throwing handfuls of earth into it. Soon the boy was lost to their sight. Never before had Samir known the earth to be so sublime a source of solace.

'Whatever the sky had left, was taken over by the earth,' observed the father, his voice calm but candid.

Samir left the bungalow the same day. He forgot the demands of his health, for such thoughts seemed utterly small and insignificant.

For long thereafter, a blast of cold wind, a crack of thunder, or a glimpse of the distant horizon at some lonely moment would instantly flash the son and the father in Samir's vision. And always they looked like the elements that constituted the majesty of the horizon.

The Miracle

Although five miles away from the nearest bus stop and twenty-five miles from the railway station, our village could not be called obscure any longer, for a blessed son of the soil had been promoted to the rank of a sub-divisional officer and another one had just become a lecturer in a college.

But, even in wildest dreams, no one had thought of a Mahatma or a holy soul emerging in our village.

I, a junior teacher in a high school, had seen Bulu for the first time two years ago while spending the summer vacation in the village. Haridas, the boy's father, was leading him along the village road. 'Salute him!' Haridas directed the boy, calling his attention to me, and demonstrating how he should do it. But the boy remained stubbornly aloof.

I had the creeps. Who wouldn't have at the sight of a wee beard and moustache on the face of a boy aged eight or nine? What was more, one of his eyes was bigger than the other, arousing the suspicion that he could see what others could not.

'I must have sinned in an earlier life to be condemned with an offspring like this, totally dumb and unable to comprehend a thing. I wish it had been stillborn,' moaned Haridas.

'You ought not to say so,' I admonished the hapless father. Obviously accustomed to such sage words, he nodded, probably to mean that people not encumbered with a burden of this kind had every right to treat him to such advice.

The situation changed unexpectedly. Bulu came to the notice of Braja Sadhu alias Braja Vaishnav alias Brajagopal Das, another wonderful character, a soul continuously drunk with mystic devotion according to some and a madcap according to some others. If the second opinion had not gained wider currency, it was because whoever came in his personal contact began to like him. Not that he could overwhelm anybody, but he looked overwhelmed himself, continuously under the spell of the holy name of Krishna. A widower and issueless, but inheritor of a hundred acres of land, he had allowed himself to be exploited by whoever pretended to be a devotee of Krishna.

Brajagopal was never tired of singing bhajans, often himself playing the mridangam. I had heard him two or three times and cannot say that his musical talent had impressed me, but his screaming recitations certainly inspired a sort of awe and reverence.

One day, Haridas dragged Bulu into Brajagopal's courtyard and ordered the boy to prostrate himself before the gathering of pious Vaishnavs. Bulu knelt down and, his gaze fixed on Brajagopal's eyes, laughed.

That was the first ever time anybody saw him laughing. It was rumoured that the laughter had an occult language, which Brajagopal alone could decipher.

'Where were you all these days, my lord? Should you have taken such a long time to remember this humble servant of yours?' This had been the theme of the poignant lyric Brajagopal was singing when Bulu surprised him. He changed over to prose, but without introducing any change in the theme, and hugged Bulu tightly, tears rolling down his cheeks and laving the boy's uneven forehead.

Bulu continued to laugh, making some odd gurgling sound, and Brajagopal continued to weep. The few devotees present on the scene were amazed. Soon they realized that there was nothing absurd in the situation. Who but a goldsmith could identify pure gold! Bulu was one of those concealed Mahatmas who, in their inscrutable whim, roamed about the earth, assuming deceptive forms. But he could not deceive Brajagopal!

Bulu became Bulu Baba. He had been born on a full-moon

night. Hence devotees began to collect around him on Brajagopal's courtyard on every full-moon night.

Their number was limited to twenty or twenty-five until the day a certain clerk at the local Zainindar's office won a case in the court and offered a hundred rupees to Bulu Baba because he had selected his lawyer by drawing lots muttering the Baba's name. Thereafter the crowd of devotees began to swell. Parties involved in litigations paid offerings of a rupee or two in advance. People with other kinds of desires and problems followed suit.

Some men and women beset with gout and colic confessed to having found considerable relief after making prayful submissions to Bulu Baba. The loudest among them was the tall and robust Namdar Khan, a *goonda* of considerable reputation endowed with a voice as terrifying as the thunderclaps. The carbuncle that had humbled a formidable man like him must have been the monarch among carbuncles, the people were sure. Short of an avatar, who could have cured it?

Before long, Bulu Baba's reputation assumed a special colour—that he was the avatar incarnated to fight the evil of carbuncles. This did not mean that his supernatural power was not effective against other evils.

Once the gout-ridden zamindar decided to summon the little Baba to his mansion in order to prostrate before him in the privacy of his own house. He sent his manager and his bullock cart to fetch him. While Brajagopal, disapproving of such summons, was locked in an argument with the manager, Bulu Baba toddled towards the cart and stood looking at the handsome bullocks.

'Look here, the Baba himself is ready to go!' announced the manager, and in an unforeseen move, lifted the Baba and dumped him in the cart and ordered the carter to start.

The carter duly shouted at the bullocks and whipped them and twisted their tails in great earnest; but the bullocks refused to budge.

Brajagopal laughed. The manager, red in the face, set the Baba sheepishly on the ground. The bullocks began to move.

'Who—who—who on earth can kidnap the Baba? Which vehicle can move him unless he himself consented to move?' the

Baba's devotees, basking in his newly acquired glory, demanded of all and sundry.

Clad in ochre silk, garlands flowing down to the floor, his forehead marked by sandalwood paste and vermilion, Bulu Baba occupied the centre of the throng of devotees and curious would-be recruits. The offerings collected were spent in feeding the poor. However, Brajagopal had no interest in publicizing the wonderful powers of Bulu Baba. One or two merchants, hopeful of earning fast bucks if Bulu Baba attracted more people, proposed to print a booklet in verse narrating the Baba's miracles, but Brajagopal rejected their proposal.

Alas, the full-moon nights were not destined to pass smoothly forever, thanks to Professor (even a junior lecturer enjoyed that honorific in the liberal popular parlance) Navin Ray, the lecturer who had brought glory to our village. He was struck by the inspiration for redeeming the earth from its superstitions with a bang. Since it was summer vacation and both of us were in the village, he enrolled my support in his mission. Reports of the goings-on around Bulu Baba used to reach me in the town. But 'There are more things in heaven and earth, Horatio, than are dreamt of in your philosophy' was the attitude I had nurtured in regard to him.

Navin Ray, however, changed my outlook. Two or three other young men of the village joined us.

We entered Brajagopal's courtyard almost unnoticed, for the congregation was in an ecstatic state of collective singing.

'Brajagopalji, which one the scriptures declare that the new avatar will prove his divinity by sprouting a goatee at the age of nine?' asked Ray as soon as the singing ended.

Brajagopal sat still entranced. It was difficult to say if his mind recorded Navin Ray's question.

'How did you conclude that Bulu was a prodigy with regard to the science of gout and carbuncle?'

'*Hari bol!*' shouted Brajagopal in a choked voice and slapped the mridangam. At once, the other devotees started a new song. Bulu Baba, who sat decorated like a bridegroom, looked at Navin Ray with his extra-large right eye, keeping the left one shut. Ray felt extremely awkward and we grew impatient. We tarried for a few minutes more. There was no sign of the singing coming to an end. We quit the place.

'Light carries no value in this land of the blind,' commented Ray with some anguish. 'Let India be free. Then we will see!'

We too found it convenient to repose our trust in that bright future and let Brajagopal and Bulu Baba in peace for the last phase of the British rule in India.

The vacation was over and we were back in the town. Before we had come together once again, the chapter in the history of our village dominated by Bulu Baba came to an abrupt end. This is the summary of the report I received:

Brajagopal set out for Vrindavan with Bulu Baba and twelve other members of his inner circle. While Bulu Baba rode a bullock cart, the pilgrims and those out to see them off deposited their luggage in the cart and launched a marathon walk for the railway station, for the lone bus that plied between the station and the market eight miles away from our village remained suspended during the monsoon. No more than four or five trains passed through the station in a day, and only two of them, running in opposite directions, stopped there.

The pilgrims as well as the bullock cart were still plodding through a meadow when the train steamed into the platform. The pilgrims decided to run. Since the cart was incapable of coping with them, a giant-like devotee carried Bulu Baba on his shoulder and ran. Only three or four more devotees could keep pace with him. The forward party had just stepped into the platform when the train whistled and made jugging sounds indicating motion.

The successful runners, sweating and tightening their loins, were anxious about their friends trailing half a kilometre behind. A grand idea flashed in the roomy encephalon of the giant devotee. Once Bulu Baba ascends the train, it cannot move away according to its own free will, just as the zamindar's cart had failed to do.

'Look here, fellows, the passenger train has already left. This is an Express making a halt for technical reasons. Don't board it!' the stationmaster cautioned them.

The four devotees were in no condition to heed the warning. They were agog with excitement at the prospect of hypnotizing the train, partly to prove Bulu Baba's power and partly for the sake of their comrades who were now running like cattle scared by a wolf, carrying their luggage along. They managed to push Bulu Baba into a compartment and, with bated breath, waited to see the miracle.

The train began to pull out. The devotees almost pitied the engine, for, they were sure, the poor thing will hardly be able to drag Bulu Baba farther than a few feet.

At last, Brajagopal and the rest of the party caught up with the forerunners. They looked on, flabbergasted and dumbfounded, as the train gathered speed and disappeared at a distant turn of the passage.

Yet another flash of idea now set the giant devotee on the run. Perhaps he intended to pull the train back by holding on to the bar of the last compartment. But he fell down, struck by an epileptic fit.

The bewildered devotees walked up and down the platform for an hour. Some of them cried. The next day, by the regular passenger train, Brajagopal and two other knowledgeable villagers left for the city, the final destination of all the locomotives running in that direction. They came back after a week, of course without Bulu Baba.

Brajagopal did not seem quite perturbed. 'Leela, the play,' he said, his arms raised towards the heavens, and slipped into a trance-like silence. 'He came of his own will; of his own will he parted!' said his near ones in the way of interpreting their leader.

The rumour that Bulu Baba had somehow landed in a city orphanage, where he died a year later, may not be directly relevant to this narration. We were once again in the village about a month after the episode. Professor Navin Ray found it difficult to control his laughter. The next day the professor, myself and another friend were on our way to a former student's home for dinner, when the sound of devotional music, coming from Brajagopal's courtyard, brought the professor to a halt.

'Let's hear how Brajagopal explains the episode,' he

proposed, his voice lively with mischief. We followed him even though his intent appeared rather frivolous to me. Brajagopal stood up the moment he saw us entering.

'About Bulu Baba, will you please . . .'

But Ray could not finish his query. Brajagopal hugged him. 'Where were you, my beloved, my lord?' he demanded, 'Must you play with me like a naughty little child?' His eyes tearful, Brajagopal led the luckless Ray into the midst of the throng and dabbed sandalwood paste on his forehead and cheeks.

The devotees resumed singing with greater gusto. Brajagopal exerted pressure on Ray's shoulders, obliging him to sit down. Ray tried to get up, but gave up after a second futile effort. Patting him on the back, Brajagopal held out a banana to his lips. Ray kept his mouth shut, but the devotees sang with great fervour how when the child Krishna refused to eat, Mother Yasoda caught hold of him and fed him forcibly. Ray swallowed the banana, though keeping his eyes shut. Someone put a garland of jasmine flowers around his neck. He did not protest. We too were entertained to bananas and pieces of coconut.

It took us an hour to come out to the street again. I was surprised that Ray did not care to wipe out the sandalwood paste or take the garland off.

'Brajagopal is somewhat wonderful,' I suddenly observed, spontaneously. 'He commands some power,' said the other friend.

Ray still kept quiet.

The Assault

'I completed eighty yesterday. It took me rather long, the first sixty years of my life, to realize that I was not different from anyone else in my desires, ambitions, attractions and repulsions—call it ordinary or whatever you please. I had taken it for granted, I do not know when, how and why, that I was unique. How easily could praise gladden me and make me crave for more, and how spontaneously would I reject any criticism of my actions or wishes! Little did I care to remember that so many in this world had been a hundred times braver, nobler and more talented than I. What is more, there were so many who were less egoistic and, consequently, less stupid than I!

'Alas, dear Avani, it took me six long decades to realize that I was hardly different from those who I thought were inferior to me. How at last this realization dawned on me is a matter too personal. It brought me surprise mixed with remorse, but was followed by a sense of peace. To be free from the obligation to appear special in one's speech and conduct—is that not a bliss? Avani, I am happy at your success. You sought my good wishes. Well, all I can do is pray that you don't wait till you're sixty for a similar realization. I know that you have some truly noble qualities in you. Hence this rather unusual response to your kind communication.'

This was from a venerable freedom-fighter and a former leader.

A response like this to Avani's formal, printed appeal for goodwill dispatched to several such distinguished men and women after his victory in the elections appeared rather uncalled for, and somewhat irrelevant. But Avani was not surprised that the letter should flash in his vision today and bring him some comfort as he gazed at the serene sunset across the garden, from his bed in the nursing home.

He had remained lost in an opaque mist of surprise for days. In his befuddled mind, the mist had, at one stage, changed into an ocean. He lay floating on it, at times overwhelmed by fresh waves of surprise. Perhaps he had given vent to his feelings in a state of delirium.

'Father, you are lying in your bed, not floating on the sea,' his son told him.

'Never mind. We must allow him a little more time to gain normalcy,' the doctor told the son, politely but firmly.

'But how long? Doctor, I don't mind his being in the nursing home as long as he or you wish. But, I'm sure you realize the urgency of his making a coherent statement. Please do all that's necessary for that to be possible.'

The son meant it to be an appeal to the doctor though anxiety made him sound a bit rude.

'We are doing our best.' The doctor was curt.

'Thank you. Yes, any delay would only prolong the uncertainty, the confusion.'

Avani heard them. No more did he care for any confusion. He was no longer under any confusion himself. How could his son—even such a worthy son—know about the churnings he had silently gone through? The worthy son was not merely a successful contractor, but also a model citizen, acutely sensitive to his rights and duties. He had obliged an editor, who had alleged his receiving undue favours from the government because of his father's clout, to come out with a distinctly printed apology on the front page of his journal. Avani, excited at his son's success, had thrown a banquet, although under a different pretext, and was heard observing before his own friends, but within the hearing of his son's pals, 'We are lucky that our sons are not in politics. If they were, how long would they take to consign us to the dustbin of history?'

The light of the setting sun was fading out of the garden. Avani had observed that the garden had only a few birds, looking quite urbanized, to twitter and hop about in style from branch to branch. At the moment, however, there was only one bird present and its voice betrayed monotony and dejection. And Avani did not know why it reminded him of the ominous warning chanted by his old Sanskrit teacher time and again: never be proud of either your wealth or your authority or your youthfulness; in the twinkle of an eye, Time can strip you of everything!

'Father, can you make out where you are?' the worthy son asked anxiously. The daughter-in-law had just come in and was poring over him, the velvet edge of her vanity bag tickling his cheek. 'Can you now recollect the events, Daddy?' she asked.

'I can.'

'Excellent. Unless you are feeling extremely tired, will you please tell us in brief who assaulted you in that remote village and how? The press, the police and the people are all thirsting for the facts; we are dying with anxiety.'

But the lady's voice betrayed more curiosity than anxiety.

Avani closed his eyes. Let them think he was tired. The daughter-in-law appeared more restless than the son. She had been preparing to make her debut on the public arena, leaving it to her husband to earn enough to fuel her self-propelled launching into the firmament of politics and, as a warming up exercise, had found her way to the leadership of a couple of women's organizations. Her reeking ambition was offensive even to the seasoned nostrils of Avani. She told her companion, an elderly social worker, 'Can you imagine, Aunty, the alacrity and method with which the conspirators planned their operation? Daddy was visiting the village just for a night and only a few knew about it. To gather the intelligence and dispatch goondas in advance, and to lure him to a lonely place and beat him up was no small villainy!'

'Certainly not, my daughter. It cannot but be the outcome

of a sinister conspiracy. I won't be surprised if there was a nasty foreign hand behind it all!' the elderly lady commented gravely.

'I wish there were a few more ladies in this vast country as far-sighted as you are, Aunty. There's a demand for a judicial enquiry. But would they expose all the hidden hands?' mused the daughter-in-law.

She was one of the most valuable trophies won by Avani. He was in power when his son became enamoured of this nymph. The indulgent Avani duly sent a formal proposal to the girl's father who could not have been happier if the chariot of Indra had suddenly descended to transport him to paradise.

But Avani was to receive the shock of his life just a day before the wedding. He was sipping tea with the bride's father at the latter's house, finalizing a few arrangements. The postman handed over a few letters to the would-be relative who opened one of them and, glancing through it, handed it over to Avani with a meaningful beam.

Avani had encountered numerous varieties of shameless smiles but never anything so nauseating as this one.

'Well, it seems to be what they call . . . well . . . a sort of love letter. For whom is it meant? Why should I read it?' The puzzled Avani sought some light.

'Hah! Don't you understand? The writer is pursuing his higher studies abroad. There was a proposal for my daughter's marriage with him. Hence he had started writing this silly stuff to her. But the moment I received your message, I told my daughter point blank that nothing doing . . .'

'Scoundrel!' uttered Avani in a muffled voice, though he was well-known for keeping his emotions to himself.

'Well—er—I should say he is not a bad guy. But what relevance the question of good or bad had once there was a proposal from you?' said the proud father, casting glances at his gate where some people had collected to have a glimpse of his VIP guest.

He was perhaps feeling guilty for his inability to give any spectacular dowry, ostensibly because of Avani's routine, statutory warning against the practice, but really because he was not that wealthy. Hence he was bent on proving the sacrifices he had made to accommodate Avani's proposal. His smile lingered on in expectation of a nod of appreciation from Avani.

Avani felt suffocated but, as a principle, he kept his mouth shut on situations that were no longer amenable to alteration. That helped keeping the catalogue of enemies or disgruntled friends shorter.

But before long he had begun to fear his daughter-in-law. Why should she not avenge herself at an opportune moment? By and by, he had realized that she was far more mature than he had thought her to be. Hers would be a refined revenge. She would make a thorough and gleeful use of the standing and authority he had earned with decades of labour. The secret realization sometimes chilled him.

Avani opened his eyes. A couple of streetlights flashed on the other side of the road. They were yellow. Suddenly he had the feeling that yellow was the colour of fear. He would very much like those lights switched off. But that was not possible.

He looked for his son and understood that the daughter-in-law and her 'Aunty' had left.

'Why are the windows open? Who stopped the aircon?' he demanded.

'At your instruction, Father. Have you forgotten how you were keen on having natural breeze?'

'Oh!'

'Father, there is nobody else here. Will you please tell me everything in brief? You can't imagine the sensation the incident has created all over the state! Papers carrying the news and the editorial comments are all here. Your doctors have forbidden us to read them out to you now. And while you lay unconscious, what a rush of celebrities was there to enquire about your condition and to wish you speedy recovery! They included practically all the ministers of our state, and most of the MPs, MLAs and editors. There are heaps of get-well messages and bouquets in the outer room. Now, tell me, Father, who assaulted you?'

Assault! Was it not he who was an adept at it, who had refined the act to the level of art? What is art if not the capacity to appear assaulted while meting out assaults? Maybe, dramatic art.

'Father!'

'Let me recollect the sequence.'

'Did you know those hoodlums? Can you at least identify them when they are paraded? Or was it only one fellow? Do you remember his face?'

Avani felt amused and sad at the same time. The sensation was bizarre and upsetting.

Of course he remembers the face and shall always remember it. In fact, excepting for the times when he lay asleep or unconscious, it continued to dominate his memory—the sombre face, grim and adamant. He was reading numerous shades of significant messages in it. The face continued to inspire awe in him, but from the core of that gloomy feeling emerged a luminous flame. In it he recognized a very personal communication. For him it was the dawn of wisdom.

But he would still get spasms and shivers—result of an eerie mixture of horror, humiliation and helplessness—whenever he would recollect the first moment of his meeting with his tormentor. To foresee any benefit in that crisis would have been a wild dream. But once the crisis proper was over, its memory was doing miracles in him.

'Father!'

Avani did not respond. 'Father, here is Jayantji!' the son whispered in a meaningful tone.

Jayantji alone among the leading figures in the state politics had not paid him a visit till then. He had been the latest rival to be humbled by Avani.

'Well, let's not disturb his repose. We may, at times, fight each other on issues and ideals. That is inevitable in democratic politics. But we are friends. And friendship brooks no formality. I was in Delhi and was scheduled to return after yet another week. But concern for Navin Babu got the better of me and I obliged my friend, the civil aviation minister, to get me a seat in the flight at an hour's notice.'

He then lowered his voice, 'Well, how deep is the wound? Nothing irreparable, I hope.'

'We'll get all the reports only tomorrow. He seems to have

been attacked with a forked weapon on his chest. Besides there were numerous bashings all over his body!' The son sighed.

'How incredibly fast things are going from bad to worse!' Jayantji lowered his voice further and asked, 'Someone told me about the fear of a partial paralysis. I hope it is baseless.'

'Was he a doctor?'

'Forget about it, friend. Let us do our duty. And that is to pray for his full recovery, and at the earliest. Can the president of the party, within a week of his assuming office, afford to become invalid? Secondly, the criminal must be ruthlessly punished. From CBI to Interpol, we should leave no stone unturned to bring the culprits to book. Thirdly, kindly don't forget to inform your father that I had come, and that my heart bleeds for him and I will come again.'

'I won't forget, sir.'

It was Jayantji whom Avani had defeated in the race for the party's presidentship. Avani felt that the rival's receding footsteps were unusually resounding.

By then Avani had been able to recollect the entire sequence.

He had paid an unpublicized, private visit to his native village at his son's behest. Adjacent to their ancestral compound was a small plot of land owned by an old widow. She had no direct heir, but she was about to will her property in favour of a young relative lately looking after her.

'Father, that land must come to us. Here is the plan for the house I intend to build in the village. Its environment would be marred if someone sets up a hut or a cowshed only twenty yards away. Once you speak to the widow personally, there'll be no hitch. And, Father, the sooner the better.'

Avani had reached his village at sundown. He was keen to avoid any public gaze. It was a calm twilight when he left his house for the widow's hut, situated on a hillock-like mound of earth beyond a marshland. The old woman, no doubt, would be thrilled to see before her the great man, to meet whom crowds of people wait for hours. He would be kind to her and offer a generous price for her land. He was sure of the success of his mission.

Maybe the young relative of the old woman would feel disappointed, but he banished such thoughts from his mind. And he remembered how once beforehand too he had banished another uncomfortable thought—of a certain young man preparing for his examinations abroad suddenly receiving the news of his beloved marrying a VIP's son.

He felt remorseful. The aura of the setting sun—whatever of it was still left on the bushes and the trees or the mound— looked yellow. And as soon as he had reached the top of the mound and looked up, his eyes met with a pair of yellow eyes.

And they seemed to be fast changing into two yellow flickers, ready to leap on to him and destroy him. He grew panicky.

The creature facing him was a billy goat, enormous and tough. Its beard reminded him of a demoniac wizard in the Arabian Nights. He could read in the beast's eyes an uncanny resolution to knock him down and pound and pulverize him if possible.

Jackals broke the silence of the hour, spraying a certain despair and cynicism in the atmosphere.

Not a soul was in sight. Every atom of Avani's body froze. He assured himself, desperately, that he was no coward, that he had confronted numerous enemies—formidable and brilliant ones at that—and had vanquished them, that he could even activate the armed forces if warranted.

But such assurances were of no avail. He stood perplexed. How at all could such a situation arise? He reflected, at the speed of lightning, on as many protective strategies as possible. Panic even prompted him to appease the adversary with some such words: 'Your He-goatish Majesty, did you by any chance think that I'm here to buy you off the old granny for a ritual sacrifice? Oh no!'

He could have also said, 'Perhaps you don't know me. I am a VIP, rather a VVIP. Please be reasonable and ask yourself before taking the next step: should a man of my status go down in history as one trampled by a billy goat?'

The goat took two forward steps.

Avani trembled.

The beast lowered its head and made a dash at him. He

stumbled, face down, right on its back, and then slipped to the ground. The beast tried to gore him. He began rolling down the mound. And with each turn of his body was peeled off of a certain value he cherished, each collision with a shrub or a clod of hardened earth demolished one of the numerous monuments of his achievement. That is how he felt.

He had fainted before reaching the bottom of the mound.

'Father, come on. Let me hear your story now. The home minister has already telephoned three times. They are all set to act on a hint from you.'

Avani tried to smile. He sat up, leaning on two bolsters, and calmly narrated the bare truth to his son. The talking tired Avani and he fell asleep.

When he slowly woke up, he heard the son softly telling the daughter-in-law, 'What a farcical predicament! Think of the press conference in the offing! Think of the anti-climax! Oh no!'

'And do you know about the medical report? I'm afraid, Daddy would no longer be able to stand straight or walk by himself. I wonder if, for a dynamic person like him, it would be at all worth living . . .' the daughter-in-law observed in a whisper.

Right. It would be better to die, not because he would be unable to lead the party and consequently people would look down upon him, but because he no longer expected to learn much more in this life after the lesson imparted to him by the billy goat. And, just as he had no longer any reason to stand up or walk, he had no longer any reason to keep lying either.

The yellow eyes of the giant goat flashed in his memory once again, like the embrace of the all-swallowing Time.

'Open the windows! Let me go,' he cried out to the surprise of his son and his daughter-in-law.

The Crooked Staff

Whenever I remember that autumn evening on the river, I feel that the distant planets indeed exercise a lot of influence on the creatures of the earth and sometimes a weird conjunction among them could wreak havoc in our lives. Of course, by our lives, I mean a limited sphere of her mankind extending from Tom, Dick and Harry to men like, say, Mr Thomas Jacob who retired as an Additional Secretary to the government, and over the years, through the sheer force of repetition of his complaint that a bureaucratic conspiracy stopped his promotion, had managed to cultivate in his acquaintances the respect due to a full-fledged Secretary, or Mr Jagu Singh who, after continuing with his black gown and his status as a fourth-grade lawyer for twenty years, put on a white cap and made a first-rate minister, or Harish Goswami, almost the professional good man of the town who spent his days generously presiding over public meetings of all kinds. I am not speaking of geniuses or of spiritually advanced souls.

Let me return to the autumn evening. There was nothing unusual about it. All that should happen was happening: the hawkers were doing their usual rounds with roasted groundnuts, tea and balloons, and pairs of male and female of different age groups were strolling and inhaling litres of river-cooled air, and we three friends were about to settle down on the most conveniently situated cement bench, which we looked upon as our private property and occupied every evening as we sat for an hour or two inhaling the perfumes exuded by the fashionable ones among the passing pairs and talking of mice and men.

But we could not sit down because the bench had already been occupied by the venerable octogenarian Rudranath, his hands and head resting on his crooked walking stick.

Among the students of the earlier generation, Rudranath had gained notoriety as a tyrant of a principal, quite different from the professors and principals of our time who were so meek and accommodative. Listening to the anecdotes of his toughness from our uncles, we were astonished that he could live through the whole tenure of his professorship and principalship without even a scratch on his broad bald head.

We were obliged to occupy a bench opposite him. But however we tried to engage ourselves in our usual ritual of munching nuts and gossiping, we could not help sulking under Rudranath's latest tyranny—his uprooting us from our strategic retreat.

Well, we should have been sensible enough to do nothing more than mere sulking, but among us was Kishore, always bubbling with ideas as hot and as tempting as the nuts we were cracking. Who could have thought that his offer of a cup of tea to Rintoo, if the latter could sufficiently annoy the old man to leave the bench, would produce consequences so different from the limited fun we expected of it?

Rintoo kept bargaining till Kishore, afraid that the professor might leave the bench without giving them a chance to pull his leg, agreed to entertain him to a complete dinner in one of our favourite minor restaurants.

Rintoo set out on his mission. He ambled around for a minute, the took position before the professor and coughed. The professor looked up, sported a cordial smile and was about to lower his head again on the handle of his stick when Rintoo began, 'Good evening, sir. What attracted me to you is your walking stick. It appeared to me . . .' Rintoo hurriedly glanced at us while the professor raised his head and nodded with a smile. Rintoo resumed, 'It appeared to me, for its slimness, mature look and gait, that it could very well be your twin brother—or—ah—could it be a sister?'

The old man kept nodding for a moment more and broke his silence after some hesitation, or, probably reflection: 'No, the stick and I are not twins. We were seven brothers; no sister; three were older than I. The eldest, Harihar, was a deputy magistrate. I wonder if you have heard of him—clean bald, but also a clean officer. Next to him was Mahesh, the headmaster. He limped a little, and after retirement, grew delicious mushrooms. The third, Mahindra, was a PWD contractor working in the remote villages. Once the narrowly escaped being gored to death by a naughty bull notorious for its wrath against men using umbrellas. Silly, isn't it? But all the three are gone. Even from the younger lot . . .'

'Sir, all I wanted to say was, your stick looked exactly like you. The bend on its upper half is a perfect imitation of your stooping gait.'

'Well, this cane, since the beginning of its career as a walking stick, had been crooked like this, but not I. In fact, at the beginning of my career as a lecturer, I was as straight as a mark of exclamation. But age has reduced me to looking like a mark of interrogation. Do you follow me, young man?' The professor laughed in silence.

There was no sign of the old man's legendary rages. He was bent upon removing Rintoo's misconception as dispassionately and seriously as a barber removed a customer's unwanted hair.

Rintoo looked utterly undone.

We pitied him.

'Long live—you and your crooked stick, sir!' Rintoo saluted him and returned to us. We laughed at his discomfiture.

'So, Rintoo dear, be reasonable. Buy me a dinner,' demanded Kishore.

'Absurd! There had been no stipulation that my failure will oblige me to entertain you!' protested Rintoo.

'But that is understood! Whoever accepts a challenge must pay the penalty for his failure!' said I, for I was not prepared to let go the chance of sharing the dinner as a witness to the deal.

But our argument came to a dead stop. Before us stood the professor, glaring at us through his thick glasses, the metal knob at the top of the bent handle of his walking stick confronting us like an inquisitor.

'So young yet so wise! You saw my stick as my twin, didn't you? The occult truth uniting me with my stick revealed itself to you. One who can realize the mystery of similes is on the pathway to Brahma-realization. No, I am not joking. This is a truth. We often compare a smile with a flower. What physical or logical similarity is there between the two? But then we not only accept the simile as natural, but also appreciate it, don't we? Well, there is certainly something common between the two—something subtle and significant—and we feel that secret oneness at a plane of our sensibility that transcends the rational. Are you a student of philosophy?'

'No, sir, we are students of law.' We stood up.

'Inmates of this hostel?' The professor's stick was raised pointing at our abode.

'Yes, sir.'

'Come, let's go.'

The professor kept us buttonholed for a full hour at the portico of our hostel before quitting us, half-hugging each one of us.

We did not know whether to laugh or to weep. The dispute as to who should host the dinner had died a natural death. We were content with our worthless meals at the mess.

Someone knocked on Rintoo's door early in the morning. An incorrigible late riser, Rintoo was naturally annoyed. But upon reluctantly opening the door, whom should he see but Rudranath and his walking stick! Both the man and his stick seemed to have taken an early morning oil bath. Both looked bright and holy.

'Come, my young friend, let's enjoy a morning walk. I'll tell you more about the unity pervading two apparently diverse objects.'

'Sir, I'm yet to take bath.'

'I don't mind waiting,' said the professor, stepping into Rintoo's room.

Rintoo was obliged to get ready at the earliest and go out with the professor.

'Young man, you might have forgotten about your other important observation—when you wished me and my walking stick a long life. That is to say, you attributed a certain deep intimacy to our apparently casual relationship. The more I reflected on your observation, the more enlightened I felt. In fact, I felt the thrill of a new discovery. Indeed, how is one's stick inferior to one's son or one's grandson? You imagine that your son loves you. It is because of your imagination that he is dear to you, not because of his true attitude towards you of which you really know nothing. Since in any case you derive your satisfaction from your imagination, why not imagine that your walking stick loves you? The idea that your son is your support is rather figurative as well as hypothetical. But can I deny the fact that the stick is my practical support? Once in a while, my son comes and stands by my side for a minute or two. But my stick? Just fork out your hands and its head is in your left or right grip. Surely, for all practical purposes, I depend more on my stick than on my son!'

The old man justified his thesis from several angles.

In the evening, we abandoned our old familiar bench and selected another, almost a furlong away from it, half hidden behind a kiosk. Our engaging conversation was interrupted by a sort of eureka. 'So, friends, you are here!'

The professor's stick danced in his hand for a moment and he virtually drove us back to our hostel with his flowing speech.

Morning after morning, the inevitable knock would oblige Rintoo to accompany the professor on his walk. Our examination was approaching. Hints of it, first made indirectly and then directly, made no difference to the professor's zeal.

Rintoo was becoming a nervous wreck. He cursed Kishore, the original cause of his predicament. And Kishore, I could see, was truly repentant. He proposed that Rintoo should stay away from the hostel for some days. We talked to a day scholar who gladly put up Rintoo in his house.

But the irony of ironies! On the third day, the day scholar's father, a former student of Rudranath, met his old professor on the road and brought him over to his house for a cup of tea. 'Hello, young man, should you have kept me in the dark about your change of residence? And what kind friends were the other two to be totally ignorant of your new address? You cannot imagine how many miles I have walked, looking for you! Wait.'

The tea over, he led Rintoo into a nearby park. How he saw his own image in his walking stick and how the stick had inaudibly begun to talk to him, were the themes of his confidential report to Rintoo. 'I will come tomorrow,' he promised while taking leave of Rintoo.

There were only ten days left for the examination. Rintoo was banking on the fortnight preceding the examination to make up for his year-long truancy. Who could have foreseen how a little innocent mischief indulged in one autumn evening would land him in such a crisis?

But the next day brought the most unexpected news. The old professor had peacefully passed away in sleep. For a moment Rintoo was unable to read his own feelings. Was it good news for him? He wondered. But the next moment he was a sad man. He returned to the hostel.

Two days later, a posh car stopped in front of our hostel. The middle-aged gentleman who descended from it introduced himself as Rudranath's eldest son, a senior executive in a multinational enterprise. His lawyer accompanied him.

'Are you Mr Bhuvan Acharya?' the gentleman addressed Rintoo by his official name. He brought the familiar walking stick out from his car and respectfully handed it over to Rintoo. 'According to the will which Father made only a couple of days before his departure to heaven, this is his gift to you. I know that it was nothing more than his whim and this is of no use to you. But so far as we are concerned, it is our duty to execute his will faithfully,' explained the dutiful son.

He invited all three of us to his father's funeral feast.

Rintoo gazed at the stick vacantly and then carried it into his room as if carrying a baby.

My room was beside Rintoo's and I knew that after dinner he sat poring over the Indian Penal Code. At midnight, I heard a suppressed cry and dashed into his room. He had the book opened before him, but his gaze was fixed on Rudranath's walking stick standing in a corner of his room.

'What's the matter?' I queried anxiously. Rintoo came back to senses and looked embarrassed. Upon my insistence, he disclosed that for a moment he had an illusion—he saw Rudranath in his stick.

Kishore joined us. He laughed and so did I. Honestly, we were not amused, but we were eager to amuse Rintoo. We sent him to bed and dispersed.

It was still dark when Kishore woke me up. He signed me to follow him. We saw Rintoo out for a morning walk, such the stick in his hand. And if both of us were not mistaken, he clearly displayed Rudranath's gait. Kishore and I looked at each other. Then, in a few bounds, we caught up with Rintoo. He was taken aback.

'When did you develop such a keen love for morning walks, baby?' demanded Kishore. Rintoo's eyes betrayed confusion. Kishore suddenly snatched the stick and hurled it into the river. It floated on, its hooked upper end swaying rhythmically once to the left and once to the right. It reminded me of Rudranath's movements despite my efforts to block my memory. We kept looking at it till it disappeared from our sight.

'Come on, Rintoo, let's have tea.' I gave a shake to Rintoo and dragged him into a nearby restaurant.

Later, often I argued with Kishore that his inspiration to throw the stick away was rather irrational, but whenever the memory of the floating stick flashed in my vision, I had the creeps, I must confess.

The Vengeance

Vilas Singh stood dazzled for a moment. A hundred fingers of fire rent asunder the huge heart of darkness. He felt a yard or two of the lightning creeping into his veins, sparking off a double-edged sensation. Among the fiery designs that flashed along the horizon he saw Bahadur's face. And, the suddenness and the sharpness of the blaze reminded him of his own dagger. Surely, he could be equally sudden in handling it, in driving it across Bahadur's breast—he assured himself.

He could not sleep a wink. Despite his vigorous attempts at dispelling it, his mind remained filled with the ominous presence of Bahadur. Even the memory of the sweet little face peeping out of his home in the faraway village failed to make a little room for itself.

He left the mat and began strolling along the narrow veranda of the inn. His legs were tired. But he could not afford to rest, not until he had wreaked his vengeance on Bahadur. On the verge of weeping, he repeated his oath. He must finish Bahadur off. If he had ever had one mission in life, it was this.

There was yet another flare along the horizon. Vilas Singh shut his eyes. Lightning was a disturbing reminder. It flashes and disappears. One cannot catch it. So was Bahadur, who had, time and again, given him the slip. But Vilas Singh had not given up. Defeat had only made him tougher. Morning was still a couple of hours away when he resumed walking. And it was just at the crack of dawn that he reached Shashikala's hut.

'Did you get him? Are you avenged and satisfied?' asked Shashikala as she handed out a mugful of tea.

'No.' Vilas Singh's reply sounded like an explosion. He was sprawling on the veranda. The jerk wrought by his own roar made him sit up straight.

'I have always hoped that one day you would happen to pass this way and I could avail of the opportunity to persuade you to give up your mad pursuit. You are yet to cross your youth. Your whole life is before you. The battle is no more than a memory; you ought to also allow all that went with it to be buried in the past. Besides, it is hardly a year since you got married. Is it sensible for you to leave your sweet home behind and pursue an unfortunate wretch?' Shashikala's voice was soaked in kindness.

Vilas Singh reacted like a tickled serpent. He was ready to splash Shashikala's face with his hot tea, but checked himself and gasped.

'A brazen face like mine does not get scorched easily,' Shashikala crooned and then burst into a sonorous laughter.

The meadow before the hut was marked by hedges and bushes. They had just begun recovering their individual forms out of the darkness. Against the sky over the eastern horizon could be made out the flight of the first covey of early birds.

'Listen, Singh, pay heed to my advice. Look how the night is nearing its end. View those two years in the frontier as a night that is over. Take note of the fresh dawn. Begin a new phase of life, as fresh as the dawn.' Shashikala placed her hand on Vilas Singh's shoulder. But Vilas Singh flung it aside and stood up.

'Please finish your tea,' pleaded Shashikala. Vilas Singh laughed. The laughter combined, in a dramatic fashion, hatred and sarcasm. 'Shashi! Such words surely don't befit you! Hadn't it been your dharma, throughout, to carry the cup right up to one's lips only to take it away? It is you who had led me to Sumati. Then, just when I had become entirely possessed by her, you introduced her to Bahadur. And the scoundrel bewitched her.'

A smile, like a flitting butterfly, had suddenly left Vilas Singh's lips and alighted on Shashikala's where it looked much more elegant and purposeful.

'Singh, while complaining, you seem to forget all about my role during those evil days. I used to bestow my attention equally on all. It was not with any greater affection that I had led Bahadur to Sumati. Needless to say, others had preceded you just as you preceded Bahadur. Sumati too was expected to be impartial in doling out her favour. But the poor girl deviated miserably. She fell for Bahadur. She did not realize how dangerous it was to fall for anyone in the kind of life that she had been obliged to lead. To fall once meant to fall again. The poor creature had to pay dearly for her error. You know about that, don't you?'

'I know. In fact, I came to know about it the very day Bahadur murdered her.'

Shashikala had come closer to Vilas Singh. Stroking his back, she whispered, 'Let me tell you what you do not know. If you are seeking to kill Bahadur, it is not because he took Sumati away from you, but because he killed Sumati and thereby asserted his ultimate right on her—something that you failed to do.'

'Never. I would have been the last man to murmur even if Sumati were to be torn asunder by a dozen hounds,' shouted Vilas Singh. 'How do you forget that Bahadur snatched not only Sumati away from me but also my savings of a decade?' Vilas Singh motioned as if he was protecting himself from some invisible enemy.

'I'm no child, Singh, to accept your explanation. However, let me tell you that it is just impossible to claim the ultimate victory on someone by killing the person. Bahadur killed Sumati spurred by a mad desire to possess her entirely. But one who is dead has slipped away. You cannot have the satisfaction of exercising your authority on one who is not there to revolt against it. And how on earth can you possess one who is dead? Is it not rather the privilege of the dead to possess you? I know for certain that Bahadur, after killing Sumati, has not passed a moment without longing for her. He lives in a hell of anguish.'

'I don't care. I told you, didn't I? That Bahadur's crime against

me was not limited to his eloping with Sumati!' groaned Vilas
Singh.

'I insist, Singh, that the loss of money cannot be the inspiration
behind your mission. If it were, you would have got satisfied
a year ago when you wounded him on the head,' asserted
Shashikala.

Vilas Singh laughed gleefully. 'Shashi! Have you ever
met him after my inflicting that wound on him? Do you think
the wound might heal up in his lifetime?' He looked at her
imploringly.

'I don't think so.'

'Thanks!' Vilas Singh burst into a fresh peal of laughter,
more lusty than ever and, from the fold of his clothes, flashed
out a dagger. He raised it for Shashikala to see it fully. Against
the silent and serene dawn, the dagger looked ghastly. Shashikala
was beset with melancholy.

✛

Evening had just set in when Vilas Singh stood on the outskirts
of the bazaar. He straightened his limbs. He knew that he was
on the verge of success, at the end of a chase for that had
continued for five months. Its true beginnings, of course, went
back five years—years of anguish, wandering and frustration,
interrupted only by a brief though dreamy period at home when
he got married.

Time and again, when he was almost sure that his net was
closing in on the enemy, the latter had escaped. But something
like intuition informed Vilas Singh that there was no escape for
the fellow this time. Bahadur was under the impression that
Vilas Singh, married and declared heir to an unexpected estate
in the village, had given up the chase. In fact, it was Vilas Singh
who had arranged to give him this impression. The fellow
ought to be caught quite unawares at last!

By the time Vilas Singh strolled into the tavern at the far
end of the sleepy little town, it was past the first quarter of the
night. The tavern was Bahadur's haunt. He and his gang visited
it regularly. Vilas Singh's disguise was perfect. He mingled easily
with the few other customers, but occupied a seat right at the

entrance. He must do his job as soon as Bahadur stepped in. Not a second, not a word were to be wasted. Behind the tavern stretched a valley with dark ravines. There should be no difficulty in his making off. It was not likely that Bahadur's comrades would raise a hue and cry or launch a hunt for him, for an investigation would only disclose the victim's identity, inevitably leading to an exposure of the gang.

But the only ritual Vilas Singh proposed to observe was to let the dying enemy have a glimpse of his true face. The beard he wore was easily detachable.

Others in the tavern were drinking. Vilas Singh only pretended to drink. His eyes were glued to the door. But he knew that two or three fellows inside the tavern had begun casting suspicious glances at him. He was growing impatient.

An hour passed. Suddenly the doors of the tavern, left ajar till then, flung open. Vilas Singh stood up hurriedly. But none of the two visitors was Bahadur, though one was his closest collaborator. It was due to this one that Bahadur had narrowly escaped death in the hands of Vilas Singh on the last occasion.

The cluster of drinkers looked at the door. Even the dim light revealed their anxiety, and the two visitors looked distressed.

'What's the news?' asked one from the cluster.

'Finished!' they replied.

From the reaction of the listeners it was evident that the news was not unexpected. Even then, some of them sighed and all stood up. Vilas Singh followed them.

A vague fear was overtaking him. The road was uneven and rocky. He stumbled over several boulders as he walked behind the silent gang, shadow-like. They climbed a hillock and entered the small house atop it.

The dead body lay on an old rope cot. There were a number of medicine bottles and glasses around. The fellow must have suffered for long. He had been reduced to a wreck.

Someone raised a lantern.

And, at once, the deep wound on the corpse's forehead glimmered in the light.

There was a shriek. It was from Vilas Singh, the author of that wound. He fumbled his way out into the open. He sat down and cried, looking helplessly at the darkness and the forest around. He rolled on the ground, seething with frustration, muttering curses.

Those who cared could make out what he had to say: The rascal Bahadur had given him the final slip, suddenly rendering his five-year-old enterprise futile. What was he to do? How to satisfy the demand of his smouldering wrath?

Those who heard him hardly understood the significance of his outburst.

Vilas Singh kept on sitting on the hillock for the whole night. Neither the mist soaked in the peace of the stars nor the breeze conveying the calm of the forest could cool down the fire within him.

It was a little before sunrise, while his eyes were still fixed on the forest, that he remembered Hidamba Baba. The Baba's abode in the forest, at the foot of Mount Luvurva, was not far.

Vilas Singh felt the weight of the accumulated sleep he had managed to keep at bay as soon as he had reached the periphery of his village. Two months of stay with Hidamba Baba had diminished his inner fire, although his urge for vengeance had not been rooted out.

And he did not wish it to be rooted out. The opportunity for taking revenge on Bahadur, despite his death, was still open. It is only Hidamba Baba who could have given such an assurance.

Of course, he must wait.

'Vilas! You are back at last!' He was greeted warmly by the villagers.

'There is hardly anything left of your mother. She has been continuously weeping on your account.'

'And what about that unlucky girl your mother brought home? How could you muster the cruelty to desert so beautiful a wife within months of the wedding? What was her fault? What had she done to deserve this?'

Vilas Singh pushed forward, head hung, through a shower of comments at once sweet and bitter. He alone knew what his newly-wed wife's fault was. She was gradually casting a spell on him. Had he submitted himself to her magic for a little while longer, he would have forgotten his mission. That is why he had to flee suddenly.

'Come home. You have proved yourself sneaky and treacherous. But come and see the surprise we have in store for you,' said an elderly lady.

At last he realized, while climbing the steps, that he had become a father a month ago. He was being led to have the first glimpse of his son.

He felt delighted. Instantly, he took a decision to do his best to sustain that delight forever. For that, it was necessary to drive all the corroding impulses out of his heart.

He was willing to do that.

A number of women were there to welcome him into the inner apartment. His wife stood up, pulling down her veil to cover her face.

The child lay asleep in a swing.

His heart throbbing in excitement, Vilas Singh cast his first ever look on the child.

Suddenly he felt as if a dozen thunderbolts were blasting his head. He rubbed his eyes and looked again. No, his eyes had not deceived him.

Still he made a desperate attempt to appear composed, and brooded upon the geographical situation of his village. Was it really in the north-eastern direction when viewed from Luvurva? Indeed, it was.

Hidamba Baba, the *tantrik*-astrologer, had assured him that Bahadur's soul would creep into an infant that was about to be born in a village situated to the north-east of the forest. Further, with a meaningful snicker he had whispered to him that it should not be difficult for him to recognize Bahadur in that infant, for the newborn soul would reveal its identity by sporting a mark which Vilas Singh cannot miss.

Vilas Singh looked at the infant's forehead for the third time. The mark was a delicate miniature of the wound he had once inflicted on Bahadur.

He tried to retreat into a room, but could not. He collapsed, while the women were tickling the infant to make it smile.

The Dusky Horizon

Where do all the butterflies go during a storm? I wondered in my childhood and have continued to wonder over the decades past.

And birds caught up in a gale always saddened me. The sight of their pell-mell flight would bring to my mind a kind of modern poetry—its crazy violence against rhythm.

And if a sudden gust sent a handful of dead leaves spiralling up, I felt myself shot up too and gone with them!

But it was rather strange that storms, birds and dead leaves should tickle my memory while I read a fairytale.

'Atop the hill on the horizon lived a certain ogre, quite afraid of the world,' stated the novella, beginning on a somewhat unusual note.

There was a time when I had great curiosity about ogres. Some of my childhood pals claimed to have bumped into an ogre or two. I did not challenge their claim. All I desired was to gather some intimate details about the ogres—their social and family background, the reasons for their invariably wearing black looks, their eyes and nostrils spouting sparks, their teeth rattling non-stop, and their not taking to farming or bee-keeping or some such blameless vocation as our fathers and uncles did.

No sooner had I read about the hill on the horizon than I

remembered the hill on the outskirts of my village. Because of its resemblance to a peacock with spread-out tail it was called the Peacock Hill, and though not very high, to us kids it was the Himalayas.

Although I have passed all my days since my early youth in cities where darkness meant only the lights turned off, I have never forgotten the grandeur of rural darkness, awfully alive, like a surging flood throbbing with impulses and emotions of its own, which, in my childhood, used to assume its most impressive and terrifying stance on the Peacock Hill.

From time to time, when the moon hung over the hill, the tall trees atop it looked like a solemn committee of supernatural beings in session, with the moon's future and several other equally important issues on their agenda.

I had heard, right from the age I was able to make out the meaning of words, that an ogre dwelt in the thicker part of the forest on our hill. Although no one ever told me much about him, I knew that thunder was his mother tongue and that his breakfast often included a naughty little fellow like me.

Peacock Hill, naturally, was a forbidden world for us despite all our fascination for it.

When I grew up and came to look upon myself as a young man with progressive ideas, I strung together such facts that, I felt, explained the genesis of the ogre legend.

It must have been long before I was born, at a time when there was no restriction on gathering wood from the forest. One winter evening, on their way home after the day's work, some woodcutters saw a column of smoke coiling up above a clump of trees. On reaching the spot, they discovered a stranger—to be identified later as the ogre—huddling over a fire. The stranger had probably looked up with some surprise and let out a scream.

I analysed the sequence:

The stranger's eyes must have reflected the flames, thereby giving an impression that they spouted sparks. His scream, combined with the howling wind, must have sounded eerie and blood-curdling. Since no human being was known to live on the hill, the woodcutters promptly concluded that the stranger was an ogre, or at least did not contradict their listeners when some of them identified him as one.

But this was by no means the only rumour about the stranger on the hill. He was believed by some to be a fugitive from the law, an absconding gallant who had murdered ten or twenty rogues for the sake of the lady he loved. Grannies, who took a more liberal view of realism, stretched the number of his victims to one hundred and one.

My father's generation, in its youth, took pride in pointing out to their visiting relatives or friends this great attraction of our neighbourhood—the round clump of forest on the hill. But the legend of the stranger hiding there received a most unexpected turn from one an ambitious village lad, a budding scholar in history.

Like the *tulsi* plant giving out its holy fragrance from its very first sprouting, this lad had shown the signs of his distinctiveness right from his childhood. While still a student in the Middle English School, he had begun practising Pranayam with nostrils closed, or the Tratok—gazing at a lamp for hours on end—always choosing a conspicuous as well as meaningful spot for his practice, such as the temple courtyard or the cemetery.

Most of the villagers believed that he would do great things when he grew up. And it augured well for such predictions when he became the first-ever youth from our area to proceed to the town for higher studies.

My father recalled that the bamboo-legged, pipe-necked youth always looked agog with exciting ideas. One summer vacation, he descended on the village with the notion, which he 'confided' to every second man he met, that the dweller on the hill was none other than the legendary Nana Sahib, the hero of the Sepoy Mutiny.

He must have read the accounts of Nana's mysterious disappearance, and the arrest by the British of several lunatics and mendicants suspecting them to be the legendary leader in disguise, of Nana's wife refusing to live like a widow, and the rumour that Nana met her secretly on the holy Shivaratri night, year after year.

The youth explained, with the help of a map he had drawn, the logic leading to his conclusion. Stammering or choking with excitement, he indicated where Nana had last been seen fighting. He then proceeded to show how in the course of his retreat Nana must have taken to a river-way and, his boat led by the north wind of the season, must have touched a certain town, and the town then being under the control of the East India Company, he must have followed a certain forest route and reached the outskirts of our village, and, at last, found a haven on Peacock Hill.

But the youth's mind must have been ruptured by a formidable conflict. He had gathered the intelligence that Nana carried with him a fabulous treasure. Should he make his way into Nana's presence, befriend him, and in due course, inherit his property, or should he inform the government and go satisfied with a promised reward of ten thousand rupees only?

He had at last decided in favour of the second course of action, which held out not only the certainty of a reward but also the prospect of a high-level friendship with the British which might, when matured, yield him a knighthood.

The youth secured an appointment with the English collector-cum-magistrate of our district. The sahib listened to him patiently, but finally said, 'Baboo! Please leave the poor old Nana in peace. Goodbye, baboo, goodbye!'

This obliged the youth to take recourse to the other option—that of befriending Nana. If only he had so requested, my father or any of his friends would have readily accompanied him to the hill. But he kept the adventure all to himself.

Though after his return from the hill he spoke no more of Nana, to those who cared to observe him he seemed even more worked up.

In fact, a new revelation had dawned on him: the hill contained rich ores of varieties of precious metals. On the condition of being allowed a regular share of the profit from their mining, he was willing to reveal his discovery to any reputable firm.

Eventually he succeeded in luring an expert from Bird & Co., a well-known British enterprise, to our village. After passing a hard day on the hill with the youth for his guide, the exhausted Englishman suddenly expressed a desire to meet his father.

In broken Hindi, the sahib whispered to the eager old man: 'There is something wrong with your boy's head. You should arrange for his treatment. And, confidentially, nothing would be a better cure than giving him a wife. He will forthwith stop exploring the hills. Ha ha!'

The youth continued loitering on the hill for a week or so more. Nobody saw him thereafter. His old father, too sick to go looking for him, lay on a cot under a banyan tree in front of his house and asked all and sundry if they had by any chance seen his son. By and by, his mind became so feeble that he put the question even to monkeys if his dim vision spotted one on the tree.

He did so for a long time and then gave up.

With the youth's disappearance, the speculation about the dweller on the hill entered a new phase; some asserted that he was a wizard, engaged in secret rites, and the youth must have come in handy to him to be sacrificed at the altar of his deity. Some others were of the opinion that he was a Yaksha, guardian of the immeasurable wealth lying buried in the hill. Since the youth coveted the wealth, the Yaksha had whisked him off to the netherworld.

By the time I was old enough to appreciate legends, the Yaksha had been reduced to an ogre once again.

Had our people's imagination been tempered by a little more empathy, they would not have let the ogre seethe in the sun and soak in the rain and shiver in the cold all alone, but would have found an ogress to keep him company. As I pursued the fairy tale, I could not stop the solitary ogre of Peacock Hill from entering my mind again and again.

✛

The epoch-making downfall of Shri Jagatbandhu Das, a distinguished young man of our village, had occurred nearly half a century before my birth. But the episode was still discussed from time to time, often with so much animation and in such confident tones that the speakers appeared to know the details of the event down to the exact second of its occurrence.

Jagatbandhu's father had a small zamindari comprising two nearby villages. Being the only son of a reasonably affluent father, handsome and a medical student to boot, he had become a bright flame towards which the guardians of the girls of marriageable age rushed like moths, only to be thrown off with their enthusiasm singed. Before some of them the proud Jagatbandhu would feign lunacy, while before others he would behave like one inflamed with an insatiable greed for dowry. When in a serious mood, he would confide to the appalled parents that he had managed to banish or neutralize the planets in his horoscope, which had conspired to bring about his marriage!

But, alas, no sooner had Jagatbandhu qualified as a doctor than he fell in love with a Christian nurse. For at least a fortnight from the day of that ominous news reaching our village, the solemn ones among our elders were seen walking the roads with their heads hung and their faces pulled long like rotten cucumbers.

They straightened their heads only when the progressive and ever-optimistic Jagatbandhu, appearing in the village with his bride, was not only obliged by his father to take shelter in their cowshed but was also completely ostracized by the villagers, who showed exemplary unity on this issue.

In the cowshed, Jagatbandhu's wife took ill. Nobody came to their aid. The young man was even forbidden the use of the village ponds and had to fetch water from the river himself. Respectable men from several nearby villages, umbrellas stuck under their arms, came to steal glimpses of Jagatbandhu's plight. And, of course, those among them who tried to catch his attention with meaningful coughs were the fathers of girls earlier refused by him.

At last, one midnight, when Jagatbandhu's father secretly entered the cowshed with a pair of blankets, some milk, fruits, and two streams of tears on his pale cheeks, Jagatbandhu could not help blurting out, 'Father! I've reconciled myself to your heartlessness, but I'm afraid your cowardice and hypocrisy will drive me mad!'

Leaving the gifts untouched, Jagatbandhu left for the town as soon as it was dawn, his wife limping behind him to the bus stop several miles away.

The father took to bed, shocked at his son's failure to realize that in the prevailing circumstances he could have hardly done anything better than revealing his tears to him only at midnight. He died a heartbroken man.

His Christian daughter-in-law followed suit. But she left behind her a son.

The son grew up into a brilliant scholar and duly married and produced a daughter. Then, along with his wife, he too bade a sudden farewell to the world.

Jagatbandhu continued to live amidst an abundance of deaths. To see him was to feel the impact of a full three-act tragedy. He wore a long gown, a round khaki cap and thick glasses. His face looked blurred behind the puffs of smoke from his cheroot. I suspect he wished to hide himself. We saw very little of him anyway, for he rarely visited the village.

The world had taken great leaps forward since the time of Jagatbandhu's revolutionary romance half a century ago, and their impact on our village was obvious. For example, several well-to-do villagers had led their families on exploratory trips to the town and had returned with family photographs with flowery frames, which decorated the walls of their homes along with the colourful portraits of gods, goddesses and King George the Sixth. One bespectacled gentleman subscribed to a weekly and carried a bundle of the back numbers of the periodical wherever he went.

To top it all, a post office and a government dispensary had opened in a village notorious for its modern lifestyle, only three miles away from ours. Several gentlemen of the surrounding villages, who had no reason whatever to expect a letter, made it a practice to pay occasional visits to the post office and to exchange courtesies with the postmaster, thus keeping pace with the times.

At the dispensary, not only did those running high

temperatures press the thermometer under their armpit and thereby transferred their surplus heat into it, but also others with pains from a cut or a boil pleaded with the doctor's assistant—whose designation was Compounder but who was called Kuru-Pandav—to be treated with that magic glass stick. They felt great relief when obliged.

In such a changed climate, there was no question of boycotting Jagatbandhu any longer. He was, rather, treated with some reverence.

But this time, Jagatbandhu had not come alone. It had become easier for the elders to accept Jagatbandhu, but for us village boys, the girls did not count, the question of accepting Lily, Jagatbandhu's granddaughter, whom we saw for the first time, was absurd.

Firstly, she was a girl. Secondly, she wore a frock at eleven, by which age all our sisters in the village had outgrown their first sarees.

Then, she was in the habit of surveying us from top to toe through her gold-rimmed glasses without the slightest regard for our budding maleness.

Moreover, she knew English and had several other dubious qualities which went with that.

Though we village boys often quarrelled and fought among ourselves, we belonged to a single world, after all. And I have often questioned the wisdom of Providence in suddenly springing amidst us a girl from a different culture, almost an alien world, thereby wreaking havoc in our lives.

But I did not understand why, in my eighties, the memory of Lily should disturb me while I was trying to enjoy a fairy tale.

The main character in the fairy tale was a shy and lonely girl. The author had cleverly avoided telling us why on earth a sweet little thing like that should be required to live, all alone, in a forest.

At first the girl's playmates were a few squirrels and butterflies. When she grew up a little, several hares befriended her. Later she got to know a herd of antelopes. These friends imparted to her the art of lightning quickness in her movements. A swarm of bees were her early music teachers; but soon they placed her

in charge of a flock of cuckoos who, when they had taught her all
they knew, guided her to a gorge amidst a row of caverns deep
in the forest where the wind composed extraordinary symphonies,
with a murmuring brook contributing to the melody.

Stars taught her the alphabet and she learnt love from the
rainbow, smiles from the flowers, aspirations from the sunrise,
sadness from the sunset and dreams from the moonlight.

Although we had no hares or antelopes in our village, we
had plenty of butterflies and a notable number of squirrels.
From time to time, rainbows were observed and cuckoos heard.
We had a river flowing by, if not a brook. And we had sunrises,
sunsets, moonlight, stars and flowers galore. But I do not know
if Lily was impressed.

I was away in my maternal uncle's village when Lily had
arrived. On my return two days later, I found the atmosphere
in our boys' world tense. Our natural leader, Hatakishore alias
Hatu, and the deputy leader, Navin, sat under the banyan tree
on the river bank, our usual place of meeting at twilight, with
faces drawn as if it were the eve of the school opening after a
vacation.

'When did you return?' asked an agitated Hatu, and before
I could replied, asked again, 'Have you seen the creature?'

'What?' I asked, suspecting that some new teacher had
descended on us.

'Stupid!' muttered Hatu.

Hatu, being the leader, had the prerogative of making such
arbitrary comments. Even so, I felt a bit humiliated. My father
had lately acquired a new bullock cart and had also become
the secretary of our primary school. I had expected Hatu to
take note of the elevation in my status brought about by such
developments.

But I always avoided quarrelling with him, partly because
I was physically weaker and partly because I believed that Hatu
would bully his way into a bright future.

But as they described the totally unforeseen menace that
was Lily, my sense of inadequacy grew more and more acute.

'As she passed this way the other day, looking at things
through her glasses with that insufferable vanity, Hatu followed
her stealthily and when quite close, gave out such a terrific

scream that her spleen could have burst like a watermelon,' reported Navin.

'And would you like to know what Navin did? The little smarty had put on a dazzling new frock. Navin passed by her at great speed, in the process emptying a shell-full of babul juice on it. Be sure, the stain will never vanish even if the frock is boiled down to a pulp!' added Hatu.

I understood that every member of our company worth his salt had already done his best to teach the proud Lily a lesson. I alone was lagging behind.

'So, that's all you fellows could do, eh? Had I been here, I would have, well, eh . . .' I tried to be aggressive in a bid to make up for my backwardness, but my brain, weakened by frequent bouts of malaria, failed to come up with the necessary idea to complete my sentence.

'Well, well, you are very much here now, aren't you, baby? Why don't you do what you should have already done?' retorted Navin.

'Done, eh? What could a funk, a sissy, a nanny goat like him do?' Hatu spoke to Navin, pointing at me.' With one look through her glasses she could teach even an expert shiverer like him how to shiver better!'

I used to feel awfully embarrassed at any reference to my shivering. God alone knew how much will power I had to muster to still my limbs when a friend or a relative visited me while I was under an attack of malaria.

'She'd look through her glasses at me? Look at me? At me? Why, don't I know how to smash her glasses?' I asserted myself.

'Cheerio, sonny, but take my advice, approach her with your shorts off. You might catch cold, for you are certain to wet your linen.' Navin laughed, inspired by his own wit.

'Never! You are welcome to feel my shorts after I have done my job!' I put a lot more vigour into my voice and that generated some self-confidence.

We set out at the crack of dawn. The crows had just begun their trial flights through the fog. Catapult in hand, I advanced slowly and took position behind a palm tree. Hatu and Navin crouched under a huge bush a few yards away.

I had spent the first half of the night without any sleep and the latter half with bizarre dreams. Hatu and Navin had passed on the intelligence to me that Lily regularly appeared on her balcony a little before sunrise and enjoyed gazing at the eastern horizon. Although I had proclaimed my determination to smash her glasses, my leaders were considerate enough not to demand that I do it standing face to face with her. My talent in bringing down guavas and mangoes with shots from the catapult, however, was well recognized in the village, and they had told me that it would do if I adopted the same method for achieving the current objective.

The door and the window on Lily's balcony were already open before we took our position. Faces flushed with excitement, my captains signalled me to keep my catapult ready, for the sun was about to rise and it was time for Lily to appear on her balcony.

I tried to keep my hands steady, but they were trembling like those of one possessed by a spirit. In a nook of my heart I felt awfully unhappy at what I was going to do, but I had come to realize that on the success of this—my holy mission against the aggressive urban femininity—rested not only the hoary tradition of our bravado, but also the entire edifice of masculine superiority.

Hatu and Navin suddenly seemed anxious to convey some urgent message to me with frantic movements of almost all their limbs. In my nervousness, I concluded that the target had already been sighted. With my weapon raised, I strained my eyes to locate her.

In the twinkling of an eye my catapult was gone—snatched away! I whirled around.

The earth seemed to have drastically increased its rotation. Soon everything dimmed before my vision and faded out.

When I began to see again, I found myself being dragged along by a luminous being whom I could have mistaken as supernatural had she not been wearing glasses.

Thus was I kidnapped, and from the very midst of those in whose power of protection I had until then an unqualified faith.

After we reached a spacious room on the upper floor, Lily

loosened her grip on my wrist and pushed me towards a grandfatherly chair. I dropped into it like a sandbag.

'Whom did you want to aim at—Grandpa or myself? And why? What harm have we done to you?' asked Lily, in a voice that was sharp and clear as a whistle, while rubbing her glasses on her apparel.

I did something terribly embarrassing before I was aware of it. I burst into tears. And that came as such a surprise to Lily that for some time she could do nothing except rub her glasses more vigorously and mumble, 'Sorry, but I'm so sorry!' Then, in a flash, she brought out a colourful tin box and opened its lid, holding it close to my eyes.

I took time to identify as toffees what at first looked like a swarm of well-dressed bees about to take off. Not that toffees were not available in the nearest market, but I had never seen them donning dazzling paper frocks.

I quickly overcame my misgivings and picked up three of them, one after another. I felt a thrill even before I tasted them. We were under the impression that the townsfolk summoned the police even to drive flies from the tips of their noses. But Lily's gesture reassured me that she did not intend to hand me over to any such fearsome agency.

'Missing your two followers left behind under the bush?' Lily asked and smiled. She looked beautiful.

I warmed up. Oppressed by Hatu and Navin all my life, today I was being looked upon as their leader. My satisfaction was great.

Indeed, soon I began to feel pity for Hatu and Navin. At the same time, there was a feeling of revolt against them. Though they did nothing to stop Lily from catching me, they would nevertheless ridicule me savagely for my inability to escape. Little would they realize that while they stood in the damp, suffering horrendous mosquitoes, I was being feasted on the choicest toffees, being addressed respectfully and regarded as the leader of the gang. They would not believe me even if I were to swear by the presiding goddess of our village.

Lily repeated her question.

'They are Hatu and Navin, I mean Shri Hatakishore Das and Shri Navinchandra Mishra,' I replied, wiping my eyes.

'Why not call them here?'

I welcomed the idea but found myself on the verge of tears again.

'What's the matter?' enquired Lily anxiously, looking at my contorted face. Although ashamed, I made bold to confess my fear that she might inform them about my crying. Lily promptly assured me under oath that she would never would such a thing.

We then sat in a serious discussion, trying to hatch a scheme to win over Hatu and Navin. I wrote a note: 'I'm taken prisoner. I will be let off only if you two present yourselves here. Otherwise Lily's Grandpa will telephone to the police and that will mean our arrest as well as of our parents'! I have been offered delicious toffees. The same good luck awaits you. I am hale and hearty!'

That important people of the town took recourse to a magic instrument called telephone had lately become a part of our general knowledge. And I could terrify my friend swearing by its name because we were yet to learn that wires and posts were required for the system to operate.

At Lily's advice, I rolled up two toffees in the scrap of paper carrying the message. Looking through the window, I could see Hatu and Navin, agape and drooling, gazing up at me. I signalled them to come nearer. That only enlarged the size of their gaping. They did not stir.

I smiled, relishing this diminution in their status.

After some exchange of signals, I hurled the small bundle at them. They opened it, examined the toffees with amazement and read the note with keen interest and, casting doubtful glances at me, slowly advanced towards the house. I went down to receive them.

'Let us get away, now that you are free,' proposed Hatu in a suppressed tone at the door.

'That would be sheer cowardice,' I said. 'And what would stop them from calling the police, anyway?' Then I whispered, 'Tasted those toffees? She has a lot more. Think of that! And, believe me, she is an angel despite her specs.'

I led them up the stairs, enjoying the proudest moment in my life.

Lily greeted them with smiles and matronly pats. Then, holding a hanky under Hatu's nose, she commanded, 'Blow; do not leave it hanging like icicles!'

The idea of using a clean, scented hanky for removing his nasty mucus was a little too much even for Hatu. He biinked and did nothing.

'I love to nurse patients in Grandpa's clinic,' said Lily, herself wiping Hatu's nose and then throwing the hanky to a corner.

Next, her gaze was fixed on Navin.

'Unbutton your shorts, please!' she directed him.

Even I blushed, what to speak of the hapless Navin.

But Hatu's natural instinct for leadership was toning up after its momentary languor.

'Open, I say!' he bellowed at Navin.

'Don't be rude!' Lily took Hatu to task and began unbuttoning Navin's shorts herself. Before I had grasped her intention, she pushed the soiled lower portion of Navin's shirt into his shorts and buttoning them up, observed, 'This is how it should be. Don't you look smarter now?'

'I always insert my shirt in that fashion,' declared Hatu with a snigger, although he hardly ever wore a shirt. At the moment, both he and I sported bare chests.

'You couldn't have had any time for breakfast, I bet. Why should you be nibbling your nails otherwise?' asked Lily, looking at Hatu.

'Better I bring something to eat.' She disappeared into an ante-room.

Biting his nails and spitting them out was a habit with Hatu, but now he lost no time in boasting, 'Do you see how I am making her get me breakfast?'

But I had suddenly stopped being impressed by Hatu's glib talk and trickery. Lily's charm, manners and speech had started widening my horizon.

She returned with a packet of biscuits and four or five oranges. I knew that Hatu was getting ready to say something extraordinary. 'I can't eat much, for I took a plateful of *halwa* and four laddoos only half an hour ago,' he said, fixing his greedy eyes on the plate.

Hatu's breakfast generally consisted of a bowlful of leftover rice from the previous night mixed with water, salt, an onion, and a chilli pod. But it was no use challenging him. His head could always produce an explanation like a magician producing a pigeon from his hat.

'But you must finish at least these oranges. They will rot otherwise. We brought a basketful of them with us,' said Lily. That was the first time ever someone was coaxing us to eat such delicacies.

We complied with her request without qualms. Oranges and biscuits have never tasted the same during the next six decades of my life.

'Do you drink tea?' asked Lily.

'No,' said Navin.

'Oh, yes,' Hatu replied smartly. 'But I don't mind going without it.'

Lily and Hatu were soon drinking tea. Hatu, no doubt, singed his lips and tongue with the first sip, but carried on with commendable composure.

Navin and I sat stunned. Until then we had regarded tea as a luxury belonging to the category of wine, enjoyed only by the elderly aristocrats. Nobody drank tea in our village. The nearest tea-drinker, one Natbar, belonged to the modern village mentioned earlier. He had served for a while in the city, where he contracted the habit. To distinguish him from his several namesakes, people called him Natbar the tea-drinker.

The only child of Natbar, a girl, had married a peasant belonging to our village. The unfortunate woman did not bear any child and I had heard our aunties attributing her barrenness to a congenital defect in her system resulting from her father's addiction to tea.

It was only when her husband failed to father a child even after marrying twice more that the aunties stopped blaming Natbar the tea-drinker for the situation.

We took leave of Lily after promising to come again in the afternoon.

For some time we walked in silence. Once on the river bank, Hatu suddenly began hobbling and staggering and circling. His eyes took on a funny, glazed look. Although none of our villagers had ever got drunk, we had once seen a drunkard in a drama in the aforementioned modern village. Navin and I exchanged meaningful glances, sure that the tea had begun to act on Hatu.

We sat down under the banyan tree suppressing our amusement as well as anxiety. Hatu gambolled for a while and then jabbered meaningless phrases and boxed our ears and tore our hair. We put up with his conduct and blushed with a faint pride to see one of us experiencing a state of high intoxication.

At last, Hatu sprawled on the grass. After some brisk consultation we two picked up a coconut shell and fetched water from the river and sprinkled it on his face. He opened his eyes, feigned bewilderment and then grinned and went away.

✛

The modern village had a Middle English School. We had heard that on Sundays the boys in the hostel indulged in a game called ludo. Lily was going to give us lessons in that pastime in the afternoon. We had all come with the bottoms of our shirts tucked into our shorts. Our mothers, proud that we had struck friendship with Lily, had wiped our faces with wet cloths and combed our hair.

Lily was in *salwar* and *kameej*, a dress we had never seen before.

Jagatbandhu once entered our room and threw an affable smile at us. It was only Hatu, hats off to his remarkable presence of mind, who could manage to offer him a prompt salutation.

Since that was the only double-storeyed house in the village, we enjoyed surveying the landscape through the window. The sun was setting and Navin suddenly clapped his hands in ecstasy, mumbling, 'All gold, all gold, the rippling river and the fields beyond!'

Lily looked at him with admiration. 'You should grow into a writer or a poet. Your ears are so big!' she observed.

Navin had to frequently undergo humiliation for his big ears, for every teacher would box them till his cheeks turned red with pain. But today they turned red for a totally different reason, though because of his ears again.

We were treated to fried cashewnuts and cheese-sweets. Hatu again joined Lily in drinking tea.

'Should we go to the riverside for a stroll?' suggested Lily.

'Why not!' Navin and I jumped at the idea. In fact, we were most eager for the village folk to see us in the company of Lily. But Hatu seemed determined to sabotage the plan. He said that a certain dog had lately been observed behaving rabidly and that the sight of a stranger like Lily might provoke it to attack. Also, he said, an unusually large number of snakes had lately taken to visiting one another's holes in the evening.

As Lily did not appear frightened, Hatu brought in ghosts. He narrated the story of the young widow who had been murdered along with her infant child, and whose ghost was sometimes seen washing her baby in the river on moonlit nights. Any new mother who happened to see her was doomed to lose her own child. There was also the famous old miser who forgot where he had buried his jar of gold and went on digging all over his compound till his death, whose ghost could occasionally be seen or heard, digging and searching.

'Is there a population of ghosts in the town too?' I asked, trying to sound chaste.

Lily answered rather sadly, 'Yes, but perhaps not as big as you have here. I know of only one case. Years ago, there was a fair in the suburb. A photographer had camped there. One evening, a gentleman, holding his infant granddaughter in his lap, posed for a picture. He did so on an impulse, for he could have surely visited a better studio. However, when the picture was ready, the photographer observed, 'I don't understand why the lady's picture should come so indistinct.'

'"But there was no lady with me unless you refer to this big venerable one!" commented the gentleman showing the child.

'"Who then was standing behind you, holding on to your chair?"' asked the surprised photographer, and showed the picture to the gentleman who, as soon as he looked at it, shrieked and almost fainted. The phantom figure was his dead daughter-in-law, that is to say, my mother. Grandpa was the gentleman and I was the baby he held.'

Lily wiped her eyes. We sat in silence while the twilight turned into evening.

'I wish I had seen that figure. But by the time I was capable of distinguishing between things natural and supernatural, the figure had completely faded out.'

However, Lily appeared to get over her gloom in a moment. 'You have so many ghosts here. Can't you show me one?' she asked with a giggle.

We welcomed the change in her mood, and while we were unable to promise showing her a ghost, we were eager to tell her about the many wonders of Peacock Hill. In the dusk, the hilltop looked like an island floating on the horizon. The forest assumed a new, even more forbidding aspect and one just could not doubt that unearthly creatures galore—goblins, ghosts or demons, corporeal or ethereal—crowded there. Perhaps they peeped at you if you thought of them.

There was another spell of silence during which we saw a swarm of stars emerging above the hill.

Lily stood up all of a sudden, the ends of her thin *dupatta* flying in the breeze like two flames, and exclaimed, 'And can't we go there—to the hill?'

The daring suggestion startled us. At the same time, her fascination with the hill and her reckless call to adventure sent a subtle thrill coursing through our veins.

We explained to her that visiting the hill at that late hour was not practical. However, if she was keen about it, we could start early in the afternoon the next day and return before evening.

'Well, then, you may leave now for playing *hu-tu-tu*. I no longer feel like strolling on the river bank,' she said as she stood up without looking at us.

We left her reluctantly. I had a strong feeling that she wanted to be alone in order to weep.

Hatu began to stagger as soon as we were on the road. I was in a solemn mood and Hatu's clowning disgusted me.

'Stop your tomfoolery!' I shouted.

Hatu, taken aback, became sober.

'It is a bluff that one could get drunk on tea! In the morning, you showed signs of intoxication immediately. How is it that this time the signs waited for two hours to show up? And it is only because you desired to enact this farce that you dissuaded Lily from coming out for a stroll, didn't you? You are a wretched liar. Lily would be the last person to drink tea if it had such a bad effect!' I blurted out.

Hatu flinched and couldn't reply for a few seconds. He must have felt the very ground on which his hitherto unchallenged leadership, his false superiority rested, slipping away.

'Shut up,' he shouted back finally. 'Lily would not drink tea if its effect were this bad? As if you know every bit of Lily! Is she a nincompoop like you? How do you forget that she is a town girl? She can drink even wine! Yes, wine! It is called—I bet you have never even heard the word—brandy! How much of the goings-on of this wide world do you know?'

'Stop.' Navin joined me in shouting Hatu down. 'We will ask her tomorrow! She never takes wine, I'll pledge my head to prove it.'

'Ask her, would you? I'll murder you!' yelled Hatu with appropriate histrionics.

'But what about those signs of drunkenness in you?' I demanded with a chuckle.

'Why, here they are!' Hatu resumed staggering and humming to himself.

We let him stagger and went our way.

Throughout the forenoon I was in a state of exhilaration—the kind of feeling which in later years has visited me only for brief moments, at a sudden touch of the spring breeze or at a whiff of the fragrance of some forgotten flower.

We had visited Peacock Hill only twice or thrice before, needless to say through the courtesy of the elders and under their stewardship. To launch an independent expedition was an event of untold significance in the process of our personal evolution. We could not have dreamt of the adventure but for Lily's inspiration.

Hatu's face looked as fresh as morning, unmarred by any trace of discomfiture or embarrassment. People born to be leaders must be endowed with a special kind of forgetfulness.

The sun had just begun its westward slant when we set out upon our journey, giving no hint of our plans to anyone else. Lily, with a winning smile, told Jagatbandhu, 'Grandpa! I'm going for an outing with these my most dependable friends. You should not worry if I am a bit late in coming home. Is that all right?'

'Well, well, worry of course I must. But you can go,' he replied, returning the smile.

We put the biscuits and the last few oranges into a bag and left. We followed an unused track and, after crossing the village, abandoned it and took a short cut through the paddy fields.

It must have been quite trying for Lily. But she never murmured, not even while climbing the hill.

Midway to the top, we relaxed on a rock and ate the oranges. Below, the green crops in the fields rippled and swayed without losing their tranquillity. A couple of birds flew by at our level.

In keeping with the mood of the hour, Lily narrated to us the adventures of Robinson Crusoe, which were like nothing we had ever heard and hence even Hatu listened with rapt attention. At our demand, Lily told us a few other stories as well.

I had a feeling that we were floating weightlessly high above the earth, wafted by the erratic breeze. Until then we had not realized how treacherously swift the hours could be if they got a chance. By the time we reached the top, the sun was already disappearing at the remote edge of the forest.

But the sun, pursued by an armada of ominous clouds, looked very pale, as if it knew that with its declining prowess it could hardly withstand their attack.

There were some clouds, like a few shovelfuls of dust flung into the sky, even when we had set out. We had chosen not to notice them. But now they had swelled to menacing proportions.

'We had better hurry back,' I was prompted to suggest.

Navin supported me. But Hatu silenced us, saying, 'Cowards, what then are we going to show her? Now that the biscuits and oranges are finished, you are ready to hurry back, aren't you? Why did you come at all?'

We understood that he had not quite forgotten his humiliation of the previous evening and was now determined to take it out on us.

Lily looked embarrassed. No doubt she appreciated our fear, but since Hatu opposed us swearing by her name and also perhaps because she was curious to see a bit more of the hill, she proposed a compromise: 'Let us just have a peep into the forest and then we'll leave.'

We had hardly spent fifteen minutes when the wind suddenly turned cold and cruel. The trees raised a terrific chorus of a thousand hissing voices and waved their branches frantically, signalling us to flee immediately. We huddled under a big tree.

'Are you all afraid? This is only a passing phenomenon,' announced Hatu like a master in all the secrets of the elements.

Soon came lightning and thunderclaps. I had never seen such dazzling flashes nor heard such deafening sounds before. The rain falling like cascades followed them. The familiar fields at the foot of the hill and the faint contours of our village beyond them disappeared completely. And as soon as that happened we felt cut off, as if deprived of our sole link with life.

The wind was intent on tearing us away from our shelter, but we had nowhere else to go. We clung on to the tree trunk.

Suddenly, Lily cried out, 'My glasses! O God, they are gone.' Then the downpour became even heavier and I stood blinded.

A large branch of the tree came crashing down.

'We must get away and descend through the Snail's Route,' proposed Hatu, 'lest the whole tree should fall.'

The so-called Snail's Route that was too difficult to climb from the foot of the hill, but provided a short cut down, was quite near our shelter. We took Hatu's advice and followed him. He was relatively more familiar with the route.

'Forget your glasses. Let us first get out,' I advised Lily when I located her, screaming to be heard above the storm.

'But I am practically blind without them!' she cried in

despair. I could hear nothing more, for the howling wind swallowed up her words.

'Hold on to me,' I shouted and extended my right hand. She caught it and followed me, stumbling again and again.

We reached the descent. Climbing down was not possible with the use of only one hand. We had to clutch at plants and rocks. I freed my hand from Lily's.

'Follow us and do as we do,' we told her and began the difficult and risky negotiation with all the concentration we could muster. The rain and wind continued unabated while one cloud after another seemed to burst on us like a shell.

Separated from one another, and with our limbs strained, cramped and badly bruised, we continued our descent, for the most part keeping our faces towards the slippery rock and holding on as tightly as we could to the bushes that did not spare us their biting thorns.

At last we reached the base. It was far too dark to see anything at all. Hatu tried to grasp my hand with his stiff fingers and asked, 'Where is Lily?'

I did not know. Even my memory seemed frozen. The storm, after barely a minute's respite, was evidently entering a new phase through the display of a fresh series of lightning. And every time the lightning flashed, it seemed to reveal to us the tribe of demons, the beings of darkness, chuckling around us, as if they could throttle the lot of us and fling us into some darker pit like worthless dead lizards, any moment.

I sat on my bed, tucked under a blanket, drinking a glass of hot milk and refusing to reply to any of the numerous questions asked by my parents.

A torch flashed on our veranda. Father went out and held the lantern high. I saw Jagatbandhu, slightly stooping, water dripping from his raincoat. The storm had subsided.

'Where is Lily?' he aimed his question at me. Behind him stood Hatu and Navin, their fathers and a few other villagers. I did not know what my friends had said. As soon as my eyes met Navin's, we both burst into wailing. Hatu wiped his eyes repeatedly without looking at us.

Jagatbandhu did not ask us many questions. Accompanied by a dozen men including Hatu, Navin and myself and half a dozen lanterns protected by palm-leaf raincoats, he advanced towards the hill. Two young men stayed on at his house. One of them was to run and inform us, shouting his utmost all the while, in case Lily managed to return home on her own.

Hatu, Navin and myself—brave explorers only a few hours ago—were now carried on the shoulders of three able-bodied villagers. We had no strength to walk.

The climb was grim and long. They began by searching the small area on the top of which our movement had been limited. Jagatbandhu called out for Lily repeatedly and frantically, his voice growing louder and louder till it cracked.

And then all was silent except for the big drops of water dripping from the upper layers of leaves to the lower and, from some distance in the woods, an intermittent moaning of some beast in agony.

The party started descending through the Snail's Route. We three boys had to repeat our performance. All the bushes and dark areas on the way were thoroughly searched. Jagatbandhu had fallen silent, but the others had resumed calling out for Lily.

Midway down the route was a precipice on one side, perhaps made by a landslip in the primeval past. Jagatbandhu focused his torch down it. It slipped from his trembling hand.

But it continued to focus on the object he had located even when it lay on the patch of grass below. And looking down, we could see Lily's small face, quiet as a flower.

All hurried down, Jagatbandhu with the support of others. He sat down and examined his granddaughter—perhaps the last case in his career as a physician—and continued to sit still.

It drizzled for a while even after that. The lanterns gave out one by one. The moaning from the forest appeared to come closer. But Jagatbandhu, Lily's head in his lap, sat like a statue. None dared to disturb him.

The next day, Lily was buried on that very spot. Jagatbandhu then left the place and, in a few hours, the village. It was a cloudy morning and the whole village lay as though in a stupor, fallen under a spell of silence.

Once before too he had left our village, in a somewhat similar situation, half a century ago. But then he had in him the spirit of a rebel, the dream of leading a life free of everything rotten he was leaving behind.

It was so different today! We stood at a distance and looked on as he got into a bullock cart. Later in life, often when I had an occasion to pray to God, I said, 'Grant me, Lord, that never again should I see a man as lonely as Jagatbandhu!'

The fairy tale lay in my lap, I don't know for how long, while Lily dominated my mind as the full moon dominates the sky.

Then I forced myself to finish the book.

Upon the hill, skirted by a deep wood, lived the strange ogre. Once every year, the people of the kingdom came there to enjoy tormenting the creature who hid in a cavern to save himself from the fireballs they hurled at him. Not that the people really wanted him to come out. But his roars of agony pleased them.

The people dispersed after sunset.

One day, the sweet little girl who lived in the forest came upon the scene, attracted by the crowd. She stood on a rock and observed the festival and shed tears silently.

She stood there even after the crowd had left, the hullabaloo receding farther and farther.

At midnight, the wounded ogre emerged from the cavern. It was a full-moon night and the ogre could read the empathy in the girl's eyes. Her beneficent influence dissolved the curse that lay upon him and he was transformed into a charming lad.

Deer and hares and peacocks and squirrels saw them strolling towards the golden clouds on the horizon, hand in hand, and they never saw the two again.

That was the gist of the fable. I did not know when and how the lonely girl of the story became identified with Lily in my memory.

A good deal of time spent on a stroll up and down my veranda failed to tame my restlessness, which grew more and more intense as the day wore on.

Late in the afternoon, I drove along one of the main roads of the city and stopped in front of 'Good Morning Publications'.

They were about to close. A smart gentleman as old as myself, somehow reminding me of a white eagle, was skipping down the steps. His portfolio sported his designation—Manager.

'Excuse me, I wonder if I could meet the author of this publication of yours,' I said, respectfully showing him the novella.

'Who is the author?' he asked me like a quizmaster.

'Well, the book carries a strange name, "Butterfly"! Obviously a pseudonym!' I replied.

'Even so you don't understand, or do you? If the author wanted every Brown, Jones and Robinson to be able to haul him out and give him a hug, why on earth would he use a pseudonym?' the manager, his eyes twinkling in appreciation of his wit, dared me to give a fitting reply.

'To be honest, that had not struck me,' I fumbled.

'Naturally.' The manager resumed hopping down the steps.

I was about to drive off when a young lady, who was a witness to my encounter with the manager, gracefully signalled me to wait. 'May I know in which direction you are going?' she asked most politely.

'Towards the lake.'

'Would you mind giving me a lift? I have an important appointment and it is so hard to get a cab at this hour!'

'With pleasure.'

The smiling little lady, who turned out to be one of Good Morning's editors, sat down by my side.

'I will tell you where our author, Butterfly, lives. Our manager has queer ideas. I have yet to know an author who is not delighted to meet an admirer.' She gave me elaborate instructions for locating Butterfly's residence.

She got down near the lake and there was no difficulty in my driving to Butterfly's doorstep. I did not encounter any hurdle in meeting the author either. We shook hands and I asked calmly, 'How are you, Navin?'

'Butterfly' gazed at me for a full minute and then hugged me. 'I cannot say why, but I had a strong feeling that in discovering the author of this novella I was going to discover something truly wonderful,' I said.

Navin had no words. He hugged me again and again.

Fifty years ago, I had taken up a job with a foreign shipping company and had been abroad for the most part of my life. I had managed even the sale of our small property in the village, after my parents' death, through a power of attorney. There had neither been an occasion nor any need for me to be there. When I had time after I retired, my interest had died. I had lost track of Hatu and Navin.

I found out that Navin had done well as an author and an editor. As for Hatu, all I could gather from Navin was, while in college he had joined a group of political anarchists and had spent a term in prison. After release, he had simply vanished!

We talked on till midnight. I learnt that our village was now linked with the town by a good road.

'Why don't we take a trip to Peacock Hill?' I proposed. Navin was enthusiastic. There was no need for rationalizing our decision.

It was twilight when, on the following day, we were near the hill.

A small crowd was gathered around a newly built hut. We learnt that a hermit had been dwelling there for some weeks. He had sensed the presence of a goddess at the foot of the hill and wished to erect a small shrine to her. The villagers were only too willing to help him.

We were amazed to find that the spot marked for the shrine was the very spot at the bottom of the precipice where, about seventy years ago, Lily had been buried.

We caught a glimpse of the hermit and returned to our car. I drove slowly, savouring the exhilarating breeze to my heart's content.

'Stop!' Navin shouted suddenly. 'We must go back!'

'Why?' I slowed down.

'The hermit. I'm afraid, we did not have a close enough look at him,' Navin stammered with excitement.

'Suppose,' I said with a smile, 'your guess is right and the hermit is none other than Hatu, what do you propose to do? Nobody can recognize me. But people know you. If you talk to Hatu and his identity is revealed, do you think he will thank you for it? Give it a second thought. We can always return some other day when Hatu is more or less alone, if you so desire.'

Navin kept quiet and I drove faster. Soon the hill was lost in the fog and the dusk.

'Hatu is doing penance in his own way. You paid your tribute to Lily by recreating her as the charming heroine of your fairy tale. But what about me?' I asked, and to my own great surprise, began to weep.

'If only I could weep like you! It is not so easy at eighty, you know!' said Navin with a sigh.

The Tiger at Twilight

One

For three long days and nights our lonely little valley was churned by a violent gale. The frequent claps of thunder that echoed in the surrounding hills seemed to be playing hide-and-seek; sometimes they made such a terrific noise that I plugged my ears and shut my eyes and imagined myself trapped in a desolate and dreary wasteland, its last blade of grass licked away by thunderbolts. At relatively sober times, the rumbling of the thunder was like the anxious cries of a brood of lion cubs lost in the hills, yearning for their mother.

The heavy downpour and dark clouds either blotted out the world beyond my window, or revealed it only in fragments, inspiring me to fill up the blank spaces with my own ideas of the shape of things. The good old meditative hills were metamorphosed into fantasies, sometimes looking like a colonnade of the citadel of the gods and, at other times, giants in a conference.

In the still of the night, the wailing gusts sounded like incantations of a demoness who, in frenzy, rocked and swung the valley. I was afraid of looking out too long into the night lest I should catch a glimpse of her weird face. In fact, every flash of lightning across the clouds threatened to reveal it—a huge face with a sinister laugh, even though the golden raindrops, whenever lightning showed them, looked like dust of stars knocked down by thunders.

The intensity of the cyclone began to wear itself out on the fourth day. When not engrossed in a fairy tale—the stuff I enjoyed reading most—I had little to do except sit close to the window and gaze at the woods and at the distant hamlets appearing and disappearing like mirages, depending on the density of the downpour, and leaves and tiny branches caught up in updraughts shooting high and then spiralling down.

During one of those days of confinement I stepped into my twenty-fifth year. But there was no one to remember my birthday now that both my parents were dead. I passed the day quietly lost in nostalgia. One of my earliest memories bore the imprint of a storm. A mere child of four, I had suddenly found the sky growing dark and clouds gathering ominously before dashing against a stubborn peak and breaking into turmoil. That had been followed by a loud booming sound capable of shaking the earth's foundations. I had made a beeline for my mother and dived into her lap. I missed my mother.

Horizon, the mansion I had now come to own, stood on a hill four thousand feet above sea level. Behind it was a mountain, named Nagdev, its barren peak raised like the hood of a cobra, looming protectively over my mansion. On moonlit nights, the ashen peak radiated a bluish hue. Fairies played on it, asserted a local legend. On a full-moon night, when it looked particularly resplendent, I would gaze at it for long hours, in the hope of stealing a glimpse or two of those supernatural beings. I loved to believe that they would peep out of the peak or the clouds surrounding it at any moment. Except at such moments when I brooded over my loneliness, I relished my status as the master of the mansion. With an extensive forest to its west and a river to its east, its location was enchanting. A rocky road meandered through innumerable rocks covered by bushes, and tribal villages hiding from one another, for fifty kilometres or so, linking our valley, Nijanpur, with the headquarters of the district, Samargarh. Before India won freedom and the princely states were liquidated, Samargarh, now an ordinary small town, was the capital of the small principality known by the same name. Unlike some of the bigger states ruled by ambitious or progressive princes, Samargarh had hardly any link with the world beyond its boundaries, most of its habitable areas tucked in jungles and nooks of hills and half of its population consisting of different hill tribes. I doubt if, barring the last of the rajas, who was away, and his father, any earlier ruler of the dynasty had ever stepped out of his territory and the neighbouring territories of his close relatives.

Some primary and 'minor' schools remained scattered over wide areas and a few students reached the only high school in the state, situated in Samargarh proper. There was a dispensary, but no hospital. There was neither a college nor any printing press. Nobody felt the absence of such institutions to be of any consequence.

Lately, of course, things had begun to change. The authorities had built a hospital and also a college at Samargarh.

But hardly anything had changed in my valley.

My happiness in owning a mansion here was tinged with pride. It had been built by the last Raja of Samargarh shortly before he lost his state, designed by an English architect who claimed to have studied the landscape well and, in his plan, had achieved some kind of a synthesis between the Greek and the Indian styles. It stood on an elevation and was spacious and imposing, an acre of green lawns surrounding it. The site was always breezy, but seldom beyond a certain degree, for the fierce wind was always checked by the guardian-like Nagdev.

The young Raja had christened the mansion Heera Mahal in honour of a young lady named Heera, somewhat of a legend and an enigma during that era, when gossip had an uncanny way of circulating over and over again, yet remaining green, and seldom reaching the ears of those who figured in them. Heera was the subject of many a weird rumour, some juicy and some fearsome.

Our Raja's father, on a visit abroad, had acquired a mistress who had just ceased to be a European nobleman's consort. The Raja, if he was in a good mood, said that he had lawfully wedded her; but very few had heard it directly from him. She lived in the Raja's bungalow in a distant city and was never seen at Samargarh. Heera, born to her in undue haste, was declared to be the old Raja's daughter, though nobody took her official genesis seriously.

Even before the old Raja had passed away, Heera was found to be exercising an ever-greater influence on the prince, the heir to the throne, older than her by ten years. The prospect of India winning freedom or the hoary feudal system coming to an end was not yet in sight. Hence, as was the custom, on the death of the old Raja, the young prince ascended the throne amidst the traditional ceremony.

It was on that festive day that Heera was first seen in public. She dominated the scene with her dazzling gaiety and glib tongue and proved a far greater attraction than the prince in the process of his metamorphosis into a raja.

There were even people who firmly believed that she was a fairy child, trapped by the late Raja from the clouds once while aboard a plane. Later, he had tamed her with the help of wizards. My father's old servant swore that his brother-in-law had seen milk instead of blood oozing out of her toe when a blade of grass cut it.

Soon the fairy seemed to hold the new Raja in thrall. He did not take much interest in the affairs of state and spent most of his time in the cities in accordance with the whims of the restless fay.

Those who had seen Heera agreed that she was charming. But those who had not seen her were more effusive about her charm and some of them attributed a certain magical quality to it. That way it was easier to explain her hold on the young Raja who was otherwise known to be intelligent, level-headed and sensible.

I had never seen Heera, but her portrait stared me in the face when I first entered Heera Mahal. It was an oil painting executed by a gifted hand and it looked so lifelike that when I ordered my servant Subbu to remove it, I felt guilty of forcibly dislodging a lady from her seat.

The rajas had an old castle at Nijanpur, a colossal structure containing several suites, a big hall and spacious corridors. It lay almost deserted, looked after by a lone watchman.

The Raja's ancestors were accustomed to passing their summers at Nijanpur. It was not so much for the beauty and excellent climate of the place as much as for the ancient deity, Vaneswari, a representation of the primeval goddess, that was housed in an old stone temple on a small lake behind the castle.

Once Vaneswari had been the family deity of my forefathers. Though they had ruled a very small state, they were proud of their ancestry, which they traced to an illustrious sage who fell in love with a princess, married her and inherited her father's kingdom. When, generations ago, a ruler of Samargarh usurped our state as the climax of a long-drawn conspiracy he had hatched in collaboration with some other feudal lords, the deity's wrath struck his family and death began to stalk its members. Several died inexplicably—one of them in horror of his own shadow which he found to be headless!

The then Raja of Samargarh did everything prescribed by his priests and astrologers to propitiate the deity, but to no avail.

One moonless night, the chief priest of Vaneswari knocked on the doors of the Raja's bedchamber. Even the palace guards had not dared to stop him—so obvious was it from his appearance that he was not himself, but was possessed by some supernatural power. He whispered something in the Raja's ear. The Raja sat up, stunned. One or two confidants, who had followed the priest into the bedchamber and who had overheard a few random words from his strictly private message to the Raja, stood horrified. The priest left the palace, laughing and shrieking wildly, leaving a stupefied Raja behind.

What the priest had said did not remain a secret for long. If Vaneswari was to be appeased, the Raja must sacrifice one of his sons at her altar.

Needless to say, the priest was believed to have been possessed by the spirit of the deity. But I remember my father saying, 'It was neither Goddess Vaneswari nor, for that matter, any other goddess who possessed the poor chap, but some fiendish vampire.'

The Raja was in a fix. Of his nine sons, seven had already died in quick succession. He must either sacrifice one of the remaining two and save the other, or be ready to see his dynasty come to an end. After some hesitation, he took the painful decision to follow the priest's advice. A month later, upon the recurrence of the moonless night, under some pretext, the meeker and milder of the two princes was led into the temple and was told that unless he was sacrificed, not even a kitten belonging to the Raj family would survive the deity's curse.

The prince was beheaded before he could speak. But the horror reflected on his face even after his head had rolled off his neck so overwhelmed the priest that he went mad and began confessing his terrible deed to all and sundry. No wonder the Raja was obliged to dispatch him too!

'And that was the last bit of fun the diabolical power which possessed the priest had,' my father, a staunch believer in the manifold occult forces at work in our life, would comment.

The rulers of succeeding generations continued the practice, but in a modified manner. They would not sacrifice their sons, but would adopt an infant, generally an orphan, and sacrifice it before the child had grown up enough to understand what was in store for him. The rite was practised in absolute secrecy and the priests seemed to have grown bolder than their ancestor who had initiated the rite. I do not know if they relished their status as performers of such an extraordinary function, but all feared them.

We do not know how and at which point of time the original curse was lifted, for the dynasty did not become extinct; but the anguish and bewilderment of its victims must have ripened into another curse that struck the family of the priests. The last of them died rather young, leaving no heir behind. The secret practice was discontinued.

That must have been decades ago. Then a priest continued performing the daily rituals of the deity for some years. That too had stopped for at least two generations now. The royal family had lost its awe of the deity.

Between the castle and the temple was a small lake, which remained ice-cold for a greater part of the year. It was said to be the abode of a Yaksha, one of the demigodly guardians of the buried treasures of the earth. Each raja, after his coronation at Samargarh, would pay a visit to Nijanpur, offer obeisance to

Goddess Vaneswari and throw a piece of gold or silver into the lake as his contribution to the treasure in the Yaksha's custody. In return, whenever a raja faced a financial crisis, the Yaksha would come to his aid—he would stumble upon a jarful of gold ingots or a box filled with jewellery. Since Vaneswari was no longer worshipped, probably the last two Rajas had not performed this rite either.

My forefathers, even when bereft of their state, continued the ceremonies, which characterized a ruling family till the time of my father who stopped such practices. Among the Kshatriyas, our line ranked higher than that of the Rajas of Samargarh. They held us in esteem mixed with the kind of pity a felled elephant inspired. Had they not been very poor, they would have restored our affluence to us, if not our lost authority, with liberal shares from their own wealth.

After years of ineffective hostility towards the Samargarh rajas, our sires reconciled themselves to their fate. But they would not tolerate any show of sympathy from the descendants of the enemy. The rajas of Samargarh were ready to grant us numerous favours, including an indefinite lease of estates, only if we agreed to a marital alliance with them. But my proud patriarchs refused the offer.

The downward trend in the fortunes of our family, which had touched the point of penury by my great-grandfather's time, was at last arrested by my grandfather, who had the singular luck of marrying into three noble families, each one of which had only one daughter as its heir. Thus he became the sole inheritor of three properties. His only child, my father, had been able to effectively shake off the feudal hangover. He was enterprising and had succeeded in consolidating his father's gains. But I had overheard him telling my mother more than once, 'The ghost of our past may shun me, but it is doubtful if it will spare our son.' In me, he must have detected an atavistic appearance of the signs of inertia that had plagued his illustrious forefathers!

The last Raja of Samargarh had gone broke years before surrendering his state to the government of free India. And, with his state gone, he found living among the people who had overnight ceased to be his subjects extremely uncomfortable. He sold his ancestral palace, which stood as an imposing backdrop to the small town of Samargarh, to the government, and dismissed his personal staff and dependants, giving each of them a generous gift in cash or kind. The Provincial Government, as provided for in the Instrument of Accession to the Indian Union, absorbed his officers.

After putting his affairs in order, he left for some undisclosed destination. His nearest kinsmen were two cousins, neither of whom lived in Samargarh, and we seldom heard of his whereabouts.

My father, though friendly with the Raja, had been quite pragmatic in his dealings with him. He lent a substantial sum of money to the Raja with Heera Mahal pledged to him as security. The Raja expected a handsome compensation in lieu of his forfeited state, but what he received, after the government had deducted its dues on several accounts, fell far short of his expectations. He was unable, or did not care, get to Heera Mahal released. The mansion became ours.

Meanwhile, Nijanpur had begun to gain in importance. The range of hills around the valley was found to be rich in mineral deposits. Added to that, an age-old spring with a natural pool was found to have contained several beneficent mineral properties. An Englishman, a retired member of the British Indian Civil Service, camped in the valley for some weeks, fell in love with it and, before leaving for home, sent his prophecy to a newspaper saying that Nijanpur was going to be the health resort of the future.

It dawned upon me that I could take advantage of the situation. I entrusted my lands and house in our village to a benevolent old uncle and moved over to the Mahal. It was exciting. I changed the mansion's name to Horizon and advertised it as an ideal lodge for nature-lovers, the health-conscious as well as for holiday-makers. My staff consisted of a cook, a servant and a gardener, with myself ready to act as the manager-cum-clerk-cum-receptionist.

But tourism was still a remote concept. We received guests rarely, but they were enthusiastic about the place and promised to return with their families or friends. I ran the establishment, subsidizing it with the income I received from my property in the village. I had nothing better to do.

'Are you happy?' my uncle once asked me.

'Well, I have never thought about it,' I fumbled.

'That means you are happy. If you ask a fish what water is, it will not be able to tell you, though it is always in water,' observed my uncle, pleased with his conclusion.

Four days of vigorous rinsing and scrubbing by the cyclone had given the valley the elegance of an autumn star. The silence that had always pervaded the place, but which I became aware of only after the storm, made me feel as though the valley had really been flung into some remote region of space—resembling a lone star.

It was late in the afternoon when a sleepy sun resumed shining over the valley. The hilltops and forests looked like exchanging meaningful smiles at one another.

Two

A dozen stunned pigeons and sparrows had been sitting in our skylights and in other safe nooks all these stormy days. Now, one after another, they flew out in search of their nests—or to rebuild them.

Coming out into the open was stepping into a kind of freedom. The wind had calmed down so that its touch was as soothing as that of the water lilies and it carried the mild fragrances of wet earth and crushed leaves. There was a rejuvenating freshness in the atmosphere.

I strolled on my lawns surveying the valley and the landscape, washed anew. It was like seeing the place with different eyes, like meeting a familiar village maiden who suddenly looked different when she emerged from bathing in the river. Soon I was out on the road.

The sun was dipping behind the forest. It looked very weak, as if it could be blown out by a child. Yet it draped the valley in tender gold. The few clouds floating around it looked so detached, innocent and remote that nobody would believe they had anything to do with the havoc just wrought on the valley or if they knew about it at all!

Particularly active were the partridges, flitting between the bushes. Several cranes flew across the sky, their milk-white wings brilliantly gilded by the sun, a privilege denied to the trees and creatures below them in the valley.

I ambled along absent-mindedly and would have loved to have gone on doing so indefinitely but for a jolly shout, 'Hello, Dev!'

It was Rao approaching from the opposite direction. He was accompanied by Pandit Indranath Sharma.

Rao owned a small mine on the outskirts of Nijanpur and had become almost a permanent resident of the valley. Sharmaji, an erudite scholar, hailed from Nijanpur, but served as headmaster in the high school at Samargarh. As a young man, he had even been honoured for his scholarship by the Raj durwar. When vacations brought him home to Nijanpur, he and Rao, the latter a graduate and a great lover of English poetry, constituted the intelligentsia of the valley.

They came closer. I bowed to Sharmaji. I had once been his student in the village school. And he had hated me. But that was because my friends and I had cut off the holy plaited hair-roll at the back of his head while he enjoyed a midsummer noon's nap on his table. Although the operation was a part of our routine mischief and was secular in spirit, it had been considered an outrageous sacrilege and had created a commotion. No wonder Sharmaji continued to frown at me for a long time.

Even after I had passed out of the village school and Sharmaji had taken up a higher position at Samargarh, he never failed to advise me, whenever we met, on the ethics of living and the value of rectitude. He did not approve of my wearing trousers. Once or twice I told him that while I had great respect for the dhoti and the kurta, I somehow felt that they were meant for good men only and not for people of an uncertain nature like me.

Once he told me with some anguish, 'When I see people smoking cigarettes, what I really see is their souls going up in smoke!' Someone had informed him that I had taken to smoking.

That was the first ever time I contradicted him with the help of a couplet I remembered from my father's daily recitation of the *Gita*. 'Sir,' I said, 'the soul can neither be dissected nor burnt. It cannot even be drowned. How can it then go up in smoke?'

'Stand up on the bench!' he yelled, prompted by his habit of punishing students in the classroom although we stood in the open. 'How dare you quote the *Gita* to me?'

Years had passed and Sharmaji, now in his forties, had mellowed.

I was still in the process of greeting Sharmaji with folded hands when Rao took hold of them and shook them with the vigour natural to a budding mine-owner. 'So, Dev, how is the weather? Water, water everywhere but no pot to drink, eh?—I read the other day in a college poetry book I found in the town,' he said, giving me a pull to induce me to change my direction in favour of theirs. 'Sahoo!' Rao then pointed at the man of enormous size descending from another ridge and clapping and drawing his attention to us. I rarely had any occasion to talk to Sahoo though, as a child, I was obliged to hear of him often. A prosperous merchant, he was also widely acknowledged as frugality personified. Fathers and uncles liberally cited the example set by him to teach worldly prudence to their young. Hyperboles like his squeezing out molecules of his stolen property from the tummies of ants found in the sugar bags in his shop were in wide circulation.

'Out for a stroll? So am I. Nowadays I become an ascetic the moment the sun goes down. Indeed, the sun and I stop work together,' said a beaming Sahoo. 'In my sixty years, I had never seen such rain. I wondered if the earth was about to be submerged! And I wasn't wrong. A couple of hamlets down the valley, to the south of the forest, have been washed away.'

'I wish the rain could wash away the sins of man!' commented Sharmaji. Sahoo chortled in appreciation of the sagacious statement.

Sahoo had lately begun spending much of his time at Nijanpur, entrusting his equally prudent sons with his business at Samargarh. Camping here enabled him to supervise his growing timber business. He was also a moneylender to the tribals who never cheated and were always ready to be cheated. Besides, he had begun to speculate in the real estate business; foreseeing Nijanpur's growth into a busier locality, he was buying plots of land.

The sun had set. The roseate elegance of the hour was fast fading. A rain-soaked dusk, heavy as wet wool, was slowly spreading over the woods and the rocks around the valley. Birds were circling over the battered treetops in an uncertain manner.

We advanced along the meandering slope, talking of things big and small, Rao frequently quoting and misquoting poetry and Sharmaji coming out with their Sanskrit equivalents whenever possible. A furlong down, in the bushes between the lake and the deserted shrine of Vaneswari, the jackals had just resumed their ceremonial howling, after a lapse of three days, heralding the advent of darkness. Suddenly, Rao stopped and checked us from stepping on some marks on the damp sand. Curiosity was writ large on his face as he bent down, his gaze fixed on the ground. Then he swore in a suppressed tone.

'Why this sudden departure from poetry, Mr Rao?' I asked.

But Rao had become very serious. He squatted and drew our attention to his discovery.

I recognized the soft but distinct imprints on the damp reddish sand.

Rao looked at me, still squatting. 'What is this?' he asked.

'Surely you know—the pug marks of the royal beast!'

The tiger had passed from the bushes on the right to those on the left, obviously at a leisurely pace. It must have done so after the rains had stopped; not long before we chanced upon those imprints. Sahoo and Sharmaji seemed to freeze on the spot. If silence had volume, it had suddenly increased ten-fold.

I looked into the thickets on our left. After glistening a vivid green in the late afternoon light, they were now growing pale in the dusk. Their quietness seemed to be the outcome of a conspiracy between them and their rare guest, the tiger.

'We ought not to tarry here. The creature may still be close by. Who knows if it is not the very beast which struck at Dinpur the other day?' Rao observed, standing up.

The rain had made us forget all about the tiger's havoc at Dinpur, the seat of the only weekly market in the area.

A farmer who was returning from the market at sundown was under the impression that someone else was walking behind him. He even made a comment or two regarding the unprecedented rain and the hasty approach of darkness along the lonely road, but did not care to check why no response came from the fellow following him. At one point, a narrow lane from a tribal village joined the main road. A villager emerging from the lane suddenly let out a shriek, and the next moment the farmer saw a tiger pouncing on the villager and carrying him away. The tiger had stalked the farmer for quite some time, but the one to fall prey to it finally was someone else.

'This is what you call the play of fate!' was the invariable comment of those, including Rao, whom I heard discussing the tragedy.

Although Dinpur was miles away, it suddenly appeared to have telescoped and come closer to us. Sharmaji and Sahoo grew pale. The nearest house was the castle. Its caretaker, once known for his sinewy strength, had grown fat through sitting most of the time, leaning against a wall and dozing, and occasionally breaking into a song to relieve the monotony. He had probably taken to opium as well. Even then, as an antidote to the fear inspired by the tiger, we instantly thought of him and advanced towards the gate involuntarily.

'Whom do you wish to see, gentlemen?'

The strange voice from within the mossy portals took us by surprise.

'Come in,' the castle itself seemed to gurgle out the command.

My companions faltered towards the gate, as though hypnotized. I followed them. I did not remember having come so close to the castle ever before. In fact, I used to avoid it like shunning a haunted house.

From the other side of the gate emerged an extraordinary face, big and bright, dominated by a bold moustache. It was Sahoo who first recognized the stranger. Before I guessed what he was up to, he had thrown himself on the ground in an extravagant display of reverence. 'Get up, will you?' asked the stranger tenderly. Sahoo stood up, but his palms remained joined.

'Aren't you the trader Sahoo? How hard old habits die!' the stranger commented, chiding Sahoo affectionately.

I realized that we were in the presence of the Raja of Samargarh. We were to learn later that he had arrived there during the rains, driving straight from the Samargarh Railway Station in vehicles provided by the district collector, who alone had been notified of his arrival. The Raja was keen on staying out of the public eye.

Rao, always ready to shake hands, for once forgot to extend his hand, and bowed quite low; Sharmaji, accustomed only to blessing others, bowed even lower.

I gazed at the Raja with great curiosity for I had never seen him before. He was in pyjamas and a silken kurta, his figure fittingly framed by the impressive portal. Rao, Sahoo and Sharmaji seemed to shrink in size and volume in his awesome presence.

'Come in,' said the Raja once again. I heard in his voice the roar of a tiger, but of an affable one. I shook off my hallucination and entered into a dusky hall along with the others.

Three

A dozen chandeliers, wrapped in black linen, were suspended like sleeping giant bats, from the high ceiling of what was once the Raja's audience hall. Only one of them had been unwrapped and lit. The castle had not been electrified. I felt awkward about Horizon dimly shining two furlongs up the road with a single bulb focused on its small signboard. The poles toppled by the cyclone had been set right and the power supply restored minutes ago.

'The collector had ordered temporary electric connections to my house without my asking for it. But I prefer to spend my evenings by candlelight and with whatever breeze comes from the woods,' said the Raja showing us to the thickly cushioned old sofas scattered over half the hall. He sat down in the most archaic one of them, a sort of throne, and signalled us to occupy those before him.

I sat down immediately, but the Raja had to ask twice before any of my companions would even touch the seats. They tried to drag the sofas backwards, but were embarrassed by the screeching sound emanating from their actions. They sank into them one by one looking awkward.

I had seen printed copies of the Raja's standard portrait in the households of some of his former subjects, who retained a distant loyalty towards him or the feudal institution. The picture showed him adorned with a bejewelled *choga* and a colourful turban. While his left hand rested on his waist, the fingers of his right hand, weighed down by diamond-studded rings, were spread on the hilt of an ornate sword.

But people had obviously realized that to display the picture any longer was an anachronism. One by one, all the copies in existence had disappeared.

The Raja, however, looked quite different in real life; not so much because of the intervening years or the absence of his regal costume and the diamond rings, but because of his disarming smile, which was absent in his portrait. The smile looked capable of betraying everything he had in mind—intrigue and mischief included.

'Years ago I knew you all, didn't I? Let me test my memory,' said the Raja.

His eyes were fixed on Sahoo. 'You have grown remarkably healthier. Right?' The Raja seemed to enjoy his euphemism.

Sahoo looked at his own bulging belly and laughed gratifyingly. 'How can you be wrong, Raja Sahib?' he said with great humility. 'You have the memory of a god.'

The Raja now concentrated on Sharmaji.

'Pundit! You've hardly changed except for growing wiser, I suppose.' The Raja pointed at Sharmaji's receding hairline. Sharmaji obviously took the comment literally and looked thrilled. 'This humble subject of yours, sir, has never stopped devoting himself to the study of scriptures, classics and . . .'

'And you are . . .' the Raja strained his memory, fixing a curious gaze on Rao.

'I know, Khasu the butcher. No doubt, you've prospered. I am happy about that,' the Raja exclaimed with joy, chuckled and closed his eyes. I waited impatiently for someone to correct him. But even Rao himself seemed to have quietly accepted the Raja's pronouncement on his identity. I was amazed.

'Raja Sahib, this gentleman is not Khasu the butcher, but Mr Rao, an up-and-coming mine-owner and an ardent lover of poetry—English poetry,' I pointed out.

'How stupid of me! Much of my memory of the olden days has been washed clean and the rest is hazy. But who are you, young man?'

'Devdas, son of Gautam Dev. They call me Dev. You knew my father rather well.'

The Raja straightened up and surveyed me with renewed interest. 'Knew your father?' he protested, 'We are friends! Yes, I knew that he had a son. Glad to meet you. How's Gautam and where is he?'

'Dead.'

'Oh!' The Raja shut his eyes and stroked his forehead. 'Good God! I should have known!' he muttered in a tone of taking himself to task.

I could feel his anxiety to get over his uneasiness as soon as possible. His eyes still closed, he said, 'Our relationship was always tinged with embarrassment, a hangover from the past which we understood so little. Is it not an irony that sometimes the so-called achievements of our ancestors should become matters of regret for us?'

He paused and opened his eyes and resumed, 'My ancestors are believed to have usurped the possessions of your ancestors. Thank God, a flash of lightning in the firmament of recent times and I stand bereft of any vestige of them, earned or usurped. I can regard you with a clear—or is it empty—conscience, can't I?' The Raja smiled gingerly.

I had not expected him to dwell on this subject at our very first meeting. Some of the embarrassment he had just shed crawled up my spine. I felt awkward too.

'Your Highness, may we know the expected length of your sojourn here?' asked Rao.

'I don't know.' The Raja's poignant voice betrayed a mild despair. 'I cannot say that I have reached my destination. At the same time' I do not know what my next stop will be. I have a sick daughter. Doctors, failing in everything else, suggested a total change of climate and atmosphere. What can be a more radical departure from our life in the city than a retreat to Nijanpur? Besides, since our fleeing what was once our domain,

Heera has continued to miss Nijanpur, though not Samargarh.'

The Raja stopped abruptly, probably because he became conscious that he had been speaking more about himself than was necessary. He looked at Sahoo. 'Why are you at Nijanpur, Sahoo? In quest of still richer health?'

'Yes, huzoor, the climate here suits me fine. It is partly for health . . .'

'And, of course, partly for wealth, Your Highness. Sahooji is busy buying plots of land, to sell them later when Nijanpur gains importance,' I said.

'I knew him as a pragmatist, but he is also a futurist!' commented the Raja.

'His speculations rarely fail, Your Highness,' said Rao. 'I'm afraid, it will not fail in this case either—to Nijanpur's ultimate ruin. On my way here, even through the rains, I could see the forest line receding.' The Raja sounded sad. 'That is a sign of the shape of things to come, or to happen, to our old, obscure Nijanpur.'

'Sahooji has made some contribution to that too. He is in the timber business,' I informed the Raja. But his eyes had gone over to one of the doorways opening into the interior of the castle. I noticed a sudden crisis breaking out on the faces of my companions. They were unable to decide whether to stand up or to remain seated.

I had no difficulty in recognizing the one who sailed in with a smile, for the only picture that had adorned Heera Mahal and which I had removed to a lumber room in the process of reshaping the mansion into Horizon was a portrait of hers in oil, executed by some European painter. She must have been in her teens when she sat for it, yet she did not look any different now. Her pink cheeks were still youthful and her hair was still the vivid auburn that it used to be.

The Raja gestured us to remain seated as Heera came nearer. Dazzlingly fair, she was in jasmine-soft white saree. A pair of diamond earrings gave her shining eyes the company of two tiny stars.

'Heera, meet our old friends—Sahoo, Rao and Sharma.' The

three almost blushed. 'And this young man,' continued the Raja, 'is Devdas, son of the Devs and, I suppose, the present lord of Heera Mahal.'

The Raja looked at me expecting either confirmation or denial. I nodded confirming his guess.

My eyes met Heera's. I gave a start. I hope nobody observed it. I had the sudden eerie feeling that a flash from her eyes leaped at me like a serpent's forked tongue.

Was it my imagination, or could it be the glint of her diamonds?

Heera sat down beside the Raja. Her gaze fixed on me, she asked in a resonant but acid tone, 'Does the mansion retain its old name?'

'No, but for the first letter. Now it is Horizon,' said Rao bursting into a forced laugh. Since it met with only grins from the rest of us and nothing at all from Heera, he laughed more loudly and nervously.

'The wonderful site once inspired a dream in me,' Heera reminisced. 'All I wanted was to have a cottage built of that very stuff . . .'

Sharmaji who was bursting with eagerness to speak and had been clearing his throat for the past one minute, cut in, 'Of what kind of valuable stuff, please?'

There was a faint frown on Heera's face. She did not answer Sharmaji and continued, 'But the Raja built me a miniature palace—with the usual stuff of stone and mortar.'

'A castle in the air!' Rao butted in. Heera turned grave. Sharmaji's full-throated guffaw in appreciation of Rao's wit petered out like a damp cracker.

A few minutes passed during which Heera subtly goaded my companions to sing each other's glory. Rao spoke of Sharmaji as an elephantine pundit and Sharmaji returned the compliment by describing Rao as a man whose heart was as soft as butter— and both projected Sahoo as a philanthropist! I knew that Rao had borrowed large amounts of money from Sahoo at critical phases of his business and Sharmaji was perhaps just enamoured of his wealth. Or, maybe, they were all anxious to reduce the gap between themselves and the Raja.

Outside the castle, the wind had started moaning again. And the chandelier swung ominously. I was suddenly aware of our dancing shadows on the wall looking like a committee of hobgoblins in session.

'I hope it does not rain again!' said the Raja.

'Let me see,' I said and went out briskly. Though the wind was erratic, there were only a few clouds and they seemed to have fallen asleep. A palm tree flapped its fronds vigorously as if it was ready for a take-off.

'Young man, wait a while. What the weather has in mind will become clear.'

The Raja summoned me back to my seat. Sharmaji suddenly burst into a popular Sanskrit verse saying that in a duel between goats, in the funeral ceremony of a hermit, in the storm that gathers at dawn, in a fight between a married couple, much ado culminates in precious little! He then commented, in a bid to import some relevance into his show of scholarship, 'Since this is not dawn, but evening, the storm may break, after all.'

'We should leave before that,' I proposed.

'Will you kindly initiate me into a study of the ancient Sanskrit works?' Heera suddenly asked Sharmaji.

Sharmaji was visibly nervous. 'I know too little to be of any use to you. I'm only a small teacher. I'm . . .'

'I have a volume of the *Panchatantra* with me. When do we begin?' Heera was not interested in Sharmaji's protestations.

'Since you are inspired, you are already initiated. Nevertheless, Sharmaji should not refuse to be your guide. Sharmaji, can't you report tomorrow? She has already begun to feel bored.' It was the Raja.

'Maharaja, even Brihaspati, the guru of the gods, will feel honoured to be of any assistance to her,' Rao said unctuously.

'Oh yes! I'll gladly put myself at her disposal,' announced Sharmaji. 'I've nothing much to do here during my vacation and I'll be at your beck and call,' he said, turning to Heera.

'Thank you. I will expect you tomorrow afternoon.'

Heera stood up and walked towards one of the windows. 'Will there be yet another storm? How much I wish I could fly into its heart!' she added in a hiss as if to invisible elements listening to her appreciatively in the darkness. Perhaps she gazed at Horizon, faintly outlined against the hillock, Nagdev.

Four

The evening was deepening into night when we left the castle. There was a refreshing coolness in the atmosphere and the sharp-edged moon gnawing through the clouds seemed to have descended a number of steps on an invisible ladder and come quite close to our hills.

A massive desolation was the soul of Nijanpur at night. Behind us the castle lay like a huge carcass, a streak of yellow light creeping out through the slightly open door registering its faint desire to return to life.

The wind had suddenly subsided and was now no stronger than a whisper. Was it a deceptive lull? A spell seemed to hold the hills and woods in its grasp. The sorcerer, of course, was the lurid moon.

The Raja had seen us off to the portals of his castle. In his presence, my companions had behaved like a bewitched group, agreeing with whatever he said, or making irrelevant and inane comments. The Raja had waved at us and I alone had waved back; my companions had just looked on.

'Good Heavens! We forgot to bow to Raja Sahib!'

The dismay in Sahoo's voice brought Sharmaji and Rao to a dead halt.

They seemed to contemplate going back and making good the omission, but since I did not stop, they were obliged to resume walking, confining their lament to their wrinkled brows and a self-reproachful silence. Each of them, otherwise so proud of himself, had suddenly grown so humble that were they able to sprout tails, they would have run back into the castle and wagged them before the Raja for a while to atone for their omission. I giggled at my propensity for such a bizarre visualization.

'What's the matter?' demanded Sharmaji gravely. 'Why must you laugh?'

'Sometimes the imp of laughter tickles my sides, that's all,' I answered, and since that amounted to impudence before my former teacher, I hastened to add, 'Can't Sharmaji apologize on our behalf tomorrow?' reminding Sharmaji of his most important commitment.

'Oh yes, I'll do that,' Sharmaji agreed sprightly, like a soda bottle opened with a jerk. He was lapsing into reverie. 'Could anyone have imagined just an hour or so ago that I would be required to tutor Heera—the legendary Heera? How unpredictable are the tides of time! Like the real tides of the sea, they can toss you, roll you, tumble you down or lift you!'

'Sharmaji, you can greet Raja Sahib with as much respect as you please, but not Heera. She is now your student. Now it is your privilege to receive her obeisance without having to return them. You can, however, bless her aplenty.'

Before Sharmaji could react to my advice, some little creature hopped from one slender branch to another of a jackfruit tree bending over the road.

Sharmaji clasped my hand immediately. Although nobody had mentioned it, we all knew that we had suddenly remembered the tiger.

'It must be a naughty squirrel or a bird showing disapproval at our intrusion into its monopoly over the hour and its right to total quietude,' I said and Sharmaji released my hand. 'But the tiger could very well be near about, at a more convenient place to spring upon a passer-by than the branch of a jackfruit tree,' I observed. Once again Sharmaji's hand groped for mine. We walked in silence through the moonlight and shadows; for a moment Sharmaji, Rao, Sahoo and myself as well seemed as insubstantial as the chiaroscuro we were crossing.

When we had come close enough to Horizon for us to be able to see one another in its light, Sharmaji's relief suddenly found expression in an explosion of laughter, ostensibly because he had sighted my childish servant, Subbu, playing with my pet doe. Subbu fetched me my gun and we escorted the three gentlemen to their houses, Subbu leading us with torchlight.

The slope from Horizon to the small village in the valley, in the direction opposite to the castle, was not absolutely desolate. A furlong down, to the right of the narrow road, a cluster of huts had sprung up housing a colony of labourers working for some timber merchants including Sahoo. Adjacent to that was a kiosk selling betel leaves, beedis and perhaps country liquor. Some of the labourers, both men and women, sat beside the kiosk around a turbaned man, who played on a drum and sang a mythological song.

'Should we tell them about danger lurking in the dark?' I asked my companions in a whisper.

'Not necessary. I don't expect the beast to come near the light and the sound of drums,' said Sahoo.

'Just as contentment is a state of mind, so is fear. Both are within us and not in situations or factors without,' observed Sharmaji, quoting half of a Sanskrit couplet.

'But, Sharmaji, so far as the revival of the philosopher in you is concerned, much depended on the situations and factors without—a gun in Dev's hand and your increasing distance from the ominous footprints!' quipped Rao. Sahoo laughed aloud.

Sharmaji had no skill for retorts. In any case, we had reached his house—the very first in the village when viewed from Horizon. A boy stood on the veranda with a lantern in hand, probably alerted about Sharmaji's arrival by Sahoo's laughter. Since Sharmaji spent most of his time at Samargarh—at first because he had been adopted by his maternal uncle who lived there and then because of his job there—and he visited Nijanpur only during vacations to take stock of his ancestral property, no wonder his house was in a poor shape.

'Take care, Sharmaji, don't open your door if someone knocks. It may be that!' Rao's elation at our approaching his own house was evident. He had put up an elegant log cabin with a tin-roof. A little further from his was Sahoo's residence—large but clumsily built—on a grassy mound. I declined his offer to provide me with two escorts for my return journey.

Stars had begun to wriggle out of the clouds by the time Subbu and I returned to Horizon. Such nights—cool and raven-dark—lured me to bed early, but an unusual curiosity was then getting the better of me. After a quick dinner, I recovered Heera's portrait from the dump, dusted it off and carried it into my room. As I examined it, holding it closer to the light, a slight shiver ran through me. What kind of woman was she who did not change with age?

I put the portrait aside and, in order to get over my odd sensation regarding Heera, concentrated on the pale moonlight filtering through the clouds and the untimely cooing of a dove.

I could not meet Rao or Sharmaji for the next three days. My servant Subbu who had become a friend of the watchman of the castle, reported that Sharmaji had fetched a big bundle of books from Samargarh and had started imparting lessons to Heera. 'But sir, he is stuttering violently before the mem sahib,' Subbu said, feigning the innocence of an objective reporter. 'What sounds like stuttering to your friend, you fool, must be classical Sanskrit,' I told him. Subbu was not expected to answer back. But he had a mischievous twinkle in his eye.

I learnt that Rao invariably escorted Sharmaji and spent hours talking to the Raja. The Raja's presence at Nijanpur was no longer a secret. Groups of people, mostly tribals, had begun to pay regular visits to him. Most of them just bowed to him from a distance and departed after gazing at him in awe for a while.

Next to the Raja, the tiger had become the talk of the valley. My *mali* brought me this report: A small party of villagers, escorting a bridegroom to the bride's house through the forest west of the valley, suddenly saw the tiger crouching by the roadside. It had been too late for them to avoid the route. They quietly continued on their journey, stealing glimpses of the proud beast. It was big, but its slobbering lips indicated that it was tired. It viewed the passers-by with contempt; then it stood up, shook off its tiredness and began to follow them. Somehow they managed to keep their legs moving though feeling numb in the rest of their limbs; the bridegroom giving up hope of ever meeting his bride. They realized that the tiger had ceased stalking them, only after a dreadful hour of silence when they met a party of drum-beaters, commissioned to receive them, coming from the opposite direction.

It was a gentle dawn, distant ridges looking like respectable villagers with super-fine shawls of cloud adorning their necks. Still lying lazily on my bed, I imagined what great fun it would be to hang on to the daily sun when it rose on one side of my valley and to descend with it on the other side, since the valley seemed to have shrunk considerably and the rising sun had grown nearer and more familiar.

Two tiny hooves appeared on my windowsill. My doe managed to stretch its neck till its tender eyes met mine. She was desperately trying to get my attention, pressing her muzzle against the bars.

'Princess!' I called out to her. She responded with a flicker in her eyes. She lowered her head when I put my hand out and fondled her. Satisfied that it had made its presence felt, it took its legs off the window and began to prance about on the lawns.

Further down, little birds chirped in the narrow strip of a nursery my mali had nurtured. A current of inexplicable joy, reminiscent of the bright Sunday mornings of my school days, passed through me when an orange sunbeam shot into my room. I planned climbing the barren hilltop behind Horizon, something I had not done in months. This was one of the very few things I could do when I was especially happy, apart from putting a disc record on my mother's old gramophone or switching on the radio I had bought lately.

I started the gramophone to allow myself some time to assess my keenness for trekking. Suddenly, I heard hurried footsteps and agitated voices making enquiries about me. Soon Rao and Sharmaji trooped into my room.

Rao was in shorts and boots, his double-barrel gun slung across his back. But what was amazing, Sharmaji wore his dhoti in a newfangled fashion, pulling it up tightly to his knees to make it look as close as possible to breeches. Perhaps he had toyed with the idea of inserting the tails of his shirt under the dhoti at the waist but had rejected it on second thoughts, for a small part of the shirt still remained tucked under the dhoti at the back. His right hand remained clenched tightly.

'No merry-making, please!' he commanded.

At once I stopped playing the gramophone.

'Haven't you heard?' he demanded of me. I blinked.

'Don't you live at Nijanpur?' he took me to task. I felt a bit nervous.

'A tiger claimed a life last night. Right at our doorstep, I mean the outskirts of Nijanpur,' Rao informed me.

He then gave me the details of the incident:

Three kilometres from Horizon, in the plains where paddy

fields mingled with open tracts of terrain and grasslands and where temporary rivulets were formed during the monsoon, there were a number of natural pools. One of the labourers in Rao's mine, a man from a distant village who had lately moved into the slowly expanding settlement in the valley along with his family, had set a small net in a narrow breach in an overflowing pool—a style of catching fish, involving little labour, common among the villagers. Soon after sunset he had gone with his son to collect his catch. While the boy waited on the rocky embankment, the man descended to the brink of the pool to lift the net.

It was dusk. The boy noticed a wave on the top layer of the bushes. He took it for a jackal heading in their direction. Suddenly the tiger sprang on his father, dragging him away by the neck. The boy fainted and rolled down the embankment. He was lying close to the pool when his uncle, looking for them, chanced upon him.

Early in the morning, the victim's friends had followed the trail for half-a-mile into the forest. They had not dared to proceed any further.

'Should we not request Raja Sahib to do something about it? After all, he used to be a great hunter,' said Rao.

'We must—that's what I say,' Sharmaji asserted, with an emphasis on 'I'.

'But is he still the great hunter he was?' I wondered aloud.

'Once a hunter always a hunter, and a true hunter would jump at a challenge thrown by a maneater. Besides, I saw Raja Sahib cleaning his rifle the other day. Why should he do so if he did not intend using it?'

'Quite a sensible supposition, Mr Rao. Why not ask Raja Sahib?' I said.

Sharmaji had suddenly fallen silent. That seemed unnatural. I cast stealthy glances at him while talking to Rao. Sharmaji's gaze was fixed on Heera's portrait on the floor leaning against a wall. His fist was no longer clenched. The uneasy feeling I had had the other day—at realizing Heera's eerie immunity to the process of ageing—returned to me for quite a different reason now; I observed Sharmaji's face changing incredibly fast.

A mini *durbar* had already commenced by the time we reached the castle. Unlike the other day when a kind of strangeness dominated the atmosphere, it was now filled with gaiety. Those who were there to greet the Raja—among whom were two tribal *sardars* and some former officials of the Raj—squatted on the floor. The sofas and chairs were lying vacant but for the one occupied by the Raja.

'Here had we now our Nijanpur's honour roofed, were the graced person of our Sahoo present!' The Raja's jubilant parody of Macbeth amazed me, but my amazement was far greater at the high-pitched snigger that followed. It came from a slim little man sporting a goatee who sprang to his feet and greeted me with folded hands. 'Do you recognize me? I'm Ketu Singh—Ketu the sly fox,' he announced aloud and laughed again. I had never met a person who would announce such an unflattering nickname with such jubilation. The nickname had been given to him by the Raja, perhaps at an auspicious moment, for it had stuck him. And now Ketu Singh himself seemed to have accepted it as a sobriquet of honour.

Ketu Singh's presence intrigued me. He was known to be a trusted lieutenant of Mansingh, the man who spearheaded the movement against the British as well as the Samargarh Raj. Both were looked upon as the Raja's sworn enemies.

Ketu kept looking at me, perhaps expecting some exclamation of astonishment from me so that he could laugh again and explain his stand. I took care to keep my surprise to myself.

'Mr Rao, you look accoutred for war!' observed the Raja.

'Your Highness, I propose to follow you, should you be pleased to . . . '

'Thanks. I was about to send for you and this young man,' said the Raja, a bit impatient with Rao's formality and politeness.

It was obvious that he had decided to take action. He stood up and dismissed the assembly, but detained the two sardars, one armed with a muzzle-loader and the other with an impressive bow and quiver. They were to be the Raja's companions.

Heera strode into the hall in her hunting attire complete with a gun. She walked towards Sharmaji and smiled meaningfully. No doubt, Sharmaji had grown quite familiar with her, but, I was afraid, there was nothing of a pupil's homage to a teacher in her smile, but the primeval coquetry of a woman out to vanquish a man. And that too, in this case, was obviously fake. Nevertheless, Sharmaji responded with a proud simper.

My suspicion that she was amusing herself at Sharmaji's cost was confirmed when, feigning seriousness after a closer scrutiny of Sharmaji's gallant demeanour and his innovative style of dressing for the occasion, she said, 'Leading an expedition against the maneater, are you? We need not waste any bullets then. It will be an experience for us to see the tiger dying of a heart attack.'

As Rao and I chuckled, Sharmaji giggled foolishly. But Heera broke off as abruptly as she had begun laughing. 'Just a minute,' she said gravely. I marked the rapid formation of a kind of resolution in her eyes. 'Just a minute!' she said again with some suppressed excitement and disappeared into the interior of the castle.

The Raja began examining our firearms. Rao and I stood before him, answering his queries, ready to learn from his observations. Sharmaji stood apart, sort of helpless and confused, looking alternately at us and at the long dusky corridor, which had suddenly grown mysterious for him.

Heera re-emerged from the corridor in a few minutes.

'Mr Dev,' she turned to me with a modest appeal in her eyes, 'Will you please help Sharmaji to slip into these?' She handed a packet to me and showed us to an ante-room. Obediently we entered the small chamber, unused for years and smelling musty. I opened the window for some air and light. Sharmaji opened the packet and stared at its contents in disbelief—a pair of trousers and a shirt. To my knowledge, they were made of the costliest material. Although they appeared to have remained in the very state in which they had come out of the tailor's shop, they had not been made very recently.

The trousers were too loose for Sharmaji. I took off my leather belt and fastened it round his waist. He stood blinking but resigned to the operation, his arms raised in total surrender.

I could not help feeling amused at strapping Sharmaji, who was once averse even to leather shoes, into a leather belt. Sharmaji, however, seemed enchanted with his new appearance. He grinned at me over and over again, forcing me to reluctantly assure him that he looked smart indeed!

A metamorphosed Sharmaji re-entered the hall, shook hands with Rao and laughed. His laughter ate into my heart like termites.

Five

It had been taken for granted that I would join the expedition. Much against my will, I sent the Raja's watchman to fetch my gun. A Kshatriya hailing from a feudal family was expected to have developed love for hunting. My father had been a skilled shikari and had given me several chances to prove my interest in the pastime. Had my response been positive, he would have arranged to train me. My lack of inclination for it, I am afraid, was one of the reasons for his losing whatever interest he had in it.

I was nine when my father first took me out into the forest one summer morning. He and his friends shot down a number of birds, and a couple of deer. Since we could not have eaten all of them the same night, some wounded ones were allowed to live till the next day. Among them was a Kochilakhai—the Indian hornbill.

We camped in an isolated house on the western edge of the forest that belonged to a timber merchant named Vasant Singh. Outside the house was a small, picturesque lake. We lay on the veranda of the house, enjoying the cool breeze rolling out of the lake.

My father and the others soon fell asleep. But I could not. A huge bird circled the lake again, and again and from time to time dived close to the courtyard of the house. Suddenly, a little after midnight, the wounded Kochilakhai got loose and struggled out into the open. It was heading towards the lake, flapping its bleeding wings fitfully, when a servant got up and ran after it and struck it with a *lathi*. It fell dead, but almost instantly the bird circling overhead swooped down upon the servant and, with its sharp beak, tried to gouge out his eyes—or at least that was the motive the elders attributed to its determined attack. The bird then flew away into the forest shrieking indifferently, probably with a touch of satisfaction, leaving its victim behind to bleed. The second phase of the expedition, planned for the next day, was abandoned.

Although they made light of the mishap, I could understand how small the party felt because of the humiliation a mere bird had inflicted on it.

Only once had I witnessed a beat and that had been organized by Vasant Singh, because a tiger had been haunting his estate regularly and decamping with sheep and cattle. Probably the menace was due to Vasant Singh himself and others of his ilk felling the trees, thus destroying the forest at great speed and depriving the tiger of its sylvan territory and its usual supply of food. It was not a large beat like the ones the rajas used to organize, with over two thousand people participating. Vasant Singh managed to collect only two hundred tribals and placed them under Father's command.

The beat commenced early in the morning. The beaters, who had furtively made a semicircle covering the area within which the tiger was expected to be lurking, began beating drums and shouting. They slowly pressed forward towards the opening where Father sat on a *machan* ready with his gun. I sat on a taller and safer machan, designed for merely witnessing the operation, with a servant by my side.

The sky was overcast and the chilly wind somehow enhanced the fear in the atmosphere. But as the ring of the beaters came closer, the excitement mounted. A number of smaller creatures made a beeline towards the opening, but neither Father nor his assistants shot at them lest the tiger should change its direction and jump the beat in its despair.

The beating of drums and the shouts of the beaters grew louder and more frightening. They were enthusiastic because their labour was coming to an end. Suddenly the tiger sprang from a bush and headed in our direction at great speed.

Father must have remained extremely alert all the time, for he shot at the beast instantaneously. My companion on the machan saw the beast roll on the grass, but the next moment it had steadied itself and bolted out of the forest at great speed.

Father and some more experienced members of the party tried to track down the wounded tiger. Drops of blood and faint stains on the grass led them up to the emerald paddy fields beyond the forest. Thereafter the marks were no longer visible.

'It must be hiding in the paddy fields, waiting to die,' suggested Father, and that was some consolation. The beat ended—difficult to say whether in success or failure.

Vasant Singh was busy till late in the afternoon, feeding and paying up the beaters. Tired, he then entered his bedroom in his camp house by the lake.

Two or three of his employees who had stepped on to the veranda behind Vasant Singh heard a groan and rushed into his room. Vasant Singh had fainted, holding on to his door. On his low rope cot lay the tiger.

His people hurriedly dragged him out and bolted the room from outside. Father was summoned. Through a window, he fired another bullet, this time right into the tiger's forehead, though he was sure that it was already dead.

Vasant Singh took some time to regain consciousness. His happiness knew no bounds when he realized that he was alive while the tiger was dead. He fell in love with that rope cot, so much so that he would carry it to his home at Samargarh and bring it back when he came to his camp. He would not sleep on any other bedstead. Years later, he died a natural death on the rope cot and was cremated along with the cot. I do not know whether this was done in deference to his own wish or according to the decision of his family members who might have thought it proper to dispatch the spirit of the cot along with its master's to the world beyond.

Partly out of respect for the family tradition and partly to break away from the monotony of life, I used to go hunting once in a while, but never for any big game. However, my poor record of shikar come to an abrupt end the day I shot a doe, not knowing that she was then suckling her two fawns. I fell into a deep remorse. I brought home the fawns, one of which survived, nurtured by Subbu and my mali, and began to waltz and frolic in and around the mansion with abandon and learnt to climb the stairs and trot on the roof. It grew up into a pert and healthy doe. We called her Princess.

It was after more than a year that I was entering the forest, if not against my will, not with any enthusiasm either. We were on our way to the spot where the tiger had struck. The relatives of the victim led the way. The Raja and the two sardars followed them, but Heera tended to lag behind. As a courtesy, Rao, Sharmaji, and I slowed down and walked escorting her.

'I hope Mr Dev realizes that his is not a mansion, but an intoxication—an irresistible love!' Heera commented, turning round several times to steal glances at Horizon which seemed to stand helplessly blushing in the mellow sunlight two furlongs behind us. If it was her design to embarrass me, she did not quite succeed, but I felt awkward at the thought that she should have such designs at all.

A narrow rill had managed to carve a permanent passage for itself over the rocky ground, perhaps through hundreds of years of humble but relentless effort. The rill separated the forest from the valley and its small locality.

'Your Highness, all this was once yours!' said Rao, walking up to the Raja and throwing his arms wide in a burst of inspiration. He lost his balance on the mossy boulders rising over the small stream. The Raja, however, acted promptly to steady him and said, 'Alas, but the woods look poorer though now they belong to the nation!'

The Raja was fully justified. The forest had been and still was mercilessly plundered by timber merchants. They did so illegally, no doubt, in collusion with the officials appointed to protect it. They did a lot of poaching too.

An enterprising travel agency had sought to make the forest its regular market, where it could bring its affluent customers and give them the thrill of shikar. It had taken Vasant Singh's camp house on lease, renovated it and hired local hands to assist in the project. 'Babu, they are ready to hire even animals to fall to the shikari's bullet if that were possible,' Subbu had commented.

But the enterprise came to an abrupt end, when the very first adventurer brought by the agency shot at a tribal youth instead of a beast. It was an error of judgement, but a rumour spread that the agency intended giving its special customers the thrill of manhunt. There was a ferocious attack on the company's camp. Its officials fled, narrowly escaping a shower of deadly arrows.

The process of plundering the forest, however, had continued. The Raja felt that some tigers had been obliged to come away to this side of the forest, close to the valley, because the other side had grown thin. One of these refugees had somehow tasted human flesh and had developed a liking for it.

We were near the pool where the tiger had bagged its prey. On the muddy slope between the natural embankment and the water, the pug marks were still discernible. Particularly the imprint of the beast's paws formed when it took the deadly leap was distinct. The victim did not seem to have offered any resistance. He had been caught unawares, immobilized and dragged away. There was a drizzle of blood on the grass.

Sunlight had erased the fear from the atmosphere, but not completely, for it still lurked in the dusky interiors of the bushes and thickets. This part of the forest was more or less familiar to me, but it was no longer the same with a tiger hiding somewhere, probably close by. In the throbbing silence of the moment, I had the feeling that, all said and done, it was the tiger that had a natural right to the forest. We were the intruders. The tiger was only trying to partly avenge man's inhumanity towards the forest and its creatures.

The Raja warned us against making the slightest noise. He and Heera, alternately, paved the way for us and we followed them as noiselessly as possible. I was amazed to see Heera feeling as much at home in the forest as a squirrel in the bush. The deeper we went, the brighter she grew. She was certainly much more her natural self here than in the castle. I later learnt that though she had never explored the forests in this area, she had never failed to accompany the Raja on his hunting expeditions elsewhere. Perhaps it would be more correct to say that the Raja was seldom out for shikar without her.

The tiger's trail became totally indistinct a furlong or so from the rill. Thereafter, we depended on the Raja's experience distilled into intuition. For him both silence and sound—even a movement made by a tiny creature—had a message. We had failed to notice a large cobra slithering round an anthill only a few yards ahead of us, but the Raja stopped us in time to let it take the course of its choice before we could choose ours.

Beyond a range of anthills thriving over a few stumps of dead trees stood a cluster of thick, thorny bushes and clumps of tall grass. Following signals from the Raja, we slowed down before coming to a complete halt. His gesture indicated the presence of something significant inside the well-knit hedge in front of us.

I could see a piece of soiled cloth clinging to a forked twig which protruded from a shrub. The ground under our feet was slightly higher than the small turf enclosed by the hedge. Carefully following the Raja's gaze, I saw the tiger crouching at the foot of a tree, its back towards us. It was totally engrossed in devouring something, its head buried between its forelegs. Patches of light playing on its stripes imparted a dreadful vivacity to it. Heera noiselessly tiptoed closer to the Raja. The Raja raised his gun, brought it to position in very slow motion and took aim. His finger was closing in on the trigger.

But awaited us was a sort of bolt from the blue.

Till then, Sharmaji had been coping awkwardly, following Heera literally blindly, for I had observed that his attention was rarely swayed by anything else. For a while he had fallen behind us, I suppose taking out a thorn that had pierced his canvas shoe. He was too deeply immersed in his own world to reflect on the possible cause of our coming to a halt. But coming closer to Heera and following her concentrated vision, he had suddenly spied upon the tiger. Involuntarily, he burst into a cry of horror.

The tiger leapt up and spun around. Its eyes spouted fire for the lightning moment it surveyed us. Then, in one bound, it disappeared from sight. Its answer to Sharmaji—growl of disgust—came from some distance.

A troop of monkeys on a banyan tree, quiet till then, began jumping and whooping. They were obviously amused.

The Raja took some time to lower his gun. I could imagine his anguish at missing such a sure target. But the severe scowl on his face melted after he had cast a contemptuous look at Sharmaji who was still in the process of absorbing the impact of his own discovery. In fact, he was shivering.

'Tiger!' he muttered, trying some gesture with his almost paralysed arms.

Thus was the tense silence broken.

Heera peered at him, a mixture of boiling anger and utter disappointment in her eyes.

'Indeed, Pundit, how brave of you! To scare a tiger away is no joke!' she said through clenched teeth.

Sharmaji grimaced. Could he have grown so very dull as to feel uncertain about the import of Heera's observation? I wondered and let myself remain uncertain about it. In no time, the Raja had reverted to his usual mood of detachment and stepped into the deserted cover of the tiger. We followed him. The remains of the victim were a gruesome sight. Any violent destruction of a form built by nature always pointed out to me a kind of helplessness underlying our existence—and the wrecking of a human body was certainly the most poignant reminder of that reality.

'The beast has done a good job of his trophy,' said the Raja after a hurried inspection of the scene.

The victim's kinsmen collected the remains in a sack. If the tragedy had struck them dumb, the presence of the Raja stopped them from giving vent to their horror. They just looked haggard.

'What now?' I asked.

'We can go back,' replied the Raja calmly. 'Perhaps someone else is destined to end up in the tiger's jaws. We can then try our luck again.'

We began our journey back to the valley.

'Don't you remember that tantric physician's prescription? Balika should have deer meat as frequently as possible. Can't we bag a deer?' Heera asked the Raja, looking askance. Irritation made her walk faster.

'Well, okay, if we see one.'

'We can carry a deer a day to the castle, Maharaja, if you so command!' said one of the sardars eagerly. The Raja conveyed his thanks through a smile and a pat on the sardar's back, but said in a whisper, 'The problem is, my daughter refuses to touch the stuff. I'll tell you if she changes her taste.'

Now the trekking proved tedious. The sun was on the meridian and the shafts of sunlight intermittently bursting through the trees were unbearable.

It was great relief to me when we reached the rill. Sweeping bushes and the rope-like roots of a banyan tree made ripples in the tender flow. Beyond a bend, the rill produced a sound somewhat similar to that of bells on the feet of some distant dancers.

At last, one of the kinsmen of the tiger's victim spoke: 'Maharaja, but for you we would not have recovered what remained of our unfortunate cousin. Now we can at least perform his last rites in a humble manner, satisfying his spirit.' The Raja brought out some money from his pocket and pushed it into the man's unprepared hands. They were all in tears. Bowing to the Raja, they moved away with their grisly sack.

We stopped near the rill spontaneously. We badly needed some rest. The Raja descended to the edge of the rill and splashed water on his face. Heera did the same. I sat down on a rock, relishing the bracing coolness emanating from the rill.

My other companions relaxed leaning against the banyan trees.

A deer was speeding past us like a streak of lightning. Perhaps it planned to leap over the rill. But it came to a nervous dead halt when it unexpectedly confronted us.

I alone held a gun at that time. 'Shoot!' shouted Heera. The dumbfounded deer almost offered itself to me. The force of incitement in Heera's command made me raise my gun involuntarily. However, I passed the stage of reflex action in a moment and lowered my gun.

'Shoot, will you?'

The repetition of the command struck my ears like bullets as the deer resumed its loping run. Heera shifted her scorching eyes from me and probably swore in a groan. She had been rude to me, but I did not feel hurt. That I did not care to give any apology for my inaction was, I hoped, rebuff enough to her.

But Sharmaji's conduct was amusing. His angry glances

convinced me that had I still been a boy under his tutelage, he would have twisted my ears or slapped me. My audacity in disobeying Heera had upset him terribly.

We walked on in silence. Heera, seething with anger, rarely took her eyes off the ground. But suddenly, she jerked her head up and raised her gun. She fired before I had been able to comprehend her intention.

It took me a few seconds to locate her target. From the top of a grassy mound I saw my darling doe, Princess, rolling down.

I threw down my gun and ran towards her. She lay completely still at the foot of the mound. Heera's shot had broken her neck. I lifted her velvet body, now soaked in blood. She was dying. Subbu, who occasionally brought her to this extreme part of the valley and who was picking berries nearby, came running towards me. He cradled the doe on his lap and broke down like a mother over her dead child.

I looked at Heera. She stood staring at me, but immediately shifted her eyes. I shall never know whether or not Heera knew that the doe belonged to me. But her eyes betrayed the very look she had cast at me the day she had learnt that I was the owner of her Heera Mahal. Her eyes were like flashes of will-o'-the-wisp. There was no question of her laughing at that moment. But I felt her laughter pervade the air, as if the eerie vibrations it created would scald and singe the greenest of trees. For a moment I forgot that she was a human being and not a vampire. I even looked around for my gun. I had a burning desire to destroy her.

But that was also the moment I realized that I was unable to act. I felt totally crippled. I stood up, but faltered and sat down again with a reeling sensation in my head. In a sudden hallucination, I saw the dreary landscape opposite the forest catching fire. The white flames leaped high enough to burn down a solitary pale cloud floating over my Horizon.

Six

The day was so warm and sultry that it almost drove me crazy. I sat beside my window with a silent appeal to the passing clouds to sweep the acute anguish from my heart.

For the rest of the day, I remained somewhat insensitive to time.

Beyond a hillock in the direction of the forest there was a very old banyan tree. Its top, like a green round hat, could be seen from my window. Not long ago a very unusual old man, Chogan Baba, lived under it in a small hut and died there too. Considered a savant by the tribals, the old man had once confided to me that a swarm of invisible puny imps lived in the tree. He saw them and talked to them. They responded to him all right, though not through human speech. He understood them.

'What do they do?' I had asked.

'Several things. You may not be able to appreciate their activities. They evince an insatiable curiosity for human affairs; they follow men, particularly strangers, in the forest. They loathe some and are quite excited about some others. Again, don't ask me why. One of them would sit on the barrel of a hunter's gun or his arrow and decide whether the hunter should miss or hit a target. They of course could not do this to a hunter like your father, a person with a very strong will. But with lesser men they play all sorts of tricks.'

'For example?'

Then Chogan Baba would tell me stories which he would not tell others. But I had to coax him before he warmed to the subject.

'Do you remember Vir Kumar's accident?' he once asked me.

I remembered it well. Vir Kumar, a robust man in his forties, was a landlord of sorts. I particularly remembered his voice which normally sounded like the rumbling of distant thunder and, when agitated, like a regular thunderclap. Efficient in everything he did, but brutal to the core, he was a terror to many. Several people who had incurred his wrath were found dead in dubious circumstances.

He had a few equally brutal henchmen but surprisingly, the one servant whom he loved most was Bhiloo, a meek and mild young man, who could be frightened out of his wits by a springing rabbit! Bhiloo had joined Vir Kumar's household as his clerk-cum-valet, but had fast risen in his affection. Vir Kumar took an endless amount of trouble to teach him how to handle a gun, in order to make a brave lad out of a nincompoop. Once Vir Kumar was out hunting with his regular entourage. It had grown dusky by the time he had shot a bear from his machan. He jumped down and followed the wounded creature. Unfortunately, he was dressed in black. In the treacherous twilight, Bhiloo mistook him for the bear and shot at him. Vir Kumar rolled on the ground giving out the last roar of his life.

My father, who had been camping nearby, had rushed to the spot on hearing of the mishap. Years later, I overheard him telling one of his friends, 'I can never forget the bewilderment, the utter helplessness and anguish in Vir Kumar's eyes when he realized who his killer was!'

Chogan Baba told me, 'I was watching both Vir Kumar and Bhiloo. I saw how a dozen or so of those imps were busy with Bhiloo. It is they who made Bhiloo act in that way.'

'To what gain? Poor Bhiloo fled the land and nobody knows where he went!'

'What do the imps care for your calculation of gain and loss?' Chogan Baba had replied. He had several other tales to tell. Listening to him, one would get the impression that the forest we saw with its birds, beasts and reptiles was only the visible dimension of a reality that was far richer in its invisible dimensions. There was at least one more forest involved in the physical one—a forest inhabited by spooks, sprites and fairies. Chogan Baba seemed to walk along the thin line that divided both, passing into either one at will.

I would enjoy Chogan Baba's stories but dismiss them once we were out of each other's sight. In his presence, you had to accept whatever he narrated as fact; such was the credibility he imparted to his stories. His gait, his look and his voice were an audacious contradiction of all that we knew to be common sense and rational.

Now, for the first time, I thought over Chogan Baba's experiences seriously. Had Heera been suddenly possessed by those playful spooks? I had never seen any supernatural beings. My father claimed to have seen ghosts on two or three occasions.

He used to say, 'There was a time when supernatural beings mingled freely with men. But that was long ago. As man's rational faculty developed—and that was necessary—his faculty that had been open to the supernatural world became dull and then almost dead. He could not see or communicate with those beings any longer. But there were always some people in whom the faculty remained active. Others could even open up that faculty if they followed a certain discipline.'

Were Chogan Baba alive, I would have perhaps sought his help to solve my puzzle.

A little before sunset, I could see Sharmaji approaching my villa. His steps were hesitant. The prospect of having to talk to him depressed me. But I was soon relieved of my anxiety. Instead of heading straight into my bed-cum-study room, as was his wont, he asked Subbu if he could see me. Subbu turned him away with the excuse that I was tired and still asleep.

I was looking forward to the night. I hoped to fall asleep when it would be dark, quiet and cool. And sleep, I hoped, would end my torment.

I relaxed in an easy chair looking at the forest. Birds flew from different directions into the verdant treetops. I could see some of them settling down and watched their activities till dusk slowly erased them from sight.

Night came at a leisurely pace.

I sat gazing at the sky till I had counted three shooting stars. Then, after eating dinner absent-mindedly, I retired to bed, but sleep evaded me even when the whole valley had fallen into a moon-charmed stupor.

I climbed to the roof as if in a bid to climb out of the day's memory. Pacing up and down under a tender moon was surely preferable to tossing in bed.

The castle that looked like a congealed mass of darkness, containing in it a hapless Raja, an enigmatic lady and a sick girl, seemed to be meditating over the enchanted valley and exchanging some occult vibrations with the deserted temple behind it. Should the tiger be on the prowl now, probably there would not be even a dog alert enough to bark at it.

But someone was on the move. A man in black was pacing

along the road. I was intrigued, for the ambler could have no destination other than my house which lay where the road terminated. And when I recognized him, more by his gait than by his contours which were still indistinct, I was surprised.

I hurried down and opened the gate.

'Raja Sahib! And at this unearthly hour!' I fumbled while opening the gate and greeting him.

'I'm a kind of sleepwalker, you know!'

He handed over his gun to me so that he could shut the gate behind him. He followed me, practically ordering me into my house through gestures.

'I'm glad that I am not guilty of disturbing your sleep. Evidently you were wide awake,' he commented, patting me on the back.

I ushered the Raja into my drawing room. Subbu peeped in, his eyes bulging with disbelief. I asked the Raja if he would like to have some coffee or tea. 'No, thank you,' he said, but his thoughts were evidently elsewhere. I signalled Subbu to keep off.

The Raja's gaze lingered on the moonlit valley outside. Five minutes passed in silence. He straightened up on the sofa and smiled at me.

'This is the very first time in my life that I have had to apologize to anybody,' he said.

I had begun to anticipate his statement and the response, demanded by the occasion, was on my lips: 'Well, Raja Sahib, it was not your fault . . . ' But I stammered and stopped and said in a subdued but firm voice, 'Indeed, what happened was most unexpected. I am yet to get over the shock.'

'I can imagine that. I regret the incident,' he said. His voice was intensely sincere and I felt sure I had no need to be formal with him. All my anguish vanished in the silence that followed. He glanced at me and I knew that he had correctly sensed my changing mood.

'There is a reasonably bright moon over the valley. How about a walk?' he asked in the process of standing up with his gun for support.

He expected obedience. 'Why not?' I said and he looked happy.

While he stepped out into the open, I hurriedly went into my room to change my clothes and to get my gun. I joined him outside the gate in five minutes.

There was a certain majesty in the Raja's way of walking, a style suggesting that a full entourage trailed him. It was I who plodded along like a sleepwalker behind him, uncertain of the purpose as well as the destination of our excursion.

To our right was a gentle slope with a small pool of water at its base. Some tiny creature splashed into it, shattering the moon's reflection into a thousand pieces. The Raja stopped and gazed at the golden ripples that made circles on the water. 'We could spend hours gazing at such tiny marvels—a leaf, a bud or a butterfly, only if we had a mind unencumbered by agonies of hours past and fears of hours ahead. Don't you think memories and anticipations are the two most deadly enemies of our living fully in the present?' he asked haltingly and resumed walking. I was unprepared for philosophy at that hour; nevertheless his reflections had their impact on me. I woke up to the quiet wonders around me.

We were near the castle. The Raja took a narrow diversion to the right and approached the building from the rear. A beam of pale light coming from a half-open window was mildly coloured by the feeble mist outside. I could also hear a murmur, as tender as the light and the mist.

'I did not tell you about Balika, my daughter, or did I?' the Raja asked looking over his shoulder.

'I have heard that the princess is unwell.'

The Raja pushed open the postern. Perhaps he had left through them and they had remained unbolted. Standing on the threshold, he signed me to follow him.

The spacious corridor leading to several rooms was dark. The Raja stopped in front of a room with a blue curtain at its entrance. The meagre light filtering through the screen revealed a woman lying on the floor outside the room. She was obviously asleep.

The faint murmur continued. The Raja peeped through the curtain. The murmur stopped and I heard a voice, soft and sweet, each word vibrating like the notes of a *jal-tarang*.

'Where were you, Papa? I was so terrified! There are tigers and wolves all around this house, aren't there?' asked the girl reclining on the cosy bed, her childlike voice betraying an amazing degree of credulousness. A thick green shade guarded her face from the glare of the kerosene lantern. To me, she looked more like a distant mirage than a real form.

The Raja turned towards me and asked me to come in. I left my gun at the entrance and entered the room.

I was greeted by the fragrance of jasmine flowers arranged on the table and by Balika's gesture in sitting up on her old bedstead, panelled with crafted ivory. She was wrapped in a shawl up to her chin. Later I found out that she was eighteen, but her tender face with the curly locks straying over her temple could have been mistaken for an eight-year-old's.

The Raja showed me to a sofa, sat down near Balika, and began to stroke her head.

'How are you, child?' queried he, removing the shade from the lamp-stand to have a clearer look at his daughter's face. Balika looked me over quickly. In my memory flashed the eyes of my dying doe.

'A doctor?' she demanded of her father in a whisper.

'Oh no, he is Dev, the son of an old friend of mine. He is a brave, nice boy and he accompanied us into the forest in search of a tiger that had become a maneater. Hasn't aunty told you about it?'

Balika gave me another lightning look instead of answering her father.

'Can he kill a tiger barehanded as aunty does? He has no weapon!' she asked, lowering her voice further.

'He has a weapon, child, but why should he bring it into your room?' said the Raja, but he did not contradict the awesome aunty's incredible prowess.

'Papa, are we going elsewhere? This place is populated by a million tigers and vampires, isn't that so? But I like this house and the lake. I have never seen so many trees and so many birds anywhere. At noon today, two birds were perched on the lemon tree right outside the window. I presume they were asking me whether or not I had seen the forest, whether or not

I could swim in the lake, and whether or not I would like to fly with them. I could not say anything because I did not know how to talk to them. They repeated their questions and eventually flew away.'

'Why didn't you talk to them in your language as they did in theirs? They would have understood you as much as you understood them! But, Princess, don't the sweet birds prove that this place is not full of only tigers and vampires, after all? There are friendly creatures too!' I said and felt surprised at myself, for I had never spoken so many words in the Raja's presence, nor was I in the habit of speaking freely to strangers. Perhaps an irrepressible curiosity about Balika and an eagerness to gain some access into her world made me do so. And I was thrilled to be able to address someone as Princess—the name of my dead doe.

Balika blushed and stared at me with amazement, but the Raja looked pleased. 'What Dev says is so true! You must eat well and get well so that you can respond to the call of the birds,' said the Raja smiling. 'They are so concerned about you!'

'I'm glad the deer aunty bagged for me was devoured by a vampire. I swallow whatever she gives me because she loves me so much. But I hate to eat that stuff. Must I eat at all, Papa?'

'You must, child, for you can't live without eating.'

'Must I live, Papa?'

'You must, child, for we love you so much!'

I did not know that it was possible to hear a fairy tale dialogue in real life. I sat amused and charmed.

The woman who lay outside Balika's room had woken up, and standing on the other side of the curtain, peeped in.

'Come in,' the Raja called her. 'Be with Balika. We will take a stroll outside, keeping tigers and vampires at bay.'

Balika, obviously unwilling to let her father go, held on to his hand but perhaps felt shy to articulate her demand in my presence.

The Raja gently got his hand free. As I stepped out of the room, the Raja leaned towards the woman and told her in a whisper, 'Surely you know what is not to be reported to Heera!' She nodded.

We picked up our guns and I followed the Raja through the dark corridor.

'Devu!' a soft voice called out from behind. I was taken aback. Since the death of my parents there was no one to call me by this affectionate variation of my name. The voice sounded as familiar to me as my own, though I could not recall the person behind it instantly. But the sound bored its way fast and deep into my memory, and before long, a loving face surged up to the surface.

'Vimla Aunty?' I exclaimed, delighted and excited.

It was indeed my childhood nurse. She had left us on an impulse, after a misunderstanding with my mother on some petty issue. But once habituated to a feudal household a maid never felt comfortable in any other atmosphere. She would look for a similar haven. Vimla had landed in the Samargarh Raj family.

My old nurse hugged me and I felt a warm tear on my cheek.

Seven

An official from the newly formed Department of Tourism of the state government came rushing to Horizon to inform me of the impending arrival of five European visitors. I had hardly got ready to receive them when they descended on me, all smiles, enchanted with the valley, and totally unmindful of all inconveniences. They were ardent lovers of the wonder that was India and, after enjoying the Taj Mahal and Ajanta, Ellora and Elephanta, were longing for a few quiet days in solitude. One of them had read a brief reference to Nijanpur in an article by the Englishman who had spent a week at Horizon and had written a glowing account of it. For me, the article had made both exciting and amusing reading. Among other things, it said, '. . . my room, in the sole guest house of the place, overlooked the valley. I passed practically a whole moonlit night awake, marvelling at the surprisingly quiet yet vivacious nature. I fancied that the valley in fact was a chunk from the moon and it communicated with the moon, secretly, at certain phantom hours. The time I spent there was the most magical in my life. I spoke little, did little and even thought little, just like my mysterious young "innkeeper", a young man who at times appeared totally out of place there and at other times like the spirit-incarnate of the place . . .'

After some more intriguing, if kind, words on me interspersed with sweet nostalgia, he concluded his piece with this observation: 'It is not without a sense of guilt that I report this, for my write-up may result in people frequenting the place. Nijanpur will no longer be the same then. But write I must, for my farewell tribute to India will be incomplete without this reference to my finest hours. And I have a comfort. Some publicity to the almost hidden valley may bring a bit of business to my "innkeeper". But wait a little. Will it really do that? I had to force the "innkeeper's" dues into his hands!"'

There was no way the innkeeper could convey his gratitude to the writer who had left no address behind.

Horizon had never received so many guests at one time. I kept very busy arranging their lodging, and meeting their varied, though modest, needs, and answering their hundred-odd queries. My nocturnal visit to the castle—that bewildered and bewildering face in the dim light and the sudden meeting with Vimla—played in my memory like an irresistible, though distant, tune but I found no time to call on the Raja.

'Is it true, Babu, that the sahibs will come back to our country?' Subbu asked me when, on the day after the arrival of the tourists, I was having a relaxed dinner late at night.

'What makes you think so?' I asked, almost sure that he had taken the coming of these white men as the signal for a second conquest of the country by the British.

'They say there will be elections!'

'So what?'

'Why are elections necessary since the sahibs were gone and the Gandhiwallahs had taken over, if not to bring the sahibs back? This is the question our mali asks, not I.'

'Henceforth there will be elections every five years, but always with the natives in the fray, not the sahibs.'

'I understand, babu. However, sahibs or no sahibs, the Raja is surely getting his throne back,' Subbu said confidently. 'Who doesn't know that!' added the cook from the kitchen.

I found out what they had gathered—that the Raja was going to contest the elections from the parliamentary constituency covering the erstwhile state of Samargarh. They were disappointed to learn from me that the Raja recovering his throne, even if elected, was out of the question.

The constituency, till then, was represented by Mansingh. He had been the leader of the local people in their fight for freedom, which was also directed against the Samargarh Raj, for the feudal houses were regarded as the pillars of British empire. An inspiring speaker, organizer and a man of integrity, to a certain degree he had replaced the Raja in the popular imagination.

But with the sudden appearance of the Raja on the scene, nobody could predict the outcome of the poll. The common villagers, particularly the tribals who accounted for half of the votes in the constituency, were hard put to accept the reality that the rule of the rajas had ended for good—a proposition as absurd to them as an assertion that there would be no more fairies or spirits. They were prepared to forget a hundred tyrannies perpetrated by the feudatory system for the sake of the Raja's symbolic worth for them.

'Strange are the days when the son of a mere farmer like Mansingh could topple a Raja, and still more strange are the times when instead of growing old some people grow young,' observed my cook in a mysterious vein.

Unlike Subbu, he was a man of few words and hence demanded greater attention.

'Who is growing young?' I asked, a bit intrigued.

What he and Subbu told me, eager to share their amusement with me, was disturbing. Sharmaji, apparently, was changing incredibly fast. He had abandoned the dhoti and kurta, the kind of clothes to which he had been accustomed all his life, and taken to trousers and short-sleeved shirts, readymade sets which he had bought at Samargarh.

'Who would dare to think that Sharmaji—but now we should call him Sharma Sahib—was nearing fifty? He is as jolly and juvenile as a chicken experiencing the first sprouting of wings,' said Subbu, ostensibly addressing the cook, but really for my benefit.

Our rare guests were prepared to leave on the morning of the fourth day of their sojourn at Nijanpur. They had spent their time enjoyably, trekking up the hill behind Horizon and bathing in the hot springs. I had tried to do my bit as a guide for them, but for the most part they were on their own. Their only regret was they could not explore the forest. We had barred them from doing so and they had appreciated the reasons. Fascinating though it would have been to see the tiger at large, they had not come equipped for the adventure.

One of them was filming the landscape, standing on the porch of Horizon. I watched him silently, thinking to myself that it was probably a significant moment in the history of Nijanpur— its hills and forests being captured by a movie camera for the first time.

'And now a grand finale to the sequence,' mumbled the photographer, focusing on a bullock cart that halted in front of Horizon. And I wonder if a bullock cart had ever had the kind of passenger who alighted from it—a gentleman in an elegant, if dusty, suit, cropped hair and a moustache eminently forking out like two live sparks from the embers of a fire (if you could imagine a dark fire).

The youthful and sprightly Major Havelock was elated at meeting so many Europeans. He introduced himself to each one of them separately and, had they time to spare, would have liked to inform each one individually of the ailment he had developed in his heart, and how he had learnt about Nijanpur and decided to come here to spend a restful month or two.

'I feel as if I have just begun to grow a new heart,' he exclaimed, placing his hand on his chest, after I had assured him of reasonably comfortable accommodation.

The bullock cart created a fresh bout of excitement among the departing guests. There was no question of their travelling all the way to Samargarh by that vehicle, but they decided to board it for a mile or two, their van trailing it.

As they waved goodbye to my staff and me and the bullocks sped down the slope, Major Havelock clapped his hands.

I heard someone else too clapping his hands. Most unexpectedly, it was Sharmaji.

'What a metamorphosis!' I said reluctantly, for not to say

something in recognition of the radical changes in his person would be unnatural. Sharmaji was not only in trousers, but also in shoes and socks. He had also subjected his meagre hair to a modernistic cut; even more horrifying, he was growing a thin moustache.

I was a little more courteous than warranted to make good Subbu's discourtesy towards him on his earlier visit. As usual, I was going to fold my hands to greet him when he promptly shook hands with me. And no sooner had he entered my room than he reached out for the tin of cigarettes on my table.

'I've taken to smoking,' he declared without the least hesitation. 'Heera herself offers me cigarettes. Could I refuse?'

He spoke between a puff and a smile, looking at me with a newly acquired confidence which, it was obvious, would brook no argument against his explanation.

He was eager to narrate his adventures with Heera— adventures in ancient literature. Sharmaji was required to read the works of Kalidasa and explain them to Heera, passage by passage. Heera could find time to sit with him only in the evening, but Sharmaji did not fail to present himself at the castle once in the morning as well, in case his worthy student suddenly needed a couplet to be annotated or a simile to be elucidated. 'Should her progress come to a pause for even a momentary lack of guidance?' he asked me and smiled benignly upon realizing that the question was too ticklish for me to answer.

The conversation was hardly of interest to me and I became absent-minded. I opened my window wide and spent the time Sharmaji took to finish his cigarette staring at the sky. But that did not dampen his enthusiasm. He lowered his voice when he disclosed to me how embarrassed he felt when obliged to explain a few erotic passages in a classic and how Heera solved the problem for him by simply calling it a day!

'How sensible of her,' I commented mechanically.

'Shy and sensible. That's what she is. But I was preparing myself to compare her to the beautiful nymph who was the cause of the poet's ecstasy in the classic. I shall wait for another occasion to do so.' Sharmaji radiated optimism.

'There are matters in which shedding embarrassment pays,'

the indefatigable teacher in him told me. His effusiveness was checked only when his cigarette burnt down to its end, the glow touching his fingers. He flung it on the floor and smartly crushed it under his heel.

'Dev!' he said, bringing a degree of mellowness into his voice. 'Have I ever asked you for any favour?'

'No, I don't think you have,' I lied. He had asked me for numerous things, big and small, now and then, and had got them without fail.

'Right,' he patted me on my thigh. 'But, Dev, now I'm going to ask you for such a prized possession of yours, I'm afraid, you'll be hard put to grant. That is why I'd like you to first promise that you wouldn't refuse.' My look of surprise made him anxious. 'Come on, Dev, let me see in you the benevolence for which your ancestors are remembered.'

He fidgeted with the matchbox nervously.

'I don't understand you, Sharmaji, what do you want?'

He looked pained at my dry response. He stammered for a few seconds and then burst out, 'I want her. Won't you sacrifice her to me?'

'Her?' I was perfectly bewildered. 'I don't understand you at all!'

'I mean that portrait of hers, so dear to you! You will not deny it to me, or will you?' He took my reluctant hands into his.

'Do you mean the portrait of Heera you probably noticed the other day in this room?'

'Yes, yes, yes, my dear. What else!'

'Were it in a good condition I would have sent it to the castle. Take it away by all means. Right now if you wish!'

'Right now?'

Sharmaji's thrill and gratification were nauseously emphasized all over his face—the new face with a blooming moustache.

I asked Subbu to fetch the portrait from the lumber room. Obviously Sharmaji did not expect to win the bonanza so easily. In his excitement and his anxiety to please me, he said, 'Do you know? Heera felt quite bad over that incident. I was clever enough to understand that she even wanted me to convey her regrets to you. But I assured her that it was not at all necessary for her to feel guilty about it, for in the epic Ramayana, even Sita had coveted a deer!' Sharmaji laughed.

I was stunned. I was not much of a reader of epics or classics, but Sharmaji comparing Sita's fascination for the golden deer and her request to Rama to try and catch it with Heera's snatching away someone's gun and shooting down a domestic pet maddened me.

But Subbu reappeared with Heera's portrait before I had voiced my disgust—if I could have voiced it at all. I asked the boy to carry the thing to Sharmaji's house.

'No, no,' exclaimed Sharmaji. 'Don't deprive me of the opportunity to carry it myself!'

He waved Subbu out of the room and brought his face closer to my ear. 'My wife died before I could have her photographed. Let me at least have the portrait of the lady who-ah-ah-how to say it!'

'Who adores you?'

'Pass mark! You're quite close to being correct. But "she adores me" does not reveal the state of affairs exactly. It should be—ah—ah—how to say it . . .!'

'She loves you?' I made bold to ask.

'Correct!' He patted me again, more lustily, and blushed.

I felt the warm blood within my veins grown hot with anger a minute ago now turn chill. Also I hated his speaking so close to me, for his tobacco-filled mouth smelled obnoxious and that in spite of my being a smoker.

'Do you really believe that Heera loves you?' I asked matter-of-factly.

Sharmaji did not answer. Instead, he laughed soundlessly, meaningful glints in his eyes suggesting that there were more things in heaven and earth than could be dreamt of by me.

'You are intelligent, aren't you?' he observed seriously. 'You can draw your own conclusions from a sample incident. Heera was engaged to a princely young man. But all of a sudden he died. That was years ago. Till today, she had fondly preserved a set of clothes made for him—her prospective bridegroom. Now, now . . .' Sharmaji's eyebrows danced a couple of times,

'Would you believe? The trousers and the shirt she offered me the other day were from the same suit! Dev! What do you make of this gesture of hers?'

Sharmaji laughed loudly and then set forth the conclusion himself: 'Did you catch the symbolism in her action? In a most imaginative way, a way that could have been devised by her ingenious brain alone, she quietly made me slip into the position vacated by the late lamented young man—her would-be bridegroom!'

Sharmaji's radiant glance dared me to contradict him. He stooped, lifted the picture reverently and, holding it under his right arm, marched out of my room triumphantly.

Absent-mindedly, I picked up a cigarette and lit it. But the very first puff repulsed me. I tossed it away. That was the end of my smoking.

A gory dream woke me up at midnight. Sharmaji figured in it prominently. I saw his newly cultivated moustache change into a monstrous leech. It throbbed and grew fatter and fatter. I knew that what it was sucking out of Sharmaji was infinitely more precious than blood.

Eight

I was surprised to see Sahoo's dusty jeep speeding up the serpentine road to Horizon. I was even more surprised when Sahoo, all smiles, got off his vehicle and declared, 'I told myself, it was high time I paid Devji a courtesy call.'

And the legendary tightwad's driver brought out half-a-dozen pineapples and handed them over to Subbu.

'This is from my own kitchen garden, grown under my own care. Look how plump they are, apart from being juicy and sweet as nectar. They are fit for King Vikramaditya's plate,' he said, wiping his face with the dusty end of his dhoti.

'You should have sent a few to the Raja,' I said.

'I have, Devji, I have. Then, I decided to give some to the junior Raja,' he laughed. 'Devji, the old rajas are gone, but there can be no rajya without the raja. How do you think the new rajas are going to be chosen, and when?' he asked me as he walked about, taking a round of my house. It did not appear a casual query, for he repeated his epigram, there can be no rajya without the raja, and expected me to respond. I did not know why a purely academic question like this should bother him. Maybe the sudden appearance of the Raja had stimulated many novel thoughts in the minds of the people around him.

'Sahooji, surely you know that there is no question of a set of new rajas coming into being. The British Raj as well as the princely raj are abolished forever.'

'I know and I don't know, to confess to you. The rajas are still there—aren't they?—though without any power, like our Raja of Samargarh!'

'Only in their titles. And, I'm sure, the titles will soon begin to sound so hollow that the rajas themselves would be anxious to get rid of them.'

'But I knew at least two rajas who had no rajyas. They were, in fact, merchants like me, only more prosperous.'

'Right. The British used to honour their favourites with titles of different grades: Rao Sahib, Rao Bahadur, Raja Sahib, Raja Bahadur, Khan Sahib, Khan Bahadur, Companion of Indian Empire, Knight Companion of Indian Empire, Grand Companion of Indian Empire, so on and so forth.'

Sahoo's confusion over the differences between the rajas who were ruling princes and those who were honorary rajas was over, as I understood from his ready nods. He was thoughtful for a moment and then asked, 'But how does one obtain such a title?'

'No longer can one do that, Sahooji, for the British who bestowed them on those who proved their worth through philanthropy or sheer show of love for the King Emperor, are gone, as you know. The Indian government does not give such titles.'

'Why don't they?'

I laughed. 'Why worry over that, Sahooji? Even if not a raja, you can surely become a mantri! All you have to do is get elected to the legislature! You have money and you enjoy a wide reputation as a . . .'

'True, babu, true, but a raja is a raja!' he sighed. I felt immensely relieved that he did not let me complete my sentence, for absent-mindedly, I was perhaps going to name his reputation.

'Devji, one of the reasons for my calling on you is, the Raja wants to see you.'

'Any particular reason?'

I believe he plans to go on a longer hunting expedition. The tiger you were looking for the other day has turned into a regular maneater and has become a bigger menace.'

On my way to the castle with Sahoo, I heard that the beast's area of operation had gradually expanded. Its latest victim belonged to a hamlet beyond the valley, five kilometres from Nijanpur as the crow flies, though it was more than ten kilometres by a zigzagging road.

We greeted the Raja. He showed Sahoo to a sofa a little away from his, while signalling me to sit closer to him. But Sahoo confidently occupied the place offered to me.

Sharmaji popped up at the door the very next minute, ushering Havelock into the Raja's presence. I knew that misery made strange bedfellows, but it was beyond me how Sharmaji could become so chummy with the Major.

The former army officer was conspicuously excited over his meeting with the Raja who, I realized from their conversation, had done a stint in the army as was the tradition or fashion with the princes. Havelock nodded smartly and approvingly at every syllable the Raja uttered. 'What a pity,' mused the Raja, 'that we should have a Major amidst us and yet we must go. hunting without the benefit of his leadership!'

'What a pity, what a pity,' echoed Major Havelock himself and then, on second thoughts—or perhaps his first—said, 'Why, sir? I'm not disabled! I can surely accompany you! I can still crush a few enemy battalions!'

'All we need is to kill one beast and for that we ought not to bother you. Please relax. Sharma's company should be a tonic for you.'

Sharmaji grew pale. His face showed the emotions of a little boy whose parents had threatened to leave him out of a proposed picnic. 'But, sir,' he stuttered, 'I can give Major Havelock company even while he is with you in your party. What I mean is, I can also be a member of the party.'

'No, Sharma, you need not, for heaven's sake!' said the Raja and burst into a hearty laugh—a rare exercise on his part.

In my imagination, his laughter was translated into this crude statement: 'Look here, Sharma, the tiger has to first survive your shriek to be shot down by us!'

Havelock joined in the Raja's laughter without realizing its significance and exceeded him in volume.

Sahoo was fast growing interested in affairs that were not his business. He and Rao were both busy drawing up the Raja's itinerary. Obviously they were to be included in the expedition—Sahoo because of his jeep which he had placed at the Raja's disposal and Rao by virtue of his possessing a gun.

I received a detailed account of the maneater's activities from the Raja. Going after it, meanwhile, the Raja had killed a panther and a common tiger, but the rogue still remained at large. The Raja was now making a comprehensive plan to finish it off. He was preparing to spend three or four days in the forest or close by it, beginning with Dinpur, the tiger's latest haunt.

In fact, 'I intend killing two tigers with one shot,' he said in a matter-of-fact tone. 'One is the maneater; the other is—I must say he too is a tiger of sorts—Mansingh.'

I was under the impression that the Raja wanted me to join the expedition. That he did not raise the question at all intrigued me. But as the assembly was dispersing, he looked at me.

'You seem tired. I can understand. You had a number of guests. Now that they are gone, you ought to relax,' he said. I felt relieved though I had started mentally preparing myself for the expedition.

The Raja shook hands with Major Havelock and wished him a speedy recovery.

'Take care of the Major,' he told Sharmaji who had stopped talking. I was leaving the castle along with the others, still wondering why I had been summoned, when the Raja asked me to wait.

'Heera desires to talk to you,' the Raja informed me almost apologetically and went in, obviously to call her, without waiting to ascertain whether I was in a mood to see her or not. I was obliged to sit down, annoyed and not without some trepidation.

Fifteen minutes must have passed before she emerged from the corridor. For a moment she stopped at the dusky doorway, smiling. Sharmaji had once compared her to a fresh morning rose, but without thorns. I realized how appropriate the first part of his comparison was and suspected the presence of something far more galling than thorns—a scorpion or two lying in ambush behind the petals—the moment I looked into her eyes.

She resumed walking with a jerk and went over to the sofa facing me.

'I am ashamed of my conduct, Dev! I didn't know that the deer was yours.'

She spoke contritely, but her words were as irresistible as a magical incantation.

'We should forget it,' I mumbled.

'Should we?' she said unexpectedly. 'But why? Shouldn't there always be something between two persons for a dialogue or even for a momentary wrangle?'

I pretended to appreciate her philosophy through an uneasy smile. Two strangers came to my rescue. A grandfather clock had been set into motion after years and they were installing it in a corner of the hall, behind me. Heera scowled at their intrusion, but after a minute straightened up, smiled to hide her irritation and said, 'Why does it happen so often that one is suddenly reminded of time when one would love to forget it?'

Some jackals howled behind the castle announcing sunset.

'I propose to secure a bright and bonny deer for you one of these days, during our travels in the wilderness in search of the maneater. But you must cooperate with me. Honestly, I'm more interested in bagging a deer alive than the man-eater dead. When the Raja is busy mobilizing support for his human pet we can surely slip into the forest at such intervals—can't we?—to recruit a pet for you!' she said with the excitement of a child who had just discovered a new avenue of merry-making and was anxious to share it with his playmate.

'But I'm not joining the expedition.' I sounded dull.

'No? But why not?' The tone her voice suddenly assumed surprised the men handling the grandfather clock.

'I'm rather unwell,' I said, happy that I was defending the Raja's decision as mine.

'What's the problem with you?' She seemed concerned.

'Nothing serious. I'm tired; had too many guests to deal with.'

'Who's there to take care of you in your . . .' she completed her question after a slight pause, 'Horizon?'

'My servant Subbu, my cook, my mali . . .'

She stood up. I followed suit. She seemed to laugh silently.

'Well, I can do nothing about it, anyway! I hope you really have somebody to look after you!'

She was interrupted by the grandfather clock which chimed after years. The Raja was back in the hall, looking at the clock and beaming.

'I wish you could join us,' Heera said concluding the interview and left the hall abruptly.

It was nearly evening. I bowed to the Raja and stepped out on to the portico.

'We'll meet,' the Raja whispered behind me. I looked back. His smiling face had disappeared from the doors left ajar.

Alone on the lonely road to Horizon, I wondered if the Raja had yet another nocturnal stroll in mind.

'Babu!'

I looked back. The two men who had fixed the grandfather clock were behind me. They introduced themselves. They had come from Samargarh to meet the Raja. Former employees of the royal family, one of them had become a petty contractor and the other the owner of a grocery in the town. They had been at the castle for the last three days doing sundry jobs for the Raja simply out of a sense of duty.

'We are prepared to extend electricity to the castle—at our cost and under our supervision. But Raja sahib is stubbornly resisting the proposal. We don't understand why,' they complained.

I did not understand either. But I told them that I would reiterate their offer to the Raja with my recommendation added to it. Reassured, they bade me goodbye having seen me to my doorstep.

After dinner, I sat near my window flipping through a book

for a while and then losing myself in the hazy landscape. Remaining awake alone, watching a sleepy little valley, had its rewards. I felt myself transported into the mild mist spread over the woods and the invisible hamlets to have become a privileged member of their secret alliance.

It was past midnight when the Raja appeared outside the gate and I hastened to open it. 'Let's take a walk,' he proposed straightaway. I was ready for it, amused that the Raja's conduct did not appear unnatural to me any more. Along the slope that gently meandered towards the castle I suddenly realized how right the Raja was in not agreeing to the proposal for the mansion's electrification. It would be an affront to the mystery of the moonlight and the majestic and innocent darkness that formed a backdrop to the castle. The castle itself, at that moment, looked like a faithful protégé of that mystery.

We were approaching the castle. But the Raja took the narrow diversion along which he had led me earlier. I followed him towards the ancient pool between the castle and the deserted temple.

'So, you are taking a plunge into politics!' I observed and almost immediately felt how alien my question was to the spirit of the hour and the situation.

'You've heard wrong,' he corrected me calmly. 'I cannot plunge into politics or, for that matter, into anything at all! I am just having a little fun—snubbing that proud little fellow—Mansingh. He had been too vociferous against the construction of Heera Mahal for Heera to live it down.' The Raja laughed softly but mischievously, and added, 'I could do very well without the fun. But, well, I believe I have reached a stage when I find little difference between doing and not doing a thing.'

'Mansingh may not dare to oppose you,' I observed.

The Raja looked at me, I suppose, with some curiosity.

'Are you under the impression that I'm planning to be a candidate for the elections?' he asked, and he must have understood that his question surprised me. 'All I'll do is a little canvassing for Ketu Singh. He can claim—and I won't mind the voters thinking—that he is my candidate.'

'Ketu Singh of all!' I could not contain my surprise any

longer. Now I understood what Heera meant by the Raja's human pet.

'Yes, Ketu the goblin, who now loudly bemoans his past opposition to us under Mansingh's instigation, as if he had really ever mattered! Besides, his repentance is fake, but I don't care. The fact is, he has the resilience and vanity of a cat, and Heera's delight lies in humbling the genuine with the help of the fake, if she hates the former. I could stomach the abolition of our rajya quite easily, but not Heera.'

I felt bizarre that Heera's whims and foolish sentiments should be a factor behind the Raja'a action. But the Raja obviously revelled in moderate roguery. If Heera was to be believed, Ketu had been fielded by the Raja himself.

We reached the emerald patch between the lake and the rear wall of the villa. Before us loomed a brooding silhouette. It was the temple.

'Dev!' The Raja suddenly came to a halt. 'Heera rarely leaves Balika behind her. If she is doing so this time it is because of the prospect of shikar combined with the thrill of wreaking her vengeance on Mansingh. Should Vimla be in need of any help, she can count on you, can't she?'

'I shall be only too happy to render any kind of help she might need and at any time,' I said and sounded like lodging a protest, for it was surely unnecessary for the Raja to remind me of my duty!

'Raja sahib, may I know the nature of Balika's illness?'

'They call it catatonic stupor, but who knows!'

He gave an account of the events leading to her present condition: She used to be the jolly little cherub of an extremely indulgent mother—the Rani. 'What a radiant change the child had brought to my wife's personality! She would forget the world and lose herself in the child; the child would do the same. Sometimes, observing them, I had the sweet feeling that they had become one—like the twilight when you cannot distinguish the day from the night.'

But the Rani took ill suddenly. She had to be removed to the hospital, and she was not to return.

Vimla and the others decided not to reveal the tragedy to

Balika. They kept assuring the child that her mother would soon be back with her.

Meanwhile Heera, unable to get on well with the Rani, had been living separately. One evening Balika was told that her mother was coming home. But the open arms into which she was expected to jump, and in her innocence did jump, were Heera's! The realization shocked Balika. She reacted as if she had been hurled into a fire. Yet the more Balika rejected Heera, the more determined Heera grew in her efforts to make the child accept her.

Did Heera succeed in her endeavour? The Raja evaded the question, or probably did not know the answer. Perhaps Heera really loved the child and she did her best to prove it, but Balika never came out of her depression. She was found to be afraid of hoping for or looking forward to anything and gradually slipped into a state of total melancholia. The world hardly existed for her beyond her room. She had been taught but little; nevertheless, she developed a voracious reading habit and that became a great support to her in her self-imposed solitude.

Since I knew Vimla, I could imagine the care she would take of Balika, and with how much love. The irony was, Heera had succeeded in making not only Balika but also the Raja believe that the girl owed her survival to her love and her love alone!

'Heera is possessive of Balika, no doubt, but she is awfully attached to the girl,' the Raja said. He seemed to be apologizing for Heera's conduct.

We strolled on the stretch between the disintegrating stone lions guarding the temple and the rear wall of the castle.

'Have you ever entered the shrine?' the Raja asked me.

'Only once, when I was very small. I remember nothing except that I felt terribly scared inside.'

'After the last priest's death nobody ever went in. It was infernal inside. I have just got it cleaned.'

'Do you propose to revive the rituals?'

'Then I have to begin with a human sacrifice. There hasn't been one for long. The elements which rejoiced in the ritual must be starving.'

He fell silent. All was quiet under a sickly moon. An otter

leapt into the pool and swam out instantly, perhaps with a catch.

'I love to loiter here at night, all alone. I am often overtaken by an irresistible and weird sense of dejection. At such moments, I have even considered the prospect of sacrificing myself. But I wonder if I'm not as hungry as those phantoms which once thrived on human blood or if the deity is not as dead as myself!' The Raja laughed. The temple and the hill returned the echoes.

'Sorry,' he muttered, forcing himself to stop laughing and as if struggling against his unearthly propensity for exploring the nocturnal solitude. With determined steps, he walked towards the rear door of the castle.

At a soft tap from the Raja, Vimla opened the door.

'Papa, a tiger roared and it sounded like your laughter!' Balika observed with some excitement.

'No, child, it was Papa who laughed and that must have sounded like a tiger's roar.'

'Oh!' She shut her eyes.

Nine

A jarring voice disturbed my afternoon nap. Someone was trying to impress upon Subbu that the nation's future depended on his waking me up at once.

I came out and found Subbu confronted by Ketu Singh who was glistening in the bright sunlight like a snake that had just shed its old skin.

If Subbu was puzzled, I was definitely surprised. Ketu almost pounced upon me in his bid to embrace me, passing on to me much of the sweat and dust he carried all over his person. He then took both my hands in his and stared into my eyes, keeping up his wide smile long enough for me to feel obliged to grin.

'Devji, it's the call of the motherland. Please respond and I guarantee that you'll be back here before nightfall,' he said, beginning to push me towards his jeep.

'I don't understand,' I said helplessly. 'Where do you want me to go?'

'Didn't I say it is the call of the motherland? Who are we to disregard it? Hurry up, sir. Raja sahib is waiting for you.'

'Where?'

'At Dinpur, of course!'

Ketu was talking and behaving like one possessed. But since I knew that the Raja was at Dinpur, I decided to give him the benefit of the doubt on the factual part of his statement. I got ready as quickly as I could and climbed into his jeep. Ketu's joy found a noisy expression in his addressing his driver in a vulgar, if endearing, way and ordering him to drive carefully. 'We are carrying a life as sacred as a jarful of Ganga water!' he cautioned the driver, giving him a pat on his back and drawing his attention to me. Then he began digging into the complex roots of an unmanageably large family tree and claimed kinship with me, mystifying me in the process.

'When some ignorant chaps ask me whether I enjoy your support or not, I shoot back at them, "Who but but this bastard Ketu has any claim on Devji's love?" My blunt answer shocks them into silence. I'm forthright and honest, am I not, Devji?'

'As if my support matters!' I tried to avoid answering his question.

'It matters as much as a priest at a wedding, Devji! Don't our people know that you are the scion of a great dynasty, though you lost its kingdom generations ago? Isn't your mud house in the village still called a palace? Let the people know that you're with me, and that'll be a heavenly boon to me,' Ketu said, mercilessly squeezing my hand. 'The truth is the truth. It must be announced at any cost.'

'What truth are you speaking of?'

'The truth, the undeniable truth that you support me!'

'But don't you think that Mansingh has all along been an honest worker and a trusted leader and he has done nothing to forfeit our support?'

'Look here, Devji,' Ketu's voice became grave. 'The question is not of personalities, but of principles. I stand for justice, honesty, integrity, equality and a lot of such other really good things, all printed and distributed for everybody to know. I will leave a hundred copies with you. Our country is passing through a grave crisis. How much can Mansingh's corrupt party do to tide us over it? Nothing, I say, nothing. It is only humble, selfless, very very good, nice, honest, and what d'you say incorruptible persons like me—I mean servants of the masses like me, who neither fear nor flatter—who can usher in a bright new era. Please, please, you kind and compassionate sir, my true brother, my well-wisher, my master, you must have pity on me, you must help me! I'm your servant, your slave, your serf. Who can appreciate a man of principle like me if not you? I'm willing to wipe the dust from your feet!'

We bumped down the rocky road, occasionally raising clouds of red dust. Ketu's voice rose higher and higher.

Groups of men and women were emerging from the forests flanking the road and were heading towards Dinpur. Most of them were tribals who lived in small hamlets scattered amidst the hills and woods. Many were in their best attire with leaves or feathers stuck in their one-band turbans. It was surprising how Ketu had managed to spread word of the meeting so fast. Although a jeep or a car was no longer a rarity for them, the young tribals greeted the vehicle with shouts of joy, and Ketu, all smiles, never failed to wave at them.

We were at Dinpur in half an hour. Even though the small village had lost two of its inhabitants to the tiger during the past week, it wore a festive look. We drove to the venue of the meeting, a grove of huge banyan trees. An impressive bamboo platform had been erected and was covered by a colourful canopy. Ketu, no doubt, had enterprising and resourceful lieutenants.

Raja sahib relaxed in a chair on the platform, hardly mindful of the multitudes approaching him in fearful silence and prostrating themselves before him. Some, too shy to come closer, bowed to him from a distance—sometimes as far as half a furlong away. They had trekked miles to have a glimpse of their Raja. Among them were naïve ones—the village chief who received me with great enthusiasm informed me—who believed that the Raja's return to his state did not mean anything less than the restoration of his throne to him.

The crowd kept gazing at the Raja reverentially. Hundreds of non-tribal women, their faces veiled, blew conch shells from time to time.

Behind the Raja sat Heera. It was difficult for me to gauge her reaction to the situation—whether she enjoyed it or felt uncomfortable. I had, however, no doubt that she was gloating over Mansingh's inevitable discomfiture.

She smiled and the Raja nodded to me, inviting me occupy the vacant chair beside him. I wished to ask him if it was he who summoned me or it was all Ketu's scheming.

But such a petty question, I was afraid, would not go well with the solemnity of the situation.

The headmen of the different villages—to be accurate, those who were headmen during the Raja's time and, though stripped of all authority, continued to be regarded by the villagers as their leaders—gathered in a cluster below the platform. Their hands folded, they were waiting for the Raja's message. The Raja's instructions were clear and precise. They were required to ensure Ketu's victory.

The strength of the audience had swelled to no less than five thousand when Ketu rose to address it. To my surprise and resentment, he proposed my name as the president of the meeting. Sahoo, in his maiden speech, stammered out a well-rehearsed sentence by way of seconding the proposal. He wished to add something extempore. But the words got stuck in his throat. He groaned and, perhaps to relieve him of his predicament, the Raja clapped his hands. Thousands of hands followed suit instantly. Amidst this, the little daughter of the headman of Dinpur put a garland of camphor beads round my neck.

The Raja was not likely to remember that I, because of the people's nostalgic regard for my ancestors, could count in Ketu's campaign for votes. The idea to impress upon the people my support for him must have been Ketu's, but in summoning me suddenly and making me preside over the meeting Ketu could not have acted entirely on his own. I viewed the treatment accorded me as yet another whim of the Raja's and decided to bear with it without a murmur.

The light from the setting sun glowed through the foliage and focused on Ketu's face, imparting a kind of aura to him. He demonstrated his knowledge of the world by making references to Britain, Russia and America, and mysteriously linking many global problems to Mansingh's failings.

Heera sat looking through her binoculars, perhaps at some ravens who were silently observing the human drama below. The Raja's eyes remained shut. I watched the audience. Most of them kept gazing at the Raja and hardly any of those who paid attention to Ketu seemed to understand him; they just enjoyed.

The Raja suddenly opened his eyes and smiled at me. 'Bored?' he asked in a whisper and standing up, took a step forward. Ketu stopped in the middle of a sentence. The Raja did not bother to give him a minute more to conclude his speech. He signalled him to sit down. Ketu, of course, kept standing with folded hands behind the chairs.

There was pandemonium, everyone anxious to alert the others about the chance of a lifetime descending on them; but only for a moment. It was followed by total silence.

'My sons and daughters,' the Raja began. I was amused, for there were many in the audience who were older than he.

'I thank you,' he continued, 'for gathering here, coming from far and near.'

The innocent faces of the people who obviously considered themselves lucky to have had a glimpse of the Raja now betrayed perplexity at having to be thanked by him.

'I am told that you would have liked me to contest the elections myself . . .'

'Yes, yes, yes, Maharaja! We will heap on you as many votes as you want, Maharaja!' said a large number of voices in unison. 'If enough votes are not available in Samargarh, we shall fetch them from elsewhere. We are ready to trek the hills and scour the forests and collect them,' said an enthusiastic old man, 'if only you tell us where they are available.'

'You are our Raja. We are fortunate that you are back! We will not let you desert us once again,' shouted a minuscule elderly man who had been lifted up by two stout youths to be seen by all. He mopped his face nervously. People applauded him. It was almost as if he had said aloud the single thing that loomed large in all their minds.

The Raja signalled them to be silent. At once all was quiet.

'I was your raja,' he said, quite unmoved by the overwhelming emotional outburst of the multitude.' Now, must you suffer your raja to become a mere mantri at best?'

The Raja paused for any possible answer from the audience. Those who understood the implication of his question were visibly embarrassed. After almost a minute, some sober voices were heard saying, 'No, Maharaja, no.'

'Good,' the Raja resumed, 'Ketu should suffice. In fact, he is great. How much do you know of America or Russia? But he knows. I say, vote for him!'

The Raja waved his right hand in a gesture of farewell as well as of blessing and returned to his chair. Amidst thunderous applause, someone raised a slogan hailing Ketu Singh. Only a few voices, obviously planted by Ketu in the audience, took it up. As the slogan was repeated, the volume continued to increase.

Crows flew nervously from tree to tree as Ketu stood on the platform, glowing with delight that was heightened by the patch of soft sunlight still focused on his face. He raised his folded palms to touch his forehead everytime the slogan was repeated.

In the advancing twilight, I witnessed the metamorphosis of the petty little Ketu into a fearful bigwig.

'My bothers and sisters, my uncles and aunties, my friends and well-wishers, please remember our noble, honourable, revered, godly Raja sahib's advice and vote for me. Now, my request to you is, disperse before it is dark. I cannot bear losing one of my dear voters to the maneater!' said Ketu Singh.

Needless to say, the meeting ended without any presidential address.

While the crowd began dispersing, albeit reluctantly—some of them bowing to the Raja and walking out backwards as turning their backs to him would be disrespectful—the Raja spoke, as if to himself but loud enough for me to hear, 'I feel sorry for Mansingh. One more meeting in the other part of the constituency and Ketu's victory is assured.'

'I wish people like Ketu were never elected,' I said in weak protest.

'Why? What's wrong with the Ketus? Don't you see how active this one is and how timid too? His timidity will check him from doing more mischief than he can get away with,' said the Raja and he laughed.

I did not laugh. He checked himself and said in a more

serious tone, 'The average man swings between two poles of
possibilities. Any of us can become either an angel's cousin or
the devil's godchild. I have seen even well-publicized angels
shedding their wings and revealing a wee bit of tail. Why can't
our Ketu shed his tail and at least hop, if not fly, with a tiny
pair of wings, newly grown or borrowed?' He paused. 'In any
case, the Ketu Singhs are a temporary phenomenon, symbolizing
a missing link in the nation's political evolution.'

Meanwhile Ketu, all smiles, had come closer to us. 'This
humble boy is ever at your service, sir!' He touched the Raja's
feet.

'Are you? I thought we were at your service!' commented
the Raja with a chuckle.

'No, sir, no. Who is this nincompoop to command your
service? You are at the service of the country, of humanity, of
God . . .'

'Good. At this rate, you are sure to end up in a comfortable
chair of power. But, for the present, be at Dev's service. Arrange
for his return to Nijanpur.'

I was in half a mind to stay back so that I could keep the
Raja company. He planned to sit the night out on a machan in
the hope of getting a shot at the maneater. But he seemed eager
to see me off. I took leave of Heera hurriedly, pretending that I
had not been able to read the strong disapproval in her eyes.

Ketu instructed his workers on their duties during his hour-
long absence and led me to his jeep. He dislodged his driver
and drove the vehicle himself, sticking his head out again and
again and smiling and waving at the crowd that had begun
breaking up into smaller groups. Undoubtedly he was keen to
demonstrate his driving skills before them.

A fog had set in after sundown. Ketu enjoyed honking
frequently and scattering the pedestrians—who also enjoyed
it—to both sides of the road.

'Devji, how much I love these children of Mother Nature!
Now I can serve them with a vengeance. Just help me to win.'
He repeated the sentiment in different words even though I sat
silent.

The jeep had trudged along for a while when he brought it

to a spluttering halt. 'Do you see?' he asked me gleefully. I thought he had spotted a dancing peacock or a lazy bear. I looked out. Old Mansingh was crossing the road with a few of his followers, two of them with lanterns and the others holding sticks. I did not understand why Ketu should find the scene attractive. He jumped out shouting a greeting to Mansingh, but betraying a Satanic grin too.

'Come on, sir, let this humble man have the honour of giving you a lift to your destination,' he said loudly.

'Thanks, Ketu, but we can walk.'

People returning from the meeting stopped and gathered around the two.

'Look here, Mansingh sahib, my dear, my respected Mansingh sahib!' Ketu's voice rose to an uncanny pitch—it had perhaps cracked during his oration—and said, 'Noble souls like you and I can go on fighting on matters of principle and still be personal friends, can't we? Why can't we? Can I bear to see you walk while I ride a vehicle? How can I?'

Ketu was getting more and more excited as he observed the crowd around them swelling. 'What do you say, uncles and aunties, brothers and sisters?' Ketu folded his hands and threw the question to his amused audience. He snatched a lantern and held it high, revealing Mansingh's face as well as his own.

I could read the strain and embarrassment on Mansingh's sensitive face. Obviously he hated Ketu. He glared at Ketu, but Ketu's eyes shifted quickly, unwilling to be caught by his.

'Ketu, apart from the fact that your help is unwarranted, how can I accept your offer and let your brazen-faced hypocrisy triumph? Do you think I am unaware of all the nasty lies you and your roguish disciples are spreading against me?' Mansingh blurted out at last.

I wish he had kept quiet, for his observation inspired Ketu to launch into a harangue: 'Uncles and aunties, brothers and sisters, you be the judges, please! I swear, in Mansinghji I see my own, very own, elder brother. Can I ride my jeep without a guilty conscience, while this senior politician keeps plodding through bushes and boulders? Can I? Isn't that against the very grain of my nature? Tell me, my uncles and . . .'

Mansingh looked pathetic. I resolved to put an end to Ketu's delinquency and got down and elbowed my way into the the throng. 'Mansingh sahib, why do you waste your time? Kindly resume your walk,' I said as I greeted the old man.

Mansingh returned my greeting and, without a word more, started walking. Ketu looked crestfallen. He hardly talked for the rest of the journey.

Ten

An unfamiliar feeling of loneliness began to haunt me with the advent of darkness; unfamiliar, because I was always at home with solitude. I had no particular friends at Nijanpur and since the Raja's descent on the valley, Rao, the only person with whom I felt at ease, had no time to spare for me.

I did not let the feeling remain vague for long. I dug down to its root, which in any case was not very deep, and knew that it emanated from a strong urge to talk to Vimla, to find out if I could be of any help to her or Balika. No sooner had I hit upon the truth than I began to feel that the castle, like a magnet, was drawing me irresistibly towards it. I was there before long.

The revived staff of the castle, rather, the rump of it—the watchman, the cook and two servants—sat on the porch around a lantern playing cards. Behind them, leaning against the door and looking towards the road, stood Vimla. She seemed to be expecting me.

She took hold of me with the intense yearning of a mother for her long-lost son. We sat in the hall. She had so many things to ask me and was so eager to know about my parents' last days that she was in a quandary as to where she should begin. She shed tears, perhaps somewhat repentant about deserting us.

An hour passed. She suddenly remembered that she ought not to have left her ward alone for such a long time. She stood up. 'Let's continue our talk in Balika's room,' she said, pulling me by the arm.

She noticed my hesitation and smiled. 'Why, Dev, wasn't it Raja sahib himself who took you into her room? And how do you fail to understand that he loves you like his son?' After a pause, Vimla added, 'It is of course different with Heera. She would not tolerate even a pussy cat befriending the girl!'

I followed Vimla through a labyrinth of passages, dimly lit by a solitary lantern, towards the other end of the castle. The passage still reeked of birds and bats, and one or two partridges flitted over our heads in a disoriented fashion. It seemed like a journey into an unreal world—into the fairy tale world which Vimla, I remembered, built around me when she used to cradle me in her arms and tell me stories.

I could hear the princess mumbling. Or was she reading aloud from some book? She fell silent as soon as Vimla parted the screen. And as we entered the room, she stared at me with the wonder in her big eyes undiminished.

'Isn't it a pity that a sweet girl like you did not have a brother till today? Here is my son, Dev. I have nursed him as I have nursed you,' said Vimla, sitting down beside Balika. Turning to me, she said, 'Won't you tell her stories? She is so fond of them! You know many stories, don't you?'

'I do.' I sat down facing the two. The shaded kerosene lamp lit only one side of Balika's face. She looked pleased.

'Dev! Is the banyan tree that leaned over the western roof of your house still there?' asked Vimla. 'Do you remember how you loved it? You would always stretch your tiny hands upwards expressing your desire to climb it.'

'I remember. Its spreading branches, the play of light and shade in its foliage, the sudden sound made by a hidden bird— my fascination for all that.'

'How many ghosts are there in that banyan tree?' Balika asked Vimla in a whisper.

'Ghosts?' My tone almost rebuked her mildly. 'None. What I saw in the tree—and beyond it in the clouds gilded by the moon—were innumerable fairies. They would play hide-and-seek and smile at one another. The tree seemed to me to be a world by itself. Yes, a world not limited to its physical form or size, for every branch of the tree was a ladder into a fascinating land. There were moments when clouds came incredibly close to the treetop, and I even faintly remember some dialogue between the tree and the clouds. Once I had dozed off in Vimla Auntie's lap. When I woke up, I saw the moon peeping through the leaves. For a moment I was bewildered. It was so big, so charmingly golden! I could not recognize it. It was then that I

heard the giggle of some fairies. Yes, I have just remembered
something sweet, something beautiful.'

I stopped.

'What's that?' For the first time Balika asked me a question
directly.

'One of them looked like you.'

She was listening to me with wide-eyed wonder. Vimla was
all smiles, though, I suspect, her eyes were moist with tears once
again.

I was surprised, for I had never talked so much at a stretch
to anybody! But I did not feel embarrassed. Perhaps Balika's
obstinate, cloistered existence dared me to bring her out of it!

'Can he show me fairies?' she asked Vimla in a whisper.

'No,' I replied without waiting for Vimla to transmit her
question to me. 'Perhaps I could have if you were near me when
I saw them. But I can still tell you when the hour of the fairies
strikes. It is when the moon and the breeze and the clouds are
together in a special mood that the fairies descend from nowhere.
Did I say I don't see them any longer? I see them, rather feel
them, in flowers and sometimes in stars and sometimes in the
moonlit clouds or on hilltops. To be able to see them as I do, one
must roam about in the open and wait with patience. You must
come out into the sunlight for flowers and into the moonlight
for the fairies.'

'Did you hear that? How can you see fairies unless you leave
your room?' Vimla asked Balika mildly. Balika resolved the
issue by swiftly hiding her face in Vimla's lap.

Never before had I felt so deeply interested in talking to
anybody. But I checked my temptation and asked Vimla, 'Why
is she like this?'

My question seemed to surprise even Vimla for a second.
Perhaps she had got so accustomed to Balika that her condition
had ceased to appear abnormal to her. But, of course, before
long she began to give me an explanation of the phenomenon
as well as an account of the events leading to it.

It was a strange story—a story still in search for a
denouement.

The Raja had hardly begun to take an interest in matters of

the state when his father died. If his ritual coronation was a subdued affair, it was not because of any lack of popular enthusiasm, but because of his own awareness of the changing times. Then, with the state gone, the Raja and Heera left Samargarh in a haste. Unsure of any destination, they moved from hill station to hill station and from one city to another. 'I will marry you to a real Prince Charming,' the old Raja used to tell Heera. The young Raja had probably taken it upon himself to fulfil his father's ambitious promise.

The pity is, Heera found those who came to court her anything but charming, though some of them were members of former ruling families. What was worse, she would humiliate one, the moment she found him foolish or boring.

Vimla felt that Heera was a curse on the Raj family. Misfortune had stalked the dynasty since her arrival. The old Raja died; the rajya was gone; the new Raja, approaching forty, was yet to marry. He would not entertain any proposal for his marriage until Heera had been married.

'I'm not sure about Heera's relationship with the Raja,' I said after some hesitation.

'She is either the Raja's stepsister or no blood relation at all, remote or otherwise,' Vimla said. Then, lowering her voice, though there was no need for it, she added, 'And I can assure you that there is no question of her being the old Raja's daughter.'

'So, the Raja knows that she is not his stepsister. And yet he cares for her so much! Surprising.'

'Rather intriguing,' Vimla corrected without trying to hide her own puzzlement. I had a suspicion that the two loved each other, but would not dare to destroy the myth the old Raja had done his best to perpetuate—that Heera was his daughter!

I suggested my theory through guarded words to steer it clear of Balika's comprehension. But Vimla had no inhibitions. What she said only reinforced her first spontaneous observation— that the relationship between the Raja and Heera was intriguing indeed. The Raja was much more indulgent towards her than an elder brother or even a lover should be, but Vimla did not believe that he really loved her in an amorous sense, or in any other.

'She keeps him under a spell,' Vimla concluded.

I laughed.

'Vimla, were you a little more sophisticated, you would have perhaps discovered in that spell the mystery of feudal India's surrender to white rule!' I observed.

Vimla was sure the sooner the Raja got rid of the enigmatic Heera's hold over him, the better it would be for him. And marrying her off was possibly the only chance for the Raja to throw her off his shoulders.

Two or three ex-princes had feigned an interest in her, but they had quietly slipped away upon realizing that Heera would neither make herself available to them beyond a certain degree of companionship before marriage, nor would bring a sizeable dowry.

At first thrilled with her freedom, more so because she could unstring the Raja's purse at her will, Heera had gradually become disillusioned with her own dreams of an exciting future.

At last, a chance meeting with a gentle, if impecunious, prince of a small frontier state had rekindled her dying hopes. After months she smiled, conducting herself beautifully in her manners and speech. That was the finest phase of her life. And the Prince Charming who rarely spoke, had all the time to listen to the chatterbox. His smile, like the vivid bougainvillaea, never faded. Heera seemed to have found her man at last.

'Why don't you say something?' Heera would condescend to ask sometimes, but would resume her own chatter before he had opened his mouth.

The prince had a younger sister who was beautiful but melancholic. 'Only in fairy tales do you meet such maidens,' said Vimla with some emotion. Born when her parents had lost practically everything, her bearing, unlike that of Heera, was marked by a serene humility. The Raja who had seen her only once, consented to marry her with the tacit understanding that the prince would marry Heera.

Unknown to the Raja, the prince sold his last castle in his native town and performed his sister's marriage. It was now the Raja's turn to get ready for Heera's wedding to the prince. He began his preparations in right earnest. But what followed was perplexing. The prospective bridegroom grew increasingly cool and shy. He avoided the Raja as much as he could, and whenever Heera went to see him, he was found inebriated. 'Or at least he pretended to be so—if he was capable of pretending.' Vimla said.

The Raja, nevertheless, went ahead with the preparations for the ceremony. Luckily, it was not to be elaborate. The Raja had always remained aloof from his relatives. Those who maintained a nominal contact with him from their side, had no reason to feel enthusiastic about Heera's marriage. The Rani, the new member in the Raja's small household, was so good that she did not have the slightest hesitation in surrendering her jewellery to be recast to suit Heera's needs.

Came the wedding day. The Raja's party went to fetch the bridegroom. But the prince's room in the hotel was found latched from within, a 'Do Not Disturb' sign hanging outside.

When knocks and shouts failed to elicit response and the management was forced to break open his door, the prince was found lying unconscious. He died in a nursing home around the time set for the ceremony.

He had literally drunk himself to death, probably aware of what he was doing.

Heera appeared to take it well, if with a certain disdain for her unfortunate fiancé. She threatened to shoot herself if the Raja called off the dinner scheduled to take place after the wedding. And apparently, she found great amusement in announcing the death of her prince to the guests. The more awkward they felt, the greater seemed to be her amusement.

That of course was only a facade. Once the party was over, she refused to talk to anybody and sat the night out in a fearful silence. 'I still remember her silhouette on the rooftop, against the night sky. She sat like a statue, though her hair flew about her like dark flames. Yes, I had the queer and fearful feeling that she was being consumed by those dark flames,' Vimla reminisced. But it appeared from what she said subsequently that Heera, like a phoenix, was emerging rejuvenated from that dark fire-bath.

Soon she began darting like a bitten snake from place to

place. After six months, she was back with the Raja, as if determined to avenge her tragedy. Alone, the unlucky Rani had to swallow all the poison Heera spat forth in every word she uttered. The Raja remained indifferent. In her shyness and her reluctance to speak, the Rani was like her brother. 'But she was growing lovelier day by day.' said Vimla.

Then was born Balika, driving Heera to the height of her madness. Perhaps it was beyond her to bear the Rani's elevated status as the mother of the Raja's child. Perhaps life could have been somewhat tolerable for her if the Rani had occasionally fought back and if there were quarrels in the household. But the Rani had no enthusiasm even for a mild argument. Surely, things would have been different if her brother were alive.

Heera shifted to a hotel under the pretext of feeling insulted by the Rani's insolent silence. For five years, she remained the reigning queen of a circle of lazy aristocrats, snobs and the extravagantly wealthy. The impact of her prodigal living was clear on the Raja's lifestyle. "We were changing houses continually—from large bungalows to smaller flats." Vimla said sadly.

Heera was back with the Raja as soon as the Rani died. She took charge of the princess and developed a frenzied attachment to her. At first Vimla thought that it was like a child's fondness for its lifeless doll, but soon she realized that it was a boa constrictor's coiling grasp round its hypnotized prey.

The princess herself was listening to Vimla with rapt attention, but I do not know if she regarded this tale as being any different from the fantasies she loved to read or hear.

'It is time for Balika to take her supper,' Vimla said and she stood up. 'Will you join her? But how stupid it is of me to be formal with you. She just won't eat in your presence!'

I bade her and the silent princess a hurried goodbye and stepped out of the room. I was groping through the dingy corridor, when Vimla whispered from behind, 'When are you coming back to tell her your stories? She insists on knowing.'

My eyes had grown accustomed to the darkness. I could see Vimla smiling. 'This is the first time she has even shown any interest in anything. Devu, my son, I've assured her that you'll come again. Should you prove me wrong?'

'I shall come again.'

A surge of happiness almost choked me as I made the promise.

Once in the open I felt that I had just woken up from a magical dream.

Thereafter the sunset would signal to me the call of the castle, inaudible but irresistible. The vague and bewildered look of the princess would change into one of joy as I told her story after story. Depending upon the note on which a story ended, she would show signs of cheerfulness or sadness.

'All these years she had heard tales of horror only—of bloodthirsty vampires, brutal killers and ferocious tigers—tales Heera chose to narrate to her. There were occasions when the frightened child would shriek and Heera would clasp her and put her to sleep. Then Heera would retire to her own room. Once asleep she would be no different from her pillow. But the poor child would wake up in the middle of the night, shaking with fright because of some nightmarish dream. Raja Sahib or I would have to spend the rest of the night sitting by her bedside,' Vimla said, graphically describing the Raja's predicament which she shared.

Only once in a while, as I told her my stories, would Balika ask a question. At first routed through Vimla, she slowly began putting them directly to me. And her questions were not always easy to answer. For example, once when I told her how inside the giant's desolate castle on the tiny island the captive princess lay asleep the whole day, under the spell of the silver stick with which her captor had touched her, Balika's query was, 'What dreams did the princess dream the whole day?'

My grandmother or Vimla had never told me about the dreams of the sleeping beauty. I fumbled, but Balika helped me out with her own suggestion: 'Of tigers?'

'Oh no, for there were no tigers on that island.'

'Of vampires?'

'Oh no, for there were no vampires either. But, there were numerous birds, squirrels and butterflies in the gardens and groves around that lonely castle.'

'I'll ask Papa to take us to that island,' she had eagerly told Vimla.

'It may not be easy to locate that island even for your Papa, but you can meet plenty of birds, squirrels and butterflies if you take just a little walk. And, walking about a little, you will breathe the wonderful breeze carrying the blessings of the hills, the forests, the flowers and even the clouds! When were your eyes last filled with stars? All you have to do for that to happen is to climb to the roof of this castle!'

I was gradually able to induce her to venture out to the roof. The joy her face recorded under a clear starry sky was unforgettable. Her eyes seemed to become friends of the stars and her flowing hair intimate with the breeze.

The concluding part of the story of the enchanted princess— the straying young traveller waking her up by touching her with the golden stick—remained unsaid for a while. Strangely, I did not feel that usual dissatisfaction which goes with one's inability to complete a story. But she reminded me about it as she climbed down the stairs, supported by Vimla. I had to finish the story.

I spent almost the whole of that night in Balika's room. We had fewer tales and more silence. Vimla fell asleep. But Balika was wide awake. The moment I would look at her, she would smile and take her eyes off me, but then they would stealthily return to me.

Eleven

Nothing could quite explain the blossoming friendship between Major Havelock and Sharmaji, even though the former was as affable and companionable as a pussy cat. They were often seen reclining on the lawns of Horizon and chatting, or sitting on the parapet in a Bohemian manner. When Havelock spoke, Sharmaji listened with rapt attention, chewing blades of grass and spitting them out. When Sharmaji spoke, Havelock focused his gaze on him like an owl, pouring tea from a flask and sipping it with visible relish.

Havelock had confessed to me that he had become an alcoholic and was now in the process of curing himself.

'For Heaven's sake, don't tell me if there is a bar or liquor shop nearby,' he had warned everybody. The warning was not necessary. Nijanpur did not have such a shop.

I would usually see the pair in the distance, and I would always notice how happy Sharmaji looked. He would raise his hand in greeting, with a wink and a fleeting smile to match—a totally new gesture. As far as Havelock was concerned, he always looked agog with excitement. That was rather puzzling. What could Sharmaji say to a war veteran who had also lived a full life, to keep him so engrossed? The Raja and Heera returned to the castle after five days. Though the Raja had never been a man of hectic activity, whatever he did in few days amounted to an upheaval in the area.

According to the reports that reached us, the crowd that had turned out to hear him—or maybe only to see him—was unprecedented. Hundreds of men and women shed tears when they heard that he had refused even to have a look at what was once his palace at Samargarh. The Raja had himself offered to sell the building to the government and the latter had obliged him by buying it. It now housed a college. But, curiously, the Raja acted, and the people reacted, as though he had been deprived of his ancestral properpy, as if it were because he had no house to live in that he was reduced to wandering from place to place!

A handful of Mansingh's followers tried to stage a black flag demonstration against the Raja. At first, the crowd mistook the demonstrators for devotees of a local deity whose shrine traditionally displayed black flags—a shrine that was previously maintained by the Raj family. The demonstrators were cheered lustily. That encouraged them, and their inspired spokesman began a fiery speech, telling the crowd that the Raja was not only a reminder of the inglorious colonial and feudal rule, but also a symbol of all that was reactionary in history.

Once the mob had understood what the demonstrators actual represented, it pressed towards them menacingly. They would have been crushed, but for the Raja's timely arrival on the scene and his strict injunction to the crowd to leave the demonstrators alone.

The episode practically sealed Mansingh's political fate. The stable base the leader had built for himself over the years, through his continuous service to the common man and exemplary sacrifices, crumbled overnight.

Thus the Raja destroyed, more or less peacefully, one of his two targets. The maneater, however, was still at large. Its latest victim was a cowherd youth. His was a tragic story.

He had waded into a pool in a meadow to pluck red lilies for a peasant girl whom he loved and who had stood coyly by the bank. Suddenly, he noticed the tiger approaching the girl. In a shaky and subdued voice, he asked her to jump into the pool, but the girl perhaps thought that it would be too romantic a plunge for her to take at that stage. She blushed but did not move. There was no time to lose. The young man splashed water furiously, shouted and made a dash at the tiger in a desperate bid to scare it away. He was dragged away to his death, but his beloved was saved.

I was being pestered by the members of a government-sponsored committee lodged in Horizon to fix up for them an appointment with the Raja. They were required to prepare a report on Nijanpur's potential as a hill resort. But I delayed calling on the Raja, for Subbu had passed word that the Raja was tired and was resting.

It was nearly evening when I finally set out to meet the Raja. The first person I saw as I left Horizon was Sharmaji. He stopped me through a lively gesture and reached the portico in long, hurried strides. Some kind of a premonition made me uncomfortable.

'Where are you going, Dev?' he demanded anxiously and holding on to my shirt, added, 'I won't allow you to move forward even an inch until I have opened my heart to you.'

His voice sounded as ominous as the clang of a firebrigade's bell. He exuded an exotic fragrance, a perfume which Major Havelock used.

'Well,' I said unhappily, 'Let us then move backwards—into my room.' He was happy.

'Thank you, thank you.' He thanked me probably for the first time in his life. He must have received such lessons in deportment from Major Havelock, though the source of his inspiration for educating and updating himself at this stage of his life, I had begun to feel, was his contact with Heera and the Raja.

'You've grown plump, Sharmaji,' I observed as he settled down in a chair facing mine.

'Well, that was only natural, wasn't that?' he asked, smiling in gracious appreciation of my observation and adding, with a kind of brazen-faced frankness that upset me, 'Heera desired that it should be so.'

It was embarrassing to look him in the face, for his smile proclaimed his witless infatuation with Heera.

'So, Heera wished you to grow fat!' I tried to sound as unenthusiastic as possible, in order to impress upon him that I was too unromantic to appreciate the subtle and special nature of the law operating behind his prompt ascent to health.

'And here I am, fat enough to fit into the garments she presented to me, in keeping with her injunction that if. . .'

Sharmaji stopped and blushed.

'If what?' I asked, more in my eagerness to put an end to the interview than with any real curiosity.

'If what?' he repeated, disappointed. 'Can't you guess the situation, Dev? Why then have you stuffed your racks with novels?'

'I'm sorry, Sharmaji, I really fail to guess.'

'If I loved her, my friend, if I loved her. Believe me, Dev, that is exactly what she told me,' he simpered and giggled.

'And you think you love her, do you?' I asked in a deadpan tone.

'Dev!' Sharmaji appeared emotional. 'Is it merely a question of my thinking? Haven't I put on weight enough to fit into those garments as tightly as a pigeon fits into its feathers? Is this not one of those miracles of love?'

A feverish dejection ran through my veins. His glazed and flitting eyes, like those of one possessed, suggested he was in pretty poor shape. I had never known passion and self-reproach to twinkle so distinctly together. I wished I could run away from him.

'Dev!' His voice began choking.

'Yes, Sharmaji, anything more to tell me, anything in particular?'

'Dev! Haven't I already told you? Now it is for you to tell

her, Dev, and you must tell her—and the sooner the better,' Sharmaji implored, taking my hands in his.

As I sat speechless, he increased the pressure of his grip on my hands almost violently.

'Tell her? Do you expect me to tell Heera about your love for her?' I cried out my question, with the force of my suppressed anguish.

'At last Dev, at last you understand!' He smiled with great relief. Perhaps he was even wondering if he was not granting me a rare privilege. Clearing his throat while smiling on me graciously, he resumed,' Dev, the situation is like this: not that she is not aware of my love. In fact, she is as aware of my love as I am of hers. But all said and done, she is a woman!' And he recited a Sanskrit dictum asserting that shyness adorned a woman more than her jewellery.

'Sharmaji, how can you be so sure about it?'

'Dev, in such matters, only fools wait for tangible proof, the wise are guided by their intuitions.' He was beginning to recite yet another verse in support of his theory, but I stopped him saying impatiently, 'I know you are a wise man, Sharmaji, but, pardon my impudence, are you sure that you are as wise in your drawing conclusions in this matter as you are in quoting the classics?'

'Absolutely sure. Between Heera and myself, all that is left is a formal declaration of love. The only question is, whether I should do it first or allow her to steal a march on me. Is it not the male lover's duty to take the initiative? It is, I need hardly assert. That is pure common sense; right? But I cannot perform that duty properly as my voice chokes every time I begin and she asks me with concern if I should not cleanse my throat by gargling with salted water. She smiles at my plight. Somebody has to lend his throat to voice my sentiments. Well, Dev, who but you can perform that task for me? There is, of course, another gentleman who could be entrusted with the job. He has guided several people in love as efficiently as he has manoeuvred battalions through wars. He is Major Havelock, my greatest moral support; you are no less a support though.'

'That would be just wonderful—I mean Major Havelock,

in his impeccable manner, accent and style, singing out your heart to Heera!' I said enthusiastically.

But Sharmaji impatiently shook his head.

'Do you think we have not weighed the pros and cons of the possibility? We found it impractical. Heera is not used to him. It will be a Herculean task for him to bring up a topic of such tremendous import unless they had talked of mice and men over a pretty long time. Secondly, he is a cardiac patient. If over-emotional, he may swoon right away, slumping on the lady. No, Dev, there is no alternative to your taking up this sacred mission and I have already paved the way for it.'

'How?' My heart began to palpitate violently.

'I've told her this very morning that you were yearning for a private meeting with her. Believe me, she understood at once. In fact, she fixed her gaze on me and I could feel the intensity of her expectations. When she asked me when you would like to meet her, I suggested that it could be this very evening!' Sharmaji squeezed my hand again.

'Have you ever observed a cat about to lap up milk?' he asked me assuming the grave stance so natural to him in his role as a teacher.

'I don't think I have. Why?'

'She looked as ecstatic as that.'

'Sharmaji, the simile is giving me the creeps, I must confess. What do you propose to do?' I asked impatiently.

Sharmaji looked at me with some frustration. 'Don't be naïve, Dev! How do all the love affairs culminate? Don't you read classic romances?' he demanded of me.

'The lovers marry and live happily ever after.'

'Exactly.'

'You don't propose to marry Heera—or do you?'

'What else?'

The precision and unambiguity of his response staggered me.

'But how?' I managed to ask.

'What do you mean by how?'

'Don't you think it would be rather unnatural, awkward . . .?'

'What is unnatural or awkward in love, Dev?'

His lucidity, strengthened by a certain dreamy idealism, dazed me.

'Sharmaji, I don't know what kind of response you expect from me, but please give me some time. Let me reflect on the issue,' I stood up, hopeful of some respite.

'Not necessary, Dev. All the reflection has already been done by our valued friend, Havelock. You won't have to waste time. Yes, Dev, time is the thing. As Havelock observes so wisely, there is a time for everything: a time to conquer, a time to retreat, a time to propose. And for the last feat, now is the time, most propitious. And Dev, can I be frank with you?'

I was surprised that he still had a secret to deliver. He lowered his voice, half closed his eyes and revealed it lugubriously, 'I shall die if you let this moment slip away.'

I felt like shouting, 'Is that all? So what? Who cares?' But my failure to shout and the silence that followed his proclamation convinced him that he had impressed me. He clucked and nodded in appreciation of what he imagined to be my deep concern for him.

I stood up and crossed the door before he could stop me. He followed.

On the road, I controlled my impulse to take to my heels. Did he suspect my motive? Probably he did, for he kept pace with me, guarding me like a hound! Surprisingly, I read in his eyes the horror one notices in the eyes of goats on their way to slaughterhouses, although it was my condition which was comparable to that.

His expression, however, convinced me that with him it was a matter of life and death. I did not wish to become the immediate cause of his death by refusing to undertake his errand. I gritted my teeth and continued to walk towards the castle.

Sharmaji's garrulousness and speed began to decrease as the castle loomed nearer. He began clutching at my arm or tugging at my sleeve. He was obviously growing nervous.

'Raja sahib was thinking of sending me to fetch you, sir,' Sahoo's driver whispered to me. He was dusting the jeep which, it seemed, Sahoo had placed at the Raja's disposal.

I regained my poise to a considerable extent on meeting

the Raja. His hands resting on my shoulders, he surveyed me more than once. Perhaps he felt a little more drawn towards me. Maybe Vimla had spoken to him warmly about my humble contribution to his daughter's happiness. Or could it be that the princess herself had spoken?

Sharmaji was mute but restless, stealing glances at the doors leading to the inner suites. I conveyed to the Raja the visiting committee's desire to meet him and learn from him as much as he would care to speak on the antiquity of the temple of Vaneswari. The Raja showed no interest in it but drawled on the legends and lores surrounding the deity and the shrine. He was lost in a loud reverie, more as a recreation for himself after a few strenuous days than with any intention to enlighten me.

Sharmaji was getting fidgety. I too heard the Raja only in parts, all the while wishing that I could get away with meeting the Raja alone.

A saving idea struck me. Yes, I could postpone meeting Heera if I could satisfy Sharmaji with the argument that in my novel role as a matchmaker, etiquette demanded that I spoke to the Raja, the legal guardian of the bride-to-be, before I carried my embassy to Heera.

But this avenue of escape was blocked when Heera sailed into the hall, looking vibrant in a dazzling orange saree with accessories to match. 'Can I have a word with Dev?' she asked the Raja sweetly, though abruptly.

'He's here!' said the Raja mechanically, but his brows were raised.

'But you must be tired and we can...' I made one last attempt to wriggle out of the ordeal.

'Will you please follow me?' she cut in and, beckoning me with a nod, turned away from us. As I got up to comply with her direction, my eyes fell on Sharmaji. Was it an illusion that I saw his hair appeared to be standing on end?

I followed Heera with faltering steps. She led me into her suite. I had never been there before but I was in no mood to observe anything, for I felt as if I had been suddenly dumped in a cell reserved for prisoners awaiting execution.

She tried to make me comfortable in a sofa, pressing me to

accept an extra pillow for my back, and sat down facing me and smiled. She readjusted the lamp on her table to keep her face in shade. I sweated profusely. Though light did not fall on her eyes, they held me in their grip like a pair of claws.

My head reeled. I passed a few seconds trying to locate an elusive moth around my face. The hands of the clock on the wall did not seem to move at all while its 'tick-tock' was magnified. I tried to persuade myself that since there was no retreat from the situation, the quicker the business was over the better.

'I wonder if you can guess what's on my mind. I'm not even sure that I'm doing the right thing. Perhaps I should have first spoken to Raja Sahib!' I fumbled out.

'Why? If it concerns me, am I not grown up enough to listen to it or participate in the dialogue personally?' she protested, feigning offence.

'I do not know how to put it. I have absolutely no experience in such matters . . .'

'Don't I know that?' Heera, to my surprise, spoke softly and tenderly. And I don't know why the uneasiness that had momentarily left me, returned. The screech of an owl behind the castle, though faint, added to my feeling of discomfort.

'I knew how innocent you were the very evening we met for the first time,' Heera shifted her gaze from me and fixed it on the floor.

'You know and that's my sole strength at the moment.' I stopped to take a deep breath and cast a lightning glance at her. Our eyes met.

'Well, Dev, I don't know if I really know what you think I know. I have suddenly begun imagining so many things rather too exciting to be true. But please go on.'

'How glad I am that you have already imagined what I'd say. I was feeling so awkward and I had such terrific misgivings! I must have read a full dozen books of a certain kind to realize that the way of—what d'you call it—love—is mysterious . . .'

'O Dev! You'd kill me with surprises!'

'Surprises? You're being polite. Didn't I hear you say you had already guessed what I intended saying? Well, I take it that we can proceed to make the necessary arrangements . . .'

'Arrangements?' Heera's voice trembled.

'That's right, arrangements, for the wedding, of course!'

Heera gave a start. Absent-mindedly I turned the lamp and her face became clearly visible. She did not look unhappy; but seemed intrigued. Then she clutched her head with both her hands and shook it. Obviously she was trying to resolve some confusion.

'Dev, I knew you to be naïve, but I never expected you to be so rash. You'll turn me mad-mad-mad!'

I decided to remain calm in the face of her excitement. I assumed the tone of a mentor.

'To be honest, I had also thought that there were formidable difficulties in the way of a formal marriage. In fact, I am a bit orthodox in my ideas, and I was even going to suggest that perhaps both would do well to live as simple lovers. But I have just discovered the astounding fact that Sharmaji is nothing short of a revolutionary. I'm sure, you're no less progressive. I must confess that I feel rather small before you two!'

I paused and looked at Heera. She looked rather shaken, but I interpreted it as modesty. I was keen to draw my mission to a quick close and to go out and breathe the fresh air. 'Once known to be somewhat conservative,' I continued, 'Sharmaji has now reached a stage—hats off to the miracle of love—when he does not care two hoots for worn-out conventions and anything that does not conform to the avant-garde ideas he has lately developed. The only thing that matters to him is his love for you and yours for him. He is determined to wed you, come what may, to wed you against all odds.'

Throwing the last ounce of burden off my mind, I heaved a sigh of relief and congratulated myself for having accomplished a ticklish mission reasonably well. I did not look at Heera in order to save her the embarrassment of being caught blushing.

'I had better leave now and carry the happy tidings to Sharmaji.' I stood up.

Suddenly, and I cannot recollect how it began, everything seemed to fade and I was wrapped in extreme bewilderment. Heera seemed to have disappeared. Where was she?

There she was, standing a little away from me, perhaps shivering. It could not but be Heera, but was it her face? Was it a human face at all?

Suddenly she cried out. But a kind of roar was all I could hear. Did she show me the door? Perhaps she did.

I tottered out of the room, my head reeling, and immediately stumbled on somebody who fell down, but managed to get up promptly. It was Sharmaji. Obviously he had been eavesdropping.

Sharmaji ran along the corridor and I followed him. To my horror, I could hear clumsy footsteps behind me.

No sooner had we staggered into the hall than Heera caught up with us. Like a wild cat she chased Sharmaji. Poor Sharmaji continued scurrying from one corner of the hall to another even after she had given up the chase and had collapsed into a chair, gasping and fuming.

Sharmaji looked an utter wreck. I stood thunderstruck, expecting worse if Heera left her seat. But soon the Raja appeared at one of the doorways. Sharmaji's instinct for self-preservation came to his rescue. He ran and hid behind him.

Before the Raja had a chance to comprehend this strange turn of events and its rationale, there was a thudding sound. Sharmaji had fainted. The Raja and I tried to lift him. By then, Vimla and a servant had arrived on the scene. The Raja asked Vimla for smelling salts and the servant for water.

Heera left the hall without a word. Under the silent care of the Raja and Vimla, Sharmaji opened his eyes, but his was a blank stare.

'Should I take him to Horizon? We can look after him till he is fit enough to go home,' I said, anxious to leave the place as soon as possible. I did not know how to explain the situation to the Raja. And I feared Heera's reappearance in the hall.

'That's better. He will feel more comfortable there,' said the Raja and he assisted me in carrying Sharmaji to Sahoo's jeep.

Silently, I thanked Sharmaji for his latest exercise. None could have done anything better in the prevailing circumstances for all concerned.

Twelve

'You should have thought twice before carrying such a grotesque message to Heera, even though commissioned by the venerable Sharma.' The Raja said at our midnight rendezvous. This was the first time he had ever taken me to task.

I had been squirming with embarrassment while trying to put up a brave face, but his mild but straight criticism considerably soothed my feelings.

'But Sharmaji was so sure of her love for him!' I defended myself and then added, 'In fact I was literally driven to committing that blunder. I realize that it was my stupidity, but looking back I do not see how and when I could have backed out. Things happened at such speed!'

'The imp that presides over stupidity is not stupid; it is quick and cunning. It takes care to see that its victim is under a kind of spell, before any better sense in him has had a chance to check the process. Poor Sharma! How easily he let himself be fiddled about by misplaced passion!'

'And, sir, what havoc my own stupidity wrought on me, leading me to believe, even momentarily, that Heera would love and desire to marry Sharmaji! Now I wonder if I should not feel more puzzled by my own conduct than by Sharmaji's!' My voice betrayed more surprise than regret. My embarrassment had quickly changed into amazement. I do not know why I did not feel truly repentant. While the whole incident was extremely ludicrous in some crude part of my being, I enjoyed the comic in it!

Since my confession failed to provoke the Raja to come out with any word of sympathy or indulgence, I decided to argue on with facts.

'Isn't it true that the suit Heera offered Sharmaji had been stitched for the one who was to be her bridegroom? Can Sharmaji be blamed if he took her gesture of making a gift of the suit to him as symbolic? I think anybody else in his position would have interpreted it more or less in the same way!'

'No Dev, Sharma ought to have understood and behaved differently—a bit more prudently. Passion can be given a lot of concessions, but one cannot reduce one's adventure to anarchy. It was unpardonable of Sharma to forget the vast gulf between him and Heera in matters of personal and social culture. He had begun to live in a fool's paradise and built up his trust in the impossible; he knit a chimera out of some kind of eerie darkness he had nurtured within.'

'But his wild fancy was so real for him!'

The Raja fell silent for a moment. 'That shows,' he observed, his articulation directed more at himself than at his listener, 'that we shall never know enough about men. Just now I said that Sharma should have conducted himself differently. But could he have really?'

'But surely, there are exceptions to this general rule of vulnerability! For example, I can never imagine you losing your cool over anything!' I was suddenly roused to praise him. It was a very sincere offering to one whose company filled me with pride. He understood and was not anxious to contradict me. 'I've just learnt enough from life to not to react to its vicissitudes; at least not through impulse,' he said.

'Why can't others learn that much?' I asked impatiently.

'I don't know. At some point of time in my youth, I must have realized that while I could not forestall events or alter situations, the way I reacted to them remained my prerogative. We always try to make others understand us; little do we try to understand ourselves. If we did, we would no doubt become wiser. But what I have stated is a principle. Don't jump to the conclusion that I am a wise man. Wisdom is a ladder that touches the sky, its higher rungs almost hidden from our eyes. What pushes us up are often kicks or whips from below. A new kick may strike me any moment. But one day in the past, I stopped being shocked or even surprised by them.'

I decided to bring the conversation down to a pragmatic plane: 'Sir, you are yet to tell me why she should offer a prized possession of hers to Sharmaji unless she had developed some very special warmth for him!'

'If by prized possession you mean the suit Heera presented to Sharma, that was Heera's original, if peculiar, way of avenging the man who, having promised to wed her, chose death instead. Heera has not pardoned him. It has been her fond pastime— though she indulges in it very rarely—to identify the clown in the crowd around her and to adorn him with something or other bearing the memory of the only young man she had probably loved in her life.' The Raja's statement came like a revelation to me. He paused—was it to allow me time to absorb the shock?—and resumed, 'Once she persuaded a millionaire buffoon to shave his head—yes, the whole of it; and the chap had the most luxuriant mop of hair I had ever seen—so that her prince's hat could fit it. Another time she obliged a fellow, a vainglorious sycophant, to put on the pair of shoes I had got made for her would-be husband. The fellow had enormous feet and they must have been tormented like the jinn inside the jar. She has just been doing the same thing with poor Sharma.'

'What a pity!'

'Indeed. You pity Sharma; I pity both Sharma and Heera. I have my own theory about the conduct of men, though it's a bit funny. You know the absurdity and whimsicality for which the rajas were notorious. Do you know what my father once did to an eminent poet who had come a long way to seek some favour? He led him on an elephant into the forest under the pretext of showing him some rare trees and flowers, and left him in a dense and dangerous part of the forest and quietly slipped away. The poet passed an unforgettable night, perched on a tree, shivering with fear all the time, only to be rescued by my father's officials early in the morning and be informed that the Raja expected a new poem from him out of the inspiration he ought to have received in the sylvan silence of the night. But I doubt if the poet ever wrote again!'

The Raja laughed and I echoed his laughter.

'The motive for such mischief, I believe, is generated by a genre of naughty little imps. No, I'm not joking. In our palace at Samargarh, during those idle days between my return from college and my father's death, I spent hours in an odd research: I would try to assess whether the thoughts and actions of the past left any lasting impact on the atmosphere around their occurrence. My conclusion was, they did. Some vibrations, very subtle, are left by such thoughts and actions that involve a certain intensity of emotion, be it of agony or joy, but of agony in particular.'

'Did you ever catch such vibrations?'

'Rather the vibrations caught me. It began by chance. My father's guests, an Englishman from the Civil Service and a Raja, were keen to take me with them for shikar. I was in no mood to oblige them. Deciding to hide temporarily, I slipped into a remote chamber in the older wing of the palace used as a lumber room. Though it had a small window, it was obviously designed to be a place shut out from the world, for there stood a thick wall only inches away from the window. But a part of the wall had crumbled and some light broke in. I dusted off an antique chair and sat on it, reading a book.

'Soon I dozed off. What occurred next was terrifying. A pale face, I don't know whether a man's or a woman's, came close to me and snarled at me. It was a scary nightmare. Not that the face tried to frighten me; it was only expressing anguish, anger and perplexity. The air was charged with deafening, blood-curdling cries—though inaudible—demanding answers to questions which were unanswerable.

'An hour must have passed before an old servant, seeing the door ajar, peeped in. He gave a shout of surprise upon discovering me there. I woke up. From him I learnt that for long the room used to serve as a secret torture chamber to punish the rebellious, the disobedient, or the criminal. Some of them never came out of it alive. A few did not come out even dead. They were buried right there.'

We were strolling on the lawns outside Horizon. The Raja leaned over the parapet overlooking the dark valley. His face was hardly visible, but I imagined that he had closed his eyes.

Perhaps he was engrossed in his recollections of the nightmare. Soon, however, he came out with the theory he had formulated out of his experience: 'There are beings, supernatural ones needless to say, who feed on these vibrations of human anguish and hapless suffering or, maybe, these beings are actually born out of the ambience of violence, shock, treachery and similar abominable acts of men. And once born, they wish to thrive on more and more such vicious situations. They starve when they don't find any. They grow vengeful and look for preys. They catch some people in their weaker moments. I won't be surprised if

Sharma was possessed by a legion of such phantoms, as effective as microbes.'

I was about to ask: 'Why Sharmaji alone? Wasn't Heera also possessed when she decided to play with the sentiments of Sharmaji, of all persons?'

The Raja had perhaps anticipated my question, for he said, even though my question was unpronounced,' Something must have deeply incensed Heera. Could it be Sharma's audacity in aspiring to woo her? I wonder.'

'But Heera did not know of Sharmaji's motive! I put forth his proposal before her only now!'

The Raja looked askance at me. A shaft of light reflecting from the interior of Horizon revealed a twinkle in his eyes. If that was not my imagination, it must have meant his pity at my failure to appreciate human nature.

'Look here, my boy, Sharma's cheek might have borrowed your voice only now, but it was there brewing in his puckish mind from the beginning. Every human being has in him or her something canine which can smell certain things concerning himself or herself, which others cannot. Heera must have smelt Sharma's hopeless and strange desire.'

'But, to the best of my knowledge, Sharmaji had never betrayed any weakness for women.' I tried to defend my old teacher.

'How much do you know of yourself that you would know what was inside Sharma?' the Raja laughed. 'In any case, did I not take sufficient precaution by terming Sharma's desire as strange? Like you, I too could not have imagined such hunger in him!'

The waning moon was effective enough only to reduce the darkness to a lemon-green shade. We walked on slowly. We were not far from the castle when the Raja put a hand on my shoulder and said softly, 'But, Dev, I can assure you that the Sharma episode has not disturbed my happiness; it is so deep!'

The statement was unexpected, but it gave me a great deal of satisfaction. The faint feeling of guilt I still had in my mind on account of my role as Sharmaji's 'cloud-messenger' vanished.

'I'm glad to hear that. I'm sure there are some strong reasons for your happiness.'

'You've made Balika smile—something she had not done for years. She now smiles at everything,' he said in matter-of-fact manner, but it thrilled me and made me blush.

He took his hand off my shoulder. 'My daughter had become only a symbol for me, a memory of my wife, my past, and a reminder of my bleak future, from the day she ceased to be the jolly little cherub that she was, pestering me with her babbling and her antics. Yes, she had become a symbol like a distant moon. You feel close to the moon without knowing whether it knows you or not. On a realistic plane, I felt that she, my only dream of joy, would continue to remain a dream.'

I had never heard the Raja's voice tinged with such sadness. Oblivious of my movements, I had already followed the Raja, not only into the castle, but also into Balika's room. Only then did I become conscious of my surroundings, now dominated by a smiling princess so beautifully different from the picture of gloom she had been. The cool light from the flickering lamp had a rare sweetness about it, for the louvres of the large window had been left open allowing a generous passage to the breeze from the wilderness.

'Sit down, Dev, and tell her more stories. I shall be back after a while,' said the Raja.

'Where are you going?'

'I've a secret errand. But more of that later.' He smiled mysteriously and waved to us before disappearing into the dark.

Vimla sat leaning against the wall. I sat in a chair facing the princess who, instead of lying on her bed, sat up. Minutes passed. I believe Vimla kept deliberately quiet, to force me to speak to Balika directly.

'Would you like to hear more stories?' I asked Balika at last.

She said nothing, but smiled. I opened the windows fully and sat idle, looking alternately at the fog-covered landscape bewitched by a deceptively weak moon and the princess, and consciously let myself be entranced by her smiles which appeared spontaneously whenever our eyes met. I did not keep my gaze fixed on her so that I could have more smiles.

Time passed for me as blissfully as it used to years ago when, my head resting on my mother's lap, I would watch the moon appearing and disappearing amidst velvet clouds—looking more and more golden with every fresh appearance.

Suddenly, I saw the old look of bafflement and panic back on Balika's face. I followed her look. At the door, like an apparition, stood Heera. Her silent and stern stance chilled my blood. My eyes searched for Vimla. She had dozed off.

Heera rushed up to the princess and slapped her on the cheek. I stood up, trembling with anger and disgust. The sensation was intolerable. I cannot say what I would have done had Heera not perplexed me once again with yet another unexpected action; she fell on Balika and began sobbing hysterically.

'How dare you linger here!' she shrieked, raising her head for a second or two to blurt out her command.

I walked out. Vimla stood at the door, dumbfounded. I brushed past her and walked on through the open door. I saw the Raja emerging from the fog.

'Was that Heera shrieking?'

'Yes. She slapped Balika.'

The Raja turned to look at me for a moment. But I could not read his eyes. He bade me a hasty goodnight and rushed in. I was surprised to see his clothes wet and plastered with patches of mud. I waited with bated breath to hear what would transpire between the Raja and Heera. But all was quiet.

Thirteen

I was fast falling in love with the midnight at Nijanpur. It was a wonderful feeling to walk alone through the silence which had a heart and I could feel its throbs; it had a soul and I could feel its serene majesty. Even my maddening encounter with Heera could not detract me from the bliss I had learnt to experience.

Back from the castle, I passed some time in front of my gate. From time to time my eyes returned to the castle submerged in a slender darkness, but as if I could penetrate the distance and locate at least one face—Balika's. But in the new vision I was developing, a vision that showed me a wondrous fusion of things real with those of fancy, she was a part of the landscape of the valley, with a single floating cloud and the wild flowers shining faintly under the stars.

The moonlight looked more intense at certain places than at others. I found it intriguing and tried to trace the cause of the phenomenon, as it had often been a recreation for me to indulge in such pointless reflections. I could have easily spent an hour in pondering this but was distracted by the sound of footsteps coming from Horizon, growing louder behind me. It was Havelock. He marched towards me, his arms stiffly locked on his chest.

A jackal howled close by. Havelock at once unlocked his arms and picked up a couple of pebbles and hurled them at the bushes. He was obviously agitated.

'I did not expect you to be awake at this hour!' I said.

'It's going to be scandalous,' he rejoined, ignoring my observation.

I could see Subbu standing at the portico. What could be amiss at my Horizon, which stood aloof from all events, good or bad?

'Going to be scandalous. Better be prepared to accept the inevitable when it occurs. Therein lies prudence.' The excitement he betrayed was tempered with a certain amount of satisfaction.

'What's going to be scandalous, Mr Havelock?'

'Our friend, Mr Sharma, our dear Mr Sharma, has resolved to put an end to his life.' Mr Havelock's hands were restless inside his pockets like two captive birds. His facial muscles twitched.

I was least prepared for the intelligence. Standing face to face with Mr Havelock, my hands too began to tremble like his and, I'm afraid, to some extent my face also began to twitch.

'Is this true?' I asked after a while.

'It is. He may do so any moment,' Mr Havelock announced like a physician withdrawing from a patient's bedside, folding up his stethoscope and his kit, absolutely certain about the futility of any further treatment.

'Mr Havelock, he loves you so much. Surely you could prevent him from taking such a drastic step!'

'Pardon me, but I don't see what else is left for him to do!' Mr Havelock coughed and added, 'I hate to mince words.'

Mr Havelock's pronouncement fell on my ears like a few blows from a hammer. A chill ran down my spine. His silhouetted figure, standing still before me, suddenly ceased to be human. It became a cold outline as stubborn and immovable as death.

I went over to Subbu who exuded panic. Before I had even asked him where Sharmaji was, he showed me his room. 'He has bolted the door from inside,' Subbu reported in a shaky voice.

I knocked on the door. Sharmaji did not respond.

'What's this I hear, Sharmaji? Must you do such a horrible thing?' I cried out in anguish.

'I will, Dev, I will. Nothing can stop me. Perhaps there are better ways of doing the job but, as Mr Havelock rightly observed, there is a time for everything. The time has come for me to end my wretched life. All—all is dark for me, and extremely painful too. Death alone can take me beyond this unbearable condition.' Muffled by the closed doors, Sharmaji's voice sounded like the desperate articulation of a creature from the remote Ice Age.

'Sharmaji, will you please open the door?'

'Naturally, he is reluctant to show his face to you!' commented Mr Havelock. I had not noticed him standing behind me. I ignored him and, banging the door, shouted again, 'Sharmaji! Will you please come out of the room?'

'I wonder if it is right on our part to interfere with his plan. He is feeling awfully embarrassed. He may blush to death before us,' said Mr Havelock in a determined bid to justify his policy of total non-intervention. There was no trace of anxiety in his voice. He appeared determined to let Sharmaji go his way.

'Blushing to death should be preferable to any other way of dying.' I deliberately sounded a bit stern, as I wanted to silence him. I renewed my pleas to Sharmaji with knocks on the door, 'Please come out, will you?'

'Dev, I will not. I am getting ready to step into the world beyond. Did I not tell you that death alone could end my agony?'

'But are you sure, Sharmaji, that it could? You ought to know better, but to the best of my knowledge, death in this manner is more likely to prolong your agony than end it. Don't you know of scriptural injunctions against suicide? Sharmaji, think of the helpless state of your being when the body is gone. All your desires, all your disappointments will remain intact, but you would have deprived yourself of the protection your physical sheath is giving you. A tribe of hobgoblins will mercilessly poke fun at you and heckle you and torment you. Must you let that happen, Sharmaji?'

This time Sharmaji's silence encouraged me to come out with the last ounce of knowledge I had lately gathered from a book on the subject of life after death: 'No godly power will come to your rescue because you have sinned against the sacred law of life by destroying your body!'

There was still no response, but Mr Havelock took a step forward. 'I've told him, precisely, all there was to be told. There is no point in your wasting your breath over him. All said and done, birth and death are matters of destiny. This is common sense,' he said. I wondered about the manner in which Sharmaji proposed to execute his plan. Perhaps Subbu could enlighten me. I beckoned to him and began climbing the staircase so that I could get away from Havelock. His presence and attitude made me distinctly uncomfortable.

'Babu, he had gathered poison. It was in a small phial in the room he had occupied. But while he was talking to Hablu Sahib, I removed it,' he whispered to me.

I felt partly relieved. There was not even a ceiling fan in that particular room from which Sharmaji could hang himself. The bathroom attached to it had no shower rod. 'Lock the room,' I instructed Subbu. Surely, that would foil Sharmaji attempting to look for other means to kill himself. I also instructed Subbu to sleep on the veranda in front of the room.

After a brief and restless stroll on the terrace, I returned to my room and sank into my bed.

A bat which had forgotten its resting place beat its wings restlessly overhead, but could not stop me from falling into a sort of stupor.

Jackals were announcing the end of the night when Subbu woke me up.

'Sharmaji is not responding to our knocks and calls.'

'So what?'

'Hablu sahib thinks that . . .'

'What does he think?'

'That Sharmaji has left his mortal frame and has departed to heaven!' Subbu was on the verge of tears.

'How could Mr Havelock be so precise about Sharmaji's destination?' I asked angrily, but within me anxiety was fast turning into fright. I hurried out despite all my reluctance to face the unavoidable. Subbu ran ahead of me and banged Sharmaji's door. I too did the same in utter despair.

Mr Havelock stood behind me like a sentinel over Fate, arms locked across his chest. I looked to him for help, but swiftly took my eyes away. He looked too formidable and remote.

'Subbu, we have no option but to break open the door. Fetch the crowbar. Or wait, we should perhaps inform the police,' I said, beginning to feel dizzy. I regretted bringing Sharmaji to Horizon.

Just then there were indications of life behind closed doors. They opened slowly. Sharmaji staggered out of the room, his eyes swollen and sleepy, and grinned sheepishly, like an adult caught in an infantile act.

I heaved a sigh of relief, feeling like a shipwrecked sailor suddenly chancing upon a lifeboat.

'O Sharmaji, thank you so much!' I said.

'Thank God,' Subbu exclaimed.

I was groping for words when Mr Havelock greeted Sharmaji in the most unexpected manner: 'So, you did not do it, after all! But you made me go without a wink of sleep the whole lonely night!' He broke into a fit of coughing and suddenly giving up his usual stiff facade, doubled up. His resentment shocked me and his coughing, echoing against the roof, sounded like laughter, at once eerie and tragic.

Sharmaji looked at me with mortification.

'Mr Havelock had every right to take me to task. We had discussed the situation at some length and he had rightly observed that suicide was the only course open to any sensible man in my position. But Dev, you have always been so nice to me; I did not have the heart to do it in your house,' he squeaked.

'I'm grateful, Sharmaji, but please don't do it anywhere else either,' I told him in all sincerity.

Mr Havelock suddenly turned and marched into his room. Sharmaji lowered his eyes.

'Sharmaji, I think you need a bath and then a heavy breakfast, for I'm afraid, you did not eat any food last night. Maybe, you need more rest too,' I said. But Sharmaji insisted on going home. The fact that he did not miss the phial, believed to contain poison, which Subbu had stolen from his room, assured me that he had abandoned his plans. Later, we learnt that the phial contained some medicine left by a guest and no poison.

I accompanied him to the gate. The green slope descending towards the lower valley was still dusky, but mild sunlight flooded the hilltops and spilled over to the trees rising on the other side of the rocky fields and hamlets. A crow, which had some grievance against a kite, swooped down on its awkwardly flying prey again and again. I called for Subbu to bring his catapult. I wanted to scare away the crow.

'Dev! The pebble you shoot may hit the kite instead of the crow. In any case, the kite will be as scared as the crow, for it is not likely to understand that you were out to protect it. Better leave nature to its own course,' said Sharmaji while crossing the gate.

I was more happy than surprised. If Sharmaji had been swept off his feet by a tumultuous attack of passion, the equally forceful shock, received by him last night, had restored to him his temporarily lost balance. He was wise once again. I bade him goodbye, wishing him a restful day.

An hour later, I was summoned urgently by Mr Havelock. He lay sprawled on his bed, looking utterly distraught.

'I'm sure, I'm getting a heart attack,' he muttered in a parrot-like, broken voice. 'Is there any doctor nearby?'

Such an eventuality had never arisen before. It took a little time for me to collect myself. 'Yes,' I remembered, 'there is one downhill. I'll send for him.'

'But what can a rustic doctor do? Mine is a case for specialists. Can you arrange to send me to the railway station at Samargarh? When can I catch a train for the city?'

He became impatient like a child. Luckily, I knew that Sahoo was on his way to Samargarh. There was no difficulty in arranging a seat in his jeep for Mr Havelock.

Sahoo informed me later that as Mr Havelock's condition

appeared to worsen on the way; he admitted him in the town hospital.

The days that followed were filled with such hectic activity and bewildering experiences that despite all my anxiety for Mr Havelock, I had no opportunity to enquire after him. It was not until a week later that I learned of his death, though it had occurred the very day after he had been admitted to the hospital.

Fourteen

I had had a restful day. It was sundown and I was enjoying a stroll on my lawns when I saw Sahoo alighting from his jeep. As I received him outside my gate, I suddenly realized how warm and affectionate I had grown towards him on account of his devotion to the Raja.

Ostensibly he met me to report about Havelock's condition and his admission into the hospital at Samargarh, but suddenly he grew jovial, looking at the dusky castle.

'It's a castle, isn't it? I mean, not only does it look like a castle, but it is a true castle; right?' His words were were interspersed with flashes of a mysterious smile.

I could not have expected a more unusual statement from Sahoo, for he spoke nothing but matters gross.

'It had to be a true castle, for it was built by the rajas,' I said.

'Right. Rajas build castles and those who live in castles are rajas! But I am not a raja and still it was so ordained that I must own a castle! What is a freak of fate if not this? What do you say?'

I looked at him blankly. His smile changed into a laugh as rapidly as the hiss of a cracker changes into a loud and fiery burst. 'I am going to own it. Yes, I have concluded negotiations with the Raja for buying it!'

I was taken aback and felt sad at the same time. The Raja must have been in dire need of money to sell away his last shelter. But clever as Sahoo was, he must have bought it cheap and the Raja must have agreed to the deal because he could have hardly expected any other customer to come forward with any lucrative bid for an unwieldy mansion in a lonely place.

'I've paid him the money and obtained a temporary receipt.

Today I've entrusted my lawyer with the task of preparing a regular document for registration.' His flabby face twitched with pride and joy.

'I must apologize, my well-wisher, for keeping the deal a secret from you till today. But, believe me, you are the first person outside my family to be told about it. It is not wise to divulge an auspicious move before it matures, you know!'

'To win a castle is no joke!' I tried to invent at least a poor epigram that would match his happiness to some degree.

He became grave at once. 'No joke,' he affirmed. 'Did I not say it is fate? My horoscope indicated that I will be crowned a king. For a long time, I thought that when I had enough money, I would buy some estates and become a zamindar and, if I was lucky, earn the title "Raja" from the British government. But by the time I had enough money, the zamindari system had vanished! I was disappointed, but not disheartened. I traced the astrologer, the author of my horoscope. The old man, living in a dilapidated hut, was dying for lack of proper food and medical care. I arranged for all his needs and when he had sufficiently recovered, I asked him to re-examine my horoscope. To my pleasant surprise, he confirmed his prediction. Now, I believe, in the changed circumstances, my owning the castle is the nearest that could happen to my winning a crown. What do you think?'

'Fantastic.' He laughed, gratified. 'Merely knowing what's in store is not enough. One must lend a helping hand to destiny to fulfil itself. What do you say?'

Sahoo, of course, was too sure of his philosophy to need any formal endorsement from me. After disclosing a few more secrets of his life, he fixed his look once again on the castle. Evening had turned it into a massive silhouette and it was a different Sahoo who stood erect, his hands on his waist, surveying the property that symbolized his enormous destiny.

Once again it was an occasion for me to reflect on how little I knew of human nature.

It was getting dark. Sahoo had just got on to his jeep when a piercing cry, fading into the hills, startled us. It emanated from the darker area behind the castle. It was followed by the sound of two gunshots. 'What could have happened?' an anxious Sahoo asked, getting down from his jeep.

'We must go and see.' No less astonished, I fetched my gun and jumped on to the jeep. Sahoo got in reluctantly, but chose to occupy a rear seat.

Soon the headlights of our jeep focused on the veranda of the castle. We saw the Raja, gun in one hand and a torchlight in the other, as if waiting for us. He asked us to remain in the jeep and squeezed himself in hurriedly beside me and directed the driver to take the vehicle to the meadow behind the castle.

He gave us an outline of the sequence of events. He had sensed the presence of a tiger in the forest behind the temple. Then, at sunset, he noticed a covey of patridges darting away in panic. He had climbed on to the roof of the castle and surveyed the area. But that was an exercise in futility. He did not even have a pair of binoculars.

He had come down when evening set in. A while ago he saw through a window, someone rambling about on the banks of the lake. The man seemed uncertain and awkward in his movements. The Raja was intrigued. There was no habitation between the castle and the forest; the mysterious rambler, as was evident from the clothes he wore, was not a tribal who could have come from some hamlet in the forest.

The Raja was watching the figure when, all of a sudden, his view was eclipsed. For a fleeting second, a weak beam of light from one of the windows of the castle lit up the spot and the Raja saw a pair of intensely bright eyes. He knew whose they were!

The man emitted a long howl while being dragged away. Through his window the Raja fired two shots into the darkness in a desperate bid to scare away the beast. He did not think that his action could have meant anything more than satisfying his own impulse to do something at the moment.

We had stopped talking and were driving at a snail's pace along the grassy banks of the lake. I signalled the driver to stop. The engine silenced, the stillness of the place was broken only by the buzzing of cicadas. There was a faint splash in the water. Some small creature swam across the lake.

A thin spray of fog covered the region, a physical corollary to the shadow of fear in our minds.

'Why did you stop?' the Raja broke the silence. I took the

torchlight from the Raja's hand and focused it on the ground to our right. Two sandals lay not far from each other.

'But are they not Sharmaji's?' I cried out.

'Oh no!' the Raja sounded horrified.

'Are they?' asked Sahoo from his seat behind us, more prepared than the Raja or myself to face reality.

'I'm almost sure they are,' I replied. The Raja swore in disbelief.

'They may not be Sharma's, after all. How can we be sure that no one else used similar sandals? But the question is, whoever be their owner, what was he doing here?' The Raja's query was not directed at anybody in particular.

For a while my mind refused to record anything. Thoughts of Sharmaji monopolized my memory, my whole being. His childish insistence on my playing his emissary, the excitement writ large on his face while waiting for me as I was led away by Heera, his pathetic strutting about to save himself from her wrath, and the apologetic smiles he sported for his inability to stand up to Havelock's expectations and to commit suicide— a jumble of scenes formed a sobbing surrealistic apparition in my mind. Could the tiger have put an end to all that in a single sweep? The Raja and Sahoo probably had some doubts about the victim's identity. Somehow I had none. I smelled Sharma in the atmosphere—rather I smelled his death, fresh and bloody, with every breath I took. I was bewildered by the sudden turn of events, but had no illusions about Sharmaji's fate.

'Should we proceed?' asked the driver.

'Go on,' said the Raja.

The jeep started again. The hill loomed large in the forest beyond the deserted temple, leaving a narrow passage to its right. We took it till we reached a ravine not far from the temple.

It was not possible for the jeep to go any further. There was a gust of wind and the tall trees swaying over the uneven rocks jostled one another, warning us against plunging into the ocean of surging darkness before us.

The jeep came to a halt once again. I felt Sahoo's trembling fingers grabbing my shoulder. 'Let's go back,' he whispered. I realized that if he had sounded a bit less nervous a little while ago, it was because he had been too stupefied to react normally. Alas, the experience could not but have been an anticlimax to his elation minutes earlier at surveying from a higher altitude the castle he had come to own that very day, a fulfilment of his dream of being crowned a potentate, in some small measure.

If I was a degree less frightened, it was because of my faith in the Raja's capacity to handle the situation should it turn critical. The Raja, who sat beside me with one of his legs dangling outside, did not seem to know fear.

The silence exercised a paralytic effect on us and the darkness pressed in, almost freezing us.

'Le's go back,' said Sahoo once again, this time a little louder; his voice was like a scratch on the colossal hush.

We waited for a few seconds, but the Raja did not respond. Perhaps all his attention had gone over to the darkness of the forest; he was trying to detect a ripple or two, if there were any, in that fearful stillness.

'Shouldn't you fire another shot?' Sahoo asked impatiently.

'What for?'

'To frighten the beast!' Sahoo stammered out after giving a little thought to the question.

'You cannot frighten it enough to make it offer its prey to you. No, Sahoo, there is no chance of our rescuing the man, whoever he be, from the clutches of death,' the Raja said with some anguish. 'The creature might forget and forgive my earlier shots in its excitement over its prey, but firing even a single shot now may destroy our chances of tracing it in the daylight.'

'Let's go back,' Sahoo pleaded. 'To be frank. I'm afraid.'

'Don't fear. For the time the beast will remain satisfied and busy with what it has bagged. Also, it must have dragged the prey farther into the forest on hearing the shots,' the Raja said. 'But, of course, there is no point in our stopping here. Let's go back and hope we meet Sharma alive.' We returned to the spot on the edge of the lake where lay the sandals. The Raja himself got down and collected them. We drove to Horizon. Subbu identified the sandals as Sharmaji's. He also told us that Sharmaji had not been seen in the afternoon.

We then drove to Sharmaji's house. Only an orphan nephew

lived there, working for him. The boy had not seen his uncle since the evening. We learnt that Sharmaji had not spoken to anybody for the whole day and had eaten no food either. He had devoted a long time to making a neat packet of something and then left home late in the afternoon.

Sahoo held out the sandals before the boy. 'They are uncle's!' he exclaimed and looked at us agape in bewilderment.

'You won't fear staying alone at night; am I right?' I asked the boy.

He shook his head. 'Uncle was not here last night and I was not afraid. But I have cooked for him. He must come and eat,' he mumbled.

I visualized the tiger having its meal somewhere in the dark forest and had the creeps.

'Well, boy, eat your supper and go to bed. Your uncle may not need any food,' said the Raja kindly, patting the boy on the back.

Leaving the boy to his loneliness, we headed towards the police outpost. The young officer-in-charge recorded our suspicions and offered to assist the Raja in tracking down the tiger.

We drove the Raja to the castle and then Sahoo dropped me at Horizon. Subbu probably had had some premonition. 'What happened, babu? Is Sharmaji all right?' he queried.

'I don't know.' I was too depressed to say anything more. I remembered a group photograph of our school days. Sharmaji sat in the first row among our other revered teachers. What a solemn demeanour was his!

'Is it to meet with this end that you saved the tiger the other day by your shriek?' I wished I could ask Sharmaji.

Fifteen

I passed an uneasy night. Sharmaji's face and that of the tiger appeared and disappeared like bubbles in an ocean of darkness. Try as I might, I could not curb my imagination from visualizing Sharmaji's last moments. His face took on bizarre shapes in my mind's eye, matching his last cry which continued to echo in my ears—waking me every time I fell asleep.

What was Sharmaji doing behind the castle? I had no clear answer to that question, but was sure that he had been doing something foolish; maybe he was trying to catch a glimpse of Heera. Or, maybe, he hoped that Heera would take pity on him seeing him in that distraught condition.

As decided when we had dispersed at night, Sahoo picked me up early in the morning. I was happy that he had brought with him our friend Rao, who had been away to his hometown for some days. The Raja joined us as soon as we reached the castle. The police officer was already there. We parked the jeep in the portico and walked down to the site of the disaster. The Raja instructed me to remain alert and concentrated on the marks on the ground.

'It's a tigress,' he said, examining the few visible pug marks. Before long our eyes fell on a parcel, not far from the spot where Sharmaji's sandals had been found. It had rolled close to the water where it had got entangled in a jasmine plant.

I opened the neatly made parcel. It contained the trousers and the shirt Heera had presented to Sharmaji.

I stood staring at it. Sharmaji had grown plump in his uncanny zeal to fit into these garments. Obviously, in a highly sentimental moment, the jilted lover in him had resolved to slip the parcel into the castle when all was dark and silent. There was no other explanation for his hovering about there carrying the parcel.

As I held that parcel in my hands, a strange sensation, one of seething anger, overwhelmed me. I knew how foolish Sharmaji had been. Even then I wept for him in the privacy of my inner self, and I felt like slamming those clothes on Heera's face as forcefully as I could. Perhaps, had I chanced upon Heera, I would have really done that. But Heera, I understood, was unwell. She refused to come out of her room or to talk to anybody ever since my fateful interview with her as Sharmaji's emissary.

There was no discussion on our discovery. Perhaps the Raja's reading of the situation had not been different from mine.

'Let's proceed!' he commanded, without giving Sahoo or Rao an opportunity to raise any protest. The farther we went, the more grave Sahoo grew. He did not like our entering the forest at all, but silently suffered it, looking back again and again to measure the extent of the risk we were taking.

It was on the other side of the ravine behind the temple, only half a furlong away from it, that the tiger had feasted on Sharmaji. The beast had chosen the spot well; it was difficult to find and there was little danger of anyone disturbing it. There was a profusion of bushes and anthills marking the spot, and waist-high rocks and several bushy trees ringed it.

The Raja kept staring at the spot in silence. Sahoo did the same, but he looked perfectly horrified and mopped his face repeatedly. Observing the state he was in, I decided not to look at the scene at all.

'The beast will come back. The memory of a hearty peaceful meal will prove irresistible for her,' the Raja predicted confidently.

'Must we wait around here?' Sahoo asked anxiously.

The Raja laughed. 'Don't you worry, Sahoo, the tigress would need time to grow hungry enough for any of us—particularly for you. Meanwhile, we can set up a machan and get ready to receive her,' he said.

Work on the machan began immediately. A pair of well-formed branches of a big banyan tree that projected towards a stunted date palm came in handy for the purpose.

Since it was the Raja's need, even though the need had not been publicized, three bony goats were offered to serve as the bait by the residents of the hamlet near Nijanpur. I observed the Raja's momentary predicament—his painful hesitation in passing a death sentence on one of the innocent three. I was glad that he was no longer a ruling prince. With the sort of mind he had, he would have hardly been a success as a ruler.

Rao came to the Raja's rescue and arbitrarily chose one of the goats.

It was decided that the Raja and I would occupy the machan, and Rao, Sahoo and the police officer would take position on the roof of the temple.

The machan was ready in two hours. For a rehearsal, the Raja and I climbed on it with the help of a ladder while the others were still debating the length of the rope with which the bait was to be tied to the date palm tree.

The Raja caught hold of my arm while balancing himself on the machan. His hand was as hot as a kettle fresh from the fire. 'You are running a temperature!' I observed with some anxiety. I had not noticed earlier, but his eyes were red and he seemed quite unsteady.

'Is it not funny,' he asked me, making light of his condition, 'that my diving in a cool lake for so many nights should make me hot instead of cold?'

I at once remembered having seen him, the other night, returning to the castle drenched and with smudges of mud on his clothes. I had not had any opportunity to ask him about it earlier.

'May I know the mystery behind your diving in the lake, Sir?'

'Yes, indeed, I ought to tell you all about it. And I cannot think of a more unusual situation than this to confide in you my unusual—and I must confess—abnormal activity. But keep it a secret. The fact is, I have been exploring the old hallowed lake.'

'For what?'

'For wealth.'

'Sir, you're still talking in riddles.'

There were wrinkles on the Raja's brow. Perhaps he was pondering over the best way to explain his action to me, although I did not wish him to tire himself by talking.

'Why, Dev, haven't you heard about our ancestors stumbling on buried treasures uncovered to them by the presiding spirit of the lake—a certain kind-hearted, if whimsical, Yaksha? Why shouldn't the supernatural being realize that I need his patronage most? I threw this question at him again and again while groping for a gold-filled jar or two in the waters. Should we be surprised if he responds?'

The Raja looked at me quizzically.

'What do you think of my adventures?' he asked me when I did not speak.

'I don't know, but your expectations appear so far-fetched—almost fantastic!'

I was sorry for saying so, but felt relieved to notice that my scepticism had no perceptible effect on the Raja. He lowered his already weakened voice and said, 'For your information, my groping, digging and diving have not gone in vain.'

I gaped at him in disbelief.

'Just when I was about to give up, frustrated, came the reward!'

'Reward?' I could not check my surprise.

'I should think so.'

'Am I to understand that you hit upon some hidden treasure?'

'I did. But I'm yet to know its exact form and assess its value. It was rather heavy, though not very large. My shoulders are still aching.'

The Raja squeezed his shoulders with his tired hands.

'What exactly was it that proved so heavy, Sir?'

'The chest. With great difficulty, I carried it into the temple the night before last. It was a queer experience—to emerge from an enchanted lake at midnight, carrying a chest deposited by some scheming ancestor. I felt almost convinced that not only the moon, but also a number of invisible beings looked on from the treetops and the precincts of the temple.'

The Raja laughed and continued with his description of what he had seen: 'They were of somewhat sinister shapes and they applauded my feat. Amazingly, I could hear their applause, though I was sure it would have been inaudible to anybody else. The sound grew and reached a crescendo, almost deafening me by the time I dumped the chest inside the sanctum sanctorum. Then it stopped.'

'Why didn't you open the chest?' I asked eagerly.

'For the same reason for which the applause stopped—Heera's shriek. That made me rush back home. I wanted to open it last night but, as you know, Sharma quietly walked into the doom that awaited me.'

I sat speechless. The Raja laughed with great satisfaction, though not very loudly.

'Sure I was perplexed,' he explained. 'The Yaksha may be a myth. And there is nothing really fantastic about my stumbling upon a treasure or two if you know about the habits of the Ranis of yore. Many of them took care to bury their private wealth in the pools and tanks within their reach, in the hope of retrieving them at a propitious time. For some of them the propitious time never came. For some others even if the time came, the treasure proved elusive.'

The Raja's eyes were growing bleary. He had forgotten the purpose of our climbing the machan. He did nothing to examine its strategic suitability or to see how freely he could move his gun. He was in a mood to talk. He wiped the perspiration from his forehead and resumed, 'I've a plan . . .'

His condition alarmed me. I was anxious to stop him and suggest that he had better give up the proposed all-night vigil. But we were interrupted by Rao who sought the Raja's advice on the arrangements made on the roof of the temple to camouflage their presence.

'Stay here Dev, and check if you can see us clearly when we are on the temple,' said the Raja, descending from the machan.

'There should be some moonlight, though late, if those few patches of cloud do not disturb it. It is necessary that we settle down in our allotted places before dusk, allowing our eyes to get accustomed to the growing darkness,' the Raja said while moving away with the others towards the temple.

The sun had just set. A few enthusiastic cicadas had already begun chirping. Homing birds circled some taller trees, preparing to settle down for the night. Their simple movements were the only vibrations my otherwise vacant and still mind recorded. The Raja, no doubt, had left me a bit dazed. I ought to have felt thrilled over his luck, but I did not. The urgency and the despair that must have forced him to grope for some help from his ancestors, in the mud and mire, depressed me.

The twilight was taking possession of the forest rapidly, if stealthily. The colour of the hour was in perfect harmony with my mood—pensive and passive.

I do not know how long I sat sealed in a state of vacuity. I woke up with a terrific jolt. It must have taken me a second or two to realize that what disturbed my peace was a shrill human cry. But I could not trace its origin instantly. Perhaps my sudden shock, together with the dusk, blinded me for another second.

Then I discerned the figure of Heera, standing alone, petrified and staring at some object in a dazed manner.

I followed her gaze and saw a giant beast facing her— probably the tigress we awaited. They seemed transfixed by each other.

I forced my gun into position. The maneater roared and Heera gave a blood-curdling shriek—simultaneously. The terrific impact of the sound shook me and I was sucked into a state that will ever defy my attempt at describing it. It must have been a combination of utter bafflement and stupefaction— though it could not have lasted more than a lightning moment—when I failed to distinguish between Heera and the beast. Looking at Heera I wondered if she was not the tigress, and looking at the tigress I wondered if she was not Heera.

It was dreadful; the sensation was simply maddening. I felt like dashing my head against the tree. I thought I wept blood. But I could not know the human from the beast.

I do not trust the accuracy of my vision or my memory of that moment, but I think I saw them springing on each other with equal frenzy and fury. At once, my power of discrimination was restored. I shot, aiming at the beast, before I fell into a dead faint.

Sixteen

I do not know when and how I was carried to Horizon. Memory returned to me in stages and with feverish jerks. When I remembered the scene and the situation that preceded my losing consciousness, I cried out in horror.

Subbu and Rao were by my side. I kept staring at them, afraid of asking them about the outcome of the weird encounter between Heera and the tigress. Subbu looked too stupefied to say a thing, but Rao had prepared himself to tell me all about it.

'You did your job very well. Your shot hit the left temple of the maneater and penetrated it. It died almost instantly,' he said.

I found some relief in the knowledge that I had not hit Heera accidentally. But I sensed that Rao was speaking in an extremely guarded manner.

'And how is Heera?'

'Well, the beast mauled her badly.'

'So?'

'Nothing could have saved her. Her end came an hour later.'

Rao left, promising to return after a while. I asked Subbu to switch off the light and concentrated on recollecting the sequence of events in as orderly a manner as possible. Soon I was in a position to assure myself that I had no reason to feel guilty for any lapse in my conduct, however harrowing a crisis I might have experienced within me. My eerie confusion had lasted no more than a few seconds—practically the time I took to bring the gun to the right position and take aim at the beast. I would have needed that much time anyway, confusion or no confusion.

Even then the memory of the bizarre episode weighed on my chest like a vampire, sucking at my spirit. I could not muster enough strength to even sit up. Futile thoughts oppressed me: the situation would have been different if only I knew that Heera was visiting the spot; I ought not to have sat so absorbed in my rumination over the Raja's nocturnal adventures and what he claimed to be their successful outcome.

Heera's was an incredible end both for its suddenness and for the manner in which it came. No doubt I had developed an unreasonable dread of her, at least partly because of my own foolishness, but she had become a formidable presence for me, greatly influencing my thought, conduct and attitudes; she was as alive for me as the midnight hours I paced through; as trenchantly real as the death of my dear doe or the slow death of Sharmaji, I mean his real death preceding his physical death; she was as unforgettable as the slap she had planted on Balika's cheek which, I felt, had struck my jowl.

My mind had become a blind alley, with the worst-ever jam of confused thoughts and with little hope of an arrow of sunray infiltrating it.

Soon, however, it became a vacuum, unable to accommodate or absorb any more distress and remorse.

Poor Subbu, who had been peeping into my room again and again, finally plucked up courage and walked in. My condition frightened him, but his desire to break the news to me and see me react normally was stronger.

'Babu, the carcass of the maneater is lying at the police outpost. It needed no less than eight able-bodied men, some constables included, to carry it there. Even so, the bearers staggered, perhaps more because of their own nervousness than from their burden. It looked so fearful! You should have seen the crowd swelling around it. People are still arriving, some from distant villages, bringing their supper along with them, for they will not be able to return home at night.'

He fell silent when his report failed to provoke my interest.

'And, babu,' he said gravely after a while, perhaps realizing that it was improper for him to totally blackout the tragic aspect of the event, 'the lady is to be buried in front of the temple. Preparations are afoot. Raja Sahib wants to finish with the matter without delay.'

Rao returned around midnight. Heera had been given a burial in keeping with the traditions of the Raj family, he informed me, while Sharmaji's remains had been cremated not very far from her grave. A priest who had been promptly secured from a nearby village had performed the last rites for both.

'How has Raja sahib taken it?' I asked, overcoming my hesitation.

'He looks very pale and we have all impressed upon him the need for rest. But he feels anxious about your condition. He told me that were he not drained of all vigour he would have paid you a visit. He has advised you to take it easy and relax,' said Rao, injecting some authority into his otherwise weak voice.

The Raja's message overwhelmed me. I knew the state of his mind and body better than anybody else. His concern for me assured me that he retained some of his composure.

I passed the night tossing and turning. My desire to meet the Raja and to feel the atmosphere of the castle, now that Heera had gone, was mounting, but after I had taken a bath early in the morning, sleep, which had eluded me all night, descended on me with a vengeance.

Late in the afternoon, my anguish was topped by a fresh wave of annoyance. A letter from the government—the outcome of the expert team's visit to Nijanpur some days ago—stated that they were contemplating taking over my mansion and converting it into a sanatorium. They offered reasonable compensation and expected my cooperation.

For a moment I had the strange feeling of living inside a bubble about to burst. I tore up the letter on an impulse, but when I realized how childish and impotent that was, I felt even more annoyed and frustrated. I lost the desire to move out of my room. And, as darkness fell, a dreadful thought crept into me: this mansion had been built at Heera's instance. Was her death anything to do with it slipping through my fingers? For what fault of mine should I lose the house I love? At which point of my drift along the stream of events could I have swum against the current or broken away and climbed ashore and looked at it as a mere bystander?

Night deepened as I kept staring vacantly at the dark hills. Yet another sleepless night awaited me. My tired eyes closed a little before dawn. But I was woken by Subbu. The watchman of the castle, gasping and sweating, had brought me summons from Vimla. I must see her at once.

The sun was yet to climb over the range of hills. As I walked towards the castle, my old familiar road, surprisingly, looked different. Was it a projection of my experiences, my encounter with the unfamiliar aspects of my own self?

Vimla stood at the portals. 'Where is Raja sahib?' she asked me anxiously.

The question was most unexpected. The last I had met the Raja was on the machan when he spoke to me of his mysterious discovery. Thereafter he must have seen me, but when I was in a swoon.

Vimla did not expect a reply; she was merely sharing her anxiety with me. She told me how the Raja had almost collapsed, beset with high fever and exhaustion, soon after Heera's burial, and had become delirious. By midday he had looked better, but would not let Vimla send for me or anybody else. Throughout the day, he had tossed in bed or walked up and down the castle restlessly, peering through the windows at the temple again and again. He fell asleep late in the evening, but was found missing from the castle early in the morning. Vimla was aware that he had a habit of roaming around at night, but was now apprehensive because of his condition.

'He must have slipped out, as usual, through the rear door, soon after midnight, for I was awake throughout the last quarter of the night. He could not have gone unnoticed then,' said Vimla.

Her observation suddenly reminded me of the Raja's secret quest and the point of the narration at which he had stopped.

'Don't worry. I'll find him in no time.' She looked consoled, though intrigued.

I made straight for the deserted temple, passing by the fresh mounds near the still lake—the grave of Heera and the cold funeral pyre of Sharmaji—bathed in the early morning light. Two squirrels were running around them at great speed, chasing each other. I did not allow the unearthly sensation that was creeping into me to grow. A soft glow of sunlight filtering through the trees on the southern side of the lake had begun to play on the temple. The doors were bolted from within. I stood confirmed in my guess.

'Raja sahib!' I called out in a subdued voice. There was no response.

'Raja sahib, it is Dev,' I called out again, louder, and knocked on the doors. There was no response. I increased the volume of both my voice and the knock, but to no avail.

I lost patience and pushed the doors with all my strength. The wooden bar on the other side gave way and one of the two dilapidated frames almost fell off. I stormed in, to the consternation of a number of bats. One of them, flitting by me, clashed against my head. An owl screeched and flew away through a hole on a wall.

Despite streaks of light piercing the forlorn space through the broken door-frame, it was dark inside. A putrid smell hung in the air, suffocating me.

I stood before the image of the forsaken idol till my eyes grew accustomed to the murkiness. The Raja was not in the sanctum sanctorum. I peeped into the narrow wing behind the seat of the deity. There he was—leaning against the wall, his legs outstretched. By his side lay a torch still switched on, but the light was too dim to reveal anything beyond its surface glass.

'Raja Sahib! Are you awake?'

He was not. I knelt down and shook him gently by the shoulders, calling him again. I realized that he was in a deep faint. For a moment, I did not know what to do. I hurried out, opened the doors wide to let a little more light and air in. Then I ran to the lake, soaked my handkerchief in water, and came back and squeezed it on his face. His eyelids rippled.

By then objects inside the temple had become distinct. I saw the submerged chest he had salvaged. It lay upside down beside him, close to a dark nook, its mystery scattered on the floor.

It did not take me long to identify the contents. It was a human skeleton, now lying crumbled amidst clods of mud that had penetrated the chest.

I forgot my duty towards the Raja and stood gaping at it, shivers running up and down my spine. These could have been the remains of a rebel punished by an ancestor of the Raja, or of a country lass who had inspired the passions of a prince but had endangered his honour.

The victim had wreaked its vengeance on the last of the Rajas.

Seventeen

I did not want anyone else to see the Raja in that condition. I mustered all my strength and tried to lift him.

'Devu! Did you find him?'

It was Vimla. She had seen me dipping my handkerchief in the lake and entering the temple for the second time, and had come as quickly as possible. Together we managed to carry the Raja to the castle before any of the attendants saw us.

Nijanpur was not connected with Samargarh by telephone or a telegraph line. Sahoo's jeep was the speediest means of transport and communication available to us. Rao took it and rushed to Samargarh, returning with an ambulance, a doctor and two medical assistants. Three hours had passed. The Raja had shown some signs of improvement. He had opened his eyes several times, but seemed to slip into a deeper slumber each time.

Vimla went to inform Balika that it was necessary to take the Raja to the hospital at Samargarh. I followed her and asked her in a whisper, 'Does Balika know of Heera's death? What is her reaction?'

'She is bewildered, as usual,' replied Vimla.

I could not hear what Vimla told Balika, but I saw the girl getting off her bed and struggling to walk. Vimla left the room in haste, for she found it difficult to keep her tears in check and a weeping Vimla was sure to shock Balika.

The doctor and his assistants transferred the unconscious Raja into the ambulance with great care. I sat by his side. Rao and Sahoo followed us in the jeep.

We had barely crossed Nijanpur when, to our joy, the Raja opened his eyes. 'He should recover soon,' said the doctor with a reassuring smile.

The Raja surveyed us. He was obviously trying to comprehend the situation. 'Where are we going?' he asked, softly but distinctly.

'To the hospital at Samargarh,' I replied.

He closed his eyes for a while. 'Is it you who found me?' he asked. His mind had become alert incredibly fast. He was reconstructing the events.

'That is correct.'

He let a minute pass. 'Dev, I had no time to tell you of my plan!' He seemed to be murmuring his protest against the chain of events which ran contrary to his wishes.

'You will tell me, sir, when you have fully recovered. There will be ample time for that.' I tried to sound absolutely confident of such a time arriving before long.

'What if I don't recover?' His feebly uttered question had an ominous ring to it. He looked at the doctor and his assistants and tried to smile.

'Can we do anything for you, sir?' asked the doctor.

'Will you mind leaving me alone with Dev for a moment?'

The ambulance was stopped. The doctor and one of the assistants went over to the driver's side. The third member of the team moved to the jeep which had also come to a halt.

Alone with the Raja, I told him again, 'I'm afraid, talking will be a strain on you now. We can wait, can't we, for a better time!'

He paid no heed to my words. 'Dev,' he said taking a deep breath, 'would you mind selling your mansion to me?'

While the abruptness of the proposition startled me, his next statement did not help me to recover my poise either.

'But I propose to give it back to you—with one addition. My daughter. Won't you look after her when I am gone?' He paused and added, 'Vimla, of course, will be a great asset to you. She is so good!'

I was at a total loss for words.

'But I forget my daughter's condition. How can I inflict her on you?' he sighed.

'Sir,' I managed to say at last, 'I am at your disposal along with my house. You trust me, don't you? Please don't worry about Balika and Vimla.'

He looked relaxed and then rolled and strained his eyes perhaps to ascertain that nobody else heard him.

'Dev, will you check if there is a key in my pocket?'

I searched his pockets and found it.

'Will you please keep it with you?'

'If that pleases you.' I put the key in my pocket.

'Good,' he spoke with some satisfaction. 'It is the key to the chest in my bedroom. You will find in it an envelope containing money, the amount I received from Sahoo for selling my mansion to him, and it is entirely for you. I had other plans. But the Yaksha failed me, as you must have found out yourself.'

'We can discuss matters later. Please do not tire yourself,' I pleaded again.

A faint smile seemed to play on his lips.

'Yes,' he said, 'I shall speak no more. God bless you.' He closed his eyes.

I sat resigned to an assault on my heart and mind by a jumble of emotions. I did not know when we entered Samargarh. I woke up to a multitude of grim faces when our vehicle came to halt before the hospital. The news of the Raja's sudden illness and his home-coming had spread like wildfire. The district collector, other officials and a large number of people were waiting to receive him.

'How is Raja sahib?' asked the collector as soon as I got down.

'He's better,' I said, 'and asleep.'

The doctor and his assistants went in to examine the patient.

There was an anxious silence. Five minutes passed. The doctor beckoned the chief medical officer of the hospital to come into the ambulance. After another five minutes, the chief was heard announcing to the collector and the rest, 'Raja sahib is no more!'

'But that cannot be!' I cried out. My voice was lost in the surging murmurs and exclamations. 'How will I face Balika and Vimla?' I asked Sahoo and Rao and broke down. My two kind companions held and consoled me.

'Young man,' said the collector in a patronizing tone,' I appreciate your sentiments, for I understand that you were very dear to Raja sahib. But who are we to question the ways of Providence? We must remain calm at such moments and perform our solemn duty to the best of our ability. You must rush to Nijanpur and break the news to the princess. There is no time to lose. I am told that the tradition of the dynasty demands a dead body to be interred before sunset if the death takes place during the day. Once the princess, the Raja's sole heir, is here, we can begin the preparations for the burial.'

The collector provided me with a car. The talkative chauffeur went on and on about the good old days of the Raj, elevating facts to the plane of fairy tales. I responded occasionally and mechanically, but heard him only when he raised his voice to a high pitch at the end of every anecdote.

His presence only obliged me to stomach my sobs. My father's death, five years ago, had been a big blow to me, but his physicians had already prepared me for the inevitable. The Raja's death was absolutely shattering, it was most unexpected. I had only begun to know him—and what a delightful adventure was it!

Vimla came out at the sound of the car. She stared at me for a moment and then began to weep.

'You've guessed it,' I said as I led her back into the hall, and reminded her of the need to appear as calm as possible for Balika's sake.

Vimla steadied herself and tried to appear composed.

'Vimla, do you think Balika would like to, or be able to, come to Samargarh with us for the funeral?'

Instead of answering my question, Vimla went into Balika's room. I had no courage to accompany her this time. A moment later, I heard an emphatic 'No' followed by sobs.

I waited for nearly half an hour outside Balika's room. But Vimla did not come out. I was growing impatient. I stepped into the room and saw Balika in Vimla's arms still crying. I lingered for a few minutes more. 'I must return to Samargarh without delay. Meanwhile, let me assure you, Vimla, that you and the princess will have no cause to worry about anything. Raja sahib has made all the necessary arrangements for your welfare. You can look upon me as his trustee and demand all my attention,' I said. My words sounded trite even to my own ears.

Vimla followed me into the hall. 'Dev,' she said embracing me, 'do you know? Once Raja sahib told me how much he would like you to marry his daughter. Poor Balika! She had wept— and that was the only time I ever saw Raja sahib emotionally moved and his eyes moist.'

I remained speechless for a moment. Then I made Vimla sit down and returned to the car.

By the time I was back at Samargarh, the whole town was plunged into mourning. All offices and shops had been closed. The Raja's body had been carried to the lawns of what had once been his palace. It lay in state on a bed of flowers. Thousands filed past it, many shed tears and some sobbed. Most of the mourners had never seen him earlier. The moving scene only informed me how painful the death of a symbol can be.

He looked serene, more like a hermit than a prince.

A procession of over thirty thousand men and women followed the cortége of the last Raja of Samargarh to the dynasty's exclusive burial ground. He was laid to rest, against a setting sun, amidst the ruins of the tombs of his ancestors. A pale twilight set in over the vast, grieving crowd.

Epilogue

It was morning. The massive castle had suddenly begun to look like a haunted house. An inaudible cry—whose could it be?—pervaded every inch of the atmosphere.

Or had it overnight become a house of cards, I wondered, for, despite its imposing solidity, I feared that a gust of wind would be enough to make it collapse. I remembered that it was no longer a Raja's residence; it was going to be the proud possession of a merchant who was perhaps still under the spell of his impossible dream.

I crossed the awfully empty hall and walked slowly down the dimly lit corridor. Vimla lay asleep in front of Balika's room and perhaps sobbed in her sleep.

I peeped into the room. Balika was awake. I stood by the door in silence. She sat up. Tears began rolling down her cheeks. I let some time pass. She wiped her face and looked at me and did not take her eyes away immediately. Our shared grief had perhaps brought us closer.

'I propose to carry out your father's wishes faithfully. You and Vimla Aunty have to leave this house and come over to Horizon. You have never seen it, but it now belongs to you. Yes, your father's last act was to buy it for you,' I said while wondering how long Horizon itself would remain with us.

She broke into tears once again.

I was immensely sad; yet, at the same time, I was waking to the thrill of discharging my new responsibilities.

My hope of evoking some response in her by talking to her directly seemed to be in vain. I must wait for Vimla to rise, I decided, and went out for a stroll along the lake.

Crickets chirped. A few cranes stood gracefully by the edge of the lake. A pair of tortoises were crawling back into the water after a sojourn on dry ground. And, from the dark green foliage glistening with dew, birds had started taking flight. The temple of Vaneswari at one corner of the lake looked fearfully desolate. The Raja's bizarre discovery must be still lying inside it. Not far from it were the hurriedly dug grave of Heera and the pyre of Sharmaji, reminders of experiences I would like to forget.

The morning was growing brighter. I sat down on a rock overlooking the lake—a few yards from the rear door of the castle—and wondered if each of the varieties of the tiny wild flowers smiling from the bushes and the grass had a name. I heard the sound of the door opening softly behind me and a rustling. I turned around and, for once in my life, could hardly believe my eyes.

There was Balika, coming down the steps. The breeze was playing with her curly hair and was blotting out her tears. She smiled.

'You have walked, and without anybody's help!' It was with much restraint that I could keep my voice—and my tears of joy—in check.

Balika was in a light blue saree. In my heart, frozen by the recent events, her image shone like a bluish flame. I felt a delightful thaw set in.

I looked up at the meandering road leading to Horizon. I may have to lose the mansion, I thought, but if she can walk up there, she will surely be able to walk further.